THE CAGED LION

CHARLOTTE M. YONGE

1st WORLD
LIBRARY
Literary Society

The Caged Lion

Charlotte M. Yonge

© 1st World Library, 2007
PO Box 2211
Fairfield, IA 52556
www.1stworldlibrary.com
First Edition

LCCN: 2007927809

Softcover ISBN: 978-1-4218-4515-9
Hardcover ISBN: 978-1-4218-4431-2
eBook ISBN: 978-1-4218-4599-9

Purchase *"The Caged Lion"*
as a traditional bound book at:
www.1stWorldLibrary.com/purchase.asp?ISBN=978-1-4218-4515-9

1st World Library is a literary, educational organization
dedicated to:

- Creating a free internet library of downloadable ebooks

- Hosting writing competitions and offering book
  publishing scholarships.

Interested in more 1st World Library books?
contact: literacy@1stworldlibrary.com
Check us out at: www.1stworldlibrary.com

1st World Library Literary Society

Giving Back to the World

"If you want to work on the core problem, it's early school literacy."

- James Barksdale, former CEO of Netscape

"No skill is more crucial to the future of a child, or to a democratic and prosperous society, than literacy."

- Los Angeles Times

"Literacy... means far more than learning how to read and write... The aim is to transmit... knowledge and promote social participation."

- UNESCO

"Literacy is not a luxury, it is a right and a responsibility. If our world is to meet the challenges of the twenty-first century we must harness the energy and creativity of all our citizens."

- President Bill Clinton

"Parents should be encouraged to read to their children, and teachers should be equipped with all available techniques for teaching literacy, so the varying needs and capacities of individual kids can be taken into account."

- Hugh Mackay

PREFACE

When the venture has been made of dealing with historical events and characters, it always seems fair towards the reader to avow what liberties have been taken, and how much of the sketch is founded on history. In the present case, it is scarcely necessary to do more than refer to the almost unique relations that subsisted between Henry V. and his prisoner, James I. of Scotland; who lived with him throughout his reign on the terms of friend rather than of captive, and was absolutely sheltered by this imprisonment throughout his nonage and early youth from the frightful violence and presumption of the nobles of his kingdom.

James's expedition to Scotland is wholly imaginary, though there appears to have been space for it during Henry's progress to the North to pay his devotions at Beverley Minster. The hero of the story is likewise invention, though, as Froissart ascribes to King Robert II. 'eleven sons who loved arms,' Malcolm may well be supposed to be the son of one of those unaccounted for in the pedigrees of Stewart. The same may be said of Esclairmonde. There were plenty of Luxemburgs in the Low Countries, but the individual is not to be identified. Readers of Tyler's 'Henry V.,' of Agnes Strickland's 'Queens,' Tytler's 'Scotland,' and Barante's 'Histoire de Bourgogne' will be at no loss for the origin of all I have ventured to say of the really historical personages. Mr. Fox Bourne's 'English Merchants' furnished the tradition respecting Whittington. I am afraid the knighthood was really conferred on Henry's first return to England, after the battle of Agincourt; but human—or at least story-telling—nature could not resist an anachronism of a few years for such a story. The only other wilful alteration of a matter of time is with regard to the Duke of Burgundy's interview with Henry. At the time of Henry's last stay at Paris the Duke was attending the death-bed of his wife, Michelle of France, but he had been several times in the King's camp at the siege of Meaux.

Another alteration of fact is that Ralf Percy, instead of being second son of Hotspur, should have been Henry Percy, son of Hotspur's brother Ralf; but the name would have been so confusing that it was thought better to set Dugdale at defiance and consider the reader's conve-nience. Alice Montagu, though her name sounds as if it came out of the most commonplace novelist's repertory, was a veritable personage—the heiress of the brave line of Montacute, or Montagu; daughter to the Earl of Salisbury who was killed at the siege of Orleans; wife to the Earl of the same title (in her right) who won the battle of Blore Heath and was beheaded at Wakefield; and mother to Earl Warwick the King-maker, the Marquis of Montagu, and George Nevil, Archbishop of York. As nothing is known of her but her name, I have ventured to make use of the blank.

For Jaqueline of Hainault, and her pranks, they are to be found in Monstrelet of old, and now in Barante; though justice to her and Queen Isabeau compels me to state that the incident of the ring is wholly fictitious. Of the trial of Walter Stewart no record is preserved save that he was accused of 'roborica.' James Kennedy was the first great benefactor to learning in Scotland, and founder of her

Charlotte M. Yonge

earliest University, having been himself educated at Paris.

The Abbey of Coldingham is described from a local compilation of the early part of the century, with an account of the history of that grand old foundation, and the struggle for appointments between the parent house at Durham and the Scottish Government. Priors Akefield and Drax are historical, and as the latter really did commission a body of moss-troopers to divert an instalment of King James's ransom into his own private coffers, I do not think I can have done him much injustice. As the nunnery of St. Abbs has gone bodily into the sea, I have been the less constrained by the inconvenient action of fact upon fiction. And for the Hospital of St. Katharine's-by-the-Tower, its history is to be found in Stowe's 'Survey of London,' and likewise in the evidence before the Parliamentary Commission, which shows what it was intended by Queen Philippa to have been to the river-side population, and what it might have been had such intentions been understood and acted on—nay, what it may yet become, since the foundation remains intact, although the building has been removed.

C. M. YONGE.

November 24, 1869.

CHAPTER I

THE GUEST OF GLENUSKIE

A master hand has so often described the glens and ravines of Scotland, that it seems vain and presumptuous to meddle with them; and yet we must ask our readers to figure to themselves a sharp cleft sloping downwards to a brawling mountain stream, the sides scattered with gray rocks of every imaginable size, interspersed here and there with heather, gorse, or furze. Just in the widest part of the valley, a sort of platform of rock jutted out from the hill-side, and afforded a station for one of those tall, narrow, grim-looking fastnesses that were the strength of Scotland, as well as her bane.

Either by nature or art, the rock had been scarped away on three sides, so that the walls of the castle rose sheer from the steep descent, except where the platform was connected with the mountain side by, as it were, an isthmus joining the peninsula to the main rock; and even this isthmus, a narrow ridge of rock just wide enough for the passage of a single horse, had been cut through, no doubt with great labour, and rendered impassable, except by the lowering of a drawbridge. Glenuskie Castle was thus nearly impregnable, so long as it was supplied with water, and for this all possible provision had been made, by guiding a stream into the court.

The castle was necessarily narrow and confined; its massive walls took up much even of the narrow space that the rock afforded; but it had been so piled up that it seemed as though the builders wished to make height compensate for straitness. There was, too, an unusual amount of grace, both in the outline of the gateway with its mighty flanking towers, and of the lofty donjon tower, that shot up like a great finger above the Massy More, as the main building was commonly called by the inhabitants of Glenuskie.

Wondrous as were the walls, and deep-set as were the arches, they had all that peculiar slenderness of contour that Scottish taste seemed to have learnt from France; and a little more space was gained at the top, both of the gateway towers and the donjon, by a projecting cornice of beautifully vaulted arches supporting a battlement, that gave the building a crowned look. On the topmost tower was of course planted the ensign of the owner, and that ensign was no other than the regal ruddy Lion of Scotland, ramping on his gold field within his tressure fiery and counter flory, but surmounted by a label divided into twelve, and placed upon a pen-noncel, or triangular piece of silk. The eyes of the early fifteenth century easily deciphered such hieroglyphics as these, which to every one with the least tincture of 'the noble science' indicated that the owner of the castle was of royal Stewart blood, but of a younger branch, and not yet admitted to the rank of knighthood.

The early spring of the year 1421 was bleak and dreary in that wild lonely vale, and large was the fire burning on the hearth in the castle hall, in the full warmth of which there sat, with a light blue cloth cloak drawn tightly round him, a tall old man, of the giant mould of Scotland, and with a massive thoughtful brow, whose grand form was rendered visible by the absence of hair, only a few remnants of

Charlotte M. Yonge

yellow locks mixed with silver floating from his temples to mingle with his magnificent white beard. A small blue bonnet, with a short eagle feather, fastened with a brooch of river pearl, was held in the hands that were clasped over his face, as, bending down in his chair, he murmured through his white beard, 'Have mercy, good Lord, have mercy on the land. Have mercy on my son,—and guard him when he goes out and when he comes in. Have mercy on the children I have toiled for, and teach me to judge and act for them aright in these sore straits; and above all, have mercy on our King, break his fetters, and send him home to be the healer of his land, the avenger of her cruel wrongs.'

So absorbed was the old man that he never heard the step that came across the hall. It was a slightly unequal step, but was carefully hushed at entrance, as if supposing the old man asleep; and at a slow pace the new-comer crossed the hall to the chimney, where he stood by the fire, warming himself and looking wistfully at the old Knight.

He was wrapped in a plaid, black and white, which increased the gray appearance of the pale sallow face and sad expression of the wearer, a boy of about seventeen, with soft pensive dark eyes and a sickly complexion, with that peculiar wistful cast of countenance that is apt to accompany deformity, though there was no actual malformation apparent, unless such might be reckoned the slight halt in the gait, and the small stature of the lad, who was no taller than many boys of twelve or fourteen. But there was a depth of melancholy in those dark brown eyes, that went far into the heart of any one who had the power to be touched with their yearning, appealing, almost piteous gaze, as though their owner had come into a world that was much too hard for him, and were looking out in bewilderment and entreaty for some haven of peace.

He had stood for some minutes looking thoughtfully into the fire, and the sadness of his expression ever deepening, before the old man raised his face, and said, 'You here, Malcolm? where are the others?'

'Patie and Lily are still on the turret-top, fair Uncle,' returned the boy. 'It was so cold;' and he shivered again, and seemed as though he would creep into the fire.

'And the reek?' asked the uncle.

'There is another reek broken out farther west,' replied Malcolm. 'Patie is sure now that it is as you deemed, Uncle; that it is a cattle-lifting from Badenoch.'

'Heaven help them!' sighed the old man, again folding his hands in prayer. 'How long, O Lord, how long?'

Malcolm took up the appeal of the Psalm, repeating it in Latin, but with none the less fervency; that Psalm that has ever since David's time served as the agonized voice of hearts hot-burning at the sight of wrong.

'Ah yes,' he ended, 'there is nothing else for it! Uncle, this was wherefore I came. It was to speak to you of my purpose.'

'The old purpose, Malcolm? Nay, that hath been answered before.'

'But listen, listen, dear Uncle. I have not spoken of it for a full year now. So that you cannot say it is the caresses of the good monks. No, nor the rude sayings of the Master of Albany,' he added, colouring at a look of his uncle. 'You bade me say no more till I be of full age; nor would I, save that I were safe lodged in an abbey; then might Patrick and Lily be wedded, and he not have to leave us and seek his fortune far away in France; and in Patie's hands and leading, my vassals might be safe; but what could the doited helpless cripple do?' he added, the colour rising hotly to his cheek with pain and shame. 'Oh, Sir, let me but save my soul, and find peace in Coldingham!'

'My poor bairn,' said his uncle, laying a kind hand upon him, as in his eagerness he knelt on one knee beside the chair, 'it must not be. It is true that the Regent and his sons would willingly see you in a cloister. Nay, that unmanly jeer of Walter Stewart's was, I verily believe, meant to drive you thither. But were you there, then would poor Lilias become a prize worth having, and the only question would be, whether Walter of Albany, or Robert of Athole, or any of the rest of them, should tear her away to be the lady of their fierce ungodly households.'

'You could give her to Patrick, Uncle.'

'No, Malcolm, that were not consistent with mine honour, or oaths to the King and State. You living, and Laird of Glenuskie, Lilias is a mere younger sister, whom you may give in marriage as you will; but were you dead to the world, under a cowl, then the Lady of Glenuskie, a king's grandchild, may not be disposed of, save by her royal kinsman, or by those who, woe worth the day! stand in his place. I were no better than yon Wolf of Badenoch or the Master of Albany, did I steal a march on the Regent, and give the poor lassie to my own son!'

'And so Lilias must pine, and Patrick wander off to the weary French war,' sighed Malcolm; 'and I must be scorned by my cousins whenever the House of Stewart meets together; and must strive with these fierce cruel men, that will ever be too hard for me when Patie is gone.' His eyes filled with tears as he continued, 'Ah! that fair chapel, with the sweet chant of the choir, the green smooth-shaven quadrangle, the calm cloister walk; there, there alone is rest. There, one ceases to be a prey and a laughing-stock; there, one sees no more bloodshed and spulzie; there, one need not be forced to treachery or violence. Oh, Uncle! my very soul is sick for Coldingham. How many years will it be ere I can myself bestow my sister on Patie, and hide my head in peace!'

Before his uncle had done more than answer, 'Nay, nay, Malcolm, these are no words for the oe of Bruce; you are born to dare as well as to suffer,' there was an approach of footsteps, and two young people entered the hall; the first a girl, with a family likeness to Malcolm, but tall, upright, beautiful, and with the rich colouring of perfect health, her plaid still hanging in a loose swelling hood round her brilliant face and dark hair, snooded with a crimson ribbon and diamond clasp; the other, a knightly young man, of stately height and robust limbs, keen bright blue eyes and amber hair and beard, moving with the ease and grace that showed his training in the highest school of chivalry.

'Good Uncle,' cried the maiden in eager excitement, 'there is a guest coming. He has just turned over the brae side, and can be coming nowhere but here.'

'A guest!' cried both Malcolm and the elder knight, 'of what kind, Lily?'

'A knight—a knight in bright steel, and with three attendants,' said Lilias; 'one of Patrick's French comrades, say I, by the grace of his riding.'

'Not a message from the Regent, I trust,' sighed Malcolm. 'Patie, oh do not lower the drawbridge, till we hear whether it be friend or foe.'

Charlotte M. Yonge

'Nay, Malcolm, 'tis well none save friends heard that,' said Patrick. 'When shall we make a brave man of you?'

'Nevertheless, Patie,' said the old gentleman, 'though I had rather the caution had come from the eldest rather than the youngest head among us, parley as much as may serve with honour and courtesy ere opening the gate to the stranger. Hark, there is his bugle.'

A certain look of nervous terror passed over young Malcolm's face, while his sister watched full of animation and curiosity, as one to whom excitement of any kind could hardly come amiss, exclaiming, as she looked from the window, 'Fear not, most prudent Malcolm; Father Ninian is with him: Father Ninian must have invited him.'

'Strange,' muttered Patrick, 'that Father Ninian should be picking up and bringing home stray wandering land-loupers;' and with an anxious glance at Lilias, he went forward unwillingly to perform those duties of hospitality which had become necessary, since the presence of the castle chaplain was a voucher for the guest. The drawbridge had already been lowered, and the new-comer was crossing it upon a powerful black steed, guided by Father Ninian upon his rough mountain pony, on which he had shortly before left the castle, to attend at a Church festival held at Coldingham.

The chaplain was a wise, prudent, and much-respected man; nevertheless, young Sir Patrick Drummond felt little esteem for his prudence in displaying one at least of the treasures of the castle to the knight on the black horse. The stranger was a very tall man, of robust and stalwart make, apparently aged about seven or eight and twenty years, clad in steel armour, enamelled so as to have a burnished blue appearance; but the vizor of the helmet was raised, and the face beneath it was a manly open face, thoroughly Scottish in its forms, but very handsome, and with short dark auburn hair, and eyes of the same peculiar tint, glancing with a light that once seen could never be forgotten; and the bearing was such, that Patrick at once growled to himself, 'One of our haughty loons, brimful of *outre cuidance*; and yet how coolly he bears it off. If he looks to find us his humble servants, he will find himself mistaken, I trow.'

'Sir Patrick,' said Father Ninian, who was by this time close to him, 'let me present to you Sir James Stewart, a captive knight who is come to collect his ransom. I fell in with him on the road, and as his road lay with mine, I made bold to assure him of a welcome from your honoured father and Lord Malcolm.'

Patrick's face cleared. It was no grace or beauty that he feared in any stranger, but the sheer might and unright that their Regency enabled the House of Albany to exercise over the orphans of the royal family, whose head was absent; and a captive knight could be no mischievous person. Still this might be only a specious pretence to impose on the chaplain, and gain admittance to the castle; and Patrick was resolved to be well on his guard, though he replied courteously to the graceful bow with which the stranger greeted him, saying in a manly mellow voice and southern accent, 'I have been bold enough to presume on the good father's offer of hospitality, Sir.'

'You are welcome, Sir,' returned Patrick, taking the stranger's bridle that he might dismount; 'my father and my cousin will gladly further on his way a prisoner seeking freedom.'

'A captive may well be welcome, for the sake of one prisoner,' said his father, who had in the meantime come forward, and extended his hand to the knight, who took it, and uncovering his bright locks, respectfully said, 'I am in the presence of the noble Tutor of Glenuskie.'

'Even so, Sir,' returned Sir David Drummond, who was, in fact, as his nephew's guardian, usually known by this curious title; 'and you here see my wards, the Lord Malcolm and Lady Lilias. Your knighthood will make allowances for the lad, he is but home-bred.' For while Lilias with stately grace responded to Sir James Stewart's courtly greeting, Malcolm bashfully made an awkward bow, and seemed ready to shrink within himself, as, indeed, the brutal jests of his rude cousins had made him dread and hate the eye of a stranger; and while the knight was led forward to the hall fire, he merely pressed up to the priest, and eagerly demanded under his breath, 'Have you brought me the book?' but Father Ninian had only time to nod, and sign that a volume was in his bosom, before old Sir David called out, 'What now, Malcolm, forgetting that your part is to come and disarm the knight who does you the honour to be your guest?' And Sir Patrick rather roughly pushed him forward, gruffly whispering, 'Leave not Lily to supply your lack of courtesy.'

Malcolm shambled forward, bewildered, as the keen auburn eye fell on him, and the cheery kindly voice said, 'Ha! a new book—a romance? Well may that drive out other thoughts.'

'Had he ears to hear such a whisper?' thought Malcolm, as he mumbled in the hoarse voice of bashful boyhood, 'Not a romance, Sir, but whatever the good fathers at Coldingham would lend me.'

'It is the "Itinerarium" of the blessed Adamnanus,' replied Father Ninian, producing from his bosom a parcel, apparently done up in many wrappers, a seal-skin above all.

'The "Itinerarium"!' exclaimed Sir James, 'methought I had heard of such a book. I have a friend in England who would give many a fair rose noble for a sight of it.'

'A friend in England!'—the words had a sinister sound to the audience, and while Malcolm jealously gathered up the book into his arms, the priest made cold answer, that the book was the property of the Monastery at Coldingham, and had only been lent to Lord Malcolm Stewart by special favour. The guest could not help smiling, and saying he was glad books were thus prized in Scotland; but at that moment, as the sunny look shone on his face, and he stood before the fire in the close suit of chamois leather which he wore under his armour, old Sir David exclaimed, 'Ha! never did I see such a likeness. Patie, you should be old enough to remember; do you not see it?'

'What should I see? Who is he like?' asked Patrick, surprised at his father's manner.

'Who?' whispered Sir David in a lowered voice; 'do you not see it? to the unhappy lad, the Duke of Rothsay.'

Patrick could not help smiling, for he had been scarcely seven years old at the time of the murder of the unfortunate Prince of Scotland; but a flush of colour rose into the face of the guest, and he shortly answered, 'So I have been told;' and then assuming a seat near Sir David, he entered into conversation with him upon the condition of Scotland at the period, inquiring into the state of many of the families and districts by name. Almost always there was but one answer—murder—harrying—foray; and when the question followed, 'What had the Regent done?' there was a shrug of the shoulders, and as often Sir

Charlotte M. Yonge

James's face flushed with a dark red fire, and his hand clenched at the hilt of the sword by his side.

'And is there not a man in Scotland left to strike for the right?' he demanded at last; 'cannot nobles, clergy, and burghers, band themselves in parliament to put down Albany and his bloody house, and recall their true head?'

'They love to have it so,' returned Sir David sadly. 'United, they might be strong enough; but each knows that his fellow, Douglas, Lennox, March, or Mar, would be ready to play the same game as Albany; and to raise a rival none will stir.'

'And so,' proceeded Sir James, bitterly, 'the manhood of Scotland goes forth to waste itself in an empty foreign war, merely to keep France in as wretched a state of misrule as itself.'

'Nay, nay, Sir,' cried Patrick angrily, 'it is to save an ancient ally from the tyranny of our foulest foe. It is the only place where a Scotsman can seek his fortune with honour, and without staining his soul with foul deeds. Bring our King home, and every sword shall be at his service.'

'What, when they have all been lavished on the crazy Frenchman?' said Sir James.

'No, Sir,' said Patrick, rising in his vehemence; 'when they have been brightened there by honourable warfare, not tarnished by home barbarities.'

'He speaks truly,' said Sir David; 'and though it will go to my heart to part with the lad, yet may I not say a word to detain him in a land where the contagion of violence can scarce be escaped by a brave man.'

Sir James gave a deep sigh as of pain, but as if to hinder its being remarked, promptly answered, 'That may be; but what is to be the lot of a land whose honest men desert her cause as too evil for them, and seek out another, that when seen closer is scarce less evil?'

'How, Sir!' cried Patrick; 'you a prisoner of England, yet speaking against our noble French allies, so foully trampled on?'

'I have lived long enough in England,' returned Sir James, 'to think that land happiest where law is strong enough to enforce peace and order.'

'The coward loons!' muttered Patrick, chiefly out of the spirit of opposition.

'You have been long in England, Sir?' said Lilias, hoping to direct the conversation into a more peaceful current.

'Many years, fair lady,' he replied, turning courteously to her; 'I was taken when I was a mere lad, but I have had gentle captors, and no over harsh prison.'

'And has no one ransomed you?' she asked pitifully, as one much moved by a certain patience on his brow, and in his sweet full voice.

'No one, lady. My uncle was but too willing that the heir should be kept aloof; and it is only now he is dead, that I have obtained leave from my friendly captor to come in search of my ransom.'

Lilias would have liked to know the amount, but it was not manners to ask, since the rate of ransom was the personal value of the knight; and her uncle put in the question, who was his keeper.

Charlotte M. Yonge

'The Earl of Somerset,' rather hastily answered Sir James; and then at once Lilias exclaimed, 'Ah, Uncle, is not the King, too, in his charge?' And then questions crowded on. 'What like is the King? How brooks he his durance? What freedom hath he? What hope is there of his return? Can he brook to hear of his people's wretchedness?'

This was the first question at which Sir James attempted to unclose his hitherto smiling and amused lip. Then it quivered, and the dew glittered in his eyes as he answered, 'Brook it! No indeed, lady. His heart burns within him at every cry that comes over the Border, and will well-nigh burst at what I have seen and heard! King Harry tells him that to send him home were but tossing him on the swords of the Albany. Better, better so, to die in one grapple for his country's sake, than lie bound, hearing her bitter wails, and unable to stir for her redress!' and as he dashed the indignant tear from his eyes, Patrick caught his hand.

'Your heart is in the right place, friend,' he said; 'I look on you as an honest man and brother in arms from this moment.'

"Tis a bargain,' said Sir James, the smile returning, and his eyes again glistening as he wrung Sir Patrick's hand. 'When the hour comes for the true rescue of Scotland, we will strike together.'

'And you will tell the King,' added Patrick, 'that here are true hearts, and I could find many more, only longing to fence him from the Albany swords, about which King Harry is so good as to fash himself.'

'But what like is the King?' asked Lilias eagerly. 'Oh, I would fain see him. Is it true that he was the tallest man at King Harry's sacring? more shame that he were there!'

'He and I are much of a height, lady,' returned the knight. 'Maybe I may give you the justest notion of him by saying that I am said to be his very marrow.'

'That explains your likeness to the poor Duke,' said Sir David, satisfied; 'and you too count kindred with our royal house, methinks?'

'I am sprung from Walter the Stewart, so much I know; my lands lie Carrick-wards,' said Sir James lightly, 'but I have been a prisoner so long, that the pedigree of my house was never taught me, and I can make no figure in describing my own descent.' And as though to put an end to the inquiry, he walked to the window, where Malcolm so soon as they had begun to talk of the misrule of Scotland, had ensconced himself in the window-seat with his new book, making the most of the failing light, and asked him whether the Monk of Iona equalled his expectations.

Malcolm was not easy to draw out at first, but it presently appeared that he had been baffled by a tough bit of Latinity. The knight looked, and readily expounded the sentence, so that all became plain; and then, as it was already too dark to pursue the study with comfort, he stood over the boy, talking to him of books and of poems, while the usually pale, listless, uninterested countenance responded by looks of eager delight and flushing colour.

It seemed as though each were equally pleased with the other: Sir James, at finding so much knowledge and understanding in a Scottish castle; and Malcolm, at, for the first time, meeting anything but contempt for his tastes from aught but an ecclesiastic.

Their talk continued till they were summoned to supper, which had been somewhat delayed to provide for the new-comers. It was a simple enough meal, suited to Lent, and was merely of dried fish, with barley bread and kail brose; but there were few other places in Scotland where it would have been served with so much of the refinement that Sir David Drummond and his late wife had learnt in France. A tablecloth and napkins, separate trenchers, and water for hand cleansing, were not always to be found in the houses of the nobles; and in fact, there were those who charged Malcolm's delicacy and timidity on the *nisete* or folly of his effeminate education; the having the rushes on the floor frequently changed, the preference of lamps for pine torches, and the not keeping falcons, dogs, swine, and all, pell mell in the great hall.

Lilias sat between her uncle and his guest, looking so fair and bright that Patrick felt fresh accesses of angry jealousy, while the visitor talked as one able to report to the natives from another world, and that world the hateful England, which as a Scotsman he was bound to abhor. Had it been France, it had been endurable, but praise of English habits was mere disloyalty; and yet, whenever Patrick tried to throw in a disparaging word, he found himself met with a quiet superiority such as he had believed no knight in Scotland could assume with him, and still it was neither brow-beating nor insolence, nothing that could give offence.

Malcolm begged to know whether there had not been a rare good poet in England, called Chaucer. Verily there had been, said the knight; and on a little solicitation, so soon as supper was over, he recited to the eager and delighted auditors the tale of patient Grisel, as rendered by Chaucer, calling forth eager comments from both Patrick and Lily, on the unknightliness of the Marquis. Malcolm, however, added, 'Yet, after all, she was but a mere peasant wench.'

'What makes that, young Sir?' replied Sir James gravely. 'I would have you to know that the husband's rank is the wife's, and the more unequal were their lot before, the more is he bound to respect her, and to make her be respected.'

'That may be, after the deed is done,' said Sir David, in a warning voice; 'but it is not well that like should not match with like. Many an evil have I seen in my time, from unequal mating.'

'And, Sir,' eagerly exclaimed Patrick, 'no doubt you can gainsay the slander, that our noble King has been caught in the toils of an artful Englishwoman, and been drawn in to promise her a share in his crown.'

A flush of crimson flamed forth on Sir James Stewart's cheeks, and his tawny eye glanced with a fire like red lightning, but he seemed, as it were, to be holding himself in, and answered with a voice forcibly kept low and calm, and therefore the more terribly stern, 'Young Sir, I warn you to honour your future queen.'

Sir David made a gesture with his hand, enforcing restraint upon his son, and turning to Sir James, said, 'Our queen will we honour, when such she is, Sir; but if you are returning to the King, it were well that he should know that our hot Scottish bloods, here, could scarce brook an English alliance, and certainly not one beneath his birth.'

'The King would answer, Sir,' returned Sir James, haughtily, but with recovered command over himself, 'that it is for him to judge whom his subjects shall brook as their queen. Moreover,' he added, in a different and more conciliatory voice, 'Scotsmen must be proud indeed who disdain the late King's niece, the great-granddaughter

Charlotte M. Yonge

of King Edward III., and as noble and queenly a demoiselle as ever was born in a palace.'

'She is so very fair, then?' said Lilies, who was of course on the side of true love. 'You have seen her, gentle Sir? Oh, tell us what are her beauties?'

'Fair damsel,' said Sir James, in a much more gentle tone, 'you forget that I am only a poor prisoner, who have only now and then viewed the lady Joan Beaufort with distant reverence, as destined to be my queen. All I can tell is, that her walk and bearing mark her out for a throne.'

'And oh!' cried Malcolm, 'is it not true that the King hath composed songs and poems in her honour?'

'Pah!' muttered Patrick; 'as though the King would be no better than a wandering minstrel rhymester!'

'Or than King David!' dryly said Sir James.

'It is true, then, Sir,' exclaimed Lilias. 'He doth verily add minstrelsy to his other graces? Know you the lines, Sir? Can you sing them to us? Oh, I pray you.'

'Nay, fair maid,' returned Sir James, 'methinks I might but add to the scorn wherewith Sir Patrick is but too much inclined to regard the captive King.'

'A captive, a captive—ay, minstrelsy is the right solace for a captive,' said Patrick; 'at least, so they say and sing. Our king will have better work when he gains his freedom. Only there will come before me a subtilty I once saw in jelly and blanc-mange, at a banquet in France, where a lion fell in love with a hunter's daughter, and let her, for love's sake, draw his teeth and clip his claws, whereupon he found himself made a sport for her father's hounds.'

'I promise you, Sir Patrick,' replied the guest, 'that the Lady Joan is more hike to send her Lion forth from the hunter's toils, with claws and teeth fresh-whetted by the desire of honour.

'But the lay—the hay, Sir,' entreated Lilias; 'who knows that it may not win Patrick to be the Lady Joan's devoted servant? Malcolm, your harp!'

Malcolm had already gone in quest of the harp he loved all the better for the discouragement thrown on his gentle tastes.

The knight leant back, with a pensive look softening his features as he said, after a little consideration, 'Then, fair lady, I will sing you the song made by King James, when he had first seen the fair mistress of his heart, on the slopes of Windsor, looking from his chamber window. He feigns her to be a nightingale.'

'And what is that, Sir?' demanded Lilias. 'I have heard the word in romances, and deemed it a kind of angel that sings by night.'

'It is a bird, sister,' replied Malcolm; 'Philomel, that pierces her breast with a thorn, and sings sweetly even to her death.'

'That's mere minstrel leasing, Malcolm,' said Patrick. 'I have both seen and heard the bird in France—*Rossignol*, as we call it there; and were I a lady, I should deem it small compliment to be likened to a little russet-backed, homely fowl such as that.'

'While I,' replied the prisoner, 'feel so much with your fair sister, that nightingales are a sort of angels that sing by night, that it pains me, when I think of winning my freedom, to remember that I shall never again hear their songs answering one another through the forest of Windsor.'

Patrick shrugged his shoulders, but Lilias was so anxious to hear the lay, that she entreated him to be silent; and Sir James, with a manly mellow voice, with an exceedingly sweet strain in it, and a skill, both of modulation and finger, such as showed admirable taste and instruction, poured forth that beautiful song of the nightingale at Windsor, which commences King James's story of his love, in his poem of the King's Quhair.

There was an eager pressing round to hear, and not only were Lilias and Malcolm, but old Sir David himself, much affected by the strain, which the latter said put him in mind of the days of King Robert III., which, sad as they were, now seemed like good old times, so much worse was the present state of affairs. Sir James, however, seemed anxious to prevent discussion of the verses he had sung, and applied to Malcolm to give a specimen of his powers: and thus, with music, ballad, and lay, the evening passed away, till the parting cup was sent round, and the Tutor of Glenuskie and Malcolm marshalled their guest to the apartment where he was to sleep, in a wainscoted box bedstead, and his two attendant squires, a great iron-gray Scot and a rosy honest-faced Englishman, on pallets on the floor.

In the morning he went on his journey, but not without an invitation to rest there again on his way back, whether with or without his ransom. He promised to come, saying that he should gladly bear to the King the last advices from one so honoured as the Tutor of Glenuskie; and, on their sides, Malcolm and Sir David resolved to do their best to have some gold pieces to contribute, rather than so 'proper a knight' should fail in raising his ransom; but gold was never plenty, and Patrick needed all that his uncle could supply, to bear him to those wars in France, where he looked for renown and fortune.

For these were, as may have been gathered, those evil days when James I. of Scotland was still a captive to England, and when the House of Albany exercised its cruel misrule upon Scotland; delaying to ransom the King, lest they should bring home a master.

Old Robert of Albany had been King Stork, his son Murdoch was King Log; and the misery was infinitely increased by the violence and lawlessness of Murdoch's sons. King Robert II. had left Scotland the fearful legacy of, as Froissart says, 'eleven sons who loved arms.' Of these, Robert III. was the eldest, the Duke of Albany the second. These were both dead, and were represented, the one by the captive young King James, the other by the Regent, Duke Murdoch of Albany, and his brother John, Earl of Buchan, now about to head a Scottish force, among whom Patrick Drummond intended to sail, to assist the French.

Others of the eleven, Earls of Athol, Menteith, &c., survived; but the youngest of the brotherhood, by name Malcolm, who had married the heiress of Glenuskie, had been killed at Homildon Hill, when he had solemnly charged his Stewart nephews and brothers to leave his two orphan children to the sole charge of their mother's cousin, Sir David Drummond, a good old man, who had been the best supporter and confidant of poor Robert III. in his unhappy reign, and in embassies to France had lost much of the rugged barbarism to which Scotland had retrograded during the wars with England.

Charlotte M. Yonge

CHAPTER II

THE RESCUE OF COLDINGHAM

It was a lonely tract of road, marked only by the bare space trodden by feet of man and horse, and yet, in truth, the highway between Berwick and Edinburgh, which descended from a heathery moorland into a somewhat spacious valley, with copsewood clothing one side, in the midst of which rose a high mound or knoll, probably once the site of a camp, for it still bore lines of circumvallation, although it was entirely deserted, except by the wandering shepherds of the neighbourhood, or occasionally by outlaws, who found an admirable ambush in the rear.

The spring had hung the hazels with tassels, bedecked the willows with golden downy tufts, and opened the primroses and celandines beneath them, when the solitary dale was disturbed by the hasty clatter of horses' feet, and hard, heavy breathing as of those who had galloped headlong beyond their strength. Here, however, the fore-most of the party, an old esquire, who grasped the bridle-rein of youth by his side, drew up his own horse, and that which he was dragging on with him, saying—

'We may breathe here a moment; there is shelter in the wood. And you, Rab, get ye up to the top of Jill's Knowe, and keep a good look-out.'

'Let me go back, you false villain!' sobbed the boy, with the first use of his recovered breath.

'Do not be so daft, Lord Malcolm,' replied the Squire, retaining his hold on the boy's bridle; 'what, rin your head into the wolf's mouth again, when we've barely brought you off haill and sain?'

'Haill and sain? Dastard and forlorn,' cried Malcolm, with passionate weeping. 'I—I to flee and leave my sister—my uncle! Oh, where are they? Halbert, let me go; I'll never pardon thee.'

'Hoot, my lord! would I let you gang, when the Tutor spak to me as plain as I hear you now? "Take off Lord Malcolm," says he; "save him, and you save the rest. See him safe to the Earl of Mar." Those were his words, my lord; and if you wilna heed them, I will.'

'What, and leave my sister to the reivers? Oh, what may not they be doing to her? Let us go back and fall on them, Halbert; better die saving her than know her in Walter Stewart's hands. Then were I the wretched craven he calls me.'

'Look you, Lord Malcolm,' said Halbert, laying his finger on his nose, with a knowing expression, 'my young lady is safe from harm so long as you are out of the Master of Albany's reach. Had you come by a canny thrust in the fray, as no doubt was his purpose, or were you in his hands to be mewed in a convent, then were your sister worth the wedding; but the Master will never wed her while you live and have friends to back you, and his father, the Regent, will see she has no ill-usage. You'll do best for yourself and her too, as well as Sir David, if you make for Dunbar, and call ben your uncles of Athole and Strathern.—How now, Rab? are the loons making

Charlotte M. Yonge

this way?'

'Na, na!' said Rab, descending; "tis from the other gate; 'tis a knight in blue damasked steel: he, methinks, that harboured in our castle some weeks syne.'

'Hm!' said Halbert, considering; 'he looked like a trusty cheild: maybe he'd guide my lord here to a wiser wit, and a good lance on the way to Dunbar is not to be scorned.'

In fact, there would have been no time for one party to conceal themselves from the other; for, hidden by the copsewood, and unheeded by the watchers who were gazing in the opposite direction, Sir James Stewart and his two attendants suddenly came round the foot of Jill's Knowe upon the fugitives, who were profiting by the interval to loosen the girths of their horses, and water them at the pool under the thicket, whilst Halbert in vain tried to pacify and reason with the young master, who had thrown himself on the grass in an agony of grief and despair. Sir James, after the first momentary start, recognized the party in an instant, and at once leapt from his horse, exclaiming—

'How now, my bonnie man—my kind host—what is it? what makes this grief?'

'Do not speak to me, Sir,' muttered the unhappy boy. 'They have been reft—reft from me, and I have done nothing for them. Walter of Albany has them, and I am here.'

And he gave way to another paroxysm of grief, while Halbert explained to Sir James Stewart that when Sir Patrick Drummond had gone to embark for France, with the army led to the aid of Charles VI. by the Earl of Buchan, his father and cousins, with a large escort, had accompanied him to Eyemouth; whence, after taking leave of him, they had set out to spend Passion-tide and Easter at Coldingham Abbey, after the frequent fashion of the devoutly inclined among the Scottish nobility, in whose castles there was often little commodity for religious observances. Short, however, as was the distance, they had in the midst of it been suddenly assailed by a band of armed men, among whom might easily be recognized the giant form of young Walter Stewart, the Master of Albany, the Regent Duke Murdoch's eldest son, who was well known for his lawless excesses and violence. His father's silky sayings, and his own ruder speeches, had long made it known to the House of Glenuskie that the family policy was to cajole or to drive the sickly heir into a convent, and, rendering Lilias the possessor of the broad lands inherited from both parents, unite her and them to the Albany family.

The almost barbarous fierceness and wild licentiousness of Walter would have made the arrangement abhorrent to Lilias, even had not love passages already passed between her and her cousin, Patrick Drummond, and Sir David had hitherto protected her by keeping Malcolm in the secular life; but Walter, it seemed, had grown impatient, and had made this treacherous attack, evidently hoping to rid himself of the brother, and secure the sister. No sooner had the Tutor of Glenuskie perceived that his own party were overmatched, than he had bidden his faithful squire to secure the bairns—if not both, at least the boy; and Halbert, perceiving that Lilias had already been pounced upon by Sir Walter himself and several more, seized the bridle of the bewildered Malcolm, who was still trying to draw his sword, and had absolutely swept him away from the scene of action before he had well realized what was passing; and now that the poor lad understood the whole, his horror, grief, and shame were unspeakable.

Charlotte M. Yonge

Before Sir James had done more than hear the outline of Halbert's tale, however, the watchers on the mound gave the signal that the reivers were coming that way—a matter hitherto doubtful, since no one could guess whether Walter Stewart would make for Edinburgh or for Doune. With the utmost agility Sir James sprang up the side of the mound, reconnoitred, and returned again just as Halbert was trying to stir his master from the ground, and Malcolm answering sullenly that he would not move—he would be taken and die with the rest.

'You may save them instead, if you will attend to me,' said Sir James; and at his words the boy suddenly started up with a look of hope.

'How many fell upon you?' demanded Sir James.

'Full a hundred lances,' replied Halbert (and a lance meant at least three men). 'It wad be a fule's wark to withstand them. Best bide fast in the covert, for our horses are sair forfaughten.'

'If there are now more than twenty lances, I am greatly mistaken,' returned Sir James. 'They must have broken up after striking their blow, or have sent to secure Glenuskie; and we, falling on them from this thicket—'

'I see, I see,' cried Halbert. 'Back, ye loons; back among the hazels. Hold every one his horse ready to mount.'

'With your favour, Sir Squire, I say, bind each man his horse to a tree. The skene and broadsword, which I see you all wear, will be ten times as effective on foot.'

'Do as the knight bids,' said Malcolm, starting forth with colour on his cheek, light in his eye, that made him another being. 'In him there is help.'

'Ay, ay, Lord Malcolm,' muttered Halbert; 'you need not tell me that: I know my duty better than not to do the bidding of a belted knight, and pretty man too of his inches.'

The two attendants of Sir James were meantime apparently uttering some remonstrance, to which he lightly replied, 'Tut, Nigel; it will do thine heart good to hew down a minion of Albany. What were I worth could I not strike a blow against so foul a wrong to my own orphan kindred? Brewster, I'll answer it to thy master. These are his foes, as well as those of all honest men. Ha! thou art as glad to be at them as I myself.'

By this time he had exchanged his cap for a steel helmet, and was assuming the command as his natural right, as he placed the men in their ambush behind the knoll, received reports from those he had set to watch, and concerted the signal with Halbert and his own followers. Malcolm kept by him, shivering with intense excitement and eagerness; and thus they waited till the horses' hoofs and clank of armour were distinctly audible. But even then Sir James, with outstretched hand, signed his followers back, and kept them in the leash, as it were, until the troop was fairly in the valley, those in front beginning to halt to give their horses water. They were, in effect, riding somewhat carelessly, and with the ease of men whose feat was performed, and who expected no more opposition. Full in the midst was Lilias, entirely muffled and pinioned by a large plaid drawn closely round her, and held upon the front of the saddle of a large tall horse, ridden by a slender, light-limbed, wiry groom, whom Malcolm knew as Christopher Hall, a retainer of the Duke of Albany; and beside him rode her captor, Sir Walter Stewart, a man little above twenty, but with a bronzed, hardened, reckless expression that made him look much older, and of huge height and giant build. Malcolm knew him well, and regarded him with unmitigated horror and dread, both from the knowledge of his ruffianly violence even towards his father, from fear of his intentions, and from the misery that his brutal jests, scoffs, and practical jokes had often personally inflicted: and the sight of his sister in the power of this wicked man was the realization of all his worst fears. But ere there was time for more than one strong pang of consternation and constitutional terror, Sir James's shout of 'St. Andrew for the right!' was ringing out, echoed by all the fifteen in ambush with him, as simultaneously they leapt forward. Malcolm, among the first, darting with one spring, as it were, to the horse where his sister was carried, seized the bridle with his left hand, and flashing his sword upon the ruffian with the other, shouted, 'Let go, villain; give me my sister!' Hall's first impulse was to push his horse forward so as to trample the boy down, but Malcolm's hold rendered this impossible; besides, there was the shouting, the clang, the confusion of the outburst of an ambush all around and on every side, and before the man could free his hand to draw his weapon he necessarily loosed his grasp of Lilias, who, half springing, half falling, came to the ground, almost overthrowing her brother in her descent, but just saved by him from coming down prostrate. The horse, suddenly released, started forward with its rider and at the same moment Malcolm, recovering himself, stood with his sword in his hand, his arm round his sister's waist, assuring her that she was safe, and himself glowing for the first time with manly exultation. Had he not saved and rescued her himself?

It was as well, however, that the rescue did not depend on his sole prowess. Indeed, by the time the brother and sister were clinging together and turning to look round, the first shock was over, and the retainers of Albany, probably fancying the attack made by a much larger troop, were either in full flight, or getting decidedly the worst in their encounters with their assailants.

Sir James Stewart had at the first onset sprung like a lion upon the Master of Albany, and without drawing his sword had grappled with him. 'In the name of St. Andrew and the King, yield thy prey, thou dastard,' were his words as he threw his arms round the body of Sir Walter, and exerted his full strength to drag him from his horse. The young giant writhed, struggled, cursed, raged; he had not space to draw sword or even dagger, but he struck furiously with his gauntleted hand, strove to drive his horse forward. The struggle like that of Hercules and Antaeus, so desperate and mighty was the strength put forth on either side, but nothing could unclasp the iron grip of those sinewy arms, and almost as soon as Malcolm and Lilias had eyes to see what was passing, Walter Stewart was being dragged off his horse by that tremendous grapple, and the next moment his armour rung as he lay prostrate on his back upon the ground.

His conqueror set his mailed foot upon his neck lightly, but so as to prevent any attempt to rise, and after one moment's pause to gather breath, said in a clear deep trumpet voice, 'Walter Stewart of Albany, on one condition I grant thee thy life. It is that thou take the most solemn oath on the spot that no spulzie or private brawl shall henceforth stain that hand of thine while thy father holds the power in Scotland. Take that oath, thou livest: refuse it, and—' He held up the deadly little dagger called the misericorde.

'And who art thou, caitiff land-louper,' muttered Walter, 'to put to oath knights and princes?'

The knight raised the visor of his helmet. The evening sun shone resplendently on his damasked blue armour and the St. Andrew's cross on his breast, and lighted up that red fire that lurked in his eyes, and withal the calm power and righteous indignation on his features might have befitted an avenging angel wielding the lightning.

'Thou wilt know me when we meet again,' was all he said; and for the very calmness of the voice the Master of Albany, who was but a mere commonplace insolent ruffian, quailed with awe and terror to the very backbone.

'Loose me, and I will swear,' he faintly murmured.

Sir James, before removing his foot, unclasped his gorget, and undoing a chain, held up a jewel shaped like a St. Andrew's cross, with a diamond in the midst, covering a fragmentary relic. At the sight Walter Stewart's eyes, large pale ones, dilated as if with increased consternation, the sweat started on his forehead, and his breath came in shorter gasps. Malcolm and Lilias, standing near, likewise felt a sense of strange awe, for they too had heard of this relic, a supposed fragment of St. Andrew's own instrument of martyrdom, which had belonged to St. Margaret, and had been thought a palladium to the royal family and House of Stewart.

'Rise on thy knees,' said Sir James, now taking away his foot, 'and swear upon this.'

Walter, completely cowed and overawed, rose to his knees at his victor's command, laid his hand on the relic, and in a shaken, almost tremulous voice, repeated the words of the oath after his dictation: 'I, Walter Stewart, Master of Albany, hereby swear to God and St. Andrew, to fight in no private brawl, to spoil no man nor woman, to oppress no poor man, clerk, widow, maid, or orphan, to abstain from all wrong or spulzie from this hour until the King shall come again in peace.'

He uttered the words, and kissed the jewel that was tendered to him; and then Sir James said, in the same cold and dignified tone, 'Let thine oath be sacred, or beware. Now, mount and go thy way, but take heed *how* I meet thee again.'

Sir Walter's horse was held for him by Brewster, the knight's English attendant, and without another word he flung himself into the saddle, and rode away to join such of his followers as were waiting dispersed at a safe distance to mark his fate, but without attempting anything for his assistance.

'Oh, Sir!' burst forth Malcolm; but then, even as he was about to utter his thanks, his eye sought for the guardian who had ever been his mouthpiece, and, with a sudden shriek of dismay, he cried, 'My uncle! where is he? where is Sir David?'

'Alack! alack!' cried Lilias. 'Oh, brother, I saw him on the ground; he fell before my horse. I saw no more, for the Master held me, and muffled my face. Oh, let us back, he may yet live.'

'Yea, let us back,' said Sir James, 'if we may yet save the good old man. Those villains will not dare to follow; or if they do, Nigel—Brewster, you understand guarding the rear.'

'Sir,' began Lilias, 'how can we thank—'

'Not at all, lady,' replied Sir James, smiling; 'you will do better to take your seat; I fear it must be *en croupe*, for we can scarce dismount one of your guards.'

'She shall ride behind me,' said Malcolm, in a more alert and confident voice than had ever been heard from

Charlotte M. Yonge

him before.

'Ay, right,' said Sir James, placing a kind hand on his shoulder; 'thou hast won her back by thine own exploit, and mayst well have the keeping of her. That rush on the caitiff groom was well and shrewdly done.'

And for all Malcolm's anxiety for his uncle, his heart had never given such a leap as at finding himself suddenly raised from the depressed down-trodden coward into something like manhood and self-respect.

Lilias, who, like most damsels of her time, was hardy and active, saw no difficulties in the mode of conveyance, and, so soon as Malcolm had seated himself on horse-back, she placed one foot upon his toe, and with a spring of her own, assisted by Sir James's well-practised hand, was instantly perched on the crupper, clasping her brother round the waist with her arms, and laying her head on his shoulder in loving pride at his exploit, while for her further security Sir James threw round them both the long plaid that had so lately bound her.

'Dear Malcolm'—and her whisper fell sweetly on his ear—'it will be bonnie tidings for Patie that thou didst loose me all thyself. The false tyrant, to fall on us the very hour Patie was on the salt sea.'

But they were riding so fast that there was scant possibility for words; and, besides, Sir James kept too close to them for private whispers. In about an hour's time they had crossed the bit of table-land that formed the moor, and descended into another little gorge, which was the place where the attack had been made upon the travellers.

This was where it was possible that they might find Sir

David; but no trace was to be seen, except that the grass was trampled and stained with blood. Perhaps, both Lilias and old Halbert suggested, some of their people had returned and taken him to the Abbey of Coldingham, and as this was by far the safest lodging and refuge for her and her brother, the horses' heads were at once turned thitherwards.

The grand old Priory of Coldingham, founded by King Edgar, son of Margaret the Saint, and of Malcolm Ceanmohr, in testimony of his gratitude for his recovery of his father's throne from the usurper Donaldbane, was a Benedictine monastery under the dominion of the great central Abbey of Durham.

It had been a great favourite with the Scottish kings of that glorious dynasty which sprung from Margaret of Wessex, and had ample estates, which, when it was in good hands, enabled it to supply the manifold purposes of an ecclesiastical school, a model farm, a harbour for travellers, and a fortified castle. At this period, the Prior, John de Akecliff, or Oakcliff, was an excellent man, a great friend of Sir David Drummond, and much disliked and persecuted by the House of Albany, so that there was little doubt that this would be the first refuge thought of by Sir David's followers.

Accordingly Malcolm and his companions rode up to the chief gateway, a grand circular archway, with all the noble though grotesque mouldings, zigzag and cable, dog-tooth and parrot-beak, visages human and diabolic, wherewith the Norman builders loved to surround their doorways. The doors were of solid oak, heavily guarded with iron, and from a little wicket in the midst peered out a cowled head, and instantly ensued the exclamation—

'Benedicite! Welcome, my Lord Malcolm! Ah! but this

Charlotte M. Yonge

will ease the heart of the Tutor of Glenuskie!'

'Ah! then he is here?' cried Malcolm.

'Here, Sir, but in woful plight; borne in an hour syne by four carles who said you had been set upon by the Master of Albany, and sair harried, and they say the Tutor doth nought but wail for his bairns. How won ye out of his hands, my Lord?'

'Thanks to this good knight,' said Malcolm; and the gate was opened, and the new-comers dismounted to pass under the archway, which taught humility. A number of the brethren met them as they came forth into the first quadrangle, surrounded by a beautiful cloister, and containing what was called Edgar's Walls, a house raised by the good founder, for his own lodging and that of visitors, within the monastery. It was a narrow building, about thirty feet from the church, was perfectly familiar to Malcolm, who bent his steps at once thither, among the congratulations of the monks; and Lilias was not prevented from accompanying him thus far within the convent, but all beyond the nave of the church was forbidden ground to her sex, though the original monastery destroyed by the Danes had been one of the double foundations for monks and nuns.

Entering the building, the brother and sister hastily crossed a sort of outer hall to a chamber where Sir David lay on his bed, attended by the Prior Akecliff and the Infirmarer. The glad tidings had already reached him, and he held out his hands, kissed and blessed his restored charges, and gave thanks with all his heart; but there was a strange wanness upon his face, and a spasm of severe pain crossed him more than once, though, as Lilias eagerly asked after his hurts, he called them nothing, since he had her safe again, and then bade Malcolm summon the captive knight that he might thank him.

Sir James Stewart had been left in the hall without, to the hospitality of the monks; he had laid aside his helmet, washed his face, and arranged his bright locks, and as he rose to follow Malcolm, his majestic stature and bearing seemed to befit the home of the old Scottish King.

As he entered the chamber, Sir David slightly raised himself on the pillow, and, with his eyes dilating into a bewildered gaze, exclaimed, 'My liege, my dear master!'

'He raves,' sighed Lilias, clasping Malcolm's hand in dire distress.

'No,' muttered the sick man, sinking back. 'Good King Robert has been in his grave many a day; his sons, woe is me!—Sir,' recovering himself, 'pardon the error of an old dying man, who owes you more than he can express.'

'Then, Sir,' said James Stewart, 'grant me the favour of a few moments' private speech with you. I will not keep you long from him,' he added to Malcolm and Lilias.

His manner was never one to be disputed, there was an atmosphere of obedience about the whole monastery, and the Prior added—

'Yes, my children, it is but fitting that you should give thanks in the church for your unlooked-for deliverance.'

Malcolm was forced to lead Lilias away into the exquisite cross church, built in the loveliest Early English style, of which a few graceful remnants still exist. The two young things knelt together hand in hand in the lornness of their approaching desolation, neither of them having dared to utter the foreboding upon their hearts, but feeling it all the

Charlotte M. Yonge

more surely; and while the sister's spirit longed fervently after him whose protection had been only just removed, the brother looked up to the sheltering vaults, lost in the tranquil twilight, and felt that here alone was his haven of peace, the refuge for the feeble and the fatherless.

Their devotions performed, they ventured back to the outer hall, and on their return being notified, they were again admitted. Sir James, who had been seated on a stool by the sick man's head, immediately rose and resigned his place to Lilias, but did not leave the room and Sir David thus spoke: 'Bairns, God in His mercy hath raised you up the best of guardians in the stead of your ain poor Tutor. Malcolm, laddie, you will ride the morn with this gentleman to the true head of your name, your ain King, whom God for ever bless!' His voice quivered. 'And be it your study so to profit by his example and nurture, as to do your devoir by him for ever.'

'Nay, father,' cried Malcolm, 'I cannot leave you and Lily.'

'If you call me father, do my bidding,' said Sir David. 'Lily can be safely bestowed with the good Sisters of St. Abbs, nor while you are out of Albany's reach is the poor lassie worth his molesting; but when I am gone, your uncles of Albany and Athole become your tutors, and the Prior has no power to save you. Only over the Border with the King is there safety from them, and your ruin is the ruin of your sister.'

'And,' added Sir James, 'when the King is at liberty, or when you yourself are of age, you will return to resume the charge of your fair sister, unless some nearer protector be found. Meantime,' he laid one hand on Malcolm's head, and with the other took out the relic which had had so great an effect upon Walter Stewart, 'I swear on this holy Rood of St. Andrew, that Malcolm Stewart of

Glenuskie shall be my charge, not merely as my kinsman, but as my young brother.'

'You hear, Malcolm,' said Sir David. 'You will strive to merit such goodness.'

'Father,' broke out the poor boy again, 'you cannot mean to part us! Let us abide as we have been till I am of age to take my vows! I am not fit to serve the King.'

'He is the best judge of that,' returned Sir James.

'And,' added Sir David, 'I tell you, lad, that I shall never be as I was before, and that were I a whole man and sain, riding back to Glenuskie the morn, I should still bless the saints and bid you gang.'

Rarely did the youth of the fifteenth century venture to question the authority of an elder, but Malcolm was only silenced for a moment, and though by no means understanding that his guardian believed his injuries mortal, he threw himself upon the advice of the Prior, whom he entreated to allow him to judge for himself, and to remain to protect his sister—he talked boldly of protecting her after this day's exploit. But Prior Akecliff gave him no more encouragement than did his uncle. The Benedictine vows were out of the question till he should be eighteen, and the renunciation of the world they involved would be ruinous to Lilias, since she would become his heiress. Moreover, the Prior himself was almost in a state of siege, for the Regent was endeavouring to intrude on the convent one Brother William Drake, or Drax, by his own nomination, instead of the canonical appointment emanating from Durham, and as national feeling went with the Regent's nominee, it was by no means certain that the present Prior would be able to maintain his position.

Charlotte M. Yonge

'Oh, go! yes, go, dear brother,' entreated Lilias. 'I should be far happier to know you in safety. They cannot hurt me while you are safe.'

'But you, Lily! What if this villain Drax have his way?'

'He could not harm her in St. Ebba's fold,' returned the Prior. 'The Abbess herself could not yield her; and, as you have so often been told, my young Lord, your absence is a far greater protection to your sister than your presence. Moreover, were the Tutor's mind at rest, there would be far better hope of his recovery.'

There was no alternative, and Malcolm could not but submit. Lilias was to be conducted before daybreak to the monastery of St. Abbs, about six miles off, whence she could be summoned at any time to be with her uncle in Coldingham; and Malcolm was to set off at daybreak with the captive knight, whose return to England could no longer be delayed.

Poor children! while Sir James Stewart was in the Prior's chamber, they sat silent and mournful by the bedside where their guardian lay dozing, even till the bell for Matins summoned them in common with all the other inmates of the convent; they knelt on the floor of the candle-lit church, and held each other's hands as they prayed; Lilias still the stronger and more hopeful, while Malcolm, as he looked up at those dear familiar vaultings, felt as if he were a bird driven from its calm peaceful nest to battle with the tossing winds and storms of ocean, without one near him whom he had learnt to love.

It was still dark when the service had ended, and Prior Akecliff came towards them. 'Daughter,' he said to Lilias, 'we deem it safer that you should ride to St. Abbs ere daylight. Your palfrey is ready, the Mother Abbess is warned, and I will myself conduct you thither.'

Priors were not people to be kept waiting, and as it was reported that the Tutor of Glenuskie was still asleep, Lilias had to depart without taking leave of him. With Malcolm the last words were spoken while crossing the court. 'Fear not, Lily; my heart will only weary till the Church owns me, and Patie has you.'

'Nay, my Malcolm; mayhap, as the Prior tells me, your strength and manhood will come in the south country.'

'Let them,' said Malcolm; 'I will neither cheat the Church nor Patie.'

'It were no cheat. There never was any compact. Patie is winning his fortune by his own sword; he would scorn—'

'Hush, Lily! When the King sees what a weakling Sir James has brought him, he will be but too glad to exchange Patie for me, and leave me safe in these blessed walls.'

But here they were under the archway, and the convoy of armed men, whom the exigencies of the time forced the convent to maintain, were already mounted. Sir James stood ready to assist the lady to her saddle, and with one long earnest embrace the brother and sister were parted, and Lilias rode away with the Prior by her side, letting the tears flow quietly down her cheeks in the darkness, and but half hearing the long arguments by which good Father Akecliff was proving to her that the decision was the best for both Malcolm and herself.

By and by the dawn began to appear, the air of the March night became sharper, and in the distance the murmur and plash of the tide was heard. Then, standing heavy and

Charlotte M. Yonge

dark against the clear pale eastern sky, there arose the dark mass of St. Ebba's monastery, the parent of Coldingham, standing on the very verge of the cliff to which it has left the name of St. Abb's Head, upon ground which has since been undermined by the waves, and has been devoured by them. The sea, far below, calmly brightened with the brightening sky, and reflected the morning stars in a lucid track of light, strong enough to make the lights glisten red in the convent windows. Lilias was expected, was a frequent guest, and had many friends there, and as the sweet sound of the Lauds came from the chapel, and while she dismounted in the court the concluding 'Amen' swelled and died away, she, though no convent bird, felt herself in a safe home and shelter under the wing of kind Abbess Annabel Drummond, and only mourned that Malcolm, so much tenderer and more shrinking than herself, should be driven into the unknown world that he dreaded so much more than she did.

CHAPTER III

HAL

The sun had not long been shining on the dark walls of St. Ebba's monastery, before the low-browed gate of Coldingham Priory opened to let pass the guests of the previous night. Malcolm had been kissed and blessed by his guardian, and bidden to transfer his dutiful obedience to his new protector; and somewhat comforted by believing Sir David to be mending since last night, he had rent himself away, and was riding in the frosty morning air beside the kinsman who had so strangely taken charge of him, and accompanied by Sir James's tall old Scottish squire, by the English groom, and by Malcolm's own servant, Halbert.

For a long space there was perfect silence: and as Malcolm began to detach his thoughts from all that he had left behind, he could not help being struck with the expressions that flitted over his companion's countenance. For a time he would seem lost in some deep mournful reverie, and his head drooped as if in sadness or perplexity; then a sudden gleam would light up his face, as if a brilliant project had occurred to him, his lips would part, his eyes flash, he would impel his horse forward as though leading a charge, or lift up his head with kindling looks, like one rehearsing a speech; but ever a check

Charlotte M. Yonge

would come on him in the midst, his mouth closed in dejection, his brow drew together in an anguish of impatience, his eyelids drooped in weariness, and he would ride on in deep reflection, till roused perhaps by the flight of a moor-fowl, or the rush of a startled roe, he would hum some gay French hunting-song or plaintive Scottish ballad.

Scarcely a word had been uttered, until towards noon, on the borders of a little narrow valley, the merry sound of bells clashed up to their ears, and therewith sounds of music. "Tis the toon of Christ's Kirk on the Green,' said the squire, as Sir James looked at him for information, 'where we were to bait. Methought in Lent we had been spared this gallimawfrey.'

"Tis Midlent week, you pagan,' replied Sir James. 'These good folk have come a-mothering, and a share of their simnels we'll have.'

'Sir,' entreated the squire, 'were it not more prudent of you to tarry without, and let me fetch provisions?'

'Hoot, man, a throng is our best friend! Besides, the horses must rest.'

So saying, Sir James rode eagerly forward; Malcolm following, not without wonder at not having been consulted, for though kept in strict discipline by his uncle, it had always been with every courtesy due to his rank as a king's grandson; and the cousins, from whom he had suffered, were of the same rank with himself. Did this wandering landless knight, now he had him in his power, mean to disregard all that was his due? But when Sir James turned round his face sparkling with good-humour and amusement, and laughed as he said, 'Now then for the humours of a Scottish fair!' all his offended dignity was forgotten.

The greensward was surrounded by small huts and hovels; a little old stone church on one side, and a hostel near it, shadowed by a single tall elm, beneath which was the very centre of the village wake. Not only was it Midlent, but the day was the feast of a local saint, in whose honour Lenten requirements were relaxed. Monks and priests were there in plenty, and so were jugglers and maskers, Robin Hood and Marion, glee-men and harpers, merchants and hucksters, masterful beggars and sorners, shepherds in gray mauds with wise collies at their feet, shrewd old carlines with their winter's spinning of yarn, lean wolf-like borderers peaceable for the nonce, merry lasses with tow-like locks floating from their snoods, all seen by the intensely glittering sun of a clear March day, dry and not too cold for these hardy northern folk.

Nigel, the squire, sighed in despondency; and Malcolm, who hated crowds, and knew himself a mark for the rude observations of a free-spoken populace, shrank up to him, when Sir James, nodding in time to the tones of a bagpipe that was playing at the hostel door, flung his bridle to Brewster the groom, laughed at his glum and contemptuous looks, merrily hailed the gudewife with her brown face and big silver ear-rings, seated himself on the bench at the long wooden table under the great garland of fir-boughs, willow catkins, and primroses, hung over the boughs of the tree, crossed himself, murmured his *Benedictus benedicat*, drew his dagger, carved a slice of the haunch of ox on the table, offered it to the reluctant Malcolm, then helping himself, entered into conversation with the lean friar on one side of him, and the stalwart man-at-arms opposite, apparently as indifferent as the rest of the company to the fact that the uncovered boards of the table were the only trenchers, and the salt and mustard were taken by the point of each man's dagger from

Charlotte M. Yonge

common receptacles dispersed along the board. Probably the only person really disgusted or amazed was the English Brewster, who, though too cautious to express a word of his feelings, preserved the most complete silence, and could scarcely persuade himself to taste the rude fare.

Nor when the meal was over was Sir James disposed to heed the wistful looks of his attendants, but wandered off to watch the contest in archery at the butts, where arrow after arrow flew wide of the clout, for the strength of Scotland did not lie in the long-bow, and Albany's edict that shooting should be practised on Sundays and holidays had not produced as yet any great dexterity.

Sir James at first laughed merrily at the extraordinary screwings of visage and contortions of attitude, and the useless demonstration of effort with which the clowns aimed their shafts and drew their bow, sometimes to find the arrow on the grass at their feet, sometimes to see it producing consternation among the bystanders; but when he saw Brewster standing silently apart, viewing their efforts with a scorn visible enough in the dead stolidity of his countenance, he murmured a bitter interjection, and turned away with folded arms and frowning brow.

Nigel again urged their departure, but at that moment the sweet notes of a long narrative ballad began to sound to the accompaniment of a harp, and he stood motionless while the wild mournful ditty told of the cruelty of the Lady of Frendraught, and how

'Morning sun ne'er shone upon
Lord John and Rothiemay.

Large tears were dropping from under the hand with he veiled his emotion; and when Nigel touched his cloak to remind him that the horses were ready, he pressed the old man's hand, saying, with a sigh, 'I heard that last at my father's knee! It rung in my ears for many a year! Here, lad!' and dropping a gold coin into the wooden bowl carried round by the blind minstrel's attendant, he was turning away, when the glee-man, detecting perhaps the ring of the coin, broke forth in stirring tones—

> "It fell about the Lammas tide,
> When moormen win their hay,
> The doughty Earl of Douglas rode
> Into England to catch a prey."

Again he stood transfixed, beating time with his hand, his eyes beaming, his hips moving as he followed the spirit-stirring ballad; and then, as Douglas falls, and is laid beneath the bracken bush, unseen by his men, and Montgomery forces Hotspur to yield, not to him, but

> 'to the bracken bush
> That grows upon the lily lea,'

he sobbed without disguise; and no sooner was the ballad ended than he sprang forward to the harper, crying, 'Again, again; another gold crown to hear it again!'

'Sir,' entreated Nigel, 'remember how much hangs on your speed.'

'The ballad I *must* have,' exclaimed Sir James, trying to shake him off. 'It moves the heart more than aught I ever heard! How runs it?'

'*I* know the ballad,' said Malcolm, half in impatience, half in contempt. 'I could sing every word of it. Every glee-man has it.'

'Nay—hear you, Sir—the lad can sing it,' reiterated Nigel;

Charlotte M. Yonge

and Sir James, throwing the promised guerdon to the minstrel, let himself be led away to the front of the inn; but there was a piper, playing to a group of dancers, and as if his feet could not resist the fascination, Sir James held out his hand to the first comely lass he saw disengaged, and in spite of the steel-guarded boots that he wore, answered foot for foot, spring for spring, to the deft manoeuvres of her shoeless feet, with equal agility and greater grace. Nigel frowned more than ever at this exhibition, and when the knight had led his panting partner to a seat, and called for a tankard of ale for her refreshment, he remonstrated more seriously still. 'Sir, the gates of Berwick will be shut.'

'The days lengthen, man.'

'And who knows if some of yon land-loupers be not of Walter Stewart's meine? Granted that they ken not yourself, that lad is only too ken-speckle. Moreover, you ye made free enough with your siller to set the haill crew of moss-troopers on our track.'

'Twenty mile to Berwick-gate,' said Sir James, carelessly; 'nor need you ever look behind you at jades like theirs. Nay, friend, I come, since you grudge me for once the sight of a little wholesome glee among my own people. My holiday is dropping from me like sands in an hour-glass!'

He mounted, however, and put his horse to as round a pace as could be maintained by the whole party with out distress; nor did he again break silence for many miles.

At the gates of Berwick, then in English hands, be gave a pass-word, and was admitted, he bade Nigel conduct Lord Malcolm to an inn, explaining that it was his duty to present himself to the governor; and, being detained to sup with him, was seen no more till they started the next morning. The governor rode out with them some ten miles, with a strong guard of spearmen; and after parting with him they pushed on to the south.

After the first day's journey, Malcolm was amazed to see Sir James mount without any of his defensive armour, which was piled on the spare horse; his head was covered by a chaperon, or flat cap with a short curtain to it, and his sword was the only weapon he retained. Nigel was also nearly unarmed, and Sir James advised Malcolm himself to lay aside the light hawberk he wore; then, at his amazed look, said, 'Poor lad! he never saw the day when he could ride abroad scathless. When will the breadth of Scotland be as safe as these English hills?'

He was very kind to his young companion, treating him in all things like a guest, pointing out what was worthy of note, and explaining what was new and surprising. Malcolm would have asked much concerning the King, to whom he was bound, but these questions were the only ones Sir James put aside, saying that his kinsman would one day learn that it ill beseemed those who were about a king's person to speak of him freely.

One night was spent at Durham, the parent of Coldingham, and here Malcolm felt at home, far more grand as was that mighty cathedral institution. There it stood, with the Weir encircling it, on its own fair though mighty hill, with all the glory of its Norman mister and lovely Lady-chapel; yet it seemed to the boy more like a glorified Coldingham than like a strange region.

'The peace of God rests on the place,' he said, when Sir James asked his thoughts as he looked back at the grand mass of buildings. 'These are the only spots where the holy and tender can grow, like the Palestine lilies

Charlotte M. Yonge

sheltered from the blast in the Abbot's garden at Coldingham.'

'Nay, lad, it were an ill world did lilies only grow in abbots' gardens.'

'It is an ill world,' said Malcolm.

'Let us hear what you say in a month's time,' replied the knight, lightly: then dreaming over the words.

A few days more, and they were riding among the lovely rock and woodland scenery of Yorkshire, when suddenly there leaped from behind a bush three or four young men, with a loud shout of 'Stand.'

'Reivers!' thought Malcolm, sick with dismay, as the foremost grasped Sir James's bridle; but the latter merely laughed, saying, 'How now, Hal! be these your old tricks?'

'Ay, when such prizes are errant,' said the assailant and Sir James, springing from his horse, embraced him and his companion with a cordiality that made Malcolm not a little uneasy. Could he have been kidnapped by a false Englishman into a den of robbers for the sake of his ransom?

'You are strict to your time,' said the chief robber. 'I knew you would be. So, when Ned Marmion came to Beverley, and would have us to see his hunting at Tanfield, we came on thinking to meet you. Marmion here has a nooning spread in the forest; ere we go on to Thirsk, where I have a matter to settle between two wrong-headed churls. How has it been with you, Jamie? you have added to your meine.'

'Ah, Hal! never in all your cut-purse days did you fall on

such an emprise as I have achieved.'

'Let us hear,' said Hal, linking his arm in Sir James's, who turned for a moment to say, 'Take care of the lad, John; he is a young kinsman of mine.'

'Kinsman!' thought Malcolm; 'do all wandering Stewarts claim kin to the blood royal?' but then, as he looked at Sir James's stately head, he felt that no assumption could be unbecoming in one of such a presence, and so kind to himself; and, ashamed of the moment's petulance, dismounted, and, as John said, 'This is the way to our noon meat,' he let himself be conducted through the trees to a glade, sheltered from the wind, where a Lenten though not unsavoury meal of bread, dried fish, and eggs was laid out on the grass, in a bright warm sunshine; and Hal, declaring himself to have a hunter's appetite, and that he knew Jamie had been starved in Scotland, and was as lean as a greyhound, seated himself on the grass, and to Malcolm's extreme surprise, not to say disgust, was served by Lord Marmion on the knee and with doffed cap.

While the meal was being eaten, Malcolm studied the strangers. Lord Marmion was a good-humoured, hearty-looking young Yorkshireman, but the other two attracted his attention far more. They were evidently brothers, one perhaps just above, the other just below, thirty; both of the most perfect mould of symmetry, activity, and strength, though perhaps more inclining to agility than robustness. Both were fair-complexioned, and wore no beard; but John was the paler, graver, and more sedate, and his aquiline profile had an older look than that borne by Hal's perfectly regular features. It would have been hard to define what instantly showed the seniority of his brother, for the clearness of his colouring—bright red and white like a lady's—his short, well-moulded chin, and the fresh earnestness and animation of his countenance, gave an air

Charlotte M. Yonge

of perpetual youth in spite of the scar of an arrow on the cheek which told of at least one battle; but there were those manifestations of being used to be the first which are the evident tokens of elder sonship, and the lordly manner more and more impressed Malcolm. He was glad that his own Sir James was equal in dignity, as well as superior in height, and he thought the terrible red lightning of those auburn eyes would be impossible to the sparkling azure eyes of the Englishman, steadfast, keen, and brilliant unspeakably though they were; but so soon as Sir James seemed to have made his explanation, the look was most winningly turned on him, a hand held out, and he was thus greeted: 'Welcome, my young Prince Malcolm; I am happy that your cousin thinks so well of our cheer, that he has brought you to partake it.'

'His keeper, Somerset,' thought Malcolm, as he bowed stiffly; 'he seems to treat me coolly enough. I come to serve my King,' he said, but he was scarcely heard; for as Hal unbuckled his sword before sitting down on the grass, he thrust into his bosom a small black volume, with which he seemed to have been beguiling the time; and John exclaimed—

'There goes Godfrey de Bulloin. I tell you, Jamie, 'tis well you are come! Now have I some one to speak with. Ever since Harry borrowed my Lady of Westmoreland's book of the Holy War, he has not had a word to fling at me.'

'Ah!' said Sir James, 'I saw a book, indeed, of the Holy Land! It would tempt him too much to hear how near the Border it dwells! What was it named, Malcolm?'

'The "Itinerarium of Adamnanus,"' replied Malcolm, blushing at the sudden appeal.

'Ha! I've heard of it,' cried the English knight. 'I sent to half the convent libraries to beg the loan when Gilbert de Lannoy set forth for the survey of Palestine. Does the Monk of Iona tell what commodity of landing there may be on the coast?'

Malcolm had the sea-port towns at his fingers' ends, and having in the hard process of translation, and reading and re-reading one of the few books that came into his hands, nearly mastered the contents, he was able to reply with promptness and precision, although with much amazement, for

'Much he marvelled a knight of pride
Like book-bosomed priest should ride;'

nor had he ever before found his accomplishments treated as aught but matters of scorn among the princes and nobles with whom he had occasionally been thrown.

'Good! good!' said Sir Harry at last. 'Well read, and clearly called to mind. The stripling will do you credit, James. Where have you studied, fair cousin?'

Cousin! was it English fashion to make a cousin of everybody? But gentle, humble Malcolm had no resentment in him, and felt gratified at the friendly tone of so grand and manly-looking a knight. 'At home,' he answered, 'with a travelling scholar who had studied at Padua and Paris.'

'That is where you Scots love to haunt! But know you how they are served there? I have seen the gibbet where the Mayor of Paris hung two clerks' sons for loving his daughters over well!'

'The clerks' twa sons of Owsenford that were foully slain!' cried Malcolm, his face lighting up. 'Oh, Sir, have you seen their gibbet?'

'What? were they friends of yours?' asked Hal, much amused, and shaking his head merrily at Sir James. 'Ill company, I fear—'

'Only in a ballad,' said Malcolm, colouring, 'that tells how at Yuletide the ghosts came to their mother with their hats made of the birk that grew at the gates of Paradise.'

'A rare ballad must that be!' exclaimed Hal. 'Canst sing it? Or are you weary?—Marmion, prithee tell some of the fellows to bring my harp from the baggage.'

'His own harp is with ours,' said Sir James; 'he will make a better figure therewith.'

At his sign, the attendant, Nigel, the only person besides Lord Marmion of Tanfield who had been present at the meal, besides the two Stewarts and the English brothers, rose and disappeared between the trees, beyond which a hum of voices, an occasional laugh, and the stamping of horses and jingling of bridles, betokened that a good many followers were in waiting. Malcolm's harp was quickly brought, having been slung in its case to the saddle of Halbert's horse; and as he had used it to beguile the last evening's halt, it did not need much tuning. Surprised as his princely notions were at being commanded rather than requested to sing, the sweet encouraging smile and tone of kind authority banished all hesitation in complying, and he gave the ballad of the Clerks' Twa Sons of Owsenford with much grace and sweetness, while the weakness of his voice was compensated by the manlier strains with which Sir James occasionally chimed in. Then, as Harry gave full meed of appreciative praise and thanks, Sir James said, 'Lend me thine harp, Malcolm; I have learnt thy song now; and thou, Harry, must hear and own how far our Scottish minstrelsy exceeds thy boasted Chevy Chase.'

And forth rang in all the mellow beauty of his voice that most glorious of ballads, the Battle of Otterburn, as much more grand than it had been when he heard it from the glee-man or from Malcolm, as a magnificent voice, patriotic enthusiasm, and cultivation and refinement, could make it. He had lost himself and all around in the passion of the victory, the pathos of the death. But no such bright look of thanks recompensed him. Harry's face grew dark, and he growled, 'Douglas dead? Ay, he wins more fields so than alive! I wish you would keep my old Shrewsbury friend, Earl Tyneman, as you call him, at home.'

"Tis ill keeping the scholars in bounds when the master is away,' returned Sir James.

'Well, by this time Tom has taught them how to trans-gress—sent them home with the long scourge from robbing orchards in Anjou. He writes to me almost with his foot in the stirrup, about to give Douglas and Buchan a lesson. I shall make short halts and long stages south. This is too far off for tidings.'

'True,' said Sir John, with a satirical curl of the lip; 'above all, when fair ladies brook not to ink their ivory fingers.'

'There spake the envious fiend,' laughed the elder brother. 'John bears not the sight of what he will not or cannot get.'

'I'll never be chained to a lady's litter, nor be forced to loiter till her wimple is pinned,' retorted John. 'Nor do I like dames with two husbands besides.'

'One would have cancelled the other, as grammarians tell

Charlotte M. Yonge

us,' said Harry, 'if thy charms, John, had cancelled thine hook nose! I would they had, ere her first marriage. Humfrey will burn his fingers there, and we must hasten back to look after that among other things.—My Lord Marmion,' he added, starting hastily up, and calling to him as he stood at some distance conversing with the Scottish Nigel, 'so please you, let us have the horses;' and as the gentleman hastened to give the summons, he said, 'We shall make good way now. We shall come on Watling Street. Ha, Jamie, when shall we prove ourselves better men than a pack of Pagan Romans, by having a set of roads fit for man or beast, of our own making instead of theirs half decayed? Look where I will, in England or France, their roads are the same in build—firm as the world itself, straight as arrows. An army is off one's mind when once one gets on a Roman way. I'll learn the trick, and have them from Edinburgh to Bordeaux ere ten years are out; and then, what with traffic and converse with the world, and ready justice, neither Highland men minor Gascons will have leisure or taste for robbery.'

'Perhaps Gascons and Scots will have a voice in the matter,' said James, a little stiffly; and the horses being by this time brought, Sir Harry mounted, and keeping his horse near that of young Malcolm, to whom he had evidently taken a fancy, he began to talk to him in so friendly and winning a manner, that he easily drew from the youth the whole history of his acquaintance with Sir James Stewart, of the rescue of his sister, and the promise to conduct him to the captive King of Scots, as the only means of saving him from his rapacious kindred.

'Poor lad!' said Harry, gravely.

'Do you know King James, Sir?' asked Malcolm, timidly.

'Know him?' said Harry, turning round to scan the boy

with his merry blue eye. 'I know him—yes; that as far as a poor Welsh knight can know his Grace of Scotland.'

'And, Sir, will he be good lord to me?'

'Eh! that's as you may take him. I would not be one of yonder Scots under his hands!'

'Has he learned to hate his own countrymen?' asked Malcolm, in an awe-stricken voice.

'Hate? I trow he has little to love them for. He is a good fellow enough, my young lord, when left to himself; but best beware. Lions in a cage have strange tempers.'

A courier rode up at the moment, and presented some letters, which Sir Harry at once opened and read, beckoning his brother and Sir James to his side, while Malcolm rode on in their wake, in a state of dismay and bewilderment. Nigel and Lord Marmion were together at so great an interval that he could not fall back on them, nor learn from them who these brothers were. And there was something in the ironical suppressed pity with which Harry had spoken of his prospects with the King of Scots, that terrified him all the more, because he knew that Sir James and Nigel would both hold it unworthy of him to have spoken freely of his own sovereign with an Englishman. Would James be another Walter? and, if so, would Sir James Stewart protect him? He had acquired much affection for, and strong reliance on, the knight; but there was something unexplained, and his heart sank.

The smooth line of Watling Street at length opened into the old town of Thirsk, and here bells were ringing, flags flying from the steeple, music sounded, a mayor and his corporation in their robes rode slowly forth, crowds lined the road-side, caps were flung up, and a tremendous shout

Charlotte M. Yonge

arose, 'God save King Harry!'

Malcolm gazed about more utterly discomfited. There
was 'Harry,' upright on his horse, listening with a gracious
smile, while the mayor rehearsed a speech about welcome
and victories, and the hopeful queen, and, what was still
more to the purpose, tendered a huge pair of gauntlets,
each filled to the brim, one with gold, and the other with
silver pieces.

'Eh! Thanks, Master Mayor, but these gloves must be
cleared, ere there is room for me to use them in battle!'

And handing the gold glove to his brother, he scattered
the contents of the silver one far and wide among the
populace, who shouted their blessings louder than ever,
and thus he reached the market-place. There all was set
forth as for the lists, a horseman in armour on either side.

'Heigh now, Sirs,' said Harry, 'have we not wars enough
toward without these mummings of vanity?'

'This is no show, my Lord King,' returned the mayor,
abashed. 'This is deadly earnest. These are two honourable gentlemen of Yorkshire, who are come hither to
fight out their quarrel before your Grace.'

'Two honourable foolsheads!' muttered Harry; then,
raising his voice, 'Come hither, gentlemen, let us hear
your quarrel.'

The two gentlemen were big Yorkshiremen, heavy-
browed, and their native shrewdness packed far away
behind a bumpkin stolidity and surliness that barely
allowed them to show respect to the King.

'So please you, Sir,' growled the first in his throat, 'here stands Christopher Kitson of Barrowbridge, ready to avouch himself a true man, and prove in yonder fellow's teeth that it was not a broken-kneed beast that I sent up for a heriard to my Lord Archbishop when my father died; but that he of Easingwold is a black slanderer and backbiter.'

'And here,' shouted the other, 'stands honest William Trenton of Easingwold, ready to thrust his lies down his throat, and prove on his body that the heriard he sent to my Lord Archbishop was a sorry jade.'

'That were best proved by the beast's body,' interposed time King.

'And,' proceeded the doughty Kitson, as though repeating a lesson, 'having vainly pleaded the matter these nine years, we are come to demand licence to fight it out, with lance, sword, and dagger, in your royal presence, to set the matter at rest for ever.'

'Breaking a man's head to prove the soundness of a horse!' ejaculated Harry.

'Your licence is given, Sir King?' demanded Kitson.

'My licence is given for a combat *a l'outrance*,' said Henry; but, as they were about to flounder back on their big farm-horses, he raised his voice to a thundering sound: 'Solely on this condition, that he who slays his neighbour, be he Trenton or Kitson, shall hang for the murder ere I leave Thirsk.'

There was a recoil, and the mayor himself ventured to observe something about the judgment of God, and 'never so seen.'

Charlotte M. Yonge

'And I say,' thundered Henry, and his blue eyes seemed to flame with vehement indignation, 'I say that the ordeal of battle is shamefully abused, and that it is a taking of God's name—ay, and man's life—in vain, to appeal thereto on every coxcomb's quarrel, risking the life that was given him to serve God's ends, not his own sullen fancy. I will have an end of such things!—And you, gentlemen, since the heriard is dead, or too old to settle the question, shake hands, and if you must let blood, come to France with me next month, and flesh your knives on French and Scots.'

'So please you, Sir,' grumbled Kitson, 'there's Mistress Agnes of Mineshull; she's been in doubt between the two of us these five years, and she'd promised to wed whichever of us got the better.'

'I'll settle her mind for her! Whichever I find foremost among the French, I'll send home to her a knight, and with better sense to boot than to squabble for nine years as to an old horse.'

He then dismounted, and was conducted into the town-hall, where a banquet was prepared, taking by the hand Sir James Stewart, and followed by his brother John, and by Malcolm, who felt as though his brain were turning, partly with amazement, partly with confusion at his own dulness, as he perceived that not only was the free-spoken Hal, Henry of Monmouth, King of England, but that his wandering benefactor, the captive knight, whose claim of kindred he had almost spurned, was his native sovereign, James the First of Scotland.

CHAPTER IV

THE TIDINGS OF BEAUGE

Malcolm understood it at last. In the great chamber where he was bidden to wait within 'Nigel' till 'Sir James' came from a private conference with 'Harry,' he had all explained to him, but within a curtness and brevity that must not be imitated in the present narrative.

The squire Nigel was in fact Sir Nigel Baird, Baron of Bairdsbrae, the gentleman to whom poor King Robert II. had committed the charge of his young son James, when at fourteen he had been sent to France, nominally for education, but in reality to secure him from the fate of his brother Rothsay.

Captured by English vessels on the way, the heir of Scotland had been too valuable a prize to be resigned by the politic Henry IV., who had lodged him at Windsor Castle, together with Edmund Mortimer, earl of March, and placed both under the nominal charge of the Prince of Wales, a youth of a few years older. Unjust as was the detention, it had been far from severe; the boys had as much liberty as their age and recreation required, and received the choicest training both in the arts of war and peace. They were bred up in close intercourse with the King's own four sons, and were united with them by the

Charlotte M. Yonge

warmest sympathy.

In fact, since usurpation had filled Henry of Lancaster's mind with distrust and jealousy, his eldest son had been in no such enviable position as to be beyond the capacity of fellow-feeling for the royal prisoner.

Of a peculiarly frank, open, and affectionate nature, young Henry had so warmly loved the gentle and fascinating Richard II., that his trust in the father, of whom he had seen little in his boyhood, had received a severe shock through Richard's fate. Under the influence of a new, suspicious, and avaricious wife, the King kept his son as much at a distance as possible, chiefly on the Welsh marches, learning the art of war under Hotspur and Oldcastle; and when the father and son were brought together again, the bold, free bearing and extraordinary ability of the Prince filled the suspicious mind of the King with alarm and jealousy. To keep him down, give him no money, and let him gain no influence, was the narrow policy of the King; and Henry, chafing, dreaming, feeling the injustice, and pining for occupation, shared his complaints within James, and in many a day-dream restored him freely to his throne, and together redressed the wrongs of the world. Meantime, James studied deep in preparation, and recreated himself with poetry, inspired by the charms of Joan Beaufort, the lovely daughter of the King's legitimatized brother, the Earl of Somerset; while Henry persisted in a boy's passionate love to King Richard's maiden widow, Isabel of France. Entirely unrequited as his affection was, it had a beneficial effect. Next after his deep sense of religion, it kept his life pure and chivalrous. He was for ever faithful to his future wife, even when Isabel had been returned to France, and his romantic passion had fixed itself on her younger sister Catherine, whom he endowed in imagination with all he had seen or supposed in her.

Credited with every excess by the tongue of his stepmother, too active-minded not to indulge in freakish sports and experiments in life very astounding to commonplace minds, sometimes when in dire distress even helping himself to his unpaid allowance from his father's mails, and always with buoyant high spirits and unfailing drollery that scandalized the grave seniors of the Court, there is full proof that Prince Hal ever kept free from the gross vices which a later age has fancied inseparably connected with his frolics; and though always in disgrace, the vexation of the Court, and a by-word for mirth, he was true to the grand ideal he was waiting to accomplish, and never dimmed the purity and loftiness of his aim. That little band of princely youths, who sported, studied, laughed, sang, and schemed in the glades of Windsor, were strangely brought together—the captive exiled King, the disinherited heir of the realm, and the sons of the monarch who held the one in durance and occupied the throne of the other; and yet their affection had all the frank delight of youthful friendship. The younger lads were in more favour with their father than was the elder. Thomas was sometimes preferred to him in a mortifying manner, John's grave, quiet nature prevented him from ever incurring displeasure, and Humfrey was the spoilt pet of the family; but nothing could lessen Harry's large-minded love of his brothers; and he was the idol and hero of the whole young party, who implicitly believed in his mighty destinies as a renovator of the world, the deliverer of Jerusalem, and restorer of the unity and purity of the Church.

'Harry the Fifth was crowned,' and with the full intention of carrying out his great dream. But his promise of releasing James became matter of question. The House of Albany, who held the chief power in Scotland, had bound Henry IV. over not to free their master; and it was plain that to send him home before his welcome was ensured

Charlotte M. Yonge

would be but tossing him on their spears. In vain James pleaded that he was no boy, and was able to protect himself; and vowed that when the faithful should rally round his standard, he would be more than a match for his enemies; or that if not, he would rather die free than live in bondage. Henry would not listen, and insisted upon retaining him until he should himself be at leisure to bring him home with a high hand, utterly disregarding his assurance that this would only be rendering him in the eyes of his subjects another despised and hated Balliol.

Deeming himself a divinely-appointed redresser of wrongs, Henry was already beginning on his great work of purifying Europe in preparation for his mighty Crusade; and having won that splendid victory which laid distracted France at his feet, he only waited to complete the conquest as thoroughly and rapidly as might be; and, lest his grand purpose should be obstructed, this great practical visionary, though full of kindness and gene- rosity, kept in thraldom a whole troop of royal and noble captives.

He had, however, been so far moved by James's entreaties, as to consent that when he himself offered his devotions at the shrine of St. John of Beverley, the native saint who shared with the two cordwainers his gratitude for the glories of 'Crispin Crispian's day,' his prisoner should, unknown to any save the few who shared the pilgrimage, push on to reconnoitre his own country, and judge for himself, having first sworn to reveal himself to no one, and to avoid all who could recognize him. James had visited Glenuskie within a special view to profiting by the wisdom of Sir David Drummond, and had then been at Stirling, Edinburgh, and Perth. On his way back, falling in with Malcolm in his distress, he had conceived the project of taking him to England; and finding himself already more than half recognized by Sir David, had obtained his most grateful and joyous consent. In truth, James's heart had yearned to his young cousin, his own situation had become much more lonely of late; for Henry was no longer the comrade he had once been, since he had become a keeper instead of a fellow-sufferer. It was true that he did his best to forget this by lavishing indulgences on his captive, and insisting on being treated on terms of brotherly familiarity; but though his transcendent qualities commanded love, the intimacy could be but a semblance of the once equal friendship. Moreover, that conspiracy which cost the life of the Earl of Cambridge had taught James that cautious reserve was needed in dealing with even his old friends the princes, so easily might he be accused of plotting either with Henry's immediate heir or with the Mortimers; and, in this guarded life, he had hailed with delight the opportunity of taking to himself the young orphan cousin of kindred blood, of congenial tastes, and home-like speech, whom he might treat at once as a younger brother and friend, and mould by and by into a trusty counsellor and assistant. That peculiar wistfulness and gentleness of Malcolm's look and manner, together with the refinement and intellect apparent to all who conversed with him without alarming him, had won the King's heart, and made him long to keep the boy with him. As to Malcolm's longing for the cloister, he deemed it the result of the weakly health and refined nature which shrank from the barbarism of the outer world, and he thought it would pass away under shelter from the rude taunts of the fierce cousins, at a distance from the well-meaning exhortations of the monks, and at the spectacle of brave and active men who could also be pious, conscientious, and cultivated. In the renewed sojourn at Windsor which James apprehended, the training of such a youth as Malcolm of Glenuskie would be no small solace.

By the time Malcolm had learnt as much of all this as Sir Nigel Baird knew, or chose to communicate, the King

Charlotte M. Yonge

entered the room. He flung himself on his knees, exclaiming, with warm gratitude, as he kissed the King's hand, 'My liege, I little kenned—'

'I meant thee to ken little,' said James, smiling. 'Well, laddie, wilt thou share the prisoner's cell?—Ay, Bairdsbrae, you were a true prophet. Harry will do all himself, and will not hear of losing me to deal with my own people at my own gate. No, no, he'll have me back with Southron bows and bills, so soon as this small trifle of France lies quiet in his grasp! I had nearly flung back my parole in his face, and told him that no English sword should set me on the Bruce's throne; but there is something in Harry of Monmouth that one *must* love, and there are moments when to see and hear him one would as soon doubt the commission of an angel with a flaming sword.'

'A black angel!' growled Sir Nigel.

'Scoff and chafe, Baird, but look at his work. Look at Normandy, freed from misrule and exaction, in peace and order. Look at this land. Was ever king so loved? Or how durst he act as he did this day?'

'Nay, an it were so at home,' said Baird, 'I had as lief stay here as where a man is not free to fight out his own feud. Even this sackless callant thought it shame to see two honest men baulked.'

'Poor Scotland!' sighed James. 'Woe is the land where such thoughts come readiest to gray-haired men and innocent boys. I tell you, cousin, this precious right is the very cause that our poor country is so lawless and bloody, that yon poor silly sparrow would fain be caged for fear of the kites and carrion-crows.'

'Alack, my Lord, let me but have my way. I cannot fight! Let Patrick Drummond have my sister and my lands, and your service will be far better done,' said Malcolm.

'I know all that,' said the King, kindly. 'There is time enough for settling that question; and meantime you will not be spoilt for monk or priest by cheering me awhile in my captivity. I need you, laddie,' me added, laying his hand on the boy's shoulder, with all the instinctive fascination of a Stewart. 'I lack a comrade of my own blood, for I am all alone!'

'Oh, Sir!' and Malcolm, looking into his face, saw it full of tenderness.

'Books and masters you shall have,' continued James, 'such as for church or state, cathedral, cloister, or camp, shall render you the meeter prince; and I pass you my royal word, that if at full age the cowl be your choice, I will not gainsay you. Meantime, abide with me, and be the young brother I have yearned for.'

The King threw his arms round Malcolm, who felt, and unconsciously manifested, a strange bliss in that embrace, even while fixed in his determination that nothing should make him swerve from his chosen path, nor render him false to his promise to Patrick and Lilias. It was a strange change, from being despised and down-trodden by fierce cousins, or only fondled, pitied, and treated with consideration by his own nearest and dearest friends, to be the chosen companion of a king, and *such* a king. Nor could it be a wile of Satan, thought Malcolm, since James still promised him liberty of choice. He would ask counsel of a priest next time he went to confession; and in the meantime, in the full tide of gratitude, admiration, and affection, he gave himself up to the enjoyment of his new situation, and of time King's kindness and solicitude. This

Charlotte M. Yonge

was indeed absolutely that of an elder brother; for, observing that Malcolm's dress and equipments, the work of Glenuskie looms, supplemented by a few Edinburgh purchases, was uncouth enough to attract some scornful glances from the crowd who came out to welcome the royal entrance into York the next day, he instantly sent Brewster in search of the best tailor and lorimer in the city, and provided so handsomely for the appearance of young Glenuskie, his horse, and his attendants, that the whole floor of their quarters was strewn with doublets, boots, chaperons, and gloves, saddles, bridles, and spurs, when the Duke of Bedford loitered into the room, and began to banter James for thus (as he supposed) pranking himself out to meet the lady of his love; and then bemoaned the fripperies that had become the rage in their once bachelor court, vowing, between sport and earnest, that Hal was so enamoured of his fair bride, that anon the conquest of France would be left to himself and his brother, Tom of Clarence; while James retorted by thrusts at Bedford's own rusticity of garb, and by endeavouring to force on him a pair of shoes with points like ram's horns, as a special passport to the favour of Dame Jac—a lady who seemed to be the object of Duke John's great distaste.

Suddenly a voice was heard in the gallery of the great old mansion where they were lodged. 'John! John! Here!—Where is the Duke, I say?' It was thick and husky, as with some terrible emotion; and the King and Duke had already started in dismay before the door was thrown open, and King Henry stood among them, his face of a burning red.

'See here, John!' he said, holding out a letter; and then, with an accent of wrathful anguish, and a terrible frown, he turned on James, exclaiming, 'I would send you to the Tower, Sir, did I think you had a hand in this!'

Malcolm trembled, and sidled nearer his prince; while James, with an equally fierce look, replied, 'Hold, Sir! Send me where you will, but dare not dishonour my name!' Then changing, as he saw the exceeding grief on Henry's brow, and heard John's smothered cry of dismay, 'For Heaven's sake, Harry, what is it?'

'This!' said Henry, less loudly, less hotly, but still with an agony of indignation: 'Thomas is dead—and by the hand of two of your traitor Scots!'

'Murdered!' cried James, aghast.

'Murdered by all honest laws of war, but on the battle-field,' said Henry. 'Your cousin of Buchan and old Douglas fell on my brave fellows at Beauge, when they were spent with travel to stop the robberies in Anjou. They closed in with their pikes on my brave fellows, took Somerset prisoner, and for Thomas, while he was dealing with a knight named Swinton in front, the villain Buchan comes behind and cleaves his head in twain; and that is what you Scots call fighting!'

'It was worthy of a son of Albany!' said James. 'Would that vengeance were in my power!'

'Ay, you loved him!' said Henry, grasping James's hand, his passion softened into a burst of tears, as he wrung his prisoner's hand. 'Nay, who did not love him, my brave, free-hearted brother? And that I—I should have dallied here and left him to bear the brunt, and be cut off by you felon Scots!' And he hid his face, struggling within an agony of heart-rending grief, which seemed to sway his whole tall, powerful frame as he leant against the high back of a chair; while John, together with James, was imploring him not to accuse himself, for his presence had been needful at home; and, to turn the tenor of his thought, James inquired whether there were any further disaster.

'Not as yet,' said Henry; 'there is not a man left in that heaven-abandoned crew who knows how to profit by what they have got! but I must back again ere the devil stir them up a man of wit!—And you, Sir, can you take order with these heady Scots?'

'From Windsor? no,' said James; 'but set me in the saddle, let me learn war under such a captain as yourself, and maybe they will not take the field against me; or if they do, the slayer of Clarence shall rue it.'

'Be it so,' said Henry, wringing his hand. 'You shall with me to France, Jamie, and see war. The Scots should flock to the Lion rampant, and without them the French are mo better than deer, under the fool and murderer they call Dauphin. Yet, alas! will any success give me back my brother—my brother, the brave and true?' he added, weeping again within time *abandon* of an open nature and simple age. 'It was for my sins, my forgetfulness of my great work, that this has come on me.—Ho, Marmion! carry these tidings from me to the Dean; pray him that the knell be tolled at the Minster, and a requiem sung for my brother and all who fell with him. We will be there ourselves, and the mayor must hold us excused from his banquet; these men are too loyal not to grieve for their King.'

And, with his arm round the neck of his brother John, Henry left the room; and before another word could be said, Sir Nigel was there, having only retired on the King's entrance. The news was of course all over the house, and with an old attendant's freedom he exclaimed, 'So, Sir, the English have found tough cummers at last!'

'Not too honourably,' said James, sadly.

'Hout, would not the puir loons be glad enow of any gate of coming by a clout at the man's brother that keeps you captive!'

'They have taken away one of those I loved best!' said James.

'I'm no speaking ill of the lad Clarence himself,' said Nigel; 'he was a braw youth, leal and bold, and he has died in his helm and spurs, as a good knight should. I'd wish none of these princes a waur ending. Moreover, could Swinton have had the wit to keep him living, he'd have been a bonnie barter for you, my Lord; but ony way the fight was a gallant one, and the very squire that brought the tidings cannot deny that our Scots fought like lions.'

'Would Douglas but so fight in any good quarrel!' sighed the King. 'But what are you longing to ask, Malcolm? Is it for your kinsman Patrick? I fear me that there is little chance of your hearing by name of him.'

'I wot not,' said Sir Nigel; 'I did but ask for that hare-brained young cousin of mine, Davie Baird, that must needs be off on this journey to France; and the squire tells me he was no herald, to be answerable for the rogues that fought on the other side.'

'We shall soon see for ourselves,' said James; 'I am to make this campaign.'

'You! you, my liege! Against your own ally, and under the standard of England! Woe's me, how could ye be so lost!'

James argued on his own conviction that the true France

Charlotte M. Yonge

was with poor Charles VI., and that it was doing the country no service to prolong the resistance of the Armagnacs and the Dauphin, who then appeared mere partisans instead of patriots. As to fighting under the English banner, no subjection was involved in an adventurer king so doing: had not the King of Bohemia thus fought at Crecy? and was not the King of Sicily with the French army? Moreover, James himself felt the necessity of gaining some experience in the art of war. Theoretically he had studied it with all his might, from Caesar, Quintus Curtius, and that favourite modern authority, the learned ecclesiastic, Jean Pave, who was the Vauban of the fifteenth century; and he had likewise obtained greedily all the information he could from Henry himself and his warriors; but all this had convinced him that if war was to be more than a mere raid, conducted by mere spirit and instinct, some actual apprenticeship was necessary. Even for such a dash, Henry himself had told him that he would find his book-knowledge an absolute impediment without some practice, and would probably fail for that very reason when opposed to tough old seasoned warriors. And, prudence apart, James, at five-and-twenty, absolutely glowed with shame at the thought that every one of his companions had borne arms for at least ten years past, while his arrows had no mark but the target, his lances had all been broken in the tilt-yard. It was this argument that above all served to pacify old Bairdsbrae; though he confessed himself very uneasy as to the prejudice it would create in Scotland, and so evidently loathed the expedition, that James urged on him to return to Scotland, instead of continuing his attendance. There was no fear but that his ransom would be accepted, and he had been absent twelve years from his home.

'No, no, my Lord; I sware to your father that I'd never quit you till I brought you safe home again, and, God willing, I'll keep my oath. But what's this puir callant to do, that you were set upon rearing upon your books at Windsor?'

'He shall choose,' said James. 'Either he shall study at the learned university at Oxford or at Paris, or he shall ride with me, and see how cities and battles are won. Speak not yet, cousin; it takes many months to shake out the royal banner, and you shall look about you ere deciding. Now give me yonder black cloak; they are assembling for the requiem.'

Malcolm, as he followed his king, was not a little amazed to see that Henry, the magnificent victor, was wrapped in a plain black serge garment, his short dark hair uncovered, his feet bare; and that on arriving at the Minster he threw himself on his knees, almost on his face, before the choir steps, there remaining while the *De profundis* and the like solemn and mournful strains floated through the dark vaultings above him, perhaps soothing while giving expression to the agony of his affliction, and self-accusation, not for the devastation of the turbulent country of an insane sovereign, but for his having relaxed in the mighty work of renovation that he had imposed on himself.

Even when the service was ended, the King would not leave the Minster. He lifted himself up to bid Bedford and his companions return; but for himself, he intended to remain and confess, in preparation for being 'houselled' at the Mass for the dead early the next morning, before hastening on the southern journey.

Was this, thought the bewildered Malcolm as he fell asleep, the godless atmosphere he had been used to think all that was not Glenuskie or Coldingham—England above all?

Indeed, in the frosty twilight of the spring morning,

though Henry was now clad in his usual garb, sleepless-ness, sorrow, and fasting made him as wan and haggard as any ascetic monk; his eyes were sunken, and his closed lips bore a stern fixed expression, which scarcely softened even when the sacrificial rite struck the notes of praise; and though a light came into his eye, it was rather the devotion of one who had offered himself, than the gleam of hopeful exultation. The horses stood saddled at the west door, for Henry was feverishly eager to reach Pontefract, where he had left his queen, and wished to avoid the delay of breaking his fast at York, but only to snatch a meal at some country hostel on his way.

Round the horses, however, a crowd of the citizens were collected to gaze; and two or three women with children in their arms made piteous entreaties for the King's healing touch for their little ones. The kind Henry waited, ungloved his hand, asked his treasurer for the gold pieces that were a much-esteemed part of the cure, and signed to his attendant chaplain to say the Collect appointed for the rite.

Fervent blessings were meantime murmured through the crowd, which broke out into loud shouts of 'God save King Harry!' as he at length leapt into the saddle; but at that moment, a feeble, withered old man, leaning on a staff, and wearing a bedesman's gown, peered up, and muttered to a comrade—

'Fair-faced, quotha—fair, maybe, but not long for this world! One is gone already, and the rest will not be long after; the holy man's words will have their way—the death mark is on him.'

The words caught James's ear, and he angrily turned round: 'Foul-mouthed raven, peace with thy traitor croak!' but Bedford caught his arm, crying—

'Hush! 'tis a mere bedesman;' and bending forward to pour a handful of silver into the beggar's cap, he said, 'Pray, Gaffer, pray—pray for the dead and living, both.'

'So,' said James, as both mounted, 'there's a fee for a boding traitor.'

'I knew his face,' said Bedford, with a shudder; 'he belonged to Archbishop Scrope.'

'A traitor, too,' said James.

'Nay, there was too much cause for his words. Never shall I forget the day when Scrope was put to death on this very moor on which we are entering. There sat my father on his horse, with us four boys around him, when the old man passed in front of us, and looked at him with a face pitiful and terrible. "Harry of Bolingbroke," he said, "because thou hast done these things, therefore shall thy foes be of thine own household; the sword shall never depart therefrom, but all the increase of thy house shall die in the flower of their age, and in the fourth generation shall their name be clean cut off." The commons will have it that at that moment my father was struck with leprosy; and struck to the heart assuredly he was, nor was he ever the same man again. I always believed that those words made him harder upon every prank of poor Hal's, till any son save Hal would have become his foe! And see now, the old bedesman may be in the right; poor pretty Blanche has long been in her grave, Thomas is with her now, and Jamie,'—he lowered his voice,—'when men say that Harry hath more of Alexander in him than there is in other men, it strikes to my heart to think of the ring lying on the empty throne.'

'Now,' said James, 'what strikes *me* is, what doleful bodings can come into a brave man's head on a chill

Charlotte M. Yonge

morning before he has broken his fast. A tankard of hot ale will chase away omens, whether of bishop or bedesman.'

'It may chase them from the mind, but will not make away with them,' said John. 'But I might have known better than to speak to you of such things—you who are well-nigh a Lollard in disbelief of all beyond nature.'

'No Lollard am I,' said James. 'What Holy Church tells me, I believe devoutly; but not in that which she bids me loathe as either craft of devils or of men.'

'Ay, of which? There lies the question,' said John.

'Of men,' said the Scottish king; 'of men who have wit enough to lay hold of the weaker side even of a sober youth such as Lord John of Lancaster! Your proneness to believe in sayings and prophecies, in sorceries and magic, is the weakest point of all of you.'

'And it is the weakest point in you, James, that you will not credit upon proof, such proof as was the fulfilment of the prophecy of the place of my father's death.'

'One such saying as that, fulfilled to the ear, though not in truth, is made the plea for all this heart-sinking—ay, and what is worse, for the durance of your father's widow as a witch, and of her brave young son, because forsooth his name is Arthur of Richemont, and some old Welsh rhymester hath whispered to Harry that Richmond shall come out of Brittany, and be king of England.'

'Arthur is no worse off than any other captive of Agincourt,' said Bedford; 'and I tell you, James, the day may come when you will rue your want of heed to timely warnings.'

'Better rue once than pine under them all my life, and far better than let them betray me into deeming some grewsome crime an act of justice, as you may yet let them do,' said James.

Such converse passed between the two princes, while King Henry rode in advance, for the most part silent, and only desirous of reaching Pontefract Castle, where he had left the young wife whose presence he longed for the more in his trouble. The afternoon set in with heavy rain, but he would not halt, although he gave free permission to any of his suite to do so; and James recommended Malcolm to remain, and come on the next day with Brewster. The boy, however, disclaimed all weariness, partly because bashfulness made him unwilling to venture from under his royal kinsman's wing, and partly because he could not bear to let the English suppose that a Scotsman and a Stewart could be afraid of weather. As the rain became harder with the evening twilight, silence sank upon the whole troop, and they went splashing on through the deep lanes, in mud and mire, until the lights of Pontefract Castle shimmered on high from its hill. The gates were opened, the horses clattered in, torches came forth, flickering and hissing in the darkness. The travellers went through what seemed to Malcolm an interminable number of courts and gateways, and at length flung themselves off their horses, when Henry, striding on, mounted the steps, entered the building, and, turning the corner of a great carved screen, he and his brother, with James and Malcolm, found themselves in the midst of a blaze of cressets and tapers, which lighted up the wainscoted part of the hall.

The whole scene was dazzling to eyes coming in from the dark, and only after a moment or two could Malcolm perceive that, close to the great fire, sat a party of four, playing at what he supposed to be that French game with

Charlotte M. Yonge

painted cards of which Patrick Drummond had told him, and that the rest seemed to be in attendance upon them.

Dark eyed and haired, with a creamy ivory skin, and faultless form and feature, the fair Catherine would have been unmistakable, save that as Henry hurried forward, the lights glancing on his jaded face, matted hair, and soaked dress, the first to spring forward to meet him was a handsome young man, who wrung his hand, crying, 'Ah, Harry, Harry, then 'tis too true!' while the lady made scarcely a step forwards: no shade of colour tinged her delicate cheek; and though she did not resist his fervent embrace, it was with a sort of recoil, and all she was heard to say was, '*Eh, Messire, vos bottes sont crottees*!'

'You know all, Kate?' he asked, still holding her hand, and looking afraid of inflicting a blow.

'The battle? Is it then so great a disaster?' and, seeing his amazed glance, 'The poor Messire de Clarence! it was pity of him; he was a handsome prince.'

'Ah, sweet, he held thee dear,' said Henry, catching at the crumb of sympathy.

'But yes,' said Catherine, evidently perplexed by the strength of his feeling, and repeating, 'He was a *beau sieur courtois*. But surely it will not give the Armagnacs the advantage?'

'With Heaven's aid, no! But how fares it with poor Madge—his wife, I mean?'

'She is away to her estates. She went this morn, and wished to have taken with her the Demoiselle de Beaufort; but I forbade that—I could not be left without one lady of the blood.'

'Alack, Joan—' and Henry was turning, but Catherine interrupted him. 'You have not spoken to Madame of Hainault, nor to the Duke of Orleans. Nay, you are in no guise to speak to any one,' she added, looking with repugnance at the splashes of mud that reached even to his waist.

'I will don a fresh doublet, sweetheart,' said Henry, more rebuked than seemed fitting, 'and be ready to sup anon.'

'Supper! We supped long ago.'

'That may be; but we have ridden long since we snatched our meal, that I might be with thee the sooner, my Kate.'

'That was not well in you, my Lord, to come in thus dishevelled, steaming with wet—not like a king. You will be sick, my Lord.'

The little word of solicitude recalled his sweet tender smile of gratitude. No fear, *ma belle*; sickness dares not touch me.'

'Then,' said the Queen, 'you will be served in your chamber, and we will finish our game.'

Henry turned submissively away; but Bedford tarried an instant to say, 'Fair sister, he is sore distressed. It would comfort him to have you with him. He has longed for you.'

Catherine opened her beautiful brown eyes in a stare of surprise and reproof at the infraction of the rules of ceremony which she had brought with her. John of Bedford had never seemed to her either *beau* or *courtois*, and she looked unutterable things, to which he replied by an elevation of his marked eyebrows.

Charlotte M. Yonge

She sat down to her game, utterly ignoring the other princes in their weather-beaten condition; and they were forced to follow the King, and make their way to their several chambers, for Queen Catherine's will was law in matters of etiquette.

'The proud peat! She is jealous of every word Harry speaks—even to his cousin,' muttered James, as he reached his own room. 'You saw her, though,—you saw her!' he added, smiling, as he laid his hand on Malcolm's shoulder.

The boy coloured like a poppy, and answered awkwardly enough, 'The Lady Joan, Sir?'

'Who but the Lady Joan, thou silly lad? How say'st thou? Will not Scotland forget in the sight of that fair face all those fule phantasies—the only folly I heard at Glenuskie?'

'Methinks,' said Malcolm, looking down in sheer awkwardness, 'it were easier to bow to her than to King Harry's dame. She hath more of stateliness.'

'Humph!' said James, 'dost so serve thy courtly 'prenticeship? Nay, but in a sort I see thy meaning. The royal blood of England shows itself to one who hath an eye for princeliness of nature.'

'Nay,' said Malcolm, gratified, 'those dark eyes and swart locks—'

'Dark eyes—swart locks!' interrupted the King. 'His wits have gone wool-gathering.'

'Indeed, Sir!' exclaimed Malcolm, 'I thought you meant the lady who stood by the Queen's table, with the grand turn of the neck and the white wimple and veil.'

'Pshaw!' said James; 'the foolish callant! he hath taken that great brown Luxemburg nun of Dame Jac's for the Rose of Somerset.'

However, James, seeing how confounded the boy was by this momentary displeasure, explained to him who the other persons he had seen were—Jaqueline, the runaway Countess of Hainault in her own right, and Duchess of Brabant by marriage; Humfrey, duke of Gloucester, the King's young, brilliant brother; the grave, melancholy Duke of Orleans, who had been taken captive at Agincourt, and was at present quartered at Pontefract; the handsome, but stout and heavy-looking Earl of March; brave Lord Warwick; Sir Lewis Robsart, the old knight to whose charge the Queen had been specially committed from the moment of her betrothal; and a young, bold, gay-looking lad, of Malcolm's own age, but far taller and stouter, and with a merry, half-defiant, half-insouciant air, who had greatly taken his fancy, was, he was told, Ralf Percy, the second son of Sir Harry Percy.

'Of him they called Hotspur?—who was taken captive at Otterburn, who died a rebel!' exclaimed Malcolm.

'Ay,' said James; 'but King Harry had learnt the art of war as a boy, first under Hotspur, in Wales; nor doth he love that northern fashion of ours of keeping up feud from generation to generation. So hath he restored the eldest son to his barony, and set him to watch our Borders; and the younger, Ralf, he is training in his own school of chivalry.'

More wonders for Malcolm Stewart, who had learnt to believe it mere dishonour and tameness to forgive the son for his father's deeds. A cloistered priest could hardly do

Charlotte M. Yonge

so: pardon to a hostile family came only with the last mortal throe; and here was this warlike king forgiving as a mere matter of course!

'But,' added James, 'you had best not speak of your bent conventwards in the Court here. I should not like to have you called the monkling!'

Malcolm crimsoned, with the resolution never to betray himself.

CHAPTER V

WHITTINGTON S FEAST

The next day the royal train set forth from Pontefract, and ere mounting, James presented his young kinsman to the true Joan Beaufort—fair-haired, soft-featured, blue-eyed, and with a lovely air of graciousness, as she greeted him with a sweet, blushing, sunny smile, half that of the queen in anticipation, half that of the kindly maiden wishing to set a stranger at ease. So beautiful was she, that Malcolm felt annihilated at the thought of his blunder of last night.

As they rode on, James was entirely occupied with the lady, and Malcolm was a good deal left to himself; for, though the party was numerous, he knew no one except the Duke of Bedford, who was riding with the King and Lord Warwick, in deep consultation, while Sir Nigel Baird, Lord Marmion, and the rest were in the rear. He fell into a mood of depression such as had not come upon him since he passed the border, thinking himself despised by all for being ill-favoured and ill-dressed, and chafing, above all, at the gay contempt he fancied in young Ralf Percy's eye. He became constantly more discontented with this noisy turmoil, and more resolved to insist on returning to the peaceful cloister where alone he could hide his head and be at rest.

Charlotte M. Yonge

The troop halted for what they called their noon meat at the abode of a hospitable Yorkshire knight; but King Henry, in order that the good gentleman's means should not be overtasked, had given directions that only the ladies and the princes should enter the house, while the rest of the suite should take their meal at the village inn.

King James, in attending to Joan, had entirely forgotten his cousin; and Malcolm, doubtful and diffident, was looking hesitatingly at the gateway, when Ralf Percy called out, 'Ha! you there, this is our way. That is only for the royal folk; but there's good sack and better sport down here! I'll show you the way,' he added, good-naturedly, softened, as most were, by the startled, wistful, timid look.

Malcolm, ashamed to say he was royal, but surprised at the patronage, was gratefully following, when old Bairdsbrae indignantly laid his hand on the rein. 'Not so, Sir; this is no place for you!'

'Let me alone!' entreated Malcolm, as he saw Percy's amazed look and whistle of scorn. 'They don't want me.'

'You will never have your place if you do not take it,' said the old gentleman; and leading the trembling, shrinking boy up to the door, he continued, 'For the honour of Scotland, Sir!' and then announcing Malcolm by his rank and title, he almost thrust him in.

Fancying he detected a laugh on Ralf Percy's face, and a sneer on that of the stout English porter, Malcolm felt doubly wretched as he was ushered into the hall and the buzz of talk and the confusion made by the attendance of the worthy knight and his many sons, one of whom, waiting with better will than skill, had nearly run down the shy limping Scotsman, who looked wildly for refuge at some table. In his height of distress, a kindly gesture of invitation beckoned to him, and he found himself seated and addressed, first in French, and then in careful foreign English, by the same lady whom he had yesterday taken for Joan of Somerset, namely, Esclairmonde de Luxemburg.

He was too much confused to look up till the piece of pasty and the wine with which the lady had caused him to be supplied were almost consumed, and it was not till she had made some observations on the journey that he became at ease enough to hazard any sort of answer, and then it was in his sweet low Scottish voice, with that irresistibly attractive look of shy wistful gratitude in his great soft brown eyes, while his un-English accent caused her to say, 'I am a stranger here, like yourself, my Lord;' and at the same moment he first raised his eyes to behold what seemed to him perfect beauty and dignity, an oval face, richly-tinted olive complexion, dark pensive eyes, a sweet grave mouth smiling with encouraging kindness, and a lofty brow that gave the whole face a magnificent air, not so much stately as above and beyond this world. It might have befitted St. Barbara or St. Katherine, the great intellectual virgin visions of purity and holiness of the middle ages; but the kindness of the smile went to Malcolm's heart, and emboldened him to answer in his best French, 'You are from Holland, lady?'

'Not from the fens,' she answered. 'My home lies in the borders of the forest of Ardennes.'

And then they found that they understood each other best when she spoke French, and Malcolm English, or rather Scotch; and their acquaintance made so much progress, that when the signal was again given to mount, the Lady Esclairmonde permitted Malcolm to assist her to her saddle; and as he rode beside her he felt pleased with

Charlotte M. Yonge

himself, and as if Ralf Percy were welcome to look at him now.

On Esclairmonde's other hand there rode a small, slight girl, whom Malcolm took for quite a child, and paid no attention to; but presently old Sir Lewis Robsart rode back with a message that my Lady of Westmoreland wished to know where the Lady Alice Montagu was. A gentle, timid voice answered, 'O Sir, I am well here with Lady Esclairmonde. Pray tell my good lady so.'

And therewith Sir Lewis smiled, and said, 'You could scarcely be in better hands, fair damsel,' and rode back again; while Alice was still entreating, 'May I stay with you, dear lady? It is all so strange and new!'

Esclairmonde smiled, and said, 'You make me at home here, Mademoiselle. It is I who am the stranger!'

'Ah! but you have been in Courts before. I never lived anywhere but at Middleham Castle till they fetched me away to meet the Queen.'

For the gentle little maiden, a slender, fair-haired, childish-faced creature, in her sixteenth year, was the motherless child and heiress of the stout Earl of Salisbury, the last of the Montacutes, or Montagues, who was at present fighting the King's battles in France, but had sent his commands that she should be brought to Court, in preparation for fulfilling the long-arranged contract between her and Sir Richard Nevil, one of the twenty-two children of the Earl of Westmoreland.

She was under the charge of the Countess—a stately dame, with all the Beaufort pride; and much afraid of her she was, as everything that was shy or forlorn seemed to turn towards the maiden whose countenance not only promised kindness but protection.

Presently the cavalcade passed a gray building in the midst of green fields and orchards, where, under the trees, some black-veiled figures sat spinning.

'A nunnery!' quoth Esclairmonde, looking eagerly after it as she rode past.

'A nunnery!' said Malcolm, encouraged into the simple confidingness of a young boy. 'How unlike the one where my sister is! Not a tree is near it; it is perched upon a wild crag overhanging the angry sea, and the winds roar, and the gulls and eagles scream, and the waves thunder round it!'

'Yet it is not the less a haven of peace,' replied Esclairmonde.

'Verily,' said Malcolm, 'one knows what peace is under that cloister, where all is calm while the winds rave without.'

'You know how to love a cloister,' said the lady, as she heard his soft, sad tones.

'I had promised myself to make my home in one,' said Malcolm; 'but my King will have me make trial of the world first. And so please you,' he added, recollecting himself, 'he forbade me to make my purpose known; so pray, lady, be so good as to forget what I have said.'

'I will be silent,' said Esclairmonde; 'but I will not forget, for I look on you as one like myself, my young lord. I too am dedicated, and only longing to reach my cloistered haven.'

She spoke it out with the ease of those days when the monastic was as recognized a profession as any other calling, and yet with something of the desire to make it evident on what ground she stood.

Lady Alice uttered an exclamation of surprise.

'Yes,' said Esclairmonde, 'I was dedicated his my infancy, and promised myself in the nunnery at Dijon when I was seven years old.'

Then, as if to turn the conversation from herself, she asked of Malcolm if he too had made any vow.

'Only to myself,' said Malcolm. 'Neither my Tutor nor the Prior of Coldingham would hear my vows.' And he was soon drawn into telling his whole story, to which the ladies both listened with great interest and kindness, Esclairmonde commending his resolution to leave the care of his lands and vassals to one whom he represented as so much better fitted to bear them as Patrick Drummond, and only regretting the silence King James had enjoined, saying she felt that there was safety and protection in being avowed as a destined religious.

'And you are one,' said Lady Alice, looking at her in wonder. 'And yet you are with *that* lady—' And the girl's innocent face expressed a certain wonder and disgust that no one could marvel at who had heard the Flemish Countess talk in the loudest, broadest, most hoydenish style.

'She has been my very good lady,' said Esclairmonde; 'she has, under the saints, saved me from much.'

'Oh, I entreat you, tell us, dear lady!' entreated Alice. It was not a reticent age. Malcolm Stewart had already avowed himself in his own estimation pledged to a monastic life, and Esclairmonde of Luxemburg had reasons for wishing her position and intentions to be distinctly understood by all with whom she came in contact; moreover, there was a certain congeniality in both her companions, their innocence and simplicity, that drew out confidence, and impelled her to defend her lady.

'My poor Countess,' she said, 'she has been sorely used, and has suffered much. It is a piteous thing when our little imperial fiefs go to the spindle side!'

'What are her lands?' asked Malcolm.

'Hainault, Holland, and Zealand,' replied the lady. 'Her father was Count of Hainault, her mother the sister of the last Duke of Burgundy—him that was slain on the bridge of Montereau. She was married as a mere babe to the Duke of Touraine, who was for a brief time Dauphin, but he died ere she was sixteen, and her father died at the same time. Some say they both were poisoned. The saints forfend it should be true; but thus it was my poor Countess was left desolate, and her uncle, the Bishop of Liege—Jean Sans Pitie, as they call him—claimed her inheritance. You should have seen how undaunted she was!'

'Were you with her then?' asked Alice Montagu.

'Yes. I had been taken from our convent at Dijon, when my dear brothers, to whom Heaven be merciful! died at Azincourt. My *oncles a la mode de Bretagne*—how call you it in English?'

'Welsh uncles,' said Alice.

'They are the Count de St. Pol and the Bishop of

Charlotte M. Yonge

Therouenne. They came to Dijon. In another month I should have been seventeen, and been admitted as a novice; but, alack! there were all the lands that came through my grandmother, in Holland and in Flanders, all falling to me, and Monseigneur of Therouenne, like almost all secular clergy, cannot endure the religious orders, and would not hear of my becoming a Sister. They took me away, and the Bishop declared my dedication null, and they would have bestowed me in marriage at once, I believe, if Heaven had not aided me, and they could not agree on the person. And then my dear Countess promised me that she would never let me be given without my free will.'

'Then,' said Alice, 'the Bishop did cancel your dedication?'

'Yes,' said Esclairmonde; 'but none can cancel the dedication of my heart. So said the holy man at Zwoll.'

'How, lady?' anxiously inquired Malcolm; 'has not a bishop power to bind and unloose?'

'Yea,' said Esclairmonde, 'such power that if my childish promise had been made without purpose or conscience thereof, or indeed if my will were not with it, it would bind me no more, there were no sin in wedlock for me, no broken vow. But my own conscience of my vow, and my sense that I belong to my Heavenly Spouse, proved, he said, that it was not my duty to give myself to another, and that whereas none have a parent's right over me, if I have indeed chosen the better part, He to whom I have promised myself will not let it be taken from me, though I might have to bear much for His sake. And when I said in presumption that such would lie light on me, he bade me speak less and pray more, for I knew not the cost.'

'He must have been a very holy man,' said Alice, 'and

strict withal. Who was he?'

'One Father Thomas, a Canon Regular of the chapter of St. Agnes, a very saint, who spends his life in copying and illuminating the Holy Scripture, and in writing holy thoughts that verily seem to have been breathed into him by special inspiration of God. It was a sermon of his in Lent, upon chastening and perplexity, that I heard when first I was snatched from Dijon, that made me never rest till I had obtained his ghostly counsel. If I never meet him again, I shall thank Heaven for those months at Zwoll all my life—ere the Duke of Burgundy made my Countess resign Holland for twelve years to her uncle, and we left the place. Then, well-nigh against her will, they forced her into a marriage with the Duke of Brabant, though he be her first cousin, her godson, and a mere rude boy. I cannot tell you how evil were the days we often had then. If he had been left to himself, Madame might have guided him; but ill men came about him; they maddened him with wine and beer; they excited him to show that he feared her not; he struck her, and more than once almost put her in danger of her life. Then, too, his mother married the Bishop of Liege, her enemy—

'The Bishop!'

'He had never been consecrated, and had a dispensation. That marriage deprived my poor lady of even her mother's help. All were against her then; and for me too it went ill, for the Duke of Burgundy insisted on my being given to a half-brother of his, one they call Sir Boemond of Burgundy—a hard man of blood and revelry. The Duke of Brabant was all for him, and so was the Duchess-mother; and though my uncles would not have chosen him, yet they durst not withstand the Duke of Burgundy. I tried to appeal to the Emperor Sigismund, the head of our house, but I know not if he ever heard of my petition. I was in an

Charlotte M. Yonge

exceeding strait, and had only one trust, namely, that Father Thomas had told me that the more I threw myself upon God, the more He would save me from man. But oh! they seemed all closing in on me, and I knew that Sir Boemond had sworn that I should pay heavily for my resistance. Then one night my Countess came to me. She showed me the bruises her lord had left on her arms, and told me that he was about to banish all of us, her ladies, into Holland, and to keep her alone to bear his fury, and she was resolved to escape, and would I come with her? It seemed to me the message of deliverance. Her nurse brought us peasant dresses, high stiff caps, black boddices, petticoats of many colours, and therein we dressed ourselves, and stole out, ere dawn, to a church, where we knelt till the Sieur d'Escaillon—the gentleman who attends Madame still—drove up in a farmer's garb, with a market cart, and so forth from Bruges we drove. We cause to Valenciennes, to her mother; but we found that she, by persuasion of the Duke, would give us both up; so the Sieur d'Escaillon got together sixty lances, and therewith we rode to Calais, where never were weary travellers more courteously received than we by Lord Northumberland, the captain of Calais.'

'Oh, I am glad you came to us English!' cried Alice. 'Only I would it had been my father who welcomed you. And now?'

'Now I remain with my lady, as the only demoiselle she has from her country; and, moreover, I am waiting in the trust that my kinsmen will give up their purpose of bestowing me in marriage, now that I am beyond their reach; and in time I hope to obtain sufficient of my own goods for a dowry for whatever convent I may enter.'

'Oh, let it be an English one!' cried Alice.

'I have learnt to breathe freer since I have been on English soil,' said Esclairmonde, smiling; 'but where I may rest at last, Heaven only knows!'

'This is a strange country,' said Malcolm. 'No one seems afraid of violence and wrong here.'

'Is that so strange?' asked Alice, amazed. 'Why, men would be hanged if they did violence!'

'I would we were as sure of justice at my home,' sighed Esclairmonde. 'King Henry will bring about a better rule.'

'Never doubt,' cried Salisbury's daughter. 'When France is once subdued, there will be no more trouble, he will make your kinsmen do you right, dear demoiselle, and oh! will you not found a beauteous convent?'

'King Henry has not conquered France yet,' was all Esclairmonde said.

'Ha!' cried the buxom Countess Jaqueline, as the ladies dismounted, 'never speak to me more, our solemn sister. When have I done worse than lure a young cavalier, and chain him all day with my tongue?'

'He is a gentle boy!' said Esclairmonde, smiling.

'Truly he looked like a calf turned loose among strange cattle! How gat he into the hall?'

'He is of royal Scottish blood,' said Esclairmonde 'cousin-german to King James.'

'And our grave nun has a fancy to tame the wild Scots, like a second St. Margaret! A king's grandson! fie, fie! what, become ambitious, Clairette? Eh? you were so

Charlotte M. Yonge

occupied, that I should have been left to no one but Monseigneur of Gloucester, but that I was discreet, and rode with my Lord Bishop of Winchester. How he chafed! but I know better than to have *tete-a-tetes* with young sprigs of the blood royal!'

Esclairmonde laughed good-humouredly, partly in courtesy to her hoyden mistress, but partly at the burning, blushing indignation she beheld in the artless face of Alice Montagu.

The girl was as shy as a fawn, frightened at every word from knight or lady, and much in awe of her future mother-in-law, a stiff and stately dame, with all the Beaufort haughtiness; so that Lady Westmoreland gladly and graciously consented to the offer of the Demoiselle de Luxemburg to attend to the little maiden, and let her share her chamber and her bed. And indeed Alice Montagu, bred up in strictness and in both piety and learning, as was sometimes the case with the daughters of the nobility, had in all her simplicity and bashfulness a purity and depth that made her a congenial spirit with the grave votaress, whom she regarded on her side with a young girl's enthusiastic admiration for a grown woman, although in point of fact the years between them were few.

The other ladies of the Court were a little in awe of the Demoiselle de Luxemburg, and did not seek her when they wished to indulge in the gossip whose malice and coarseness she kept in check; but if they were anxious, or in trouble, they always came to her as their natural consoler; and the Countess Jaqueline, bold and hoydenish as she was, kept the license of her tongue and manners under some shadow of restraint before her, and though sometimes bantering her, often neglecting her counsel, evidently felt her attendance a sort of safeguard and protection.

The gentlemen were mostly of the opinion of the Duke of Gloucester, who said that the Lady Esclairmonde was so like Deborah, come out of a Mystery, that it seemed to be always Passion-tide where she was; and she, moreover, was always guarded in her manner towards them, keeping her vocation in the recollection of all by her gravely and coldly courteous demeanour, and the sober hues and fashion of her dress; but being aware of Malcolm's destination, perceiving his loneliness, and really attracted by his pensive gentleness, she admitted him to far more friendly intercourse than any other young noble, while he revered and clung to her much as Lady Alice did, as protector and friend.

King James was indeed so much absorbed in his own lady-love as to have little attention to bestow on his young cousin, and he knew, moreover, that to be left to such womanly training as ladies were bound to bestow on young squires and pages was the best treatment for the youth, who was really thriving and growing happier every day, as he lost his awkwardness and acquired a freedom and self-confidence such as he could never have imagined possible in his original brow-beaten state, though without losing the gentle modesty and refinement that gave him such a charm.

A great sorrow awaited him, however, at Leicester, where Easter was to be spent. A messenger came from Durham, bringing letters from Coldingham to announce the death of good Sir David Drummond, which had taken place two days after Malcolm had left him, all but the youth himself having well known that his state was hopeless.

In his grief, Malcolm found his chief comforter in Esclairmonde, who kindly listened when he talked of the happy old times at Glenuskie, and of the kindness and piety of his guardian; while she lifted his mind to dwell

Charlotte M. Yonge

on the company of the saints; and when he knew that her thoughts went, like his, to his fatherly friend in the solemn services connected with the departed, he was no longer desolate, and there was almost a sweetness in the grief of which his fair saint had taken up a part. She showed him likewise some vellum pages on which her ghostly father, the Canon of St. Agnes, had written certain dialogues between the Divine Master and His disciple, which seemed indeed to have been whispered by heavenly inspiration, and which soothed and hallowed his mourning for the guide and protector of his youth. He loved to dwell on her very name, Esclairmonde—'light of the world.' The taste of the day hung many a pun and conceit upon names, and to Malcolm this—which had, in fact, been culled out of romance—seemed meetly to express the pure radiance of consolation and encouragement that seemed to him to shine from her, and brighten the life that had hitherto been dull and gloomy—nay, even to give him light and joy in the midst of his grief.

At that period Courts were not much burdened with etiquette. No feudal monarch was more than the first gentleman, and there was no rigid line of separation of ranks, especially where, as among the kings of the Red Rose, the boundaries were so faint between the princes and the nobility; and as Catherine of Valois was fond of company, and indolently heedless of all that did not affect her own dignity or ease, the whole Court, including some of the princely captives, lived as one large family, meeting at morning Mass in church or chapel, taking their meals in common, riding, hunting, hawking, playing at bowls, tennis, or stool-ball, or any other pastime, in such parties as suited their inclinations; and spending the evening in the great hall, in conversation varied by chess, dice, and cards, recitals of romance, and music, sometimes performed by the choristers of the Royal chapel, or sometimes by the company themselves, and often by one or other of the two kings, who were both proficients as well with the voice as with the lute and organ.

Thus Malcolm had many opportunities of being with the Demoiselle of Luxemburg: and almost a right was established, that when she sat in the deep embrasure of a window with her spinning, he should be on the cushioned step beneath; when she mounted, he held the stirrup; and when the church bells were ringing, he led her by her fair fingers to her place in the nave, and back again to the hall; and when the manchet and rere supper were brought into the hall, he mixed her wine and water, and held the silver basin and napkin to her on bended knee, and had become her recognized cavalier. He was really thriving. Even the high-spirited son of Hotspur could not help loving and protecting him.

'Have a care,' said Ralf to a lad of ruder mould; 'I'll no more see that lame young Scot maltreated than a girl.'

'He is no better than a girl,' growled his comrade; 'my little brother Dick would be more than a match for him!'

'I wot not that,' said Percy; 'there's a drop of life and spirit at the bottom; and for the rest, when he looks up with those eyes of his, and smiles his smile, it is somehow as if it were beneath a man to vex him wilfully. And he sees so much meaning in everything, too, that it is a dozen times better sport to hear him talk than one of you fellows, who have only wit enough to know a hawk from a heron-schaw.'

After a grave Easter-tide spent at Leicester, the Court moved to Westminster, where Henry had to meet his parliament, and obtain supplies for the campaign which was to revenge the death of Clarence.

Charlotte M. Yonge

There was no great increase of gaiety even here, for Henry was extremely occupied, both with regulating matters for government during his absence, and in training the troops who began to flock to his standard; so that the Queen complained that his presence in England was of little service to her, since he never had any leisure, and there were no pastimes.

'Well, Dame,' said Henry, gaily, 'there is one revel for you. I have promised to knight the Lord Mayor, honest Whittington, and I hear he is preparing a notable banquet in the Guild Hall.'

'A city mayor!' exclaimed Queen Catherine, with ineffable disgust. 'My brothers would sooner cut off his *roturier* head than dub him knight!'

'Belike,' said Henry, dryly; 'but what kind of friends have thy brothers found at Paris? Moreover, this Whittington may content thee as to blood. Rougedragon hath been unfolding to me his lineage of a good house in Gloucestershire.'

'More shame that he should soil his hands with trade!' said the Queen.

'See what you say when he has cased those fair hands in Spanish gloves. You ladies should know better than to fall out with a mercer.'

'Ah!' said Duke Humfrey, 'they never saw the silks and samites wherewith he fitted out my sister Philippa for the Swedes! Lucky the bride whose wardrobe is purveyed by honest Dick!'

'Is it not honour enough for the mechanical hinds that we wear their stuffs,' said Countess Jaqueline, 'without demeaning ourselves to eat at their boards? The *outrecuidance* of the rogues in the Netherlands would be surpassing, did we feed it in that sort.'

"Tis you that will be fed, Dame Jac,' laughed Henry. 'I can tell you, their sack and their pasties, their march-pane and blanc-manger, far exceed aught that a poor soldier can set before you.'

'Moreover,' observed Humfrey, 'the ladies ought to see the romaunt of the Cat complete.'

'How!' cried Jaqueline, 'is it, then, true that this Vittentone is the miller's son whose cat wore boots and made his fortune?'

'I have heard my aunt of Orleans divert my father with that story,' murmured Catherine. 'How went the tale? I thought it folly, and marked it not. What became of the cat?'

'The cat desired to test his master's gratitude, so tells Straparola,' said the Duke of Orleans, in his dry satirical tone; 'and whereas he had been wont to promise his benefactor a golden coffin and state funeral, Puss feigned death, and thereby heard the lady inform her husband that the old cat was dead. "*A la bonne heure*!" said the Marquis. "Take him by the tail, and fling him on the muck-heap beneath the window!"'

'Thereof I acquit Whittington, who never was thankless to man or brute,' said King Henry. 'Moreover, his cat, or her grandchildren, must be now in high preferment at the King of Barbary's Court.'

'A marvellous beast is that cat,' said James. 'When I was a child in Scotland, we used to tell the story of her

Charlotte M. Yonge

exchange for a freight of gold and spices, only the ship sailed from Denmark,'

'Maybe,' said Henry; 'but I would maintain the truth of Whittington's cat with my lance, and would gladly have no worse cause! You'll see his cat painted beside him in the Guild Hall, and may hear the tale from him, as I loved to hear him when I was a lad.

"Turn again, Whittington,
Thrice Lord Mayor of London town!"

I told my good old friend I must have come over from France on purpose to keep his third mayoralty. So I am for the City on Thursday; and whoever loves good wine, good sturgeon, good gold, or good men, had best come with me.'

Such inducements were not to be neglected, and though Queen Catherine minced and bridled, and apologized to Duchess Jaqueline for her husband's taste for low company, neither princess wished to forego the chance of amusement; and a brilliant cavalcade set forth in full order of precedence. The King and Queen were first; then, to his great disgust, the King of Scots, with Duchess Jaqueline; Bedford, with Lady Somerset; Gloucester, with the Countess of March; the Duke of Orleans, with the Countess of Exeter; and Malcolm of Glenuskie found himself paired off with his sovereign's lady-love, Joan Beaufort, and a good deal overawed by the tall horned tower that crowned her flaxen locks, as well as by knowing that her uncle, the Bishop of Winchester, the stateliest, stiffest, and most unapproachable person in all the Court, was riding just behind him, beside the Demoiselle de Luxemburg.

Temple Bar was closed, and there was a flourish of

trumpets and a parley ere the gate was flung open to admit the royal guests; but Malcolm, in his place, could not see the aldermen on horseback, in their robes of scarlet and white, drawn up to receive the King. All that way up Holborn, every house was hung with tapestry, and the citizens formed a gorgeously-apparelled lane, shouting in unison, their greetings attuned to bursts of music from trumpets and nakers.

Beautiful old St. Paul's, with the exquisite cross for open-air preaching in front, rose on their view; and before the lofty west door the princely guests dismounted, each gentleman leading his lady up the nave to the seat prepared in such manner that he might be opposite to her. The clergy lined the stalls, and a magnificent mass was sung, and was concluded by the advance of the King to the altar step, followed by a fine old man in scarlet robes bordered with white fur, the collar of SS. round his neck, and his silvery hair and lofty brow crowning a face as sagacious as it was dignified and benevolent.

It seemed a reversal of the ordinary ceremonial when the slender agile young man took in hand the sword, and laid the honour of knighthood on the gray-headed substantial senior, whom he bade to arise Sir Richard Whittington. Jaqueline of Hainault had the bad taste to glance across to Humfrey and titter, but the Duke valued popularity among the citizens, and would not catch her eye; and in the line behind the royal ladies there was a sweet elderly face, beautiful, though time-worn, with blue eyes misty with proud glad tears, and a mouth trembling with tender exultation.

After the ceremony was concluded, King Henry offered his hand to the Lady Mayoress, Dame Alice Whittington, making her bright tears drop in glad confusion at his frank, hearty congratulation and warm praise of her

Charlotte M. Yonge

husband; and though the fair Catherine could have shuddered when Sir Richard advanced to lead her, she was too royal to compromise her dignity by visible scorn, and she soon found that the merchant could speak much better French than most of the nobles.

Malcolm felt as averse as did the French princesses to burgher wealth and splendour, and his mind had not opened to understand burgher worth and weight; and when he saw the princes John and Humfrey, and even his own king, seeking out city dames and accosting them with friendly looks, it seemed to him a degrading truckling to riches, from which he was anxious to save his future queen; but when he would have offered his arm to Lady Joan, he saw her already being led away by an alderman measuring at least a yard across the shoulders; and the good-natured Earl of March, seeing him at a loss, presented him to a round merry wife in a scarlet petticoat and black boddice, its plump curves wreathed with geld chains, who began pitying him for having been sent to the wars so young, being, as usual, charmed into pity by his soft appealing eyes and unconscious grace; would not believe his assertions that he was neither a captive nor a Frenchman;—'don't tell her, when he spoke like a stranger, and halted from a wound.'

Colouring to the ears, he explained that he had never walked otherwise; whereupon her pity redoubled, and she by turns advised him to consult Master Doctor Caius, and to obtain a recipe from Mistress—she meant Dame— Alice Whittington, the kindest soul living, and, Lady Mayoress as she was, with no more pride than the meanest scullion. Pity she had no child—yet scarce pity either, since she and the good Lord Mayor were father and mother to all orphans and destitute—nay, to all who had any care on their minds.

Malcolm was in extreme alarm lest he should be walked up to the Lady Mayoress for inspection before all the world when they entered the Guild Hall, a building of grand proportions, which, as good Mistress Bolt informed him, had lately been paved and glazed at Sir Richard Whittington's own expense. The bright new red and yellow tiles, and the stained glass of the tall windows high up, as well as the panels of the wainscot, were embellished with trade-marks and the armorial bearings of the guilds; and the long tables, hung with snowy napery, groaned with gold and silver plate, such as, the Duke of Orleans observed to Catherine, no citizens would dare exhibit in France to any prince or noble, at peril of being mulcted of all, with or without excuse.

On an open hearth beneath the louvre, or opening for smoke, burnt a fire diffusing all around an incense-like fragrance, from the logs, composed of cinnamon and other choice woods and spices, that fed the flame. The odour and the warmth on a bleak day of May were alike delicious; and King Henry, after heading Dame Alice up to it, stood warming his hands and extolling the choice scent, adding: 'You spoil us, Sir Richard. How are we to go back to the smoke of wood and peat, and fires puffed with our own mouths, after such pampering as this—the costliest fire I have seen in the two realms?'

'It shall be choicer yet, Sir,' said Sir Richard Whittington, who had just handed the Queen to her seat.

'Scarce possible,' replied Henry, 'unless I threw in my crown, and that I cannot afford. I shall be pawning it ere long.'

Instead of answering, the Lord Mayor quietly put his hand into his furred pouch, and drawing out a bundle of parchments tied with a ribbon, held them towards the

Charlotte M. Yonge

King, with a grave smile.

'Lo you now, Sir Richard,' said Henry, with a playful face of disgust; 'this is to save your dainty meats, by spoiling my appetite by that unwelcome sight. What, man! have you bought up all the bonds I gave in my need to a whole synagogue of Jews and bench of Loin-bards? I shall have to send for my crown before you let me go; though verily,' he added, with frank, open face, 'I'm better off with a good friend like you for my creditor—only I'm sorry for you, Sir Richard. I fear it will be long ere you see your good gold in the stead of your dirty paper, even though I gave you an order on the tolls. How now! What, man, Dick Whittington! Art raving? Here, the tongs!'

For Sir Richard, gently smiling, had placed the bundle of bonds on the glowing bed of embers.

Henry, even while calling for the tongs, was raking them out with his sword, and would have grasped them in his hand in a moment, but the Lord Mayor caught his arm.

'Pardon, my lord, and grant your new knight's boon.'

'When he is not moon-struck!' said Henry, still guarding the documents. 'Why, my Lady Mayoress, know you what is here?'

'Sixty thousand, my liege,' composedly answered Dame Alice. 'My husband hath his whims, and I pray your Grace not to hinder what he hath so long been preparing.'

'Yea, Sir,' added Whittington, earnestly. 'You wot that God hath prospered us richly. We have no child, and our nephews are well endowed. How, then, can our goods belong to any save God, our king, and the poor?'

Henry drew one hand over his eyes, and with the other wrung that of Whittington. 'Had ever king such a subject?' he murmured.

'Had ever subject such a king?' was Whittington's return.

'Thou hast conquered, Whittington,' said the King, presently looking up with a sunny smile. 'To send me over the seas a free man, beholden to you in heart though not by purse, is, as I well believe, worth all that sum to thy loyal heart. Thou art setting me far on my way to Jerusalem, my dear friend! Thank him, Kate—he hath done much for thine husband!'

Catherine looked amiable, and held out a white hand to be kissed, aware that the King was pleased, though hardly understanding why he should be glad that an odour of singed parchment should overpower the gums and cinnamon. This was soon remedied by the fresh handful of spices that were cast into the flame, and the banquet began, magnificent with peacocks, cranes, and swans in full plumage; the tusky bear crunched his apple, deer's antlers adorned the haunch, the royal sturgeon floated in wine, fountains of perfumed waters sprang up from shells, towers of pastry and of jelly presented the endless allegorical devices of mediaeval fancy, and, pre-eminent over all, a figure of the cat, with emerald eyes, fulfilled, as Henry said, the proverb, 'A cat might look at a king;' and truly the cat and her master had earned the right; therefore his first toast was, 'To the Cat!'

Each guest found at his or her place a beautiful fragrant pair of gloves, in Spanish leather, on the back of which was once more embroidered, in all her tabby charms, the cat's face. Therewith began a lengthy meal; and Malcolm Stewart rejoiced at finding himself seated next to the Lady Esclairmonde, but he grudged her attention to her

Charlotte M. Yonge

companion, a slender, dark, thoughtful representative of the Goldsmiths' Company, to whom she talked with courtesy such as Malcolm had scorned to show his city dame.

'Who,' said Esclairmonde, presently, 'was a dame in a religious garb whom I marked near the door here? She hooked like one of the Beguines of my own country.'

'We have no such order here, lady,' said the goldsmiths, puzzled.

'Hey, Master Price,' cried Mistress Bolt, speaking across Malcolm, 'I can tell the lady who it was. 'Twas good Sister Avice Rodney, to whom the Lady Mayoress promised some of these curious cooling drinks for the poor shipwright who hath well-nigh cloven off his own foot with his axe.'

'Yea, truly,' returned the goldsmith; 'it must have been one of the bedeswomen of St. Katharine's whom the lady has seen.'

'What order may that be?' asked Esclairmonde. 'I have seen nothing so like my own country since I came hither.'

'That may well be, madam,' said Mistress Belt, 'seeing that these bedeswomen were first instituted by a country-woman of your own—Queen Philippa, of blessed memory.'

'By your leave, Mistress Bolt,' interposed Master Price, 'the hospital of St. Katharine by the Tower is of far older foundation.'

'By *your* leave, sir, I know what I say. The hospital was founded I know not when, but these bedeswomen were especially added by the good Queen, by the same token that mine aunt Cis, who was tirewoman to the blessed Lady Joan, was one of the first.'

'How was it? What is their office?' eagerly inquired Esclairmonde. And Mistress Bolt arranged herself for a long discourse.

'Well, fair sirs and sweet lady, though you be younger than I, you have surely heard of the Black Death. Well named was it, for never was pestilence more dire; and the venom was so strong, that the very lips and eyelids grew livid black, and then there was no hope. Little thought of such disease was there, I trow, in kings' houses, and all the fair young lords and ladies, the children of King Edward, as then was, were full of sport and game-someness as you see these dukes be now. And never a one was blither than the Lady Joan—she they called Joan of the Tower, being a true Londoner born—bless her! My aunt Cis would talk by the hour of her pretty ways and kindly mirth. But 'twas even as the children have the game in the streets—

"There come three knights all out of Spain,
Are come to fetch your daughter Jane."

'Twas for the King of Castille, that same Peter for whom the Black Prince of Wales fought, and of whom such grewsome tales were told. The pretty princess might almost have had a boding what sort of husband they had for her, for she begged and prayed, even on her knees, that her father would leave her; but her sisters were all espoused, and there was no help for it. But, as one comfort to her, my aunt Cis, who had been about her from her cradle, was to go with her; and oft she would tell of the long journey in litters through France, and how welcome were the English tongues they heard again at

Charlotte M. Yonge

Bordeaux, and how when poor Lady Joan saw her brother, the Prince, she clung about his neck and sobbed, and how he soothed her, and said she would soon laugh at her own unwillingness to go to her husband. But even then the Black Death was in Bordeaux, and being low and mournful at heart, the sweet maid contracted it, and lay down to die ere she had made two days' journey, and her last words were, "My God hath shown me more pity than father or brother;" and so she died like a lamb, and mine aunt was sent by the Prince to bear home the tidings to the good Queen, who was a woeful woman. And therewith, here was the pestilence in London, raging among the poor creatures that lived in the wharves and on the river bank, in damp and filth, so that whole households lay dead at once, and the contagion, gathering force, spread into the city, and even to the nobles and their ladies. Then my good aunt, having some knowledge of the sickness already, and being without fear, went among the sick, and by her care, and the food, wine, and clothing she brought, saved a many lives. And from whom should the bounties come, save from the good Queen, who ever had a great pity for those touched like her own fair child? Moreover, when she heard from my aunt how the poor things lived in uncleanness and filth, and how, what with many being strangers coming by sea, and others being serfs fled from home, they were a nameless, masterless sort, who knew not where to seek a parish priest, and whom the friars shunned for their poverty, she devised a fresh foundation to be added to the hospital of St. Katharine's in the Docks, providing for a chapter of ten bedeswomen, gentle and well-nurtured, who should both sing in choir, and likewise go forth constantly among the poor, to seek out the children, see that they learn their Credo, Ave, and Pater Noster, bring the more toward to be further taught in St. Katharine's school, and likewise to stir poor folk up to go to mass and lead a godly life; to visit the sick, feed and tend them, and so instruct them, that they may desire the

Sacraments of the Church.'

'Ah! good Flemish Queen!' cried Esclairmonde. 'She learnt that of our Beguines!'

'If your ladyship will have it so,' said Mrs. Bolt; 'but my aunt Cicely began!'

'Who nominates these bedeswomen?' asked Esclairmonde.

'That does the Queen,' said Mistress Bolt. 'Not this young Queen, as yet, for Queen Joan, the late King's widow, holds the hospital till her death, unless it should be taken from her for her sorceries, from which Heaven defend us!'

'Can it be visited?' said Esclairmonde. 'I feel much drawn thither, as I ever did to the Beguines.'

'Ay, marry may it!' cried delighted Mrs. Bolt. 'I have more than one gossip there, foreby Sister Avice, who was godchild to Aunt Cis; and if the good lady would wish to see the hospital, I would bear her company with all my heart.'

To Malcolm's disgust, Esclairmonde caught at the proposal, which the Scottish haughtiness that lay under all his gentleness held somewhat degrading to the cousin of the Emperor. He fell into a state of gloom, which lasted till the loving-cup had gone round and been partaken of in pairs.

After hands had been washed in rose-water, the royal party took their seats in barges to return to Westminster by the broad and beautiful highway of the Thames.

Here at once Alice Montagu nestled to Esclairmonde's side, delighted with her cat gloves, and further delighted

Charlotte M. Yonge

with an old captain of trained bands, to whose lot she had fallen, and who, on finding that she was the daughter of the Earl of Salisbury, under whom he had served, had launched forth by the hour into the praises of that brave nobleman, both for his courage and his kindness to his troops.

'No wonder King Henry loves his citizens so well!' cried Esclairmonde. 'Would that our Netherlandish princes and burghers could take pride and pleasure in one another's wealth and prowess, instead of grudging and fearing thereat!'

'To my mind,' said Malcolm, 'they were a forward generation. That city dame will burst with pride, if you, lady, go with her to see those bedeswomen.'

'I trust not,' laughed Esclairmonde, 'for I mean to try.'

'Nay, but,' said Malcolm, 'what should a mere matter of old rockers and worn-out tirewomen concern a demoiselle of birth?'

'I honour them for doing their Master's work,' said Esclairmonde, 'and would fain be worthy to follow in their steps.'

'Surely,' said Malcolm, 'there are houses fit for persons of high and princely birth to live apart from gross contact with the world.'

'There are,' said Esclairmonde; 'but I trust I may be pardoned for saying that such often seem to me to play at humility when they stickle for birth and dower with the haughtiest. I never honoured any nuns so much as the humble Sisters of St. Begga, who never ask for sixteen quarterings, but only for a tender hand, soft step, pure life, and pious heart.'

'I deemed,' said Malcolm, 'that heavenly contemplation was the purpose of convents.'

'Even so, for such as can contemplate like the holy man I have told you of,' said Esclairmonde; 'but labour hath been greatly laid aside in convents of late, and I doubt me if it be well, or if their prayers be the better for it.'

'And so,' said Alice, 'I heard my Lord of Winchester saying how it were well to suppress the alien priories, and give their wealth to found colleges like that founded by Bishop Wykeham.'

For in truths the spirit of the age was beginning to set against monasticism. It was the period when perhaps there was more of license and less of saintliness than at any other, and when the long continuance of the Great Schism had so injured Church discipline that the clergy and ecclesiastics were in the worst state of all, especially the monastic orders, who owned no superior but the Pope, and between the two rivals could avoid supervision altogether. Such men as Thomas a Kempis, or the great Jean Gerson, were rare indeed; and the monasteries had let themselves lose their missionary character, and become mere large farms, inhabited by celibate gentlemen and their attendants, or by the superfluous daughters of the nobles and gentry. Such devotion as led Esclairmonde to the pure atmosphere of prayer and self-sacrifice had well-nigh died out, and almost every other lady of the time would have regarded her release from the vows made for her its her babyhood a happy escape.

Still less, at a time when no active order of Sisters, save that of the Beguines in Holland, had been invented, and when no nun ever dreamt of carrying her charity beyond the quadrangle of her own convent, could any one be expected to enter into Esclairmonde's admiration and longing for out-of-door works; but the person whom she had chiefly made her friend was the King's almoner and chaplain, sometimes called Sir Martin Bennet, at others Dr. Bennet, a great Oxford scholar, bred up among William of Wykeham's original seventy at Winchester and New College, and now much trusted and favoured by the King, whom he everywhere accompanied. That Sir Martin was a pluralist must be confessed, but he was most conscientious in providing substitutes, and was a man of much thought and of great piety, in whom the fair pupil of the Canon of St. Agnes found a congenial spirit.

CHAPTER VI

MALCOLM'S SUIT

'That is a gentle and gracious slip of the Stewart. What shall you do with him?' asked King Henry of James, as they stood together at one end of the tilt-yard at Westminster, watching Malcolm Stewart and Ralf Percy, who were playing at closhey, the early form of nine-pins.

'I know what I should like to do,' said James.

'What may that be?'

'To marry him to the Lady Esclairmonde de Luxemburg.'

Henry gave a long whistle.

'Have you other views for her?'

'Not I! Am I to have designs on every poor dove who flies into my tent from the hawk? Besides, are not they both of them vowed to a religious life?'

'Neither vow is valid,' replied James.

'To meddle with such things is what I should not *dare*,' said Henry.

Charlotte M. Yonge

'Monks and friars are no such holy beings, that I should greatly concern me about keeping an innocent had out of their company,' said James.

'Nor do I say they are,' said Henry; 'but it is ill to cross a vow of devotion, and to bring a man back to the world is apt to render him not worth the having. You may perchance get him down lower than you intended.'

'This boy never had any real vocation at all,' said James; 'it was only the timidity born of ill-health, and the longing for food for the mind.'

'Maybe so,' replied the English king, 'and you may be in the right; but why fix on that grand Luxemburg wench, who ought to be a Lady Abbess of Fontainebleau at least, or a very St. Hilda, to rule monks and nuns alike?'

'Because they have fixed on each other. Malcolm needs a woman like her to make a man of him; and with her spirit and fervent charity, we should have them working a mighty change in Scotland.'

'If you get her there!'

'Have I your consent, Harry?'

'Mine? It's no affair of mine! You must settle it with Madame of Hainault; but you had best take care. You are more like to make your tame lambkin into a ravening wolf, than to get that Deborah the prophetess to herd him.'

James in sooth viewed this warning as another touch of Lancastrian superstition, and only considered how to broach the question. Malcolm, meantime, was balancing between the now approaching decision between Oxford and France. He certainly felt something of his old horror of warlike scenes; but even this was lessening; he was aware that battles were not every-day occurrences, and that often there was no danger at all. He would not willingly be separated from his king; and if the female part of the Court were to accompany the campaign, it would be losing sight of all he cared for, if he were left among a set of stranger shavelings at Oxford. Yet he was reluctant to break with the old habits that had hitherto been part of his nature; he felt, after every word of Esclairmonde—nay, after every glance towards her—as though it were a blessed thing to have, like her, chosen the better part; he knew she would approve his resort to the home of piety and learning; he was aware that when with Ralf Percy and the other youths of the Court he was ashamed of his own scrupulousness, and tempted to neglect observances that they might call monkish and unmanly; and he was not at all sure that in face of the enemy a panic might not seize him and disgrace him for ever! In effect he did not know what he wished, even when he found that the Queen had decided against going across the sea, and that therefore all the ladies would remain with her at Shene or Windsor.

He should probably never again see Esclairmonde, the guiding star of his recent life, the embodiment of all that he had imagined when conning the quaint old English poems that told the Legend of Seynct Katharine; and as he leant musingly against a lattice, feeling as if the brightness of his life was going out, King James merrily addressed him:—

'Eh! the fit is on you too, boy!'

'What fit, Sir?' Malcolm opened his eyes.

'The pleasing madness.'

Charlotte M. Yonge

Malcolm uttered a cry like horror, and reddened crimson. 'Sir! Sir! Sir!' he stammered.

'A well-known token of the disease is raving.'

'Sir, Sir! I implore you to speak of nothing so profane.'

'I am not given to profanity,' said James, endeavouring to look severe, but with laughter in his voice. 'Methought you were not yet so sacred a personage.'

'Myself! No; but that I—I should dare to have such thoughts of—oh, Sir!' and Malcolm covered his face with his hands. 'Oh, that you should have so mistaken me!'

'I have *not* mistaken you,' said James, fixing his keen eyes on him.

'Oh, Sir!' cried Malcolm, like one freshly stung, 'you have! Never, never dreamt I of aught but worshipping as a living saint, as I would entreat St. Margaret or—'

There was still the King's steady look and the suppressed smile. Malcolm broke off, and with a sudden agony wrung his hands together. The King still smiled. 'Ay, Malcolm, it will not do; you are man, not monk.'

'But why be so cruel as to make me vile in my own eyes?' almost sobbed Malcolm.

'Because,' said the King, 'she is not a saint in heaven, nor a nun in a convent, but a free woman, to be won by the youth she has marked out.'

'Marked! Oh, Sir, she only condescended because she knew my destination.'

'That is well,' said King James. 'Thus sparks kindle at unawares.'

Malcolm's groan and murmur of 'Never!' made James almost laugh at the evidence that on one side at least the touch-wood was ready.

'Oh, Sir,' he sighed, 'why put the thought before me, to make me wretched! Even were she for the world, she would never be for me. I—doited—hirpling—'

'Peace, silly lad; all that is past and gone. You are quite another now, and a year or two of Harry's school of chivalry will send you home a gallant knight and minstrel, such as no maiden will despise.'

The King went, and Malcolm fell into a silent state of musing. He was entirely overpowered, both by the consciousness awakened within himself, by the doubt whether it were not a great sin, and by the strangeness that the King, hitherto his oracle, should infuse such a hope. What King James deemed possible could never be so incredible, or even sacrilegious, as he deemed it. Restless, ashamed, rent by a thousand conflicting feelings, Malcolm roamed up and down his chamber, writhed, tried to sit and think, then, finding his thoughts in a whirl, renewed his frantic pacings. And when dire necessity brought him again into the ladies' chamber, he was silent, blushing, ungainly, abstracted, and retreated into the farthest possible corner from the unconscious Esclairmonde.

Then, when again alone with the King, he began with the assertion, 'It is utterly impossible, Sir;' and James smiled to see his poison working. Not that he viewed it as poison. Monasticism was at a discount, and the ranks of the religious orders were chiefly filled, the old Benedictine

Charlotte M. Yonge

and Augustinian foundations by gentlemen of good family who wanted the easy life of a sort of bachelor squire, and the friaries were recruited by the sort of men who would in modern times be dissenting teachers of the lower stamp. James was persuaded that Malcolm was fit for better things than were usually to be seen in a convent, and that it was a real kindness not to let him merely retire thither out of faintness of heart, mistaken for devotion; and he also felt as if he should be doing good service, not only to Malcolm, but to Scotland, if he could obtain for him a wife of the grand character of Esclairmonde de Luxemburg.

He even risked the mention of the project to the Countess of Hainault, without whose consent nothing could be effected. Jaqueline laughed long and loud at the notion of her stately Esclairmonde being the lady-love of King James's little white-visaged cousin; but if he could bring it about she had no objection, she should be very glad that the demoiselle should come down from the height and be like other people; but she would wager the King of Scots her emerald carcanet against his heron's plume, that Esclairmonde would never marry unless her hands were held for her. Was she not at that very moment visiting some foundation of bedeswomen—that was all she heard of at yonder feast of cats!

In fact, under Dr. Bennet's escort, Esclairmonde and Alice were in a barge dropping down the Thames to the neighbourhood of the frowning fortress of the Tower—as yet unstained; and at the steps leading to the Hospitium of St. Katharine the ladies were met, not only by their friend Mrs. Bolt, but by Sir Richard Whittington, his kindly dame, and by 'Master William Kedbesby,' a grave and gentle-looking old man, who had been Master of St. Katharine's ever since the first year of King Richard II., and delighted to tell of the visits 'Good Queen Anne' of

Bohemia had made to her hospital, and the kind words she had said to the old alms-folk and the children of the schools; and when he heard that the Lady Esclairmonde was of the same princely house of Luxemburg, he seemed to think no honour sufficient for her. They visited the two houses, one for old men, the other for old women, each with a common apartment, with a fire, and a dining-table in the midst, and sleeping cells screened off round it, and with a paved terrace walk overhanging the river, where the old people could sit and sun themselves, and be amused by the gay barges and the swans that expatiated there. The bedeswomen, ten in number, had a house arranged like an ordinary nunnery, except that they were not in seclusion, had no grating, and shared the quad-rangle with the alms-folk and children. They were gentle and well-nurtured women, chiefly belonging to the city and country families that furnished servants to the queens; and they applied themselves to various offices of charity, going forth into the city to tend the poor, and to teach the women and children. The appointments of alms-folk and admissions to the school were chiefly made at their recommendation; and though a master taught all the book-learning in the busy hive of scholars—eighty in number—one or more of them instructed the little girls in spinning and in stitchery, to say nothing of gentle and modest demeanour. There was a great look of happiness and good order about all; and the church, fair and graceful, seemed well to complete and rule the institution. Esclairmonde could but sigh with a sort of regret as she left it, and let herself be conducted by Sir Richard Whittington to a refection at his beautiful house in Crutched Friars, built round a square, combining warehouse and manor-house; richly-carved shields, with the arms of the companies of London, supporting the tier of first-floor windows, and another row of brackets above supporting another over-hanging story. A fountain was in the centre of a beautiful greensward, with beds of roses, pansies, pinks, stars of

Charlotte M. Yonge

Bethlehem, and other good old flowers, among which a monkey was chained to a tree, while a cat roamed about at a safe distance from him.

Alice Montagu raised a laugh by asking if it were *the* cat; to which her city namesake replied that 'her master' never could abide to be without a cat in memory of his first friend, and marshalled them into the beautiful hall, with wainscot lining below, surmounted by an arcade containing statues, and above a beautiful carved ceiling. Here a meal was served to them, and the Lady talked with Whittington of the grand town-halls and other buildings of the merchants of the Low Countries, with whom he was a trader for their rich stuffs; and the visit passed off with no small satisfaction to both parties.

Esclairmonde sat in the barge on her return, looking out on the gray clear water, and on the bright gardens that sloped down to it, gay with roses and fruitful with mulberries, apples, and strawberries, and the mansions and churches that were never quite out of sight, though there were some open fields and wild country ere coming to Westminster, all as if she did not see them, but was wrapped in deep contemplation.

Alice at last, weary of silence, stole her arm round her waist, and peeped up into her face. 'May I guess thy thoughts, sweet Clairette? Thou wilt found such a hospice thyself?'

'Say not I *will*, child,' said Esclairmonde, with a crystal drop starting in each dark eye. 'I would strive and hope, but—'

'Ah! thou wilt, thou wilt,' cried Alice; 'and since there are Beguines enough for their own Netherlands, thou wilt come to England and be our foundress here.'

'Nay, little one; here are the bedeswomen of St. Katharine's in London.'

'Ah! but we have other cities. Good Father, have we not? Hull—Southampton—oh! so many, where poor strangers come that need ghostly tendance as well as bodily. Esclairmonde—Light of the World—oh! it was not for nothing that they gave thee that goodly name. The hospice shall bear it!'

'Hush, hush! sweet pyet; mine own name is what they must not bear.'

'Ah! but the people will give it; and our Holy Father the Pope, he will put thee into the canon of saints. Only pity that I cannot live to hear of Ste. Esclairmonde—nay, but then I must overlive thee, mind I should not love that.'

'Oh, silence, silence, child; these are no thoughts to begin a work with. Little flatterer, it may be well for me that our lives must needs lie so far apart that I shall not oft hear that fond silly tongue.'

'Nay,' said Alice, in the luxury, not of castle-building but of convent-building; 'it may be that when that knight over there sees me so small and ill-favoured he will none of me, and then I'll thank him so, and pray my father to let him have all my lands and houses except just enough to dower me to follow thee with, dear Lady Prioress.'

But here Alice was summarily silenced. Such talk, both priest and votaress told her, was not meet for dutiful daughter or betrothed maiden. Her lot was fixed, and she must do her duty therein as the good wife and lady of the castle, the noble English matron; and as she looked half disposed to pout, Esclairmonde drew such a picture of the beneficent influence of the good baronial dame, ruling her

Charlotte M. Yonge

castle, bringing up her children and the daughters of her vassals in good and pious nurture, making 'the heart of her husband safely trust in her,' benefiting the poor, and fostering holy men, wayfarers, and pilgrims, that the girl's eyes filled within tears as she looked up and said, 'Ah! lady, this is the life fitted for thee, who can paint it so well. Why have I not a brother, that you might be Countess of Salisbury, and I a poor little sister in a nunnery?'

Esclairmonde shook her head. 'Silly child, *petite niaise*, our lots were fixed by other hands than ours. We will strive each to serve our God, in the coif or in the veil, in samite or in serge, and He will only ask which of us has been most faithful, not whether we have lived in castle or in cloister.'

Little had Esclairmonde expected to hear the greeting with which the Countess received her, breaking out into peals of merriment as she told her of the choice destiny in store for her, to be wedded to the little lame Scot, pretending to read her a grave lecture on the conse-quences of the advances she had made to him.

Esclairmonde was not put out of countenance; in fact, she did not think the Countess in earnest, and merely replied with a smile that at least there was less harm in Lord Malcolm than in the suitors at home.

Jaqueline clapped her hands and cried, 'Good tidings, Clairette. I'll never forgive you if you make me lose my emerald carcanet! So the arrow was winged, after all. She prefers him—her heart is touched by the dainty step.'

'Madame!' entreated Esclairmonde, with agitation; 'at least, infirmity should be spared.'

'It touches her deeply!' exclaimed the Duchess. 'Ah! to see her in the mountains teaching the wild men to say their Aye, and to wear *culottes*, the little prince interpreting for her, as King James told us in his story of the saint his ancestor.'

Raillery about Malcolm had been attempted before, but never so pertinaciously; and Esclairmonde heeded it not at all, till James himself sought her out, and, within all his own persuasive grace, told her that he was rejoiced to hear from Madame of Hainault that she had spoken kindly of his youthful kinsman, for whose improvement he was sure he had in great measure to thank her.

Esclairmonde replied composedly, but as one on her guard, that the Sieur de Glenuskie was a gentle and a holy youth, of a good and toward wit.

'As I saw from the first,' said James, 'when I brought him away from being crushed among our rude cousins; but, lady, I knew not how the task of training the boy would be taken out of my hands by your kindness; and now, pardon me, lady, only one thing is wanting to complete your work, and that is hope.'

'Hope is always before a holy man, Sir.'

'O, madame! but we peer earthly beings require an earthly hope, nearer home, to brace our hearts, and nerve our arms.'

'I thought the Sieur de Glenuskie was destined to a religious life.'

'Never by any save his enemies, lady. The Regent Albany and his fierce sons have striven to scare Malcolm into a cloister, that his sister and his lands may be their prey;

and they would have succeeded had not I come to Scotland in time. The lad never had any true vocation.'

'That may be,' said Esclairmonde, somewhat sorrowfully.

'Still,' added James, 'he is of a thoughtful and somewhat tender mould, and the rudeness of life will try him sorely unless he have some cheering star, some light of love, to bear him up and guide him on his way.'

'If so, may he find a worthy one.'

'Lady, it is too late to talk of what he may find. The brightness that has done so much for him already will hinder him from turning his eyes elsewhere.'

'You are a minstrel, Sir King, and therefore these words of light romance fall from your lips.'

'Nay, lady, hitherto my romance has been earnest. It rests with you to make Malcolm's the same.'

'Not so, Sir. That has long been out of my hands.'

'Madame, you might well shrink from what it was as insult to you to propose; but have you never thought of the blessings you might confer in the secular life, with one who would be no hindrance, but a help?'

'No, Sir, for no blessings, but curses, would follow a breach of dedication.'

'Lady, I will not press you with what divines have decided respecting such dedication. Any scruples could be removed by the Holy Father at Rome, and, though I will speak no further, I will trust to your considering the matter. You have never viewed it in any light save that of a refuge from wedlock with one to whom I trust you would prefer my gentle cousin.'

'It were a poor compliment to Lord Malcolm to name him in the same day with Sir Boemond of Burgundy,' said Esclairmonde; 'but, as I said, it is not the person that withholds me, but the fact that I am not free.'

'I do not ask you to love or accept the poor boy as yet,' said James; 'I leave that for the time when I shall bring him back to you, with the qualities grown which you have awakened. At least, I can bear him the tidings that it is not your feelings, but your scruples that are against him.'

'Sir King,' said Esclairmonde, gravely, 'I question not your judgment in turning your kinsman and subject to the secular life; but if you lead him by false hopes, of which I am the object, I tell you plainly that you are deluding him; and if any evil come thereof, be it on your own head.'

She moved away, with a bend of her graceful neck, and James stood with a slight smile curving his lip. 'By my troth,' he said to himself, 'a lordly lady! She knows her own vocation. She is one to command scores of holy maids, and have all the abbots and priors round at her beck, instead of one poor man. Rather Malcolm than I! But he is the very stuff that loves to have such a woman to rule him; and if she wed at all, he is the very man for her! I'll not give it up! Love is the way to make a man of him, whether successful or not, and she may change her mind, since she is not yet on the roll of saints. If I could get a word with her father confessor, and show him how much it would be for the interest of the Church in Scotland to get such a woman there, it would be the surest way of coming at her. Were she once in Scotland, my pretty one would have a stay and helper! But all must rest till after the campaign.'

James therefore told Malcolm so much as that he had spoken to his lady-love for him, and that she had avowed that it was not himself, but her own vows, that was the obstacle.

Malcolm crimsoned with joy as well as confusion; and the King proceeded: 'For the vows'—he shrugged his shoulders—'we knew there is a remedy! Meantime, Malcolm, be you a man, win your spurs, and show yourself worth overcoming something for!'

Malcolm smiled and brightened, holding his head high and joyously, and handling his sword. Then came the misgiving—'But Lilias, Sir, and Patrick Drummond.'

'We will provide for them, boy. You know Drummond is bent on carving his own fortune rather than taking yours, and that your sister only longs to see you a gallant knight.'

It was true, but Malcolm sighed.

'You have not spoken to the lady yourself?' asked the King.

'No, Sir. Oh, how can I?' faltered Malcolm, shamefaced and frightened.

James laughed. 'Let that be as the mood takes you, or occasion serves,' he said, wondering whether the lad's almost abject awkwardness and shame would be likely to create the pity akin to love or to contempt, and deciding that it must be left to chance.

Nor did Malcolm find boldness enough to do more than haunt Esclairmonde's steps, trembling if she glanced towards him, and almost shrinking from her gaze. He had now no doubts about going on the campaign, and was in full course of being prepared with equipments, horses, armour, and attendants, as became a young prince attending on his sovereign as an adventurer in the camp. It was not even worth while to name such scruples to the English friar who shrived him on the last day before the departure, and who knew nothing of his past history. He knew all priests would say the same things, and as he had never made a binding vow, he saw no need of consulting any one on the subject; it would only vex him again, and fill him with doubts. The suspicion that Dr. Bennet was aware of his previous intention made him shrink from him. So the last day had come, and all was farewell. King Henry had persuaded the Queen to seclude herself for one evening from Madame of Hainault, for his sake. King James was pacing the gardens on the Thames banks, with Joan Beaufort's hand for once allowed to repose in his; many a noble gentleman was exchanging last words with his wife—many a young squire whispering what he had never ventured to say before—many a silver mark was cloven—many a bright tress was exchanged. Even Ralf Percy was in the midst of something very like a romp with the handsome Bessie Nevil for a knot of ribbon to carry to the wars.

Malcolm felt a certain exaltation in being enough like other people to have a lady-love, but there was not much comfort otherwise; indeed, he could so little have addressed Esclairmonde that it was almost a satisfaction that she was the centre of a group of maidens whose lovers or brothers either had been sent off beforehand, or who saw their attentions paid elsewhere, and who all alike gravitated towards the Demoiselle de Luxemburg for sympathy. He could but hover on the outskirts, conscious that he must cut a ridiculous figure, but unable to detach himself from the neighbourhood of the magnet. As he looked back on the happy weeks of unconstrained intercourse, when he came to her as freely as did these young girls with all his troubles, he felt as if the King had destroyed all his joy and peace, and yet that these flutterings of heart and agonies of shame and fits of despair were worth all that childish calm.

He durst say nothing, only now and then to gaze on her with his great brown wistful eyes, which he dropped whenever she looked towards him; until at last, when the summer evening was closing in, and the last signal was given for the break-up of the party, Malcolm ventured on one faltering murmur, 'Lady, lady, you are not offended with me?'

'Nay,' said Esclairmonde, kindly; 'nothing has passed between us that should offend me.'

His eye lighted. 'May I still be remembered in your prayers, lady?'

'As I shall remember all who have been my friends here,' she said.

'And oh, lady, if I should—should win honour, may I lay it at your feet?'

'Whatever you achieve as a good man and true will gladden me,' said Esclairmonde, 'as it will all others that wish you well. Both you and your sister in her loneliness shall have my best prayers. Farewell, Lord Malcolm; may the Saints bless and guard you, whether in the world or the Church.'

Malcolm knew why she spoke of his sister, and felt as if there were no hope for him. Esclairmonde's grave kindness was a far worse sign than would have been any attempt to evade him; but at any rate she had spoken with him, and his heart could not but be cheered. What might he not do in the glorious future? As the foremost champion of a crusading king, bearing St. Andrew's cross through the very gates of Jerusalem, what maiden, however saintly, could refuse him his guerdon?

And he knew that, for the present, Esclairmonde was safe from retiring into any convent, since her high birth and great possessions would make any such establishment expect a large dower with her as a right, and few abbesses would have ventured to receive a runaway foreigner, especially as one of her guardians was the Bishop of Therouenne.

CHAPTER VII

THE SIEGE OF MEAUX

Wintry winds and rains were sweeping over the English tents on the banks of the Marne, where Henry V. was besieging Meaux, then the stronghold of one of those terrible freebooters who were always the offspring of a lengthened war. Jean de Gast, usually known as the Bastard de Vaurus, nominally was of the Armagnac or patriotic party, but, in fact, pillaged indiscriminately, especially capturing travellers on their way to Paris, and setting on their heads a heavy price, failing which he hung them upon the great elm-tree in the market-place. The very suburbs of Paris were infested by the forays of this desperate *routier*, as such highway robbers were called; the supplies of previsions were cut off, and the citizens had petitioned King Henry that he would relieve them from so intolerable an enemy.

The King intended to spend the winter months with his queen in England, and at once attacked the place in October, hoping to carry it by a *coup de main*. He took the lower city, containing the market-place and several large convents, with no great difficulty; but the upper city, on a rising ground above the river, was strongly fortified, well victualled, and bravely defended, and he found himself forced to invest it, and make a regular siege, though at the expense of severe toil and much sickness and suffering. Both his own prestige in France and the welfare of the capital depended on his success, and he had therefore fixed himself before Meaux to take it at whatever cost.

The greater part of the army were here encamped, together with the chief nobles, March, Somerset, Salisbury, Warwick, and likewise the King of Scots. James had for a time had the command of the army which besieged and took Dreux while Henry was elsewhere engaged, but in general he acted as a sort of volunteer aide-de-camp to his brother king, and Malcolm Stewart of Glenuskie was always with him as his squire. A great change had come over Malcolm in these last few months. His feeble, sickly boyhood seemed to have been entirely cast off, and the warm genial summer sun of France to have strengthened his frame and developed his powers. He had shot up suddenly to a fair height, had almost lost his lameness, and gained much more appearance of health and power of enduring fatigue. His nerves had become less painfully sensitive, and when after his first skirmish, during which he had kept close to King James, far too much terrified to stir an inch from him, he had not only found himself perfectly safe, but had been much praised for his valour, he had been so much pleased with himself that he quite wished for another occasion of displaying his bravery; and, what with use, and what with the increasing spirit of pugnacity, he was as sincere as Ralf Percy in abusing the French for never coming to a pitched battle. Perhaps, indeed, Malcolm spoke even more eagerly than Ralf, in his own surprise and gratification at finding himself no coward, and his fear lest Percy should detect that he ever had been supposed to be such.

So far the King of Scots had succeeded in awakening martial fire in the boy, but he found him less the companion in other matters than he had intended. When at Paris,

Charlotte M. Yonge

James would have taken him to explore the learned hoards of the already venerable University of Paris, where young James Kennedy—son to Sir James Kennedy of Dunure, and to Mary, an elder sister of the King—was studying with exceeding zeal. Both James and Dr. Bennet were greatly interested in this famous abode of hearing—the King, indeed, was already sketching out designs in his own mind for a similar institution in Scotland, designs that were destined to be carried out after his death by Kennedy; and Malcolm perforce heard many inquiries and replies, but he held aloof from friendship with his clerkly cousin Kennedy, and closed his ears as much as might be, hanging back as if afraid of returning to his books. There was in this some real dread of Ralf Percy's mockery of his clerkliness, but there was more real distaste for all that appertained to the past days that he now despised.

The tide of vitality and physical vigour, so long deficient, had, whom it had fairly set in, carried him away with it: and in the activity of body newly acquired, mental activity had well-nigh ceased. And therewith went much of the tenderness of conscience and devout habits of old. They dropped from him, sometimes for lack of time, sometimes from false shame, and by and by from very weariness and distaste. He was soldier now, and not monk—ay, and even the observances that such soldiers as Henry and James never failed in, and always enforced, were becoming a burthen to him. They wakened misgivings that he did not like, and that must wait till his next general shrift.

And Esclairmonde? Out of her sight, Malcolm dreamt a good deal about her, but more as the woman, less as the saint; and the hopes, so low in her presence, burnt brighter in her absence as Malcolm grew in self-confidence and in knowledge of the world. He knew that when he parted with her he had been a miserable little wretch whom any woman would despise, yet she had shown him a sort of preference; how would it be when he returned to her, perhaps a knight, certainly a brave man like other men!

Of Patrick Drummond he had as yet heard nothing, and only believed him to be among the Scots who fought on the French side under the Earls of Buchan and Douglas. Indeed, James especially avoided places where he knew these Scots to be engaged, as Henry persisted in regarding them as rebels against him, and in hanging all who were made prisoners; nor had Malcolm, during the courtesies that always pass between the outposts of civilized armies, made much attempt to have any communication with his cousin, for though his own abnegation of his rights had never been permitted by his guardian, or reckoned on by his sister or her lover, still he had been so much in earnest about it himself, as, while regarding it as a childish folly, to feel ill at ease in the remembrance, and, though defiant, willing to avoid all that could recall it.

Meantime he, with his king, was lodged in a large old convent, as part of the immediate following of King Henry. Others of the princes and nobles were quartered in the market hall and lower town, but great part of thine troops were in tents, and in a state of much discomfort, owing to the overflowings of the Marne. Fighting was the least of their dangers, though their skirmishes were often fought ankle-deep in mud and mire; fever and ague were among them, and many a sick man was sent away to recover or die at Paris. The long dark evenings were a new trial to men used to summer campaigning, and nothing but Henry's wonderful personal influence and perpetual vigilance kept up discipline. At any hour of the day or night, at any place in the camp, the King might be at hand, with a cheery word of sympathy or encouragement, or with the most unflinching sternness towards any disobedience or debauchery—ever a presence to be either loved or dreaded. An engineer in advance of his time, he was persuaded that much of the discomfort might be remedied by trenching the ground around the camp; but this measure proved wonderfully distasteful to the soldiery. How hard they laboured in the direct siege operations they cared not, but to be set to drain French fields seemed to them absurd and unreasonable, and the work would not have proceeded at all without constant superintendence from one of the chiefs of the army, since the ordinary knights and squires were as obstinately prejudiced as were the men.

Thus it was that, on a cold sleety December day, James of Scotland rode along the meadows, splashing through thin ice into muddy water, and attended by his small personal suite, excepting Sir Nigel Baird, who was gone on a special commission to Paris. Both he and Malcolm were plainly and lightly armed, and wore long blue cloaks with the St. Andrew's cross on the shoulder, steel caps without visors, and the King's merely distinguished by a thread-hike circlet of gold. They had breastplates, swords, and daggers, but they were not going to a quarter where fighting was to be expected, and bright armour was not to be exposed to rust without need. A visit of inspection to the delvers was not a congenial occupation, for though the men-at-arms had obeyed James fairly well when he was in sole command at Dreux, yet whenever he was obliged to enforce anything unpopular, the national dislike to the Scot was apt to show itself, and the whole army was at present in a depressed condition which made such manifestations the more probable.

But King Henry was not half recovered from a heavy feverish cold, which he had not confessed or attended to, and he had also of late been troubled with a swelling of the neck. This morning, too, much to his inconvenience and dismay, he had missed his signet-ring. The private seal on such a ring was of more importance than the autograph at that time, and it would never have left the King's hand; but no doubt, in consequence of his indisposition, his finger, always small-boned, had become thin enough to allow the signet to escape unawares, he was unwilling to publish the loss, as it might cast doubt on the papers he despatched, and he, with his chamberlain Fitzhugh, King James, Malcolm, Percy, and a few more, had spent half the morning in the vain search, ending by the King sending his chamberlain, Lord Fitzhugh, to carry to Paris a seal already bearing his shield, but lacking the small private mark that authenticated it as his signet. Fitzhugh would stand over the lapidary and see this added, and bring it back. Ralf Percy had meantime been sent to bring a report of the diggers, but he was long in returning; and when Henry became uneasy, James had volunteered to go himself, and Henry had consented, not because the air was full of sleety rain or snow, but because his hands were full of letters needing to be despatched to all quarters.

The air was so thick that it was not easy to see where were the sullen group of diggers presided over by the quondam duellists of Thirsk, Kitson and Trenton, now the most inseparable and impracticable of men; but James and his companions had ridden about two miles from the market-place, when Ralf Percy came out of the mist, exclaiming, 'Is it you, Sir King? Maybe you can do something with those rascals! I've talked myself blue with cold to make them slope the sides of their dyke, but the owl Kitson says no Yorkshireman ditcher ever went but by one fashion, and none ever shall; and when I lifted my riding-rod at the most insolent of the rogues, what must Trenton do but tell me the lot were free yeomen, and I'd best look out, or they'd roll me in the mire if I meddled with a soul of them.'

'You didn't threaten to strike Trenton?'

'No, no; the sullen cur is a gentleman. 'Twas one of those lubberly men-at-arms! I told them they should hear what King Harry would say to their mood. I would it were he!'

'So would I,' said James. 'Little chance that they will hearken to a Scot when you have put them in such a mood. Hold, Ralf, do not go for the King; he has letters for the Emperor mattering more than this dyke.'

He rode on, and did his best by leaping into the ditch, taking the spade, and showing the superior security of the angle of inclination traced by the King, but all in vain; both Trenton and Kitson silently but obstinately scouted the notion that any king should know more about ditches than themselves.

'See,' cried Percy, starting up, 'here's other work! The fellows, whence came they?'

Favoured by the fog and the soft soil of the meadows, a considerable body of the enemy were stealing on the delvers with the manifest purpose of cutting them off from the camp. They were all mounted, but the only horses in the English party were those of James, Percy, Malcolm, and the half-dozen men of his escort. James, assuming the command at once, bade these to be all released; they would be sure to find their way to the camp, and that would bring succour. Meantime he drew the whole of the men, about thirty in number, into a compact body. They were, properly, archers, but their bows had been left behind, and they had only their pikes and bills, which were, however, very formidable weapons against cavalry as long as they continued in an unbroken rank; and though the bogs, pools, sunken hedges, and submerged stumps made it difficult to keep close together as they made their way slowly with one flank to the river, these obstacles were no small protection against a charge of horsemen.

For a quarter of a mile these tactics kept them unharmed, but at length they reached a wide smooth meadow, and the enemy seemed preparing to charge. James gave orders to close up and stand firm, pikes outwards. Malcolm's heart beat fast; it was the most real peril he had yet seen; and yet he was cheered by the King's ringing voice, 'Stand firm, ye merry men. They must soon be with us from the camp.'

Suddenly a voice shouted, 'The Scots! the Scots! 'Tis the Scots! Treachery! we are betrayed. Come, Sir' (to Percy), 'they'll be on you. Treason!'

'An' it were, you fool, would a Percy turn his back?' cried Ralf, striking at the man; but the panic had seized the whole body; all were shouting that the false Scots king had brought his countrymen down on them; they scattered hither and thither, and would have fallen an easy prey if they had been pursued. But this did not seem to be the purpose of the enemy, who merely extended themselves so as to form a hedge around the few who stood, sword in hand, disdaining to fly. These were, James, somewhat in advance, with his head high, and a lion look on his brow; Malcolm, white with dismay; Ralf, restless with fury; Kitson and Trenton, apparently as unmoved as ever; Brewster, equally steady: and Malcolm's follower, Halbert, in a glow of hopeful excitement.

'Never fear, friends,' said James, kindly; 'to you this can only be matter of ransom.'

'I fear nothing,' sharply answered Ralf.

'We'll stand by you, Sir,' said Kitson to Ralf; 'but if ever there were foul treason—'

'Pshaw! you ass,' were all Percy's thanks; for at that moment a horseman came forward from among the enemy, a gigantic form on a tall white horse, altogether a 'dark gray man,' the open visor revealing an elderly face, hard-featured and grim, and the shield on his arm so dinted, faded, and battered, as scarce to show the blue chief and the bleeding crowned heart; but it was no unfamiliar sight to Malcolm's eyes, and with a slight shudder he bent his head in answer to the fierce whisper, 'Old Douglas himself!' with which Hotspur's son certified himself that he had the foe of his house before him. King James, resting the point of his sword on his mailed foot, stood erect and gravely expectant; and the Scot, springing to the ground, advanced with the words, 'We greet you well, my liege, and hereby—' he was bending his knee as he spoke, and removing his gauntlet in preparation for the act of homage.

'Hold, Earl Douglas,' said James, 'homage is vain to a captive.'

'You are captive no longer, Sir King,' said Earl Archibald. 'We have long awaited this occasion, and will at once return to Scotland with you, with the arms and treasure we have gained here, and will bear down the craven Albany.'

Kitson and Trenton looked at one another and grasped their swords, as though doubting whether they ought not to cut down their king's prisoner rather than let him be rescued; and meanwhile the cry, 'Save King James!' broke out on all sides, knights leapt down to tender their homage, and among the foremost Malcolm knew Sir Patrick Drummond, crying aloud, 'My lord, my lord, we have waited long for you. Be a free king in free Scotland! Trust us, my liege.'

'Trust you, my friends!' said James, deeply touched; 'I trust you with all my heart; but how could you trust me if I began with a breach of faith to the King of England?'

Ralf Percy held up his finger and nodded his head to the Yorkshire squires, who stood open-mouthed, still believing that a Scot must be false. There was an angry murmur among the Scots, but James gazed at them undauntedly, as though to look it down.

'Yes, to King Harry!' he said, in his trumpet voice. 'I belong to him, and he has trusted me as never prisoner was trusted before, nor will I betray that trust.'

'The foul fiend take such niceties,' muttered old Douglas; but, checking himself, he said, 'Then, Sir, give me your sword, and we'll have you home as my prisoner, to save this your honour!'

'Yea,' said James, 'that is mine own, though my body be yours, and till England put me to ransom you would have but a useless captive.'

'Sir,' said Sir John Swinton, pressing forward, 'if my Lord of Douglas be plain-spoken, bethink you that it is no cause for casting aside this one hope of freedom that we have sought so long. If you have the heart to strike for Scotland, this is the time.'

'It is not the time,' said James, 'nor will I do Scotland the wrong of striking for her with a dishonoured hand.'

'That will we see when we have him at Hermitage Castle,' quoth Douglas to his followers. 'Now, Sir King, best give your sword without more grimace. Living or dead you are ours.'

'I yield not,' said James. 'Dead you may take me—alive, never.' Then turning his eyes to the faces that gazed on him so earnestly in disappointment, in affection, or in scorn, he spoke: 'Brave friends, who may perchance love me the better that I have been a captive half my life and all my reign, you can believe how sair my heart burns for my bonnie land's sake, and how little I'd reck of my life for her weal. But broken oaths are ill beginnings. For me, so notably trusted by King Henry, to break my bonds, would shame both Scots and kings; and it were yet more paltry to feign to yield to my Lord of Douglas. Rescue or no rescue, I am England's captive. Gentles, kindly brother Scots, in one way alone can you free me. Give up this wretched land of France, whose troubles are but lengthened by your valour. Let me gang to King Harry and tell him your swords are at his service, so soon as I am free. Then am I your King indeed; we return together, staunch hearts and strong hands, and the key shall keep the castle, and the bracken bush keep the cow, though I lead the life of a dog to bring it about.'

His tawny eye flashed with falcon light; and as he stood towering above all the tall men around, there were few who did not in heart own him indeed their king. But his picture of royal power accorded ill with the notions of a Black Douglas, in the most masterful days of that family; and Earl Archibald, who had come to regard kings as beings meant to be hectored by Douglases, resentfully exclaimed, 'Hear him, comrades; he has avouched himself a Southron at heart. Has he reckoned how little it would cost to give a thrust to the caitiff who lost heart in his prison, and clear the way for Albany, who is at least a true Scot?'

'Do so, Lord Earl,' said James, 'and end a long captivity. But let these go scatheless.'

With one voice, Percy, Kitson, Trenton, and Brewster, shouted their resolve to defend him to the last; and Malcolm, flinging himself on Patrick Drummond, adjured him to save the King.

'Thou here, laddie!' said Patrick, amazed; and while several more knights exclaimed, 'Sir, Sir, we'll see no hand laid on you!' he thrust forward, 'Take my horse, Sir, ride on, and I'll see no scathe befall you.'

'Thanks,' said James; 'but my feet will serve me best; we will keep together.'

The Scottish force seemed dividing into two: Douglas and his friends and retainers, mounted and holding together, as though still undecided whether to grapple with the King and his half-dozen companions; while Drummond and about ten more lances were disposed to guard him at all risks.

'Now,' said James to his English friends; and therewith, sword in hand, he moved with a steady but swift stride towards the camp, nor did Douglas attempt pursuit; some of the other horsemen hovered between, and Patrick Drummond, with a puzzled face, kept near on foot. So they proceeded till they reached a bank and willow hedge, through which horses could hardly have pursued them.

On the other side of this, James turned round and said, 'Thanks, Sir Knight; I suppose I may not hope that you will become a follower of the knight adventurer.'

'I cannot fight under the English banner, my liege. Elsewhere I would fellow you to the death.'

Charlotte M. Yonge

'This is no time to show your error,' said James; 'and I therefore counsel you to come no farther. The English will be pricking forth in search of us: so I will but thank you for your loyal aid.'

'I entreat you, Sir,' cried Patrick, 'not to believe that we meant this matter to go as it has done! It had long been our desire—of all of us, that is, save my Lord Buchan's retainers—to find you and release you; but never did we deem that Lord Douglas would have dared to conduct matters thus.'

'You would be little the better for me did Lord Douglas bring me back on his own terms,' said James, smiling. 'No, no; when I go home, it shall be as a free king, able to do justice to all alike; and for that I am content to bide my time, and trust to such as you to back me when it comes.'

'And with all my heart, Sir,' said Patrick. 'Would that you were where I could do so now. Ah! laddie,' to Malcolm; 'ye're in good hands. My certie, I kenned ye but by your voice! Ye're verily grown into a goodly ship after all, and ye stood as brave as the rest. My poor father would have been fain to see this day!'

Malcolm flushed to the ears; somehow Patrick's praise was not as pleasant to him as he would have expected, and he only faltered, 'You know—'

'I ken but what Johnnie Swinton brought me in a letter frae the Abbot of Coldingham, that my father—the saints be with him!—had been set on and slain by yon accursed Master of Albany—would that his thrapple were in my grip!—that he had sent you southwards to the King, and that your sister was in St. Abbs. Is it so?'

Malcolm had barely time to make a sign of affirmation,

when the King hurried him on. 'I grieve to balk you of your family tidings, but delay will be ill for one or other of us; so fare thee well, Sir Patrick, till better times.'

He shook the knight's hand as he spoke, cut short his protestations, and leapt down the bank, saying in a low voice, as he stretched out his hand and helped Malcolm down after him, 'He would have known me again for your guest if we had stood many moments longer; he looked hard at me as it was; and neither in England nor Scotland may that journey of mine be blazed abroad.'

Malcolm was on the whole rather relieved; he could not help feeling guilty towards Patrick, and unless he could have full time for explanation, he preferred not falling in with him.

And at the same moment Kitson stepped towards the King. 'Sir, you are an honest man, and we crave your pardon if we said aught that seemed in doubt thereof.'

James laughed, shaking each honest hand, and saying, 'At least, good sirs, do not always think Scot and traitor the same word; and thank you for backing me so gallantly.'

'I'd wish no better than to back such as you, Sir,' said Kitson heartily; and James then turned to Ralf Percy, and asked him what he thought of the Douglas face to face.

'A dour old block!' said Ralf. 'If those runaways had but stayed within us, the hoary ruffian should have had his lesson from a Percy.'

James smiled, for the grim giant was still a good deal more than a match for the slim, rosy-faced stripling of the house of Percy, who nevertheless simply deemed his nation and family made him invincible by either Scot

Charlotte M. Yonge

or Frenchman.

The difficulties of their progress, however, entirely occupied them. Having diverged from the regular track, they had to make their way through the inundated meadows; sometimes among deep pools, sometimes in quagmires, or ever hedges; while the water that drenched them was fast freezing, and darkness came down on them. All stumbled or were bogged at different times; and Malcolm, shorter and weaker than the rest, and his lameness becoming more felt than usual, could not help impeding their progress, and at last was so spent that but for the King's strong arm he would have spent the night in a bog-hole.

At last the lights were near, the outskirts were gained, the pass-word given to the watch, and the rough but welcome greeting was heard—'That's well! More of you come in! How got you off?'

'The rogues got back, then?' said Kitson.

'Some score of them,' was the answer; 'but 'tis thought most are drowned or stuck by the French. The King is in a proper rage, as well he may be; but what else could come of a false Scot in the camp?'

'Have a care, you foul tongue!' Percy was the first to cry; and as torches were now brought out and cast their light on the well-known faces, the soldiers stood abashed; but James tarried not for their excuses; his heart was hot at the words which implied that Henry suspected him, and he strode hastily on to the convent, where the quadrangle was full of horses and men, and the windows shone with lights. At the door of the refectory stood a figure whose armour flashed with light, and his voice sounded through the closed visor—'I tell you, March, I cannot rest till I knew what his hap has been. If he have done this thing—'

'What then?' answered James out of the darkness, in a voice deep with wrath; but Henry started.

'You there! you safe! Speak again! Come here that I may see. Where is he?'

'Here, Sir King,' said James, gravely.

'Now the saints be thanked!' cried Henry, joyously. 'Where be the caitiffs that brought me their false tale? They shall hang for it at once.'

'It was the less wonder,' said James, still coldly, 'that they should have thought themselves betrayed, since their king believed it of me.'

'Nay, 'twas but for a hot moment—ay, and the bitterest I ever spent. What could I do when the villains swore that there were signals and I know not what devices passing? I hoped yet 'twas but a plea for their own cowardice, and was mounting to come and see for you. Come, I should have known you better; I'd rather the whole world deceived me than have distrusted you, Jamie.'

There was that in his tone which ended all resentment, and James's hand was at once clasped in his, while Henry added, 'Ho, Provost-marshal! to the gallows with these knaves!'

'Nay, Harry,' said James, 'let me plead for them. There was more than ordinary to dismay them.'

'Dismay! ay, the more cause they should have stood like honest men. If a rogue be not to hang for deserting his captain and then maligning him, soon would knavery be

Charlotte M. Yonge

master of all.'

'Hear me first, Hal.'

'I'll hear when I return and you are dried. Why, man, thou art an icicle errant; change thy garments while I go round the posts, or I shall hear nought for the chattering of thy teeth.'

'Nor I for your cough, if you go, Harry. Surely, 'tis Salisbury's night!'

'The more cause that I be on the alert! Could I be everywhere, mayhap a few winter blasts would not have chilled and frozen all the manhood out of the host.'

He spoke very sharply as he threw him on his horse, and wrapped his cloak about him—a poor defence, spite of the ermine lining, against the frost of the December night for a man whose mother, the fair and wise Mary de Bohun, had died in early youth from disease of the lungs.

James and the two young partners of his adventure had long been clad in their gowns of peace, and seated by the fire in the refectory, James with his harp in his hand, from time to time dreamily calling forth a few plaintive notes, such as he said always rang in his ears after hearing a Scottish voice, when they again heard Henry's voice in hot displeasure with the provost-marshal for having deferred the execution of the runaways till after the hearing of the story of the King of Scots.

'His commands were not to be transgressed for the king of anything,' and he only reprieved the wretches till morning that their fate might be more signal. He spoke with the peremptory fierceness that had of late almost obscured his natural good-humour and kindliness; and when he entered the refectory and threw himself into a chair by the fire, he looked wearied out in body and mind, shivered and coughed, and said with unwonted depression that the sullen fellows would make a quagmire of their camp after all, since a French reinforcement had come up, and the vigilance that would be needed would occupy the whole army. At supper he ate little and spoke less; and when James would have related his encounter within the Scots, he cut him short, saying, 'Let that rest till morning; I am sick of hearing of it! An air upon thy harp would be more to the purpose.'

Nor would James have been unwilling to be silent on old Douglas's conduct if he had not been anxious to plead for the panic-stricken archers, as well as to extol the conduct of the two youths, and of the Yorkshire squires; but, as he divined that the young Hotspur would regard praise from him as an insult, he deferred the subject for his absence, and launched into a plaintive narrative ballad, to which Henry listened, leaning back in his chair, often dozing, but without relaxation of the anxiety that sat on his pale face, and ever and anon wakening within a heavy sigh, as though his buoyant spirits were giving way under the weight of care he had brought on himself.

James was just singing of one of the many knightly orphans of romance, exposed in woods to the nurture of bears, his father slain, his mother dead of grief—a ditty he had perhaps chosen for its soporific powers—when a gay bugle blast rang through the court of the convent.

'The French would scarce send to parley thus late,' exclaimed James; but the next moment a joyful clamour arose without, and Henry, springing to his feet, spoke not, but stood awaiting the tidings with the colour burning on cheek and brow in suppressed excitement.

Charlotte M. Yonge

An esquire, splashed to the ears, hurried into the room, and falling on his knees, cried aloud, 'God save King Harry! News, news, my lord! The Queen has safely borne you a fair son at Windsor Castle, five days since.'

Henry did not speak, but took the messenger's hand, wrung it, and left a costly ring there. Then, taking off his cap, he put his hands over his face, uttering a few words of fervent thanksgiving almost within himself, and then turning to the esquire, made further inquiries after his wife's welfare, took from him the letter that Archbishop Chicheley had sent, poured out a cup of wine for him, bade the lords around make him good cheer, but craved license for himself to retire.

It was so unlike his usual hilarious manner that all looked at one another in anxiety, and spoke of his unusual susceptibility to fatigue and care; while the squire, looking at the rich jewel in his hand, declared within disappointment in his tone, that he would rather have had a mere flint stone so he had heard King Harry's own cheery voice.

James was not the least anxious of them, but long ere light the next morning Henry stood at his bedside, saying, 'I must go round the posts before mass, Jamie. Will you face the matin frost?'

'I am fitter to face it than thou,' said James, rising. 'Is there need for this?'

'Great need,' said Henry. 'Here are these fresh forces all aglow within their first zeal, and unless they are worse captains than I suppose them, they will attempt some mischief ere long—nor is any time so slack as cock-crow.'

James was speedily ready, and, within some suppressed

sighs, so was Malcolm, who knew himself in duty bound to attend his master, and was kept on the alert by seeing Ralf Percy also on foot. But it was a great relief to him that the young gentleman murmured in no measured terms against the intolerable activity of their kings. No other attendants went within them, since Henry was wont to patrol his camp with as little demonstration as possible.

'I would scarcely ask a dog to come out with me this wintry morn,' said he, as he waved back his sleepy chamberlain, Fitzhugh, and took his brother king's arm; 'but I could not but crave a turn with thee, Jamie, ere the hue and cry of rejoicing begins.'

'That is poor welcome for your heir,' said James.

'Poor child!' said Henry; then, after they had walked some space in silence, he added, 'You'll mock me, but I would that this had not befallen at Windsor. I had laid my plans that it should be otherwise; but ladies are ill to guide.'

'And wherefore should it not have been at fair Windsor? If I can love it as a prison, sure your son may well love it as a cradle.'

'No dishonour to Windsor,' said Henry; 'but, sleeping or waking, this whole night hath this adage rung in my ears—

"Harry, born at Monmouth, shall short time live and all get; Harry, born at Windsor, shall long time live and lose all."'

'A most choice piece of royal poesy and prophecy,' laughed James.

'Nay, do not charge me with it, thou dainty minstrel. It

　　　　　Charlotte M. Yonge

was sung to me by mime old Herefordshire nurse, when Windsor seemed as little within my reach as Meaux, and I never thought of it again till I looked to have a son.'

'Then balk the prophecy,' said James; 'Edward born at Windsor got enough, and lived long enough to boot!'

'Too late!' was the answer. 'The Archbishop christened the poor child Harry in the very hour of his birth.'

'Poor child!' echoed James, rather sarcastically.

'Nay, 'tis not solely the rhyme,' said Henry; 'but this has been a wakeful night, and not without misgivings whether I am one who ought to look for joy in his children.'

'What is past was not such that you alone should cry *mea culpa*,' said James.

'I never thought so till now,' said Henry. 'Yet who knows? My father was a winsome young man ere his exile, full of tenderness to us all, at the rare times he was with us. Who knows what cares may make of me ere my boy learns to knew me?'

'You will not hold him aloof, and give him no chance of loving you?'

'I trow not! I'll have him with me in the camp, and he and my brave men shall be one another's pride. Which Roman emperor is it that hears the nickname his father's soldiers gave him as a child? Nay—Caligula was it? Omens are against me this morning.'

'Then laughs them to scorn, and be yourself,' said James. 'Bless God for the goodly child, who is born to two kingdoms, won by his father's and his grandsire's swords.'

'Ah!' said Henry, depressed by failing health, a sleepless night, and hungry morning, 'maybe it were better for him, soul and body both, did I stand here Duke of Lancaster, and good Edmund of March yonder were head of realm and army.'

'Never would he be head of this army,' said James. 'He would be snoring at Shene; that is, if he could sleep for the trouble the Duke of Lancaster would be giving him.'

Henry laughed at last. 'Good King Edmund, he would assuredly never try to set the world right on its hinges. Honest fellow, soon he will be as hearty in his congratulations as though he did not lie under a great wrong. Heigh-ho! such as he may be in the right on't. I've marvelled of late, whether any priest or hermit could bring back my old assurance, that all this is my work on earth, or tell me if it be all one grand error. Men there have been like Caesar, Alexander, or Charlemagne, who thought my thoughts and worked them out; and surely Church and nations cry aloud for purifying. Jerusalem, and a general council—I saw them once clear and bright before me; but now a mist seems to rise up from Richard's blood, and hide them from me; and there comes from it my father's voice when he asked on his deathbed what right I had to the crown. What would it be if I had to leave this work half done?'

He was interrupted by the sight of a young knight stealing into the camp, after a furtive expedition to Paris. It was enough to rouse him from his despondent state; and the severity of his wrath was in full proportion to the offence. Nor did he again utter his misgivings, but was full of his usual alacrity and life, as though daylight had restored his buoyancy.

James, on the way back to the thanksgiving mass,

Charlotte M. Yonge

interceded for last night's offenders, as an act of grace suitable to the occasion; but Henry was inexorable.

'Had they stood to die like Englishmen, they had not lied like dogs! 'he said; 'and as dogs they shall hang!'

In fact, in the critical state of his army, he knew that the only safety lay in the promptest and sternest justice; and therefore the three foremost in accusing King James of treachery were hung long before noon.

However, he called for the two Yorkshiremen, and thus addressed them: 'Well done, my masters! Thanks for showing Scots and Frenchmen what stuff Englishmen are made of! I keep my word, good fellows. Kneel down, and I'll dub each a knight. How now! what are you blundering and whispering for?'

'So please you, Sir,' said Kitson, 'this is no matter to win one's spurs for—mere standing still without a blow.'

'I would all had that same gift of standing still,' returned Henry. 'What is it sticks in your gizzard, friend? If 'tis the fees, I take them on myself.'

'No, Sir,' hoarsely cried both.

And Kitson explained: 'Sir, you said you'd knight the one of us that was foremost. Now, the two being dubbed, we shall be but where we were before as to Mistress Agnes of Mineshull, unless of your good-will you would be pleased to let us fight out the wager of the heriard in all peace and amity.'

Henry burst out laughing, with all his old merriment, as he said, 'For no Mistress Agnes living can I have honest men's lives wasted, specially of such as have that gift of standing still. If she does not knew her own mind, one of you must get himself killed by the Frenchmen, not by one another. So kneel down, and we'll make your knighthood's feast fall in with that of my son.'

Thus Sir Christopher Kitson and Sir William Trenton rose up knights; and bore their honours with a certain bluntness that made them butts, even while they were the heroes of the day; and Henry, who had resumed his gay temper, made much diversion out of their mingled shrewdness and gruffness.

'So,' muttered Malcolm to Ralf Percy, 'we are passed over in the self-same matter for which these fellows are knighted.'

'Tush!' answered Percy; 'I'd scorn to be confounded with a couple of clowns like them! Moreover,' he added, with better reason, 'their valour was more exercised than ours, inasmuch as they thought there was treachery, and we did not. No, no; when my spurs are won, it shall be for some prowess, better than standing stock-still.'

Malcolm held his tongue, unwilling that Percy should see that he did feel this an achievement; but he was vexed at the lack of reward, fancying that knighthood would be no small step in the favour of that imaginary Esclairmonde whom he had made for himself.

'Light of the world' he loved to call her still, but it was in the commonplace romance of his time, the mere light of beauty and grace illuminating the world of chivalry.

Charlotte M. Yonge

CHAPTER VIII

THE CAPTURE

The seven months' siege ended at last, but it was not until the brightness of May was on the fields outside, and the deadly blight of famine on all within, that a haggard, wasted-looking deputation came down from the upper city to treat with the King.

Henry was never severe with the inhabitants of French cities, and exacted no harsh terms, save that he insisted that Vaurus, the robber captain, and his two chief lieutenants, should be given up to him to suffer condign punishment. The warriors who had shut themselves up to hold out the place by honourable warfare for the Dauphin must be put to ransom as prisoners of war; but the burghers were to be unmolested, on condition of their swearing allegiance to Henry as regent for, and heir of, Charles VI.

To this the deputies consented, and the next day was fixed for the surrender. The difficulty was, as Henry had found at Harfleur, Rouen, and many other places, to enforce forbearance on his soldiery, who regarded plunder as their lawful prey, the enemy as their natural game, and the trouble a city had given them as a cause for unmerci-fulness. The more time changed his army from the feudal gathering of English country gentlemen and yeomen to mercenary bands of men-at-arms, the mere greedy, rapacious, and insubordinate became their temper. Well knowing the greatness of the peril, and that the very best of his captains had scarcely the will, if they had the power, to restrain the license that soon became barbarity unimaginable, he spoke sadly overnight of his dread of the day of surrender, when it might prove impossible to prevent deeds that would be not merely a blot on his scutcheon, but a shame to human nature; looking back to the exultation with which he had entered Harfleur as a mere effect of boyish ignorance and thoughtlessness.

Having taken all possible precautions, he stood in his full armour, with the fox's brush in his helmet, under the great elm in the market-place, received the keys, accepted the sword of the captain commissioned by Charles with royal courtesy, gave his hand to be kissed by the mayor; and then, with grave inexorable air, like a statue of steel, watched as the freebooter Vaurus and his two chief companions were led down with their hands tied, halters round their necks, and priests at their sides, preparing them to be hung on that very tree. They were proud hard men, and uttered no entreaty for grace. They had hung too many travellers upon these same branches not to expect their own turn, and they were no cravens to abase themselves.

That act of justice ended, Henry mounted his warhorse and rode in at the gates. His wont was to go straight to the principal church, and there attend a solemn mass of thanksgiving; but experience had taught him that his devotions were the very opportunity of his men's rapine: he had therefore arranged that as soon as he should have arrived in the choir of the cathedral, James should take his place, and he slip out by a side door, so as to return to the scene of action.

Charlotte M. Yonge

In full procession he and his suite reached the chief door, and there dismounted in an immense crowd, which thronged in at the doors.

'Come, Glenuskie,' said Ralf Percy, as the two youths were pushed chose together in the press; 'if you have a fancy for being smothered in the minster, I have none. We shall never be missed. 'Twill be sport to walk round and see how these hardy rogues contrived to hold out.'

Malcolm willingly turned aside with him, and looked down the sloping street, which was swarming with comers and goers. The whole place was in an inflammable state. Soldiers were demanding quarters, which the citizens unwillingly gave. A refusal or expostulation against a rough entry led to violence; and ever as the two youths walked farther from the cathedral, there was more of excitement, more rude oaths of soldiers, more shrieking of women, often crying out even before any harm was done to them or their houses.

At last, before a tall overhanging house, there was an immense press, and a frightful din of shouts and imprecations, filling both the new-comers with infectious eagerness.

'How now? how now?' called Percy. 'Keep the peace, good fellows.'

'Sir,' cried a number of voices, passionately, 'the French villains have barred their door. There's a lot of cowardly Armagnacs hid there with their gold, trying to balk honest men of their ransom.'

Such was the cry resounding on all sides. 'Have at them! There's the rogue at the windows. Out on the fellows! Burn down the door! 'Tis Vaurus himself and all his gold.

Treason! treason!'

The clamour was convincing to the spirit, if not to the senses. The two lads believed in the concealed Armagnacs, or perhaps more truly were carried away by the vehemence around them; and with something of the spirit of the chase, threw themselves headlong into the affair.

'Open! open!' shouted Ralf. 'Open, in the name of King Henry!'

An old man's face peeped through a little wicket in the door, and at sight of the two youths, evidently of high rank, said in a trembling voice, 'Alas! alas! Sir, bid these cruel men go away. I have nothing here—no one—only my sick daughter.'

'You hear,' said Malcolm, turning round; 'only his sick daughter.'

'Sick daughter!—old liar! Here's an honest tinker makes oath he has hoards of gold laid up for Vaurus, and ten Armagnacs hidden in his house. Have at him! Bring fire!'

Blows hailed thick on the door; a flaming torch was handed over the heads of the throng; horrible growls and roars pervaded them. Malcolm and Ralf, furious at the cheat, stood among the foremost, making so much noise themselves between thundering and reviling, and calling out, 'Where are the Armagnacs? Down with the traitors!' that they were not aware of a sudden hush behind them, till a buffet from a heavy hand fell on Malcolm's shoulder, and a mighty voice cried 'Shame! shame! What, you too!'

'There are traitors hid here, Sir,' said Percy, in angry self-justification.

'And what an if there are? Back, every one of you! rogues that you be!—Here, Fitzhugh, see those villains back to the camp. Let their arms be given up to the Provost-marshal.—Kites and crows as you are! Away, out with you!'

Henry pointed to the broken door, and the cowed and abashed soldiers slunk away from the terrible light of his eyes. No man could stand before the face of the King.

There was a stillness. He stood leaning on his sword, his chest heaving with his panting breaths. He was naturally as fleet as the swift-footed Achilles, but the winter had told upon him, and the haste with which he had rushed to the rescue left him breathless and speechless, while he seemed as it were to nail the two lads to the spot by his steady gaze of mingled distress and displeasure.

Neither could brook his eye: Percy hung his head like a boy in a scrape; Malcolm quailed with terror, but at the same time felt a keen sense of injury in being thus treated as a plunderer, and the blow under which his shoulder ached seemed an indignity to his royal blood.

'Boys,' said Henry, still low and breathlesly, but all the more impressively, 'what is to become of honour and mercy if such as you must needs become ravening wolves at scent of booty?'

'It was not booty, Sir; they said traitors were hid here,' said Percy, sulkily.

'Tush! the old story! Ever the plea for rapine and blood-thirstiness. After the warnings of last night you should have known better; but you are all alike in frenzy for a sack. You have both put off your knighthood till you have learnt not to become a shame thereto.'

'I take not knighthood at your hands, Sir,' burst out Malcolm, goaded with hot resentment, but startled the next moment at the sound of his own words.

'I cry you mercy,' said King Henry, in a cold, short tone.

Malcolm turned on his heel and walked away, without waiting to see how the poor old man in the house threw himself at the King's feet with a piteous history of his sick daughter and her starving children, nor how Ralf hurried off headlong to the lower town to send them immediate relief in bread, wine, and doctors. The gay, good-natured, thoughtless lad no mere harboured malice for the chastisement than if his tutor had caught him idling; but things went deeper with Malcolm. True, he had undergone many a brutal jest and cruel practical joke from his cousins; but that was all in the family, not like a blow from an alien king, and one not apologized for, but followed up by a rebuke that seemed to him unjust, lowering him in his own eyes and those of Esclairmonde, and making him ready to gnaw himself with moody vexation.

'You here, Malcolm!' said King James, entering his quarters; 'did you miss me in the throng? I have not seen you all day.'

'I have been insulted, Sir,' said Malcolm. 'I pray your license to depart and carry my sword to my kinsmen in the French camp.'

'How now! Is it the way to treat an insult to run away from it?'

'Not when the world judges men to be on equal terms, my lord.'

Charlotte M. Yonge

'What! Who has done you wrong, you silly loon?'

'King Henry, Sir; he struck me with his fist, and rated me like his hound; and I will not eat another morsel of his bread unless he would answer it to me in single combat.'

'Little enough bread you'd eat after that same answer!' ejaculated James. 'Oh! I understand now. You were with young Hotspur and the rest that set on the poor townsmen, and Harry made small distinction of persons! Nay, Malcolm, it was ill in you, that talked of so loathing spulzie!'

'I wanted no spulzie. There were Armagnacs hid in the house, and the King would not hear us.'

'He knew that story too well. Were you asleep or idling last night, when he warned all, on no plea whatever, to break into a house, but, if the old tale of treachery came up, to set a guard, and call one of the captains? Did you hear him—eh?'

'I can take chiding from you, Sir, but neither words nor blows from any other king in Christendom, still less when he threatens me that I have deferred my knighthood! As if I would have it from him!'

'From me you will not have it until he have pardoned Ralf Percy,' said James, dryly. 'Malcolm, I had not thought you such a fule body! Under a captain's banner, what can be done but submit to his rule? I should do so myself, were Salisbury or March in command.'

'Then, Sir,' said Malcolm, much hurt that the King did not take his part, 'I shall carry my service elsewhere.'

'So,' said James, much vexed, 'this is the meek lad that

wanted to hide in a convent from an ill world, flying off from his king and kinsman that he may break down honest men's doors at his will.'

'That I may be free from insult, Sir.'

'You think John of Buchan like to cosset you! You found the Black Douglas so courtly to me the other day as to expect him to be tender to this nicety of yours! Malcolm, as your prince and guardian, I forbid this folly, and command you to lay aside this fit of malice and do your devoir. What! sobbing, silly lad—where's your manhood?'

'Sir, Sir, what will they think of me—the Lady Esclair-monde and all—if they hear I have sat down tamely with a blow?'

'She will never think about you at all but as a sullen malapert ne'er-do-weel, if you go off to that camp of *routiers*, trying to prop a bad cause because you cannot take correction, nor observe discipline.'

A sudden suspicion came over Malcolm that the King would not thus make light of the offence, if it had really been the inexpiable insult he had supposed it, and the thought was an absolute relief; for in effect the parting from James, and joining the party opposed to Esclairmonde's friends, would have been so tremendous a step, that he could hardly have contemplated it in his sober senses, and he murmured, 'My honour, Sir,' in a tone that James understood.

'Oh, for your honour—you need not fear for that! Any knight in the army could have done as much without prejudice to your honour. Why, you silly loon, d'ye think I would not have been as angered as yourself, if your honour had been injured?'

Charlotte M. Yonge

Malcolm's heart felt easier, but he still growled. 'Then, Sir, if you assure me that I can do so without detriment to my honour, I will not quit you.'

James laughed. 'It might have been more graciously spoken, my good cousin, but I am beholden to you.'

Malcolm, ashamed and vexed at the sarcastic tone, held his tongue for a little while, but presently exclaimed, 'Will the Bishop of Therouenne hear of it?'

James laughed. 'Belike not; or, if he should, it would only seem to him the reasonable training of a young squire.'

The King did not say what crossed his own mind, that the Bishop of Therouenne was more likely to think Henry over-strict in discipline, and absurdly rigorous.

The prelate, Charles de Luxemburg, brother to the Count de St. Pol, had made several visits to the English camp. He was one of these princely younger sons, who, like Beaufort at home, took ecclesiastical preferments as their natural provision, and as a footing whence they might become statesmen. He was a great admirer of Henry's genius, and, as the chief French prelate who was heartily on the English side, enjoyed a much greater prominence than he could have done at either the French or Burgundian Court. He and his brother of St. Pol were Esclairmonde's nearest kinsmen—'oncles a la mode de Bretagne,' as they call the relationship which is here sometimes termed Welsh uncle, or first cousins once removed—and from him James had obtained much more complete information about Esclairmonde than he could ever get from the flighty Duchess.

Her mother, a beautiful Walloon, had been heiress to wide domains in Hainault, her father to great estates in

Flanders, all which were at present managed by the politic Bishop. Like most of the statesman-secular-clergy, the Bishop hated nothing so much as the monastic orders, and had made no small haste to remove his fair niece from the convent at Dijon, where she had been educated, lest the Cistercians should become possessed of her lands. He had one scheme for her marriage; but his brother, the Count, had wished to give her to his own second son, who was almost an infant; and the Duke of Burgundy had designs on her for his half-brother Boemond; and among these various disputants, Esclairmonde had never failed to find support against whichever proposal was forced upon her, until the coalition between the Dukes of Burgundy and Brabant becoming too strong, she had availed herself of Countess Jaqueline's discontent to evade them both.

The family had, of course, been much angered, and had fully expected that her estates would go to some great English abbey, or to some English lord whose haughty reserve and insularity would be insupportable. It was therefore a relief to Monseigneur de Therouenne to hear James's designs; and when the King further added, that he would be willing to let the claims on the Hainault part of her estates be purchased by the Count de St. Pol, and those in Flanders by the Duke of Burgundy, the Bishop was delighted, and declared that, rather than such a negotiation should fail, he would himself advance the sum to his brother; but that the Duke of Burgundy's consent was more doubtful, only could they not do without it?

And he honoured Malcolm with a few words of passing notice from time to time, as if he almost regarded him as a relation. No doubt it would have been absurd to fly from such chances as these to Patrick Drummond and the opposite camp; and yet there were times when Malcolm felt as if he should get rid of a load on his heart if he were to break with all his present life, hurry to Patrick, confess

Charlotte M. Yonge

the whole to him, and then—hide his head in some hermitage, leaving his pledge unforfeited!

That, however, could not be. He was bound to the King, and might not desert him, and it was not unpleasant to brood over the sacrifice of his own displeasure.

'See,' said Henry, in the evening, as he came into the refectory and walked up to James, 'I have found my signet. It was left in the finger of my Spanish glove, which I had not worn since the beginning of winter. Thanks to all who took vain pains to look for it.'

But Malcolm did not respond with his pleased look to the thanks. He was not in charity with Henry, and crept out of hearing of him, while James was saying, 'You had best destroy one or the other, or they will make mischief. Here, I'll crush it with the pommel of my sword.'

'Ay,' said Henry, laughing, 'you'd like to shew off one of your sledge-hammer blows—Sir Bras de Fer! But, Master Scot, you shall not smash the English shield so easily. This one hangs too loose to be safe; I shall keep it to serve me when we have fattened up at Paris, after the leanness of our siege.'

'Hal,' said James, seeing his gay temper restored, 'you have grievously hurt that springald of mine. His northern blood cannot away with the taste he got of your fist.'

'Pretty well for your godly young monk, to expect to rob unchecked!' laughed Henry.

'He will do well at last,' said James. 'Manhood has come on him with a rush, and borne him off his feet; nor would I have him over-tame.'

'There spake the Scot!' said Henry. 'By my faith, Jamie, we should have had you the worst robber of all had we not caught you young! Well, what am I do for this sprig of royalty? Say I struck unawares? Nay, had I known him, I'd have struck with as much of a will as his slight bones would bear.'

'An you love me, Hal, do something to cool his ill blood, and remove the sense of shame that sinks a lad in his own eyes.'

'Methought,' said Henry, 'there was more shame in the deed than in the buffet.'

Nevertheless the good-natured King took an occasion of saying: 'My Lord of Glenuskie, I smote without knowing you. It was no place for a prince—nay, for any honest man; otherwise no hand should have been laid on my guest or my brother's near kinsman. And whereas I hear that both you and my fiery hot Percy verily credited the cry that prisoners were hid in that house, let me warn you that never was place yielded on composition but some villain got up the shout, and hundreds of fools followed it, till they learnt villainy in their turn. Therefore I ever chastise transgression of my command to touch neither dwelling nor inhabitant. You have both learnt your lesson, and the lion rampant and he of the straight tail will both be reined up better another time.'

Malcolm had no choice but to bend his head, mutter something, and let the King grasp his hand, though to him the apology seemed none at all, but rather to increase the offence, since the blame was by no means taken back again, while the condescension was such as could not be rejected, and thus speciously took away his excuse for brooding over his wrath. His hand lay so unwillingly in that strong hearty clasp that the King dropped it, frowned,

Charlotte M. Yonge

shrugged his shoulders, and muttered to himself, 'Sullen young dog! No Scot can let bygones be bygones!' and then he turned away and cast the trifle from his memory.

James was amazed not to see the moody face clear up, and asked of Malcolm whether he were not gratified with this ample satisfaction.

'I trow I must be, Sir,' said Malcolm.

'I tell thee, boy,' said James, 'not one king—nay, not one man—in a thousand would have offered thee the frank amends King Harry hath done this day: nay, I doubt whether even he could so have done, were it not that the hope of his wife's coming hath made him overflow with joy and charity to all the world.'

Malcolm did not make much reply, and James regarded him with some disappointment. The youth was certainly warmly attached to him, but these tokens of superiority to the faults of his time and country which had caused the King to seek him for a companion seemed to have vanished with his feebleness and timidity. The manhood that had been awakened was not the chivalrous, generous, and gentle strength of Henry and his brothers, but the punctilious pride and sullenness, and almost something of the license, of the Scot. The camp had not proved the school of chivalry that James, in his inexperience, had imagined it must be under Henry, and the tedium and wretchedness of the siege had greatly added to its necessary evils by promoting a reckless temper and willingness to snatch at any enjoyment without heed to consequences. Close attendance on the kings had indeed prevented either Malcolm or Percy from even having the temptation of running into any such lengths as those gentry who had plundered the shrine of St. Fiacre at Breuil, or were continually galloping off for an interval of dissipation at Paris; but they were both on the outlook for any snatch of stolen diversion, for in ceasing from monastic habits Malcolm seemed to have laid aside the scruples of a religious or conscientious youth, and specially avoided Dr. Bennet, the King's almoner.

James feared he had been mistaken, and looked to the influence of Esclairmonde to repair the evil, if perchance she should follow the Queen to France. And this it was almost certain she must do, since she was entirely dependent upon the Countess of Hainault, and could not obtain admission to a nunnery without recovering a portion of her estates.

Charlotte M. Yonge

CHAPTER IX

THE DANCE OF DEATH

The Queen was coming! No sooner had the first note of surrender been sounded from the towers of Meaux, than Henry had sent intelligence to England that the way was open for the safe arrival of his much-loved wife; and at length, on a sunny day in May, tidings were received that she had landed in France, under the escort of the Duke of Bedford.

Vincennes, in the midst of its noble forest, was the place fixed for the meeting of the royal pair; and never did a happier or more brilliant cavalcade traverse those woodlands than that with which Henry rode to the appointed spot.

All the winter, the King had heeded appearances as little as of old when roughing it with Hotspur in Wales; but now his dress was of the most royal. On his head was a small green velvet cap, encircled by a crown in embroidery; his robe was of scarlet silk, and over it was thrown a mantle of dark green samite, thickly powdered with tiny embroidered white antelopes; the Garter was on his knee, the George on his neck. It was a kingly garb, and well became the tall slight person and fair noble features. During these tedious months he had looked wan, haggard, and careworn; but the lines of anxiety were all effaced, his lustrous blue eyes shone and danced like Easter suns, his complexion rivalled the fresh delicate tints of the blossoms in the orchards; and when, with a shyness for which he laughed at himself, he halted to brush away any trace of dust that might offend the eye of his 'dainty Kate,' and gaily asked his brother king if he were sufficiently pranked out for a lady's bower, James, thinking he had never seen him so handsome, replied:

'Like a young bridegroom—nay, more like a young suitor.'

'You're jealous, Jamie—afraid of being outshone. 'Tis is your own fault, man; none can ever tell whether you be in festal trim or not.'

For King James's taste was for sober, well-blending hues; and as he never lapsed into Henry's carelessness, his state apparel was not very apparently dissimilar from his ordinary dress, being generally of dark rich crimson, blue, or russet, with the St. Andrew's cross in white silk on his breast, or else the ruddy lion, but never conspicuously; and the sombre hues always seemed particularly well to suit his auburn colouring.

Malcolm, in scarlet and gold, was a far gayer figure, and quite conscious of the change in his own appearance—how much taller, ruddier, and browner he had become; how much better he held himself both in riding and walking; and how much awkwardness and embarrassment he had lost. No wonder Esclairmonde had despised the sickly, timid, monkish school-boy; and if she had then shown him any sort of grace or preference, what would she think of the princely young squire he could new show her, who had seen service, had proved his valour, and was only not a knight because of King Henry's unkindness and

King James's punctilio?—at any rate, no child to be brow-beaten and silenced with folly about cloistral dedication, but a youth who had taken his place in the world, and could allege that his inspiration had come through her bright eyes.

Would she be there? That was the chief anxiety: for it was not certain that either she or her mistress would risk themselves on the Continent; and Catherine had given no intimation as to who would be in her suite—so that, as Henry had merrily observed, he was the only one in the whole party who was not in suspense, except indeed Salisbury, who had sent his commands to his little daughter to come out with the Queen.

'She is come!' cried Henry. 'Beforehand with us, after all;' and he spurred his horse on as he saw the banner raised, and the escort around the gate; and in a few seconds more he and his companions had hurried through the court, where the ladies had scarcely dismounted, and hastened into the hall, breaking into the seneschal's solemn reception of the Queen.

'My Kate, my fairest! Mine eyes have been hungry for a sight of thee.'

And Catherine, in her horned head-gear and flutter of spangled veil, was almost swallowed up in his hearty embrace; and the fervency of his great love so far warmed her, that she clung to him, and tenderly said, 'My lord, it is long since I saw you.'

'Thou wert before me! Ah! forgive thy tardy knight,' he continued, gazing at her really enhanced beauty as if he had eyes for no one else, even while with lip and hand, kiss, grasp, and word, he greeted her companions, of whom Jaqueline of Hainault and John of Bedford were the most prominent.

'And the babe! where is he?' then cried he. 'Let me have him to hold up to my brave fellows in the court!'

'The Prince of Wales?' said Catherine. 'You never spake of my bringing him.'

'If I spake not, it was because I doubted not for a moment that you would keep him with you. Nay, verily it is not in sooth that you left him. You are merely sporting with use.'

'Truly, Sir,' said Catherine, 'I never guessed that you would clog yourself with a babe in the cradle, and I deemed him more safely nursed at Windsor.'

'If it be for his safety! Yet a soldier's boy should thrive among soldiers,' said the King, evidently much disappointed, and proceeding to eager inquiries as to the appearance and progress of his child; to which the Queen replied with a certain languor, as though she had no very intimate personal knowledge of her little son.

Other eyes were meanwhile eagerly scanning the bright confusion of veils and wimples; and Malcolm had just made out the tall head and dark locks under a long almost shrouding white veil far away in the background behind the Countess of Hainault, when the Duke of Bedford came up with a frown of consternation on his always anxious face, and drawing King James into a window, said, 'What have you been doing to him?'—to which James, without hearing the question, replied, 'Where is *she*?'

'Joan? At home. It was the Queen's will. Of that another time. But what means this?' and he signed towards his brother. 'Never saw I man so changed.'

'Had you seen him at Christmas you might have said so,' replied James; 'but now I see naught amiss; I had been thinking I had never seen him so fair and comely.'

'I tell you, James,' said Bedford, contracting his brows till they almost met ever his arched nose, 'I tell you, his look brings back to me my mother's, the last time she greeted my father!'

'To your fantasy, not your memory, John! You were a mere babe at her death.'

'Of five years,' said Bedford. 'That face—that cough—have brought all back—ay, the yearning look when my father was absent, and the pure rosy fairness that Harry and Tom cited so fiercely against one who would have told them how sick to death she was. I mind me too, that when our grandame of Hereford made us motherless children over to our grandsire of Lancaster, it was with a warning that Harry had the tender lungs of the Bohuns, and needed care. One deadly sickness he had at Kenilworth, when my father was ridden for post-haste. My mind misgave me throughout this weary siege; but his service held me fast at home, and I trusted that you would watch over him.'

'A man like him is ill to guide,' said James; 'but he is more himself now than he has been for months, and a few weeks' quiet with his wife will restore him. But what is this?' he proceeded in his turn; 'why is the Lady Joan not here?'

'How can I tell? It was no fault of mine. I even got a prim warning that it became me not to meddle about her ladies, and I doubted what slanders you might hear if I were seen asking your Nightingale for a token.'

'Have you none! Good John, I know you have.'

John smiled his ironical smile, produced from the pouch at his girdle a small packet bound with rose-coloured silk, and said: 'The Nightingale hath a plume, you see, and saith, moreover, that her knight hath done his devoir passably, but that she yet looks to see him send some captive giant to her feet. So, Sir Knight, I hope your poor dwarf hath acquitted him well in your chivalrous jargon.'

James smiled and coloured with pleasure; the fantastic message was not devoid of reality in the days when young imaginative spirits tried to hide the prose of war and policy in a bright mist of romantic fancy; nor was he ashamed to bend his manly head in reverence to, and even press to his lips, his lady's first love-letter, in the very sight of the satirical though sympathizing Bedford, of whom he eagerly asked of the fair Joan's health and welfare, and whether she were flouted by Queen Catherine.

'No more than is the meed of her beauty,' said Bedford. 'Sister Kate likes not worship at any shrine save one. Look at our suite: our knights—yea, our very grooms are picked for their comeliness; to wit that great feather-pated oaf of a Welshman, Owen Tudor there; while dames and demoiselles, tire-women and all, are as near akin as may be to Sir Gawain's loathly lady.'

'Not at least the fair Luxemburg. Did not I see her stately mien?'

'She is none of the Queen's, and moreover she stands aloof, so that the women forgive her gifts! There is that cough of Harry's again! He is the shadow of the man he was; I would I knew if this were the step-dame's doing.'

Charlotte M. Yonge

'Nay, John, when you talk to me of Harry's cough, and of night-watches and flooded camps, I hearken; but when your wits run wool-gathering after that poor woman, making waxen images stuck full—'

'You are in the right on't, James,' said Henry, who had come up to them while he was speaking. 'John will never get sorceries out of his head. I have thought it over, and will not be led into oppressing my father's widow any more. I cannot spend this Pentecost cheerily till I know she is set free and restored to her manors; and I shall write to Humfrey and the Council to that effect.'

And as John shrugged his shoulders, Henry gaily added: 'Thou seest what comes of a winter spent with this unbeliever Jamie; and truly, I found the thought of unright to my father's widow was a worse pin in my heart than ever she is like to thrust there.'

Thus then it was, that in the overflowing joy and good-will of his heart, and mayhap with the presentiment which rendered him willing to be at peace with all his kindred, Henry forgave and released his step-mother, Joan of Navarre, whom common rumour termed the Witch Queen, and whom he had certainly little reason to love, whether it were true or not that she had attempted to weave spells against him. In fact, there were few of the new-comers from England who did not, like Bedford, impute the transparency of Henry's hands, and the hollow-ness of his brightly-tinted cheek, to some form of sorcery.

Meantime, Esclairmonde de Luxemburg, more beautiful than ever under a still simpler dress, had greeted Malcolm with her wonted kindness; adding, with a smile, that he was so much grown and embrowned that she should not have known him but for the sweet Scottish voice which he, like his king, possessed.

'You do me too much grace in commending aught that is mine, madame,' said Malcolm, with an attempt at the assurance he believed himself to have acquired; but he could only finish by faltering and blushing. There was a power of repression about Esclairmonde that annihilated all his designs, and drove him back into his bashful self whenever he came into contact with her, and felt how unlike the grave serene loftiness of her presence was to the mere queen of romance, that in her absence her shadow had become.

Alice Montagu, returning to her side, relieved while disconcerting him. Sweet little Alice had been in a continual flutter ever since commands had come from Meaux that she was to come out to meet the father whom she had not seen since what seemed like half her childish lifetime, and the betrothed whom she had never seen at all; and Lady Westmoreland had added to her awe by the lengthened admonition with which she took leave of her. And on this day, when Esclairmonde herself had arrayed the fair child in the daintiest of rose-pink boddices edged with swan's-down, the whitest of kirtles, and softest of rosy veils, the flush of anxiety on the pale little face made it so fair to look upon, that as the maiden wistfully asked, 'Think you he will flout me?' it was impossible not to laugh at the very notion. 'Ah! but I would be glad if he did, for then I might bide with you.'

When, in the general greeting, Alice had been sought out by a tall, dark-browed, grizzled warrior, Esclairmonde had, cruelly, as the maiden thought, kept her station behind the Countess, and never stirred for all those wistful backward glances, but left her alone to drop on her knee to seek the blessing of the mighty old soldier.

And now she was holding his great hand, almost as tough as his gauntlets, and leading him up to her friend, while

Charlotte M. Yonge

he louted low, and spoke with a grand fatherly courtesy:

'Fair demoiselle, this silly wench of mine tells me that you have been good friend to her, and I thank you for the same with all mine heart.'

'Silly' was a fond term of love then, and had all the affection of a proud father in it, as the Earl of Salisbury patted the small soft fingers in his grasp.

'Truly, my lord,' responded Esclairmonde, 'the Lady Alice hath been my sweetest companion, friend, and sister, for these many months.'

'Nay, child, art worthy to be called friend by such a lady as this? If so, I shall deem my little Alice grown a woman indeed, as it is time she were—Diccon Nevil is bent on the wedding before we go to the wars again.'

Alice coloured like a damask rose, and hid her face behind her friend.

'Hast seen him, sweet?' asked Esclairmonde, when Salisbury had been called away. 'Is he here?'

'Yes; out there—he with the white bull on his surcoat,' said Alice, dreading to look that way.

'And hast spoken with him?' asked the lady next, feeling as if the stout, commonplace, hardy-looking soldier she saw was scarce what she would have chosen for her little wild rose of an Alice, comely and brave though he were.

'He hath kissed mine hand,' faltered Alice, but it was quite credible that not a word had passed. The marriage was a business contract between the houses of Wark and Raby, and a grand speculation for Sir Richard Nevil, that was all; but gentle Alice had no reluctance beyond mere maidenly shyness, and unwillingness to enter on an unknown future under a new lord. She even whispered to her dear Clairette that she was glad Sir Richard never tormented her by talking to her, and that he was grave, and so old.

'So old? why, little one, he can scarce be seven-and-twenty!'

'And is not that old? oh, so old!' said Alice. 'Able to take care of me. I would not have a youth like that young Lord of Glenuskie. Oh no—never!'

'That is well,' said Esclairmonde, smiling; 'but wherefore put such disdain in thy voice, Alice? He used to be our playfellow, and he hath grown older and more manly in this year.'

'His boyhood was better than such manhood,' said Alice; 'he was more to my taste when he was meek, than now that he seems to say, "I would be saucy if I durst." And he hath not the stuff to dare any way.'

'Fie! fie! Alice, you are growing slanderous.'

'Nay, now, Clairette, own verily—you feel the like!'

'Hush, silly one, what skills it? Youths must pass through temptation; and if his king hindered his vocation, maybe the poor lad may rue it sorely, but methinks he will come to the right at last. It were better to say a prayer for his faults than to speak evil of them, Alice.'

Poor Malcolm! He was at that very moment planning with an embroiderer a robe wherein to appear, covered with flashes of lightning transfixing the world, and mottoes around—'Esclaire mais Embrase'

Every moment that he was absent from Esclairmonde was spent in composing chivalrous discourses in which to lay himself at her feet, but the mere sight of her steady dark eyes scattered them instantly from his memory; and save for very shame he would have entreated King James again to break the ice for him, since the lady evidently supposed that she had last year entirely quashed his suit. And in this mood Malcolm mounted and took his place to ride into Paris, where the King wished to arrive in the evening, and with little preparation, so as to avoid the weary length of a state reception, with all its speeches and pageants.

In the glow of a May evening the cavalcade passed the gates, and entered the city, where the streets were so narrow that it was often impossible to ride otherwise than two and two. The foremost had emerged into an open space before a church and churchyard, when there was a sudden pause, a shock of surprise. All across the space, blocking up the way, was an enormous line of figures, looking shadowy in the evening light, and bearing the insignia of every rank and dignity that earth presented. Popes were there, with triple crown and keys, and fanned by peacock tails; scarlet-matted and caped cardinals, mitred and crosiered bishops, crowned and sceptred kings, ermined dukes, steel-clad knights, gowned lawyers, square-capped priests, cowled monks, and friars of every degree—nay, the mechanic with his tools, the peasant with his spade, even the beggar within his dish; old men, and children of every age; and women too of all grades— the tower-crowned queen, the beplumed dame, the lofty abbess, the veiled nun, the bourgeoise, the peasant, the beggar;—all were there, moving in a strange shadowy wild dance, sometimes slow, sometimes swift and mad with gaiety, to the music of an unseen band of clashing kettle-drums, cymbals, and other instruments, that played fast and furiously; while above all a knell in the church tower rang forth at intervals a slow, deep, lugubrious note; and all the time there glided in and out through the ring a grisly being—skull-headed, skeleton-boned, scythe in hand—Death himself; and ever and anon, when the dance was swiftest, would he dart into the midst, pounce on one or other, holding an hour-glass to the face, unheeding rank, sex, or age, and bear his victim to the charnel-house beside the church. It was a sight as though some terrible sermon had taken life, as though the unseen had become visible, the veil were taken away; and the implicit unresisting obedience of the victims added to the sense of awful reality and fatality.

The advance of the victorious King Henry made no difference to the continuousness of the frightful dance; nay, it was plain that he was but in the presence of a monarch yet more victorious than himself, and the mazes wound on, the performers being evidently no phantoms, but as substantial as those who beheld them; nay, the grisly ring began to absorb the royal suite within itself, and an awe-stricken silence prevailed—at least, where Malcolm Stewart and Ralf Percy were riding together.

Neither lad durst ask the other what it meant. They thought they knew too well. Percy ceased not for one moment to cross himself, and mutter invocations to the saints; Malcolm's memory and tongue alike seemed inert and paralyzed with horror—his brain was giddy, his eyes stretched open; and when Death suddenly turned and darted in his direction, one horrible gush of thought— 'Fallen, fallen! Lost, lost! No confession!'—came over him; he would have sobbed out an entreaty for mercy and for a priest, but it became a helpless shriek; and while Percy's sword flashed before his eyes, he felt himself falling, death-stricken, to the earth, and knew no more.

Charlotte M. Yonge

'There—he moved,' said a voice above him.

'How now, Glenuskie?' cried Ralf Percy. 'Look up; I verily thought you were sped by Death in bodily shape; but 'twas all an abominable grisly pageant got up by some dismal caitiffs.'

'It was the Danse Macabre,' added the sweet tone that did indeed unclose Malcolm's eyes, to see Esclairmonde bending over him, and holding wine to his lips. Ralf raised him that he might swallow it, and looking round, he saw that he was in a small wainscoted chamber, with an old burgher woman, Ralf Percy, and Esclairmonde; certainly not in the other world. He strove to ask 'what it meant,' and Esclairmonde spoke again:

'It is the Danse Macabre; I have seen it in Holland. It was invented as a warning to those of sinful life, and this good woman tells me it has become the custom to enact it every evening at this churchyard of the Holy Innocents.'

'A custom I devoutly hope King Harry will break!' exclaimed Ralf. 'If not, I'll some day find the way between those painted ribs of Monseigneur de la Mort, I can tell him! I had nearly given him a taste of my sword as it was, only some Gascon rogue caught my arm, and he was off ere I could get free. So I jumped off, that your poor corpse should not be trodden by French heels; and I hardly know how it was, but the Lady Esclairmonde was by my side as I dragged you out, and caused these good folks to let me bring you in behind their shop.'

'Lady, lady, I am for ever beholden,' cried Malcolm, gathering himself up as if to fall at her feet, and his heart bounding high with joy, for this was from death to life indeed.

'I saw there was some one hurt,' said Esclairmonde in her repressive manner. 'Drink some more wine, eat this bread, and you will be able to ride to the Hotel de St. Pol.'

'Oh, lady, let me speak of my bliss!' and he snatched at her hand, but was still so dizzy that he sank back, becoming aware that he was stiff and bruised from his fall. Almost at the same moment a new step and voice were heard in the little open booth where the cutler displayed his wares, and King James was at once admitted.

'How goes it, laddie?' he asked. 'They told me grim Death had clutched you and borne you off to his charnel-house; but at least I see an angel has charge of you.'

Esclairmonde slightly coloured as she made answer:

'I saw some one fall, and came to offer my poor skill, Sir; but as the Sieur de Glenuskie is fast recovering, if you will permit Sir Nigel Baird to attend me, Sir, I will at once return.'

'I am ready—I am not hurt. Oh, let us go together!' panted Malcolm, leaping up.

'Eh, gentlemen!' exclaimed the hospitable cutler's wife; 'you will not away so fast! This gallant knight will permit you to remain. And the fair lady, she will do me the honour to drink a cup of wine to the recovery of her betrothed.'

'Not so, good woman,' said Esclairmonde, a little apart, 'I am the betrothed of Heaven. I only assisted because I feared the youth's fall was more serious than it proves.'

The bourgeoise begged pardon, and made a curtsey; there was nothing unusual in the avowal the lady had made,

Charlotte M. Yonge

when the convent was a thoroughly recognized profession; but Esclairmonde could not carry out her purpose of departing separately with old Sir Nigel Baird; Malcolm was on his feet, quite ready to mount, and there was no avoiding the being assisted to her saddle by any but the King, who was in truth quite as objectionable a companion, as far as appearances went, for a young solitary maiden, as was Malcolm himself. Esclairmonde felt that her benevolence might have led her into a scrape. When she had seen the fall, knowing that to the unprepared the ghastly pageant must seem reality, she had obeyed the impulse to hurry to the rescue, to console and aid in case of injury, and she had not even perceived that her female companions did not attempt to accompany her. However, the mischance could best be counteracted by simplicity and unconsciousness; so, as she found herself obliged to ride by the King, she unconcernedly observed that these fantastic dances might perhaps arouse sinners, but that they were a horrible sight for the unprepared.

'Very like a dream becoming flesh and blood,' said James. 'We in advance were slow to perceive what it was, and then the King merely thought whether it would alarm the Queen.'

'I trow it did not.'

'No; the thing has not been found that will stir her placid face. She merely said it was very lugubrious, and an ill turn in the Parisians thus to greet her, but they were always senseless *betes*; and he, being relieved of care for her, looked with all his eyes, with a strange mixture of drollery at the antics and the masques, yet of grave musing at the likeness to this present life.'

'I think,' said Esclairmonde, 'that King Henry is one of the few men to whom the spectacle *is* a sermon. He laughs even while he lays a thing to heart.'

These few sentences had brought them to the concourse around the gateway of the great Hotel de St. Pol, in whose crowded courtyard Esclairmonde had to dismount; and, after being handed through the hall by King James, to make her way to the ladies' apartments, and there find out, what she was most anxious about, how Alice, who had been riding at some distance from her with her father, had fared under the alarm.

Alice ran up to her eagerly. 'Ah, dear Clairette, and was he greatly hurt?'

'Not much; he had only swooned for fright.'

'Swooned! to be a prince, and not have the heart of a midge!'

'And how was it with you, you very wyvern for courage?'

'With me? Oh, I was somewhat appalled at first, when my father took hold of my rein, and bade me never fear; for I saw his face grow amazed. Sir Richard Nevil rode up on the other side, and said the hobgoblins should eat out his heart ere they hurt me; and I looked into his face as he said that, and liked it more than ever I thought to like any but yours, Clairette. I think my father was going to leave me to him and see whether the King needed some one to back him; but up came a French lord, and said 'twas all a mere show, and my father said he was glad I was a stout-hearted wench that had never cried out for fear; and then I was so pleased, that I never heeded the ugly sight any more. Ay, and when Sir Richard lifted me off my horse, he kissed my hand of his own accord.'

'This is all he has ever s aid to you?' said Esclairmonde,

Charlotte M. Yonge

smiling. 'It is like an Englishman—to the purpose.'

'Yea, is it not? Oh! is it not better than all the fine speeches and compliments that Joan Beaufort gets from her Scottish king?'

'They have truths in them too, child.'

'Ay; but too fine-spun, too minstrel-like, for a plain English maid. The hobgoblins should eat out his heart ere they touched me!' she repeated to herself, as though the saying were the most poetical concert sung on minstrel lover's lute.

Death's Dance had certainly brought this affianced pair to a better understanding than all the gayest festivities of the Court.

Esclairmonde would have been happy if no one had noticed her benevolence to the young Scot save Alice Montagu; but she had to endure countless railleries from every lady, from Countess Jaqueline downwards, on the unmistakable evidence that her heart had spoken; and her grave dignity had less effect in silencing them than usual, so diverting was the alleged triumph over her propriety, well as they knew that she would have done the same for the youngest horse-boy, or the oldest man-at-arms.

CHAPTER X

THE WHITSUNTIDE FESTIVAL

'Lady, fairest lady! Ah, suffer your slave to fall at your feet with his thanks!'

'No thanks are due, Sir. I knew not who had fallen.'

'Cruel coyness! Take not away the joy that has fed a hungry heart.'

'Lord Glenuskie's heart was wont to hunger for better joys.'

'Lady, I have ceased to be a foolish boy.'

'Such foolishness was better than some men's wisdom.'

'Listen, belle demoiselle. I have been forth into the world, and have learnt to see that monasteries have become mere haunts for the sluggard, who will not face the world; and that honour, glory, and all that is worth living for, lie beyond. Ah, lady! those eyes first taught me what life could give.'

'Hush, Sir!' said Esclairmonde. 'I can believe that as a child you mistook your vocation, and the secular life may

Charlotte M. Yonge

be blest to you; but with me it can never be so; and if any friendship were shown to you on my part, it was when I deemed that we were brother and sister in our vows. If I unwittingly inspired any false hopes, I must do penance for the evil.'

'Call it not evil, lady,' entreated Malcolm. 'It cannot be evil to have wakened me to life and hope and glory.'

'What should you call it in him who should endeavour to render Lady Joan Beaufort faithless to your king, Lord Malcolm? What then must it be to tempt another to break troth-plight to the King of Heaven?'

'Nay, madame,' faltered Malcolm; 'but if such troth were forbidden and impossible?'

'None has the right or power to cancel mine,' replied the lady.

'Yet,' he still entreated, 'your kindred are mighty.'

'But my Bridegroom is mightier,' she said.

'O lady, yet—Say, at least,' cried Malcolm, eagerly, 'that were you free in your own mind to wed, at least you would less turn from me than from the others proposed to you.'

'That were saying little for you,' said Esclairmonde, half smiling. 'But, Sir,' she added gravely, 'you have no right to put the question; and I will say nothing on which you can presume.'

'You were kinder to me in England,' sighed Malcolm, with tears in his eyes.

'Then you seemed as one like-minded,' she answered.

'And,' he cried, gathering fresh ardour, 'I would be like-minded again. You would render me so, sweetest lady. I would kiss your every step, pray with you, bestow alms with you, found churches, endow your Beguines, and render our change from our childish purpose a blessing to the whole world; become your very slave, to do your slightest bidding. O lady, could I but give you my eyes to see what it might be!'

'It could not be, if we began with a burthened conscience,' said Esclairmonde. 'We have had enough of this, Sieur de Glenuskie. You know that with me it is no matter of likes or dislikes, but that I am under a vow, which I will never break! Make way, Sir.'

He could but obey: she was far too majestic and authoritative to be gainsaid. And Malcolm, in an access of misery, stood lost to all the world, kneeling in the window-seat, where she had left him resting his head against the glass, when suddenly a white plump hand was laid on his shoulder, and a gay voice cried:

'All *a la mort*, my young damoiseau! What, has our saint been unpropitious? Never mind, you shall have her yet. We will see her like the rest of the world, ere we have done within her!'

And Malcolm found himself face to face with the free-spoken Jaqueline of Hainault.

'You are very good, madame,' he stammered.

'You shall think me very good yet! I have no notion of being opposed by a little vassal of mine; and we'll succeed, if it were but for the fun of the thing!

Charlotte M. Yonge

Monseigneur de Therouenne is on your side, or would be, if he were sure of the Duke of Burgundy. You see, these prelates hate nothing so much as the religious orders; and all the pride of the Luxemburgs is in arms against Clairette's fancy for those beggarly nursing Sisters; so it drives him mad to hear her say she only succoured you for charity. He thinks it a family disgrace, that can only be wiped off by marrying her to you; and he would do it *bon gre, mal gre*, but that he waits to hear what Burgundy will say. You have only to hold out, and she shall be yours, if I hold her finger while you put on the ring. Only let us be sure of Burgundy.'

This was not a very flattering way of obtaining a bride; but Malcolm was convinced that when once married to Esclairmonde, his devotion would atone to her for all that was unpleasant in obtaining her. At least, she loved no one else; she had even allowed that she had once thought him like-minded; she had formerly distinguished him; and nothing lay between them but her scruples; and when they were overcome, by whatever means, his idol would be his, to adore, to propitiate, to win by the most intense devotion. All now must, however, turn upon the Duke of Burgundy, without whose sanction Madame of Hainault would be afraid to act openly.

The Duke was expected at Paris for the Whitsuntide festival, which was to be held with great state. The custom was for the Kings of France to feast absolutely with all Paris, with interminable banquet tables, open to the whole world without question. And to this Henry had conformed on his first visit to the city; but he had learnt that the costly and lavish feast had been of very little benefit to the really distressed, who had been thrust aside by loud-voiced miscreants and sturdy beggars, such as had no shame in driving the feeble back with blows, and receiving their own share again and again.

By the advice of Dr. Bennet, his almoner, he was resolved that this should not happen again; that the feast should be limited to the official guests, and that the cost of the promiscuous banquet should be distributed to those who really needed it, and who should be reached through their parish priests and the friars known to be most charitable.

Dr. Bennet, as almoner, with the other chaplains, was to arrange the matter; and horrible was the distress that he discovered in the city, that had for five-and-twenty years been devastated by civil fury, as well as by foreign wars; and famines, pestilences, murders, and tyrannies had held sway, so as to form an absolute succession of reigns of terror. The poor perished like flies in a frost; the homeless orphans of the parents murdered by either faction roamed the streets, and herded in the corners like the vagrant dogs of Eastern cities; and meantime, the nobles and their partisans revelled in wasteful pomp.

Scholar as he was, Dr. Bennet was not familiar enough with Parisian ways not to be very grateful for aid from Esclairmonde in some of his conferences, and for her explanations of the different tastes and needs of French and English poor.

What she saw and heard, on the other hand, gave form and purpose to her aspirations. The Dutch Sisters of St. Bega, the English Bedeswomen of St. Katharine, were sorely needed at Paris. They would gather up the sufferers, collect the outcast children, feed the hungry, follow with balm wherever a wound had been. To found a Beguinage at Paris seemed to her the most befitting mode of devoting her wealth; and her little admirer, Alice, gave up her longing desire that the foundation should be in England, when she learned that, as the wife of Nevil, her abode was likely to be in France as long as that country required English garrisons.

Charlotte M. Yonge

To the young heiress of Salisbury, her own marriage, though close at hand, seemed a mere ordinary matter compared with Esclairmonde's Beguinage, to her the real romance. Never did she see a beggar crouching at the church door, without a whisper to herself that there was a subject for the Beguines; and, tender-hearted as she was, she looked quite gratified at any lamentable tale which told the need.

If Esclairmonde had a climax to her visions of her brown-robed messengers of mercy, it was that the holy Canon of St. Agnes should be induced to come and act the part of master to her bedeswomen, as did Master Kedbesby at home.

She had even dared to murmur her design to Dr. Bennet; and when he, under strict seal of secrecy, had sounded King Henry, the present real master of Paris, he reported that the tears had stood in the King's eyes for a moment, as he said, 'Blessings on the maiden! Should she be able to do this for this city, I shall know that Heaven hath indeed sent a blessing by my arms!'

For one brief week, Esclairmonde and Alice were very happy in this secret hope; but at the end of that time the Bishop of Therouenne appeared. Esclairmonde had ventured to hope that the King's influence, and likewise the fact that her intention was not to enrich one of the regular monastic orders, might lead him to lend a favourable ear to her scheme; but she was by no means prepared to find him already informed of the affair of the Dance of Death, and putting his own construction on it.

'So, my fair cousin, this is the end of your waywardness. The tokens were certainly somewhat strong; but the young gentleman's birth being equal to yours, after the spectacle you have presented, your uncle of St. Pol, and I myself, must do our utmost to obtain the consent of the Duke of Burgundy.'

'Monseigneur is mistaken,' said Esclairmonde.

'Child, we will have no more folly. You have flown after this young Scot in a manner fitted only for the foolish name your father culled for you out of his books of chivalry. You have given a lesson to the whole Court and city on the consequences of a damsel judging for herself, and running a mad course over the world, instead of submitting to her guardians.'

'The Court understands my purpose as well as you do, Monseigneur.'

'Silence, Mademoiselle. Your convent obstinacy is ended for ever now, since to send you to one would be to appear to hide a scandal.'

'I do not wish to enter a convent,' said Esclairmonde. 'My desire is to dedicate my labour and my substance to the foundation of a house here at Paris, such as are the Beguinages of our Netherlands,'

The Bishop held up his hands. He had never heard of such lunacy and it angered him, as such purposes are wont to anger worldly-hearted men. That a lady of Luxemburg should have such vulgar tastes as to wish to be a Beguine was bad enough; but that Netherlandish wealth should be devoted to support the factious poor of Paris was preposterous. Neither the Duke of Burgundy, nor her uncle of St. Pol, would allow a sou to pass out of their grasp for so absurd a purpose; the Pope would give no license—above all to a vain girl, who had helped a wife to run away from her husband—for new religious houses; and, unless Esclairmonde was prepared to be landless,

Charlotte M. Yonge

penniless, and the scorn of every one, for her wild behaviour, she must submit, *bon gre, mal gre*, to become the wife of the Scottish prince.

'Landless and penniless then will I be, Monseigneur,' said Esclairmonde. 'Was not poverty the bride of St. Francis?'

The Bishop made a growl of contempt; but recollecting himself, and his respect for the saint, began to argue that what was possible for a man, a mere merchant's son, an inspired saint besides, was not possible to a damsel of high degree, and that it was mere presumption, vanity, and obstinacy in her to appeal to such a precedent.

There was something in this that struck Esclairmonde, for she was conscious of a certain satisfaction in her plan of being the first to introduce a Beguinage at Paris, and that she was to a certain degree proud of her years of constancy to her high purpose; and she looked just so far abashed that the uncle saw his advantage, and discoursed on the danger of attempting to be better than other people, and of trying to vapour in spiritual heights, to all of which she attempted no reply; till at last he broke up the interview by saying, 'There, then, child; all will be well. I see you are coming to a better mind.'

'I hope I am, Monseigneur,' she replied, with lofty meekness; 'but scarcely such as you mean.'

Alice Montagu's indignation knew no bounds. What! was this noble votaress to be forced, not only to resign the glory of being the foundress of a new order of beneficence, but to be married, just like everybody else, and to that wretched little coward? Boemond of Burgundy was better than that, for he at least was a man!

'No, no, Alice,' said Esclairmonde, with a shudder; 'any

one rather than the Burgundian! It is shame even to compare the Scot!'

'He may not be so evil in himself,' said Alice; 'but with a brave man you have only his own sins, while a coward has all those other people may frighten him into.'

'He bore himself manfully in battle,' said the fair Fleming in reproof.

But Alice answered with the scorn that sits so quaintly on the gentle daughter of a bold race: 'Ay, where he would have been more afraid to run than to stand.'

'You are hard on the Scot,' said Esclairmonde. 'Maybe it is because the Nevils of Raby are Borderers,' she added, smiling; and, as Alice likewise smiled and blushed, 'Now, if it were not for this madness, I could like the youth. I would fain have had him for a brother that I could take care of.'

'But what will you do, Esclairmonde?'

'Trust,' said she, sighing. 'Maybe, my pride ought to be broken; and I may have to lay aside all my hopes and plans, and become a mere serving sister, to learn true humility. Anyhow, I verily trust to my Heavenly Spouse to guard me for himself. If the Duke of Burgundy still maintains Boemond's suit, then in the dissension I see an escape.

'And my father will defend you; and so will Sir Richard,' said Alice, with complacent certainty in their full efficiency. 'And King Harry will interfere; and we *will* have your hospital; ay, we *will*. How can you talk so lightly of abandoning it?'

Charlotte M. Yonge

'I only would know what is human pride, and what God's will,' sighed Esclairmonde.

The Duke arrived with his two sisters, his wife being left at home in bad health, and took up his abode at the Hotel de Bourgogne, whence he came at once to pay his respects to the King of England; the poor King of France, at the Hotel de St. Pol, being quite neglected.

Esclairmonde and Alice stood at a window, and watched the arrival of the magnificent cavalcade, attended by a multitude, ecstatically shouting, 'Noel Noel! Long live Philippe le Bon! Blessings on the mighty Duke!' While seated on a tall charger, whose great dappled head, jewelled and beplumed, could alone be seen amid his sweeping housings, bowing right and left, waving his embroidered gloved hand in courtesy, was seen the stately Duke, in the prime of life, handsome-faced, brilliantly coloured, dazzlingly arrayed in gemmed robes, so that Alice drew a long breath of wonder and exclaimed, 'This Duke is a goodly man; he looks like the emperor of us all!'

But when he had entered the hall, conducted by John of Bedford and Edmund of March, had made his obeisance to Henry, and had been presented by him to King James, Alice, standing close behind her queen, recollected that she had once heard Esclairmonde say, 'Till I came to England I deemed chivalry a mere gaudy illusion.'

Duke Philippe would not bear close inspection; the striking features and full red lips, that had made so effective an appearance in the gay procession seen from a distance, seemed harsh, haughty, and sensual near at hand, and when brought into close contact with the strange bright stern purity, now refined into hectic trans-parency, of King Henry's face, the grand and melancholy majesty of the royal Stewart's, or even the spare, keen, irregular visage of John of Bedford. And while his robes were infinitely more costly than—and his ornaments tenfold outnumbered—all that the three island princes wore, yet no critical eye could take him for their superior, even though his tone in addressing an inferior was elaborately affable and condescending, and theirs was always the frankness of an equal. Where they gave the sense of pure gold, he seemed like some ruder metal gilt and decorated; as if theirs were reality, his the imitation; theirs the truth, his the display.

But in reality his birth was as princely as theirs; and no monarch in Europe, not even Henry, equalled him in material resources; he was idolized by the Parisians; and Henry was aware that France had been made over to England more by his revenge for his father's murder at Montereau than by the victory at Agincourt. Therefore the King endured his grand talk about *our* arms and *our* intentions; and for Malcolm's sake, James submitted to a sort of patronage, as if meant to imply that if Philippe the Magnificent chose to espouse the cause of a captive king, his ransom would be the merest trifle.

When Henry bade him to the Pentecostal banquet, 'when kings keep state,' he graciously accepted the invitation for himself and his two sisters, Marguerite, widow of the second short-lived Dauphin, and Anne, still unmarried; but when Henry further explained his plan of feasting merely with the orderly, and apportioning the food in real alms, the Duke by no means approved.

'Feed those miserables!' he said. 'One gains nothing thereby! They make no noise; whereas if you affront the others, who know how to cry out, they will revile you like dogs!

Charlotte M. Yonge

'I will not be a slave to the rascaille,' said Henry.

'Ah, my fair lord, you, a victor, may dispense with these cares; but for a poor little prince like me, it is better to reign in men's hearts than on their necks.'

'In the hearts of honest men—on the necks of knaves,' said Henry.

Philippe shrugged his shoulders. He was wise in his own generation; for he had all the audible voices in Paris on his side, while the cavils at Henry's economy have descended to the present time.

'Do you see your rival, Sir?' said the voice of the Bishop of Therouenne in Malcolm's ear, just as the Duke had begun to rise to take leave; and he pointed out a knight of some thirty years, glittering with gay devices from head to foot, and showing a bold proud visage, exaggerating the harshness of the Burgundian lineaments.

Malcolm shuddered, and murmured, 'Such a pearl to such a hog!'

And meanwhile, King James, stepping forward, intimated to the Duke that he would be glad of an interview with him.

Philippe made some ostentation of his numerous engagements with men of Church and State; but ended by inviting the King of Scotland to sup with him that evening, if his Grace would forgive travellers' fare and a simple reception.

Thither accordingly James repaired on foot, attended only by Sir Nigel and Malcolm, with a few archers of the royal guard, in case torches should be wanted on the way home.

How magnificent were the surroundings of the great Duke, it would be wearisome to tell. The retainers in the court of the hotel looked, as James said, as if honest steel and good cloth were reckoned as churls, and as if this were the very land of Cockaigne, as Sir Richard Whittington had dreamt it. Neither he nor St. Andrew himself would know their own saltire made in cloth of silver, 'the very metal to tarnish!'

Sir Nigel had to tell their rank, ere the porters admitted the small company: but the seneschal marshalled them forward in full state. And James never looked more the king than when, in simple crimson robe, the pure white cross on his breast, his auburn hair parted back from his noble brow, he stood towering above all heads, passively receiving the Duke of Burgundy's elaborate courtesies and greetings, nor seeming to note the lavish display of gold and silver, meant to amaze the poorest king in Europe.

Exceeding was the politeness shown to him—even to the omission of the seneschal's tasting each dish presented to the Duke, a recognition of the presence of a sovereign that the two Scots scarcely understood enough for gratitude.

Malcolm was the best off of the two at the supper; for James had of course to be cavalier to the sickly fretful-looking Dauphiness, while Malcolm fell to the lot of the Lady Anne, who, though not beautiful, had a kindly hearty countenance and manner, and won his heart by asking whether the Demoiselle de Luxemburg were still in the suite of Madame of Hainault; and then it appeared that she had been her convent mate and warmest friend and admirer in their girlish days at Dijon, and was now longing to see her. Was she as much set as ever on being a nun?

Meantime, the Duke was pompously making way for the

Charlotte M. Yonge

King of Scots to enter his cabinet, where—with a gold cup before each, a dish of comfits and a stoup of wine between them—their interview was to take place.

'These dainties accord with a matter of ladies' love,' said James, as the Duke handed him a sugar heart transfixed by an arrow.

'Good, good,' said Philippe. 'The alliance is noble and our crowns and influence might be a good check in the north to your mighty neighbour; nor would I be hard as to her dowry. Send me five score yearly of such knaves as came with Buchan, and I could fight the devil himself. A morning gift might be specified for the name of the thing—but we understand one another.'

'I am not certain of that, Sir,' said James, smiling; 'though I see you mean me kindly.'

'Nay, now,' continued Philippe, 'I know how to honour royalty, even in durance; nor will I even press Madame la Dauphine on you instead of Anne, though it were better for us all if she could have her wish and become a queen, and you would have her jointure—if you or any one else can get it.'

'Stay, my Lord Duke,' said James, with dignity, 'I spake not of myself, deeming that it was well known that my troth is plighted.'

'How?' said Burgundy, amazed, but not offended. 'Methought the House of Somerset was a mere bastard slip, with which even King Henry with all his insolence could not expect you to wed in earnest. However, we may keep our intentions secret awhile; and then, with your lances and my resources, English displeasure need concern you little.'

James, who had learned self-control in captivity, began politely to express himself highly honoured and obliged.

'Do not mention it. Royal blood, thus shamefully oppressed, must command the aid of all that is chivalrous. Speak, and your ransom is at your service.'

The hot blood rushed into James's cheek at this tone of condescension; but he answered, with courteous haughtiness: 'Of myself, Sir Duke, there is no question. My ransom waits England's willingness to accept it; and my hand is not free, even for the prize you have the goodness to offer. I came not to speak of myself.'

'Not to make suit for my sister, nor my intercession!' exclaimed Philippe.

'I make suit to no man,' said James; then, recollecting himself, 'if I did so, no readier friend than the Duke of Burgundy could be found. I did in effect come to propose an alliance between one of my own house and a fair vassal of yours.'

'Ha! the runaway jade of Luxemburg!' cried Burgundy; 'the most headstrong girl who lives! She dared to plead her foolish vows against my brother Boemond, fled with that other hoyden of Hainault, and now defies me by coming here. I'll have her, and make her over to Boemond to tame her pride, were she in the great Satan's camp instead of King Henry's.'

And this is the mirror of chivalry! thought James. But he persevered in his explanation of his arrangement for permitting the estates of Esclairmonde de Luxemburg to be purchased from her and her husband, should that husband be Malcolm Stewart of Glenuskie; and he soon found that these terms would be as acceptable to the Duke

Charlotte M. Yonge

as they had already proved to her guardian, Monseigneur de Therouenne. Money was nothing to Philippe; but his policy was to absorb the little seignoralties that lay so thick in these border lands of the Empire; and what he desired above all, was to keep them from either passing into the hands of the Church, or from consolidating into some powerful principality, as would have been the case had Esclairmonde either entered a convent or married young Waleran de Luxemburg, her cousin. Therefore he had striven to force on her his half-brother, who would certainly never unite any inheritance to hers; but he much preferred the purchase of her Hainault lands; and had no compunction in throwing over Boemond, except for a certain lurking desire that the lady's contumacy should be chastised by a lord who would beat her well into subjection. He would willingly have made a great show of generosity, and have laid James under an obligation; and yet by the King's dignified tone of courtesy he was always reduced to the air of one soliciting rather than conferring a favour.

Finally, Malcolm was called in, and presented to the Duke, making his own promise on his word of honour as a prince, and giving a written bond, that so soon as he obtained the hand of the Demoiselle de Luxemburg he would resign her Hainault estates to the Duke of Burgundy for a sum of money, to be fixed by persons chosen for the purpose.

This was more like earnest than anything Malcolm had yet obtained; and he went home exulting and exalted, his doubts as to Esclairmonde's consent almost silenced, when he counted up the forces that were about to bear upon her.

And they did descend upon her. Countess Jaqueline had been joined by other and more congenial Flemish dames, and was weary of her grave monitress; and she continually scolded at Esclairmonde for perverseness and obstinacy in not accepting the only male thing she had ever favoured. The Bishop of Therouenne threatened and argued; and the Duke of Burgundy himself came to enforce his commands to his refractory vassal, and on finding her still unsubmissive, flew into a rage, and rated her as few *could* have done, save Philippe, called the Good.

All she attempted to answer was, that they were welcome to her lands, so they would leave her person free; her vows were not to man, but to God, and God would protect her.

It was an answer that seemed specially to enrage her persecutors, who retorted by telling her that such protection was only extended to those who obeyed lawful authority; and hints were thrown out that, if she did not submit willingly, she might find herself married forcibly, for a bishop could afford to disregard the resistance of a bride.

Would Malcolm—would his king—consent to her being thus treated?

As to Malcolm, he seemed to her too munch changed for her to reckon on what remnant of good feeling there might be to appeal to in him. And James, though he was certain not to permit palpable coercion in his presence, or even if he were aware that it was contemplated, seemed to have left the whole management of the affair to Esclairmonde's own guardians; and they would probably avoid driving matters to extremities that would revolt him, while he was near enough for an appeal. And Esclairmonde was too uncertain whether her guardians would resort to such lengths, or whether it were not a vain

Charlotte M. Yonge

threat of the giddy Countess, to compromise her dignity by crying out before she was hurt; and she had no security, save that she was certain that in the English household of King Henry such violence would not be attempted; and out of reach of that protection she never ventured.

Once she said to Henry, 'My only hope is in God and in you, my lord.'

And Henry bent his head, saying, 'Noble lady, I cannot interfere; but while you are in my house, nothing can be done with you against your will.'

Yet even Henry was scarcely what he had been in all-pervading vigilance and readiness. Like all real kings of men, he had been his own prime minister, commander-in-chief, and private secretary, transacting a marvellous amount of business with prompt completeness; and when, in the midst of shattered health which he would not avow, the cares of two kingdoms, and the generalship of an army, with all its garrisons, rested on him, his work would hardly have been accomplished but for his brother's aid. It was never acknowledged, often angrily disdained. But when John of Bedford had watched the terrible lassitude and lethargy that weighed on the King at times in the midst of his cabinet work, he was constantly on the watch to relieve him; and his hand and style so closely resembled Henry's that the difference could scarce be detected, and he could do what none other durst attempt. Many a time would Henry, whose temper had grown most uncertain, fiercely rate him for intermeddling; but John knew and loved him too well to heed; and his tact and unobtrusiveness made Henry rely on him more and more.

If the illness had only been confessed, those who watched the King anxiously would have had more hope; but he was hotly angered at any hint of his needing care; and though he sometimes relieved oppression by causing himself to be bled by a servant, he never allowed that anything ailed him; it was always the hot weather, the anxious tidings, the long pageant that wearied him—things that were wont to be like gnats on a lion's mane.

Those solemn banquets and festivals—lasting from forenoon till eventide, with their endless relays of allegorical subtleties, their long-winded harangues, noisy music, interludes of giants, sylvan men, distressed damsels, knights-errant on horseback, ships and forests coming in upon wheels, and fulsome compliments that must be answered—had been always his aversion, and were now so heavy an oppression that Bedford would have persuaded the Queen to curtail them. But to the fair Catherine this appeared an unkind endeavour of her disagreeable brother-in-law, to prevent her from shining in her native city, and eclipsing the Burgundian pomp; and she opened her soft brown eyes in dignified displeasure, answering that she saw nothing amiss with the King; and she likewise complained to her husband of his brother's jealousy of her welcome from her own people, bringing on him one of Henry's most bitter sentences.

Henry would only have had her abate somewhat of the splendour that gratified her, because he did not think it becoming to outshine her parents; but Catherine scorned the notion. Her old father would know nothing, or would smile in his foolish way to see her so brave; and for her mother, she recked not so long as she had a larded capon before her: nor was it possible to make the young queen understand that this fatuity and feebleness were the very reasons for deferring to them.

The ordering of the feast fell to Catherine and her train;

Charlotte M. Yonge

and its splendours on successive days had their full development, greatly to the constraint and weariness, among others, of Esclairmonde, who was always assigned to Malcolm Stewart, and throughout these long days had to be constantly repressing him; not that he often durst make her any direct compliment, for he was usually quelled into anxious wistful silence, and merely eyed her earnestly, paying her every attention in his power. And such a silent tedious meal was sure to be remarked, either with laughing rudeness by Countess Jaqueline, or with severe reproof by the Bishop of Therouenne, both of whom assured her that she had better lay aside her airs, and resign herself in good part, for there was no escape for her.

One day, however, when the feast was at the Hotel de Bourgogne, and there were some slight differences in the order of the guests, the Duke of Bedford put himself forward as the Lady Esclairmonde's cavalier, so much to her relief, that her countenance, usually so guarded, relaxed into the bright, sweet smile of cheerfulness that was most natural to her. Isolated as the pairs at the table were, and with music braying in a gallery just above, there was plenty of scope for conversation; and once again Esclairmonde was talking freely of the matters regarding the distress in Paris, that Bedford had consulted her upon before he became so engrossed with his brother's affairs, or she so beset by her persecutors.

Towards the evening, when the feast had still some mortal hours to last, there fell a silence on the Duke; and at length, when the music was at the loudest, he said 'Lady, I have watched for this moment. You are persecuted. Look not on me as one of your persecutors; but if no other refuge be open to you, here is one who might know better how to esteem you than that malapert young Scot.'

'How, Sir?' exclaimed Esclairmonde, amazed at these words from the woman-hating Bedford.

'Make no sudden reply,' said John. 'I had never thought of you save as one consecrate, till, when I see you like to be hunted down into the hands of yon silly lad, I cannot but thrust between. My brother would willingly consent; and, if I may but win your leave to love you, lady, it will be with a heart that has yearned to no other woman.'

He spoke low and steadily, looking straight before him, with no visible emotion, save a little quiver in the last sentence, a slight dilating of the delicately cut nostril; and then he was silent, until, having recovered the self-restraint that had been failing him, he prevented the words she was trying to form by saying, 'Not in haste, lady. There is time yet before you to bethink yourself whether you can be free in will and conscience. If so, I will bear you through all.'

How invitingly the words fell on the lonely heart, so long left to fight its own battles! There came for the first time the full sense of what life might be, the shielding tenderness, the sure reliance, the pure affection, such as she saw Henry lavish on the shallow Queen, but which she could meet and requite in John. The brutal Boemond, the childish Malcolm, had aroused no feeling in her but dislike or pity, and to them a convent was infinitely preferable; but Bedford—the religious, manly, brave, unselfish Bedford—opened to her the view of all that could content a high-souled woman's heart, backed, moreover, by the wonder of having been the first to touch such a spirit.

It would not have been a *mesalliance*. Her family was one of the grandest of the Netherlands; the saintly Emperor, Henry of Luxemburg, was her ancestor; and Bedford's

Charlotte M. Yonge

proposal was not a condescension such as to rouse her sense of dignity. His rank did not strike her as did his lofty stainless character; the like of which she had never known to exist in the world of active life till she saw the brothers of England, who came more near to the armed saints and holy warriors of Church legend than her fancy had thought mortal man could do, bred as she had been in the sensual, violent, and glittering Burgundy of the fifteenth century. In truth, as Malcolm had thought the cloister the only refuge from the harshness and barbarism of Scotland, so Esclairmonde had thought piety and purity to be found nowhere else; and both had found the Court of Henry V. an infinitely better world than they had supposed possible; but, until the present moment, Esclairmonde had never felt the slightest call to take a permanent place there. Now however the cloister, even if it were open to her, presented a gloomy, cheerless life of austerity, in comparison with human affection and matronly duty. And most vivid of all at the moment was the desire to awaken the tender sweetness that slept in those steady gray eyes, to see the grave, wise visage gleam with smiling affection, and to rest in having one to take thought for her, and finish this long term of tossing about and self-defence. Was not the patience with which he kept his eyes away from her already a proof of his consideration and delicate kindness?

But deep in Esclairmonde's soul lay the sense that her dedication was sacred, and her power over herself gone. She had always felt a wife's allegiance due to Him whom she received as her spiritual Spouse; and though the sense at this moment only brought her disappointment and self-reproach, her will was loyal. The bond was cutting into her very flesh, but she never even thought of breaking it; and all she waited for was the power of restraining her grateful tears.

In this she was assisted by observing that Bedford's attention had been attracted towards his brother, who was looking wan and weary, scarcely tasting what was set before him; and, after fitfully trying to converse with Marguerite of Burgundy, at last had taken advantage of an endless harangue from all the Virtues, and had dropped asleep. The Lady Anne was seen making a sign to her sister not to disturb him; and Bedford murmured, with a sigh, 'There is, for once, a discreet woman.' Then, as if recalled to a sense of what was passing, he turned on Esclairmonde his full earnest look, saying, 'You will teach the Queen how *he* should be cared for. You will help me.'

'Sir,' said Esclairmonde, feeling it most difficult not to falter, 'this is a great grace, but it cannot be.'

'Cannot!' said Bedford, slowly. 'You have taken thought?'

'Sir, it is not the part of a betrothed spouse to take thought. My vows were renewed of my own free will and it were sacrilege to try to recall them for the first real temptation.'

She spoke steadily, but the effort ached through her whole frame, especially when the last word illumined John Plantagenet's face with strange sweet light, quenched as his lip trembled, his nostril quivered, his eye even moistened, as he said, 'It is enough, lady; I will no more vex one who is vexed enough already; and you will so far trust me as to regard me as your protector, if you should be in need?'

'Indeed I will,' said Esclairmonde, hardly restraining her tears.

'That is well,' said Bedford. And he neither looked at her nor spoke to her again, till, as he led her away in the procession from the hall, he held her hand fast, and

Charlotte M. Yonge

murmured: 'There then it rests, sweet lady unless, having taken counsel with your own heart, you should change your decree, and consult some holy priest. If so, make but a sign of the hand, and I am yours; for verily you are the only maiden I could ever have loved.'

She was still in utter confusion, in the chamber where the ladies were cloaking for their return, when her hands were grasped on either side by the two Burgundian princesses.

'Sweet runaway, we have caught you at last! Here, into Anne's chamber. See you we must! How is it with you? Like you the limping Scot better than Boemond?' laughed the Dauphiness, her company dignity laid aside for school-girl chatter.

'If you cannot hold out,' said Anne, 'the Scot seems a gentle youth; and, at least, you are quit of Boemond.'

'Yes,' said Marguerite, 'his last prank was too strong for the Duke: quartering a dozen men-at-arms on a sulky Cambrai weaver till he paid him 2000 crowns. Besides, it would be well to get the Scottish king for an ally. Do you know what we two are here for, Clairette? We are both to be betrothed: one to the handsome captive with the gold locks; the other to your hawk-nosed neighbour, who seemed to have not a word to say.'

'But,' said Esclairmonde, replying to the easiest part of the disclosure, 'the King of Scots is in love with the Demoiselle of Somerset.'

'What matters that, silly maid?' said Marguerite 'he does not displease me; and Anne is welcome to that melancholy duke.'

'Oh, Lady Anne!' exclaimed Esclairmonde, 'if such be

your lot, it would be well indeed.'

'What, the surly brother, of whom Catherine tells such tales!' continued Marguerite.

'Credit them not,' said Esclairmonde. 'He never crosses her but when he would open her eyes to his brother's failing health.'

'Yes,' interrupted Marguerite; 'my lord brother swears that this king will not live a year; and if Catherine have no better luck with her child than poor Michelle, then there will be another good Queen Anne in England.'

'If so,' said Esclairmonde, looking at her friend with swimming eyes, 'she will have the best of husbands—as good as even she deserves!'

Anne held her hand fast, and would have said many tender words on Esclairmonde's own troubles; but the other ladies were arrayed, and Esclairmonde would not for worlds have been left behind in the Hotel de Bourgogne.

Privacy was not an attainable luxury, and Esclairmonde could not commune with her throbbing heart, or find peace for her aching head, till night. This must be a matter unconfided to any, even Alice Montagu. And while the maiden lay smiling in her quiet sleep, after having fondly told her friend that Sir Richard Nevil had really noticed her new silken kirtle, she knelt on beneath the crucifix, mechanically reciting her prayers, and, as the beads dropped from her fingers, fighting out the fight with her own heart.

Her mind was made up; but her sense of the loss, her craving for the worthy affection which lay within her

Charlotte M. Yonge

grasp—these dismayed her. The life she had sighed for had become a blank; and she passionately detested the obligation that held her back from affection, usefulness, joy, and excellence—not ambition, for the greatest help to her lay in Bedford's position, his exalted rank, and nearness to the crown. Indeed, she really dreaded and loathed worldly pomp so much that the temptation would have been greater had he not been a prince.

It was this sense of renunciation that came to her aid. She had at least a *real* sacrifice to offer; till now, as she became aware, she had made none. She folded her hands, and laid her offering to be hallowed by the One all-sufficient Sacrifice. She offered all those capacities for love that had been newly revealed to her; she offered up the bliss, whose golden dawn she had seen; she tried to tear out the earthliness of her heart and affections by the roots, and lay them on the altar, entreating that, come what might, her spirit might never stray from the Heavenly Spouse of her betrothal.

Therewith came a sense of His perfect sufficiency—of rest, peace, support, ineffable love, that kept her kneeling in a calm, almost ecstatic state, in which common hopes, fears, and affections had melted away.

CHAPTER XI

THE TWO PROMISES

After all, Alice Montagu was married almost privately, and without any preparation. Tidings came that the Duke of Alencon was besieging Cosne, a city belonging to the Duke of Burgundy, and that instant relief was needed. The Duke was urgent with Henry to save the place for him, and set off at once to collect his brilliant chivalry; while Henry, rousing at the trumpet-call, declared that nothing ailed him but pageants, sent orders to all his troops to collect from different quarters, and prepared to take the command in person; while reports daily came in of the great muster the Armagnacs were making, as though determined to offer battle.

Salisbury was determined not to abide the chances of the battle without first giving a protector to his little daughter; and therefore, as quietly as if she had been merely going to mass, the Lady Alice was wedded to her Sir Richard Nevil, who treated the affair as the simplest matter of course, and troubled himself with very slight demonstrations of affection. The wedding took place at Senlis, whither the female part of the Court had accompanied the King, upon the very day of the parting. No one was present, except one of Sir Richard's brothers (the whole family numbered twenty-two), his esquire; and on Alice's

Charlotte M. Yonge

side, her father, Esclairmonde, and a few other ladies.

At the last moment, however, the King himself came up, leaning on Warwick's arm, looking thin, ill, and flushed, but resolved to do honour to his faithful Salisbury, at whose request he had permitted the barony of Montagu to be at once transferred to Nevil, who would thenceforth be called by that title.

After the ceremony, King Henry kissed the gentle bride, placed a costly ring upon her finger, and gave his best and warmest wishes to the newly-married pair. Little guessed any there present what the sound of Warwick and Salisbury would be in forty years' time to the babe cradled at Windsor.

As the King passed Esclairmonde, he paused, and said, in an undertone, 'Dear lady, deem not that I have forgotten your holy purpose; but you understand that there are some who are jealous of any benefit conferred on Paris save from themselves, and whose alliance I may not risk. But if God be pleased to grant me this battle also, then, with His good pleasure, I shall not be forced to have such respect to persons; and when I return, lady, whether the endowment come from your bounty or no, God helping us, you shall begin the holy work of St. Katharine's bedeswomen among the poor of Paris.'

But while Henry V., with all his grave sweetness, spoke these words to Esclairmonde de Luxemburg, this was the farewell of Countess Jaqueline of Hainault to Malcolm Stewart:

'Look here, my languishing swain; never mind her scorn, but win your spurs in the battle that is to be, and then make some excuse to get back again to us before the two Kings, with all their scruples. Then beshrew me but she shall be yours! If Monseigneur de Therouenne and I cannot manage one proud girl, I am not Countess of Hainault!'

This promise sent him away, planning the enjoyment of conquering Esclairmonde's long resistance, and teaching her where to find happiness. Should he punish her, by being stern and tyrannical at first? or should his kindness teach her to repent? When he was a knight, he would be in a condition to assert his authority, he thought; and of knighthood both he and Ralf Percy felt almost certain, in that wholesale dubbing of knights that was wont to be the preliminary of a battle. To be sure, they had indulged in a good many unlicensed pleasures at Paris—Ralf from sheer reckless love of sport, Malcolm in his endeavour to forget himself, and to be manly; but they had escaped detection, and they knew plenty of young Englishmen, and many more Burgundians and Gascons, who had plunged far deeper into mischief, and thought it no disgrace, but rather held that there was some special dispensation for the benefit of warriors.

Malcolm and Ralf were riding with a party of these young men. King Henry had consented to make his first day's journey as far as Corbeil in a litter, since only there he was to meet the larger number of his troops, whom Bedford and Warwick were assembling. James was riding close beside him, with his immediate attendants; and the two youths, not being needed, had joined their comrades with the advanced guard of the escort.

It was always a fiction maintained by Henry, that he was marching in a friendly country; plunder was strictly forbidden, and everything was to be paid for; but unfortunately, the peasantry on his way never realized this, and the soldiery often took care they should not. Therefore, when the advanced guard came to the village that had

Charlotte M. Yonge

been marked out for their halt, instead of finding provisions and forage to be purchased, they met with only bare walls, and a few stray cats; and while storming and raving between hunger and disappointment, a report came from somewhere that the inhabitants had fled, and driven off their cattle to another village some four miles off, in the woods, on the heights above. Of course, they must be taught reason. It was true that the men-at-arms, who were under the command of Sir Christopher Kitson and Sir William Trenton, were obliged to abide where they were, much as Kitson growled at being unable to procure a draught of wine for Trenton, whom he had been nursing for weeks under intermitting fever, caught at Meaux; but the young gentlemen were well pleased to show themselves under no Yorkshireman's orders, and galloped off *en masse* to procure refreshment for their horses and themselves, further stimulated by the report that the Armagnacs had left a sick man behind them there, who might be a valuable prisoner.

By and by, a woodland path brought the disorderly party, about forty in number, including their servants and the ruffians who always followed whenever plunder was to be scented, out upon a pretty French village of the better class, built round a green shaded with chestnuts, under which, sure enough, were hay-carts, cows, sheep, and goats, and their owners, taking refuge in a place thought to be out of the track of the invaders.

Here were the malicious defrauders of the hungry warriors. Down upon them flew the angry foragers. Soon the pretty tranquil scene was ringing with the oaths of the plundering and the cries of the plundered; the cattle were being driven off, the houses and farm-yards rifled, blood was flowing, and what could not be carried off was burning. The search for the Armagnac prisoner had, however, relaxed after the first inquiry, and Malcolm, surprised that this had been forgotten, suddenly bethought him of the distinction he should secure by sending a valuable prize to Esclairmonde's feet. He seized on an old man who had not been able to fly, and stood trembling and panting in a corner, and demanded where the sick man was. The old man pointed to a farm-house, round which clouds of smoke were rolling, and Malcolm hurried into it, shouting, 'Dog of an Armagnac, come out! Yield, ere thou be burnt!'

No answer; and he dashed forward. In the lower room was a sight that opened his eyes with horror—no other than the shield of Drummond, with the three wavy lines; ay, and with it the helmet and suit of armour, whereof he knew each buckle and brace!

'Patie! Patrick! Patrick Drummond!' he wildly shouted, 'are you there?'

No answer; and seeing through the smoke a stair, he rushed up. There, in an upper room, on a bed, lay a senseless form, suffocated perhaps by the smoke, but unmistakably his cousin! He called to him, seized him, shook him, dragged him out of bed, all in vain; there was no sign of animation. The fire was gaining on the house; Malcolm's own breath was failing, and his frenzied efforts to carry Patrick's almost giant form to the stairs were quite unavailing. Wild with horror, he flew shouting down-stairs to call Halbert, whom he had left with his horse, but neither Halbert nor horse was in sight, nor indeed any of the party. Not a man was in sight, except a few hurrying far out of reach, as if something had alarmed them. He wrung his hands in anguish, and was about to make another attempt to drag Patrick down from the already burning house, when suddenly a troop of horse was among the scene of desolation, and at their head King James himself. Malcolm flew to the King, cutting short his angry exclamation with the cry, 'Help! help! he will burn! Patrick! Patie Drummond! There!'

James had scarce gathered the sense of the words, ere, leaping from his horse, he bounded up the stairs, through the smoke, amid flakes of burning thatch falling from the roof, groped in the dense clouds of smoke for the senseless weight, and holding the shoulders while Malcolm held the feet, they sped down the stair, and rested not till they had laid him under a chestnut tree, out of reach of the crash of the house, which fell in almost instantly.

'Does he live?' gasped Malcolm.

'He will not,' said the King, 'if his nation be known here. Keep out of his sight! He must hear only French!'

Remembering how inexorably Henry hung every Scotch prisoner, Malcolm's heart sank. This was why no one had sought the prisoner. A Scot was not available for ransom! Should he be the murderer of his cousin, Lily's love?

Meantime James hurriedly explained to Kitson that here was the sick man left by the enemy, summoned Sir Nigel to his side, closed his own visor, and called for water; then hung over the prisoner, anxious to prevent the first word from being broad Scotch. In the free air, some long sobs showed that Patrick was struggling back to life; and James at once said, 'Rendez vous, Messire;' but he neither answered, nor was there meaning in his eyes. And James perceived that he was bandaged as though for broken ribs, and that his right shoulder was dislocated, and no doubt had been a second time pulled out when Malcolm had grasped him by the arms. He swooned again at the first attempt to lift him, and a hay-cart having been left in the flight of the marauders, he was laid in it, and covered with the King's cloak, to be conveyed to Corbeil, where James trusted to secure his life by personal intercession with Henry. He groaned heavily several times, but never opened his eyes or spoke articulately the whole way; and James and Sir Nigel kept on either side of the cart, ready to address him in French the first moment, having told the English that he was a prisoner of quality, who must be carefully conveyed to King James's tent at Corbeil. Malcolm was not allowed to approach, lest he should be recognized; and he rode along in an agony of shame and suspense, with very different feelings towards Patrick than those with which he had of late thought of him, or of his own promises. If Patrick died through this plundering raid, how should he ever face Lily?

It was nearly night ere they reached Corbeil, where the tents were pitched outside the little town. James committed his captive to the prudent care of old Baird, bidding him send for a French or Burgundian surgeon, unable to detect the Scottish tongue; and then, taking Malcolm with him, he crossed the square in the centre of the camp to the royal pavilion, opposite to which his own was pitched.

It was a sultry night, and Henry had insisted on sleeping in his tent, declaring himself sick of stone walls; and as they approached his voice could be heard in brief excited sentences, giving orders, and asking for the King of Scots.

'Here, Sir,' said James, stopping in where the curtain was looped up, and showed King Henry half sitting, half lying, on a couch of cushions and deer-skins, his eyes full of fire, his thin face flushed with deep colour; Bedford, March, Warwick, and Salisbury in attendance.

'Ho! you are late!' said Henry. 'Did you come up with the caitiff robbers?'

Charlotte M. Yonge

'They made off as we rode up. The village was already burnt.'

'Who were they? I hope you hung them on the spot, as I bade,' continued Henry, coughing between his sentences, and almost in spite of himself, putting his hand to his side.

'I was delayed. There was a life to save: a gentleman who lay sick and stifled in a burning house.'

'And what was it to you,' cried Henry, angrily, 'if a dozen rebel Armagnacs were fried alive, when I sent you to hinder my men from growing mere thieves? Gentleman, forsooth! One would think it the Dauphin himself; or mayhap Buchan. Ha! it is a Scot, then!'

'Yes, Sir,' said James; 'Sir Patrick Drummond, a good knight, hurt and helpless, for whom I entreat your grace.'

'You disobeyed me to spare a Scot!' burst forth Henry. 'You, who call yourself a captain of mine, and who know my will! He hangs instantly!'

'Harry, bethink yourself. This is no captive taken in battle. He is a sick man, left behind, sorely hurt.'

'Then wherefore must you be meddling, instead of letting him burn as he deserved, and heeding what you undertook for me? I *will* have none of your traitor ruffians here. Since you have brought him in, the halter for him!—Here, Ralf Percy, tell the Provost-marshal—'

He was interrupted, for James unbuckled his sword, and tendered it to him.

'King Harry,' he said gravely, 'this morning I was your friend and brother-in-arms; now I am your captive. Hang

Patrick Drummond, who aided me at Meaux in saving my honour and such freedom as I have, and I return to any prison you please, and never strike blow for you again.'

'Take back your sword,' said Henry. 'What folly is this? You knew that I count not your rebel subjects as prisoners of war.'

'I did not know that I was saving a defenceless man from the flames to be used like a dog. I never offered my arm to serve a savage tyrant.'

'Take your sword!' reiterated Henry, his passion giving way before James's steady calmness. 'We will look into it to-morrow: but it was no soldierly act to take advantage of my weariness, to let my commands be broken the first day of taking the field, and bring the caitiff here. We will leave him for the night, I say. Take up your sword.'

'Not till I am sure of my liegeman's life,' said James.

'No threats, Sir. I will make no promise,' said Henry, haughtily; but the words died away in a racking cough.

And Bedford, laying his hand on James's arm, said, 'He is fevered and weary. Fret him no longer, but take your sword, and get your fellow out of the camp.'

James was too much hurt to make a compromise. 'No,' he said; 'unless your brother freely spares the life of a man thus taken, I must be his prisoner—but his soldier never!'

He left the tent, followed by Malcolm in an agony of despair and self-reproach.

Henry's morning decisions were not apt to vary from his evening ones. There was a terrible implacability about him at times, and he had never ceased to visit his brother of Clarence's death upon the Scots, on the plea that they were in arms against their king. Even Bedford obviously thought that the prisoner would be safest out of his reach; and this could hardly be accomplished, since Patrick had been placed in James's tent, in the very centre of the camp, near the King's own. And though Bedford and March might have connived at his being taken away, yet the mass of the soldiery would, if they detected a Scot being smuggled away into the town, have been persuaded that King James was acting treacherously.

Besides, the captive himself proved to be so exhausted, that to transport him any further in his present state would have been almost certainly fatal. A barber surgeon from Corbeil had been fetched, and was dealing with the injuries, which had apparently been the effect of a fall some days previously, probably when on his way to join the French army at Cosne; and the first fever of these hurts had no doubt been aggravated by the adventures of the day. At any rate Patrick lay unconscious, or only from time to time groaning or murmuring a few words, sometimes French, sometimes Scotch.

Malcolm would have fallen on his knees by his side, and striven to win a word or a look, but James forcibly withheld him. 'If you roused him into loud ravings in our own tongue, all hope of saving him would be gone,' he said.

'Shall we? Oh, can we?' cried Malcolm, catching at the mere word *hope*.

'I only know,' said the King, 'that unless we do so by Harry's good-will, I will never serve under him again.'

'And if he persists in his cruelty?'

'Then must some means be found of carrying Drummond into Corbeil. It will go hard with me but he shall be saved, Malcolm. But this whole army is against a Scot; and Harry's eye is everywhere, and his fierceness unrelenting. Malcolm, this *is* bondage! May God and St. Andrew aid us!'

When the King came to saying that, it was plain he deemed the case past all other aid.

Malcolm's misery was great. The very sight of Patrick had made a mighty revulsion in his feelings. The almost forgotten associations of Glenuskie were revived; the forms of his guardian and of Lily came before him, as he heard familiar names and phrases in the dear home accent fall from the fevered lips. Coldingham rose up before him, and St. Abbs, with Lily watching on the rocks for tidings of her knight—her knight, to whom her brother had once promised to resign all his lands and honours, but who now lay captured by plunderers, among whom that brother made one, and in peril of a shameful death. Oh, far better die in his stead, than return to Lily with tidings such as these!

Was this retribution for his broken purpose, and for having fallen away, not merely into secular life, but into sins that stood between him and religious rites? The King had called St. Andrew to aid! Must a proof of repentance and change be given, ere that aid would come? Should he vow himself again to the cloister, yield up the hope of Esclairmonde, and devote himself for Patrick's sake? Could he ever be happy with Patrick dead, and Esclairmonde driven and harassed into being his wife? Were it not better to vow at once, that so his cousin were spared he would return to his old purposes?

Almost had he uttered the vow, when, tugging hard at his

Charlotte M. Yonge

heart, came the vision of Esclairmonde's loveliness, and he felt it beyond his strength to resign her voluntarily; besides, how Madame of Hainault and Monseigneur de Therouenne would deride his uncertainties; and how intolerable it would be to leave Esclairmonde to fall into the hands of Boemond of Burgundy.

Such a renunciation could not be made; he did not even know that Patrick's safety depended on it; and instead of that, he promised, with great fervency of devotion, that if St. Andrew would save Patrick Drummond, and bring about the two marriages, a most splendid monastery for educational purposes, such as the King so much wished to found, should be his reward. It should be in honour of St. Andrew, and should be endowed with Esclairmonde's wealth, which would be quite ample enough, both for this and for a noble portion for Lily. Surely St. Andrew must accept such a vow, and spare Patrick! So Malcolm tried to pacify an anguish of suspense that would not be pacified.

CHAPTER XII

THE LAST PILGRIMAGE

The summer morning came; the *reveille* sounded, Mass was sung in the chapel tent, without which Henry never moved; and Malcolm tried to reassure his sinking heart by there pledging his vow to St. Andrew.

The English king was not present; but the troops were drawing up in complete array, that he might inspect them before the march. And a glorious array they were, of steel-clad men-at-arms on horseback, in bands around their leader's banner, and of ranks of sturdy archers, with their long-bows in leathern cases; the orderly multitude, stretching as far as the eye could reach, glittering in the early sun, and waiting with bold and glad hearts to greet the much-loved king, who had always led them to victory.

The only unarmed knight was James of Scotland. He stood in the space beside the standard of England, in his plain suit of chamois leather, his crimson cloak over his shoulder, but with no weapon about him, waiting with crossed arms for the morning's decision.

Close outside the royal tent waited Henry's horse, and those of his brother and other immediate attendants; and after a short interval the King came forth in his brightest

Charlotte M. Yonge

armour, with the coronal on his helmet, and the beaver up; and as he mounted, not without considerable aid, enthusiastic shouts of 'Long live King Harry!' broke forth, and came echoing back and back from troop to troop, gathering fervour as they rose.

The King rode forward towards the standard; but while yet the shouts were pealing from the army, be suddenly caught at his saddle-bow, reeled visibly, and would have fallen before Bedford could bring his horse to his side, had not James sprung forward, and laid one arm round him, and a hand on his rein.

'It is nothing,' said Henry. 'Let me alone.'

Ere the words were finished, he put his hand to his side, dropped his bridle, and gasped, while a look of intense suffering passed over his features; and he was passive while his horse was led back to the tent, and he was lifted down and placed on the couch he had just quitted.

'Loose my belt,' he gasped; then trying to smile, 'Percy has strained it three holes tighter.'

Alas! though it was indeed thus drawn in, his armour was hanging on him like the shell of a last year's nut. They released him from it, and he lay against the cushions with short painful respiration, and frequent cough.

'You must go on with the men at once, John,' he said. 'I will but be blooded, and follow in the litter.'

'Warwick and Salisbury—' began Bedford.

'No, no!' peremptorily gasped Henry. 'It must be you or I, I would, but this stitch in the side catches me, so that I can neither ride nor speak. Go, instantly. You know what I have ordered. I'll be up with you ere the battle.'

He brooked no resistance. His impatience, and with it the oppression and pain, only grew by remonstrance; and Bedford was forced to obey the command to go himself, and leave no one he could help behind him.

'You will stay, at least,' said John, in his distress, turning to the Scottish king.

'I must,' said James.

'You hold not your wrath?' said Bedford. 'It will madden me to leave him to any save you in this stress. Some are dull; some he will not heed.'

'I will tend him like yourself, John,' said the Scot, taking his hand. 'Do what he may, Harry is Harry still. Hasten to your command, John; he will be calmer when you are gone.'

Bedford groaned. It was hard to leave his brother at a moment when he must be more than himself—become general of an army, with a battle imminent; but he was under dire necessity, and forced himself to listen to and gather the import of the few terse orders and directions that Henry, breathless as he was, rendered clear and trenchant as ever.

The King almost drove his brother away at last, while a barber was taking a copious stream of blood from him; and as the army had already been set in motion, a great stillness soon prevailed, no one being left save a small escort, and part of the King's own immediate household, for Henry had himself ordered away Montagu, his chamberlain, Percy, and almost all on whom his eyes fell. The bleeding relieved him; he breathed less tightly, but became deadly pale, and sank into a doze of extreme exhaustion.

'Who is here?' he said, awakening. 'Some drink! What you, Jamie! You that were on fire to see a stricken field!'

'Not so much as to see you better at ease,' said James.

'I am better,' said Henry. 'I could move now; and I must. This tent will stifle me by noon.'

'You will not go forward?'

'No; I'll go back. A sick man is best with his wife. And I can battle it no further, nor grudge the glory of the day to John. He deserves it.'

The irascible sharpness had passed from his voice and manner, and given place to a certain languid cheerfulness, as arrangements were made for his return to Vincennes.

There proved to be a large and commodious barge, in which the transit could be effected on the river, with less of discomfort than in the springless horse litter by which he had travelled the day before; and this was at once prepared.

Malcolm had meanwhile remained, as in duty bound, in attendance on his king. James had found time to enjoin him to stay, being, to say the truth, unwilling to trust one so inexperienced and fragile in the *melee* without himself; nor indeed would this have been a becoming moment for him to put himself forward to win his spurs in the English cause.

Nothing had passed about Patrick Drummond, nor the high words of last night. Henry seemed to have forgotten them, between his bodily suffering and the anxiety of being forced to relinquish the command just before a battle; and James would have felt it ungenerous to harass him at such a moment, when absolutely committed to his charge. For the present, there was no fear of the prisoner being summarily executed by any lawful authority, since the King had promised to take cognizance of the case; and the chief danger was from his chance discovery by some lawless man-at-arms, who would think himself doing good service by killing a concealed Scot under any circumstances.

Drummond himself, after his delirious night, had sunk into a heavy sleep; and the King thought the best hope for him would be to remain under the care of Sir Nigel Baird for the present, until he could obtain favour for him from Henry, and could send back orders from Vincennes. He would not leave Malcolm to share the care of him, declaring that the canny Sir Nigel would have quite enough to do in averting suspicion without him; and, besides, he needed Malcolm himself, in the scarcity of attendants who had any tenderness or dexterity of hand to wait upon the suffering King.

Henry had rallied enough to walk down to the river, leaning upon James; and he smiled thanks when he was assisted by Trenton and Kitson to lie along on cushions. 'So, my Yorkshire knights,' he said, "tis you that have had to stop from the battle to watch a sick man home!'

'Ay, Sir,' said Sir Christopher; 'I did it with the better will, that Trenton here has not been his own man since the fever; and 'twere no fair play in the matter your Grace wets of, did I go into battle whole and sound, and he sick and sorry.'

Henry's look of amusement brightened him into his old

Charlotte M. Yonge

self, as he said, 'Honester guards could I scarce have, good friend.'

At that moment, after a nudge or two from Trenton, Kitson and he came suddenly down on their knees, with an impetus that must have tried the boards of the bottom of the barge. 'Sir,' said Kitson, always the spokesman, 'we have a grace to ask of you.'

'Say on,' said Henry. 'Any boon, save the letting you cut one another's throats.'

'No, Sir. Will Trenton's scarce my match now, more's the pity; and, moreover, we've lost the good will to it we once had. No, Sir; 'twas license to go a pilgrimage.'

'On pilgrimage!'

'Ay, Sir; to yon shrine at Breuil—St. Fiacre's, as they call him. Some of our rogues pillaged his shrine, as you know, Sir; and those that know these parts best, say he was a Scottish hermit, and bears malice like a Scot, saint though he be; and that your sickness, my lord, is all along of that. So we two have vowed to go barefoot there for your healing, my liege, if so be we have your license.'

'And welcome, with my best thanks, good friends,' said Henry, exerting himself to lean forward and give his hand to their kiss. Then, as they fell back into their places, with a few inarticulate blessings and assurances that they only wished they could go to Rome, or to Jerusalem, if it would restore their king, Henry said, smiling, as he looked at James, 'Scotsmen here, there, and everywhere— in Heaven as well as earth! What was it last night about a Scot that moved thine ire, Jamie? Didst not tender me thy sword? By my faith, thou hast it not! What was the rub?'

James now told the story in its fulness. How he had met Sir Patrick Drummond at Glenuskie; how, afterwards, the knight had stood by him in the encounter at Meaux; and how it had been impossible to leave him senseless to the flames; and how he had trusted that a capture made thus, accidentally, of a helpless man, would not fall under Henry's strict rules against accepting Scottish prisoners.

'Hm!' said Henry; 'it must be as you will; only I trust to you not to let him loose on us, either here or on the Border. Take back your sword, Jamie. If I spoke over hotly last night—a man hardly knows what he says when he has a goad in the side—you forgive it, Jamie.' And as the Scots king, with the dew in his eyes, wrung his hand, he added anxiously, 'Your sword! What, not here! Here's mine. Which is it?' Then, as James handed it to him: 'Ay, I would fain you wore it! 'Tis the sword of my knighthood, when poor King Richard dubbed me in Ireland; and many a brave scheme came with it!'

The soft movement of the barge upon the water had a soothing influence; and he was certainly in a less suffering state, though silent and dreamy, as he lay half raised on cushions under an awning, James anxiously watching over him, and Malcolm with a few other attendants near at hand; stout bargemen propelling the craft, and the guard keeping along the bank of the river.

His thoughts were perhaps with the battle, for presently he looked up, and murmured the verse:

"'I had a dream, a weary dream,
Ayont the Isle of Skye;
I saw a dead man win a fight,
And I think that man was I."

That stave keeps ringing in my brain; nor can I tell where

or when I have heard it.'

"Tis from the Scottish ballad that sings of the fight of Otterburn,' said James; 'I brought it with me from Scotland.'

'And got little thanks for your pains,' said Henry, smiling. 'But, methinks, since no Percy is in the way, I would hear it again; there was true knighthood in the Douglas that died there.'

James's harp was never far off; and again his mellow voice went through that gallant and plaintive strain, though in a far more subdued manner than the first time he had sung it; and Henry, weakened and softened, actually dropped a brave man's tear at the 'bracken bush upon the lily lea,' and the hero who lay there.

'That I should weep for a Douglas!' he said, half laughing; 'but the hearts of all honest men lie near together, on whatever side they draw their swords. God have mercy on whosoever may fall to-morrow! I trow, Jamie, thou couldst not sing that rough rhyme of Agincourt. I was bashful and ungracious enough to loathe the very sound of it when I came home in my pride of youth; but I would lief hear it once more. Or, stay—Yorkshiremen always have voices;' and raising his tone, he unspeakably gratified Trenton and Kitson by the request; and their voices, deep and powerful, and not uncultivated, poured forth the Lay of Agincourt to the waves of the French river, and to its mighty victor:

'Our King went forth to Normandye.'

Long and lengthily chanted was the triumphant song, with the Latin choruses, which were echoed back by the escort on the bank; while Henry lay, listening and musing; and

Malcolm had time for many a thought and impulse.

Patrick's life was granted; although it had been promised too late to send the intelligence back to the tent at Corbeil. So far, the purpose of his vow to St. Andrew had been accomplished; but with the probability that he should soon again be associated with Patrick, came the sense of the failure in purpose and in promise. Patrick would not reproach him, he well knew—nay, would rejoice in the change; but even this certainty galled him, and made him dread his cousin's presence as likely to bring him a sense of shame. What would Patrick think of his letting a lady be absolutely compelled to marry him? Might he not say it was the part of Walter Stewart over again? Indeed, Malcolm remembered how carefully King James was prevented from hearing the means by which the Countess intended to make the lady his own; and a sensation came over him, that it was profanation to call on St. Andrew to bless what was to be brought about by such means. Why was it that, as his eyes fell on the face of King Henry, the whole world and all his projects acquired so different a colouring? and a sentence he had once heard Esclairmonde quote would come to him constantly: 'My son, think not to buy off God. It is thyself that He requires, not thy gifts.'

But the long lay of victory was over; and King Henry had roused himself to thank the singers, then sighed, and said, 'How long ago that was!'

'Six years,' said James.

'The whole space from the hope and pride of youth to the care and toil of eld,' said Henry. 'Your Scots made an old man of me the day they slew Thomas.'

'Yet that has been your sole mishap,' said James.

Charlotte M. Yonge

'Yea, truly! But thenceforth I have learnt that the road to Jerusalem is not so straight and plain as I deemed it when I stood victorious at Agincourt. The Church one again— the Holy Sepulchre redeemed! It seemed then before my eyes, and that I was the man called to do it.'

'So it may be yet,' said James. 'Sickness alters everything, and raises mountains before us.'

'It may be so,' said Henry; 'and yet—Jerusalem! Jerusalem! It was my father's cry; it was King Edward's cry; it was St. Louis' cry; and yet they never got there.'

'St. Louis was far on his way,' said James.

'Ay! he never turned aside!' said Henry, sighing, and moving restlessly and wearily with something of returning fever.

"'O bona patria, lumina sobria te speculantur—"

Boy, are you there?' as, in turning, his eye fell on Malcolm. 'Take warning: the straight road is the best. You see, I have never come to Jerusalem.' Then again he murmured:

"'Hic breve vivitur, hic breve plangitur, hic breve fletur;
Non breve vivere, non breve plangere, retribuetur."

And James, seeing that nothing lulled him like song, offered to sing that mysteriously beautiful rhythm of Bernard of Morlaix.

'Ay, prithee do so,' said Henry. 'There's a rest there, when the Agincourt lay rings hollow. Well, there is a Jerusalem where our shortcomings are made up; only the straight way—the straight way.'

Malcolm took his part with James in singing the rhythm, which he had learnt long ago at Coldingham, and which thus in every note brought back the vanished aspirations and self-dedication to 'the straight way.'

For such, an original purpose of self-devotion must ever be—not of course exclusively to the monastic life; but whoever lowers his aims of serving God under any worldly inducement, is deviating from the straight way: and, thought Malcolm, if King Harry feels Agincourt an empty word beside the song of Sion, must not all I have sought for be a very vanity?

Sometimes dozing, but sometimes restless, and with the pain of breathing constantly increasing on him, Henry wore through the greater part of the day, upon the river, until it was necessary to land, and be taken through the forest in his litter. He was now obliged to be lifted from the barge; and his weariness rendered the conveyance very distressing, save that his patient smile never faded; and still he said, 'All will be well when I come to my Kate!'

Alas! when the gates were reached, James hardly knew how to tell him that the Queen had gone that morning to Paris with her mother. Yet still he was cheerful. 'If the physicians deal hard with me,' he said, 'it will be well that she should not be here till the worst is over.'

The physicians were there. A messenger had gone direct from Corbeil to summon them; and Henry delivered himself up into their hands, to fight out the battle with disease, as he had set himself to fight out many another battle in his time.

Charlotte M. Yonge

A sharp conflict it was—between a keen and aggravated disease, apparently pleurisy coming upon pulmonary affection of long standing, and a strong and resolute nature, unquenched by suffering, and backed by the violent remedies of a half-instructed period. Those who watched him, and strove to fulfil the directions of the physicians, hardly marked the lapse of hours; even though more than one day and night had passed ere in the early twilight of a long summer's morn he sank into a sleep, his face still distressed, but less acutely, and his breath heavy and labouring, though without the severe pain.

The watchers felt that here might be the turning point, and stood or sat around, not daring to change their postures, or utter the slightest word. Suddenly, James, who stood nearest, leaning against the wall, with his eyes fixed on the face of the sleeper, was aware of a hand on his shoulder, and looking round, saw in the now full light Bedford's face—so pale, haggard, and replete with anxiety, so dusty and travel-stained, that Henry, awakening at that moment, exclaimed, 'Ha, John!' And as his brother was slow to reply—'Has the day gone against thee? How was it? Never fear to speak, brother; thou art safe; and I know thou hast done valiantly. Valour is never lost, whether in defeat or success. Speak, John. Take it not so much to heart.'

'There has been no battle, Harry,' said Bedford, gathering voice with difficulty. 'The Dauphin would not abide our coming, but broke up his camp.'

'Beshrew thee, man!' said Henry; 'but I thought thou wast just off a flight!'

'Dost think one can ride fast only for a flight?' said Bedford. 'Ah, would that it had been the loss of ten battles rather than this!'

And he fell on his knees, grasping Henry's hand, and hiding his face against the bed, with the same instinct of turning to him for comfort with which the young motherless children of Henry of Bolingbroke, when turned adrift among the rude Beaufort progeny of John of Gaunt, had clung to their eldest brother, and found tenderness in his love and protection in his fearlessness; so that few royal brethren ever loved better than Henry and John of Lancaster.

'It was well and kindly done, John,' said Henry; 'and thou hast come at a good time; for, thanks be to God, the pain hath left me; and if it were not for this burthen of heaviness and weariness, I should be more at ease than I have been for many weeks.'

But as he spoke, there was that both in his face and voice that chilled with a dread certainty the hearts of those who hung over him.

'Is my wife come? I could see her now,' he wistfully asked.

Alas! no. Sir Lewis Robsart, the knight attached to her service, faltered, with a certain shame and difficulty, that the Queen would come when her orisons at Notre Dame were performed.

It was his last disappointment; but still he bore it cheerily.

'Best,' he said. 'My fair one was not made for sights like this; and were she here'—his lip trembled—'I might bear me less as a Christian man should. My sweet Catherine! Take care of her, John; she will be the most desolate being in the world.'

John promised with all his heart; though pity for cold-hearted Catherine was not the predominant feeling there.

'I would I had seen my child's face, and blessed him,' continued Henry. 'Poor boy! I would have him Warwick's charge.'

'Warwick is waiting admission,' said Bedford. 'He and Salisbury and Exeter rode with me.'

The King's face lighted up with joy as he heard this. 'It is good for a man to have his friends about him,' he said; and as they entered he held out his hand to them and thanked them.

Then took place the well-known scene, when, looking back on his career, he pronounced it to have been his endeavour to serve God and his people, and declared himself ready to face death fearlessly, since such was the will of his Maker: grieving only for the infancy of his son, but placing his hope and comfort in his brother John, and commending the babe to the fatherly charge of Warwick. 'You cannot love him for his own sake as yet; but if you think you owe me aught, repay it to him.' And as he thought over the fate of other infant kings, he spoke of some having hated the father and loved the child, others who had loved the father and hated the child.

To Humfrey of Gloucester he sent stringent warnings against giving way to his hot and fiery nature, offending Burgundy, or rushing into a doubtful wedlock with Jaqueline of Hainault; speaking of him with an elder brother's fatherly affection, but turning ever to John of Bedford with full trust and reliance, as one like-minded, and able to carry out all his intentions. For the French prisoners, they might not be released, 'lest more fire be kindled in one day than can be quenched in three.'

'And for you, Jamie,' he said, affectionately holding out his hand, 'my friend, my brother-in-arms, I must say the same as ever. Pardon me, Jamie; but I have not kept you out of malice, such as man must needs renounce on his death-bed. I trust to John, and to the rest, for giving you freedom at such time as you can safely return to be such a king indeed as we have ever hoped to be. Do you pardon me, James, for this, as for any harshness or rudeness you may have suffered from me?'

James, with full heart, murmured out his ardent love, his sense that no captive had ever been so generously treated as he.

'And you, my young lord,' said Henry, looking towards Malcolm, whose light touch and tender hands had made him a welcome attendant in the illness, 'I have many a kind service to thank you for. And I believe I mightily angered you once; but, boy, remember—ay, and you too, Ralf Percy—that he is your friend who turns you back from things sore to remember in a case like mine!'

After these, and other calm collected farewells, Henry required to know from his physicians how long his time might yet be. There was hesitation in answering, plainly as they saw that mortification had set in.

'What,' he said, 'do ye think I have faced death so many times to fear it now?'

Then came the reply given by the weeping, kneeling physician: 'Sir, think of your soul, for, without a miracle, you cannot live two hours.'

The King beckoned his confessor, and his friends retired, to return again to take their part in the last rites, the Viaticum and Unction.

Charlotte M. Yonge

Henry was collected, and alive to all that was passing, responding duly, and evidently entering deeply into the devotions that were to aid his spirit in that awful passage; his face gravely set, but firm and fearless as ever. The ceremonial ended, he was still sensible, though with little power of voice or motion left; but the tone, though low, was steady as ever, when he asked for the Penitential Psalms. Still they doubted whether he were following them, for his eyes closed, and his lips ceased to move, until, as they chanted the revival note of David's mournful penance—'O be favourable and gracious unto Sion; build Thou the walls of Jerusalem;'—at that much-loved word, the light of the blue eyes once more beamed out, and he spoke again. 'Jerusalem! On the faith of a dying king, it was my earnest purpose to have composed matters here into peace and union, and so to have delivered Jerusalem. But the will of God be done, since He saw me unworthy.'

Then his eyes closed again; he slept, or seemed to sleep; and then a strange quivering came over the face, the lips moved again, and the words broke from them, 'Thou liest, foul spirit! thou liest!' but, as though the parting soul had gained the victory in that conflict, peace came down on the wasted features; and with the very words of his Redeemer Himself, 'Into Thy hands I commend my spirit,' he did indeed fall asleep; the mighty soul passed from the worn-out frame.

CHAPTER XIII

THE RING AND THE EMPTY THRONE

No one knows how great a tree has been till it has fallen; nor how large a space a mighty man has occupied till he is removed.

King Henry V. left his friends and foes alike almost dizzy, as in place of his grand figure they found a blank; instead of the hand whose force they had constantly felt, mere emptiness.

Malcolm of Glenuskie, who had been asserting constantly that King Henry was no master of his, and had no rights over him, had nevertheless, for the last year or more, been among those to whom the King's will was the moving spring, fixing the disposal of almost every hour, and making everything dependent thereon.

When the death-hush was broken by the 'Depart, O Christian soul,' and Bedford, with a face white and set like a statue, stood up from his knees, and crossed and kissed the still white brow, it was to Malcolm as if the whole universe had become as nothing. To him there remained only the great God, the heavenly Jerusalem into which the King had entered, and himself far off from the straight way, wandering from his promise and his purpose into

Charlotte M. Yonge

what seemed to him a mere hollow painted scene, such as came and went in the midst of a banquet. Or, again, it was the grisly Dance of Death that was the only reality; Death had clutched the mightiest in the ring. Whom would he clutch next?

He stood motionless, as one in a dream, or rather as if not knowing which was reality, and which phantom; gazing, gazing on at the bed where the King lay, round which the ecclesiastics were busying themselves, unperceiving that James, Bedford, and the nobles had quitted the apartment, till Percy first spoke to him in a whisper, then almost shook him, and led him out of the room. 'I am sent for you,' he said, in a much shaken voice; 'your king says you can be of use.' Then tightening his grasp with the force of intense grief, 'Oh, what a day! what a day! My father! my father! I never knew mine own father! But he has been all to Harry and to me! Oh, woe worth the day!' And dropping into a window-seat, he covered his face with his hands, and gave way to his grief: pointing, however, to the council-room, where Malcolm found Bedford writing at the table, King James, and a few others, engaged in the same manner.

A few words from James informed him (or would have done so if he could have understood) that the Duke of Bedford, on whom at that terrible moment the weight of two kingdoms and of the war had descended, could not pause to rest, or to grieve, till letters and orders had been sent to the council in England, and to every garrison, every ally in France, to guard against any sudden panic, or faltering in friendship to England and her infant heir. Warwick and Salisbury were already riding post haste to take charge of the army; Robsart was gone to the Queen, Exeter to the Duke of Burgundy; and as the clergy were all engaged with the tendance of the royal corpse, there was scarcely any one to lessen the Duke's toil. James, knowing Malcolm's pen to be ready, had sent for him to assist in copying the brief scrolls, addressed to each captain of a fortress or town, announcing the father's death, and commanding him to do his duty to the son— King Harry VI. Each was then to be signed by the Duke, and despatched by men-at-arms, who waited for the purpose.

Like men stunned, the half-dozen who sat at the council-table worked on, never daring to glance at the empty chair at the upper end. The only words that passed were occasional inquiries of, and orders from, Bedford; and these he spoke with a strange alertness and metallic ring in his voice, as though the words were uttered by mechanism; yet in themselves they were as clear and judicious as possible, as if coming from a mind wound up exclusively to the one necessary object; and the face— though flushed at first, and gradually growing paler, with knitted brows and compressed lips—betrayed no sign of emotion.

Hours passed: he wrote, he ordered, he signed, he sealed; he mentioned name after name, of place and officer, never moving or looking up. And James, who knew from Salisbury that he had neither slept nor eaten since sixty miles off he had met a worse report of his brother, watched him anxiously till, when evening began to fall, he murmured, 'There is the captain of—of—at—but—' the pen slipped from his fingers, and he said, 'I can no more!'

The overtaxed powers, strained so long—mind, memory, and all—were giving way under the mere force of excessive fatigue. He rose from his seat, but stumbled, like one blind, as James upheld him, and led him away to the nearest bed-chamber, where, almost while the attendants divested him of the heavy boots and cuirass he had never paused all these hours to remove, he dropped into a sleep of sheer exhaustion.

James, who was likewise wearied out with watching, turned towards his own quarters; but, in so doing, he could not but turn aside to the chapel, where before the altar had been laid all that was left of King Henry. There he lay, his hands clasped over a crucifix, clad in the same rich green and crimson robes in which he had ridden to meet his Queen at Vincennes but three short months before; the golden circlet from his helmet was on his head, but it could not give additional majesty to the still and severe sweetness of his grand and pure countenance, so youthful in the lofty power that high aspirations had imprinted on it, yet so intensely calm in its marble rest, more than ever with the look of the avenging unpitying angel. To James, it was chiefly the face of the man whom he had best loved and admired, in spite of their strange connection; but to Malcolm, who had as usual followed him closely, it was verily a look from the invisible world—a look of awful warning and reproof, almost as if the pale set lips were unclosing to demand of him where he was in the valley of shadows, through which the way lay to Jerusalem. If Henry had turned back, and warned him at the gate of the heavenly Sion, surely such would have been his countenance; and Malcolm, when, like James, he had sprinkled the holy water on the white brow, and crossed himself while the low chant of Psalms from kneeling priests went up around him—clasped his two hands close together, and breathed forth the words, 'Oh, I have wandered far! O great King, I will never leave the straight way again! I will cast aside all worldly aims! O God, and the Saints, help me not to lose my way again!'

He would have tarried on still, in the fascination of that wonderful unearthly countenance, and in the inertness of faculties stunned by fatigue and excitement, but James summoned him by a touch, and he again followed him.

'O Sir!' he began, when they had turned away, 'I repent me of my falling away to the world! I give all up. Let me back to my vows of old.'

'We will talk of that another time,' said James, gravely. 'Neither you nor I, Malcolm, can think reasonably under such a blow as this; and I forbid you rashly to bind yourself.'

'Sir, Sir!' cried Malcolm, petulantly. 'You took me from the straight way. You shall not hinder my return!'

'I hinder no true purpose,' said King James. 'I only hinder another rash and hasty pledge, to be felt as a fetter, or left broken on your conscience. Silence now. When men are sad and spent they cannot speak as befits them, and had best hold their peace.'

These words were spoken on the way up the stair that led to the apartments of the King of Scots. On opening the door of the larger room, the first thing they saw was the tall figure of a distinguished-looking knight, who, as they entered, flung himself at King James's feet, fervently exclaiming, 'O my liege! accept my homage! Never was vassal so bound to his lord by thankfulness for his life, and for far more than his life!'

'Sir Patrick Drummond, I am glad to see you better at ease,' said James. 'Nay, suffer me,' he added, giving his hand to raise the knight, but finding it grasped and kissed with passionate devotion, almost overpowering the only half-recovered knight, so that James was forced to use strength to support him, and would at once have lifted him up, but the warm-hearted Patrick resisted, almost sobbing out—'Nay, Sir! king of my heart indeed! let me first thank you. I knew not how much more I owed you than the poor life you saved—my father's rescue, and that of all that was most dear.'

'Speak of such things seated, my good friend,' said James, trying to raise him; but Drummond still did not second his efforts.

'I have not given my parole of honour as the captive whose life is again due to you.'

'You must give that to the Duke of Bedford, Sir Patrick,' said James. 'I know not if I am to be put into ward myself. In any case you are safe, by the good King's grace, so you pledge yourself to draw no sword against England in Scotland or France till ransom be accepted for you.'

'Alack!' said Patrick, 'I have neither sword nor ransom. I would I knew what was to be done with the life you have given me, my lord.'

'I will find a use for it, never fear,' said James, sadly, but kindly. 'Be my knight for the present, till better days come for us both.'

'With my whole heart!' said Patrick, fervently. 'Yours am I for ever, my liege.'

'Then my first command is that you should rise, and rest,' said James, assisting the knight to regain his feet, and placing him in the only chair in the room. 'You must become a whole man as soon as may be.'

For Patrick's arm was in a sling, and evidently still painful and useless, and he sank back, breathless and unresisting, like one who had by no means regained perfect health, while his handsome features looked worn and pale. 'I fear me,' said James, as the two cousins silently shook hands, 'that you have moved over soon.—You surely had my message, Bairdsbrae?'

'Oh yes, my lord,' replied Baird; 'but the lad was the harder to hold; and after the fever was gone, we deemed he could well brook the journey by water. 'Twas time I was here to guide ye too, my lord; you and the callant baith look sair forfaughten.'

'We have had a sad time of it, Nigel,' said James, with trembling lip.

'And if Brewster tells me right, ye've not tasted food the whole day?' said Nigel, laying an authoritative hand on his royal pupil. 'Nay, sit ye down; here come the varlets with the meal I bade them have ready.'

James passively yielded, courteously signing to the others to share the food that was spread on a table; and with the same scarcely conscious grace, making inquiries, which elicited that Patrick Drummond's hurts had been caused by his horse falling and rolling over with him, whilst with Sir John Swinton and other Scottish knights he was reconnoitring the line of the English march. He was too much injured to be taken back to the far distant camp, and had accordingly been intrusted to the French farmer, with no attendant but a young French horse-boy, since he was too poor to keep a squire. He knew nothing more, for fever had run high; and he had not even been sensible of his desertion by his French hosts on the approach of the English, far less of the fire, and of his rescue by the King and Malcolm; but for this he seemed inclined to compensate to the utmost, by the intense eagerness of devotion with which he regarded James, who sat meanwhile crushed down by the weight of his own grief.

Charlotte M. Yonge

'I can eat no more, Baird,' said he, swallowing down a draught of wine, and pushing aside his trencher. 'Your license, gentlemen. I must be alone. Take care of the lads, Nigel. Malcolm is spent too. His deft service was welcome to—to my dearest brother.'

And though he hastily shut himself into his own inner chamber, it was not till they had seen that his grief was becoming uncontrollable.

Patrick could not but murmur, 'Dearest brother!'

'Ay, like brothers they loved!' said Baird, gravely.

'A strange brotherhood,' began Drummond.

But Malcolm cried, with much agitation, 'Not a word, Patie! You know not what you say. Take heed of profaning the name of one who is gone to the Sion above.'

'You turned English, our wee Malcolm!' exclaimed Drummond, in amaze.

'There is no English, French, or Scot where he is gone!' cried Malcolm. 'No Babel! O Patie, I have been far fallen! I have done you in heart a grievous wrong! but if I have turned back in time, it is his doing that lies there.'

'His! what, Harry of Lancaster's?' demanded the bewildered Patrick. 'What had he to do with you?'

'He has been my only true friend here!' cried Malcolm. 'Oh, if my hand be free from actual spoil and bloodshed, it was his doing! Oh, that he could hear me bless him for the chastisement I took so bitterly!'

'Chastisement!' demanded Patrick. 'The English King

dared chastise *you*! of Scots blood royal! 'Tis well he is dead!'

'The laddie's well-nigh beside himself!' said Baird. 'But he speaks true. This king whom Heaven assolizie, kept a tight hand over the youngsters; and falling on Lord Malcolm and some other callants making free with a house at Meaux, dealt some blows, of which my young lord found it hard to stomach his share; though I am glad to see he is come to a better mind. Ay, 'tis pity of this King Harry! Brave and leal was he; never spake an untrue word; never turned eye for fear, nor foot for weariness, nor hand for toil, nor nose for ill savour. A man, look you, to be trusted; never failing his word for good or ill! Right little love has there been between him and me; but I could weep like my own lad in there, to think I shall never see that knightly presence more, nor hear those frank gladsome voices of the boys, as they used to shout up and down Windsor Forest.'

'You too, Sir Nigel! and with a king like ours!'

'Ay, Sir Patrick! and if he be such a king as Scotland never had since St. David, and maybe not then, I'm free to own as much of it is due to King Harry as to his own noble self.—Did ye say they had streekit him in the chapel, Lord Malcolm? I'd fain look on the bonnie face of him; I'll ne'er look on his like again.'

No sooner had old Bairdsbrae gone, than Malcolm flung himself down before his cousin, crying, 'Oh, Patrick, you will hear me! I cannot rest till you know how changed I have been.'

'Changed!' said Patrick; 'ay, and for the better! Why, Malcolm, I never durst hope to see you so sturdy and so heartsome. My father would have been blithe to see you such a gallant young squire. Even the halt is gone!'

'Nearly,' said Malcolm. 'But I would fain be puny and puling, to have the clear heart that once I had. Oh, hear me! hear me! and pardon me, Patie!'

And Malcolm, in his agitation, poured forth the whole story of his having shifted from his old cherished purpose of devoting himself to the service of Heaven, and leaving lands and vassals to the stronger hands of Patrick and Lilias; how, having thus given himself to the world, he had fallen into temptation; how he had let himself be led to persecute with his suit a noble lady, vowed like himself; how he had almost agreed to marry her by force: and how he had been running into the ordinary dissipations of the camp, abstaining from confession, avoiding mass; disobeying orders, plunging into scenes of plunder, till he had almost been the death of Patrick, whom he had already so cruelly wronged.

So felt the boy. Fresh from that death-bed, the evils his conscience had protested against from the first appeared to him frightfully heinous, and his anguish of self-reproach was such, that Patrick listened in the greatest anxiety lest he should hear of some deadly stain on his young kinsman's scutcheon; but when the tale was told, and he had demanded 'Is that all?' and found that no further overt act was alleged against Malcolm, he breathed a long sigh, and muttered, 'You daft laddie! you had fairly startled me! So this is the coil, is it? Who ever told you to put on a cowl, I should like to know? Why, 'twas what my poor father ever declared against. I take your lands! By my troth! 'twould be enough to make me break faith with your sister, if I *could*!'

'The vow was in my heart,' faltered Malcolm.

'In a fule's head!' said Patrick. 'What right have babes to be talking of vows? 'Twould be the best tidings I've heard for many a long day, that you were wedded to a lass with a good tocher, and fit to guide your silly pate. What's that? Her vows! If they are no better than yours, the sooner they are forgot the better. If she had another love, 'twould be another matter, but with a bishop on your side, you've naught to fear.'

Malcolm turned away, sick at heart. To him his present position had become absolute terror. His own words had worked him up to an alarming sense of having lapsed from high aims to mere selfishness; of having profaned vows, consented to violence, and fallen away from grace; and he was in an almost feverish passion to utter something that would irrevocably bind him to his former intentions; but here were the King and Patrick both conspiring to silence him, and hold him back to his fallen and perilous state. Nay, Patrick even derided his penitence. Patrick was an honourable knight, a religious man, as times went, but he had been brought up in a much rougher and more unscrupulous school than Malcolm, and had been hardened by years of service as a soldier of fortune. The Armagnac camp was not like that of England. Warriors of such piety and strictness as Henry and Bedford had never come within his ken; and that any man, professing to be a soldier, should hesitate at the license of war, was incomprehensible to him. The discipline of Henry's army had been scoffed at in the French camp, and every infraction of it hailed as a token of hypocrisy; and to the stout Scot Malcolm's grief for the rapine at Meaux, which after all he had not committed, seemed a simple absurdity. Even his own danger, on the second occasion, did not make him alter his opinion; it was all the fortune of war. And he was not sure that he had not best have been stifled at once, since his hands were tied from warfare. And as for Lily—how was he to

Charlotte M. Yonge

win her now? Then, as Malcolm opened his mouth, Patrick sharply charged him to hold his tongue as to that folly, unless he wanted to drive him to make a vow on his side, that he would turn Knight of Rhodes, and never wed.

Malcolm, wearied out with excitement, came at last to weeping that no one would hear or understand him; but the scene was ended by Bairdsbrae, who, returning, brought a leech with him, who at once took the command of Patrick, and ordered him to his bed.

Malcolm could not rest. He was feverish with the shock of grief and awe, and absorbed in the thought which had mastered him, and which was much dwelt on in the middle ages:—the monastic path, going towards heaven straight as a sunbeam; the secular, twining its way through a tortuous difficult course—the 'broad way,' tending downward to the abyss. To his terrified apprehension, he had abandoned the direct and narrow path for the fatal road, and there might at any moment be captured, and whirled away by the grisly phantom Death, who had just snatched the mightiest in his inevitable clutch; and with something of the timidity of his nature, he was in absolute terror, until he should be able to set himself back on the shining road from which he had swerved, and be rid of the load of transgression which seemed ready to sink him into the gulf.

Those few and perfunctory confessions to a courtly priest who knew nothing about him, and was sure not to be hard on a king's cousin, now seemed to add to his guilt: and, wandering down-stairs towards the chapel, he met a train of ecclesiastics slowly leaving it, having just been relieved by a bevy of monks from a neighbouring convent, who took up the chants where they had left them.

Looking up at them, he recognized Dr. Bennet's bent

head, and throwing himself before him on his knee, he gasped, 'O father, father! hear me! Take me back! Give me hope!'

'What means this, my young lord?' said Dr. Bennet, pausing, while his brethren passed on. 'Are you sick?' he added, kindly, seeing the whiteness of Malcolm's face, and his startled eye.

'Oh, no, no! only sick at heart at my own madness, and the doom on it! O Sir, hear me! Take my vow again! give me absolution once more to a true shrift. Oh, if you will hear me, it shall be honest this time! Only put me in the way again.'

The chaplain was sorely sad and weary. He it was whose ministrations had chiefly comforted the dying King. To him it had been the loss of a deeply-loved son and pupil, as well as of almost unbounded hopes for the welfare of the Church; and he had had likewise, in the freshness of his sorrow, to take the lead in the ecclesiastical cere-monies that ensued, so that both in body and mind he was well-nigh worn out, and longed for peace in which to face his own private sorrow; but the wild words and anguished looks of the young Scot showed him that his case was one for immediate hearing, and he drew the lad into the confessional, authoritatively calmed his agitation, and prepared to hear the outpouring of the boy's self-reproach.

He heard it all—sifting facts from fancies, and learning the early purpose, the terror at the cruel world, the longing for peace and shelter; the desire to smooth his sister's way, which had led him to devote himself in heart to the cloister, though never permitted openly to pledge himself. Then the discovery that the world was less thorny than he had expected; the allurement of royal favour and great-ness; the charm of amusement, and activity in recovered health; the cowardly dread of scorn, leading him not merely into the secular life, but into the gradual dropping of piety and devotion; the actual share he had taken in forbidden diversions; his attempts at plunder; his ill-will to King Henry; and, above all, his persecution of Esclairmonde, which he now regarded as sacrilegious; and he even told how he lay under a half engagement to Countess Jaqueline to return alone to the Court, and bear his part in the forcible marriage she projected.

He told all, with no extenuation; nay, rather with such outbursts of opprobrium on himself, that Dr. Bennet could hardly understand of what positive evils he had been guilty; and he ended by entreating that the almoner would at once hear his vow to become a Benedictine monk, ere—

But Dr. Bennet would not listen. He silenced the boy by saying he had no more right to hear it than Malcolm as yet to make it. Nay, that inner dedication, for which Malcolm yearned as a sacred bond to his own will, the priest forbade. It was no moment to make such a promise in his present mood, when he did not know himself. If broken, he would only be adding sin to sin; nor was Malcolm, with all his errors fresh upon him, in any state to dedicate himself worthily. The errors—which in Ralf Percy, or in most other youths, might have seemed slight—were heavy stains on one who, like Malcolm, had erred, not thoughtlessly, but with a conscience of them all, in wilful abandonment of his higher principles. On these the chaplain mostly dwelt; on these he tried to direct Malcolm's repentance; and, finding that the youth was in perpetual extremes of remorse, and that his abject submission was a sort of fresh form of wilfulness, almost passion at being forbidden to bind himself by the vow, he told him that the true token of repentance was steadiness and constancy; and that therefore his absolution must be deferred until he had thus shown that his penitence was true and sincere—by perseverance, firstly, in the devotions that the chaplain appointed for him, and, secondly, in meeting whatever temptations might be in store for him. Nay, the cruel chaplain absolutely forbade the white, excited, eager boy to spend half the night in chapel over the first division of these penitential psalms and prayers, but on his obedience sent him at once to his bed.

Malcolm could have torn his hair. Unabsolved! Still under the weight of sin; still unpledged; still on dangerous ground; still left to a secular life—and that without Esclairmonde! Why had he not gone to a French Benedictine, who would have caught at his vow, and crowned his penitence with some magnificent satisfying asceticism?

Yet something in his heart, something in the father's own authority, made him submit; and in a tumult of feeling, more wretched even than before his confession, he threw himself on his bed, expecting to charge the tossings of a miserable night on Dr. Bennet, and to creep down barefoot to the chapel in the early morning to begin his *Misereres.*

Instead of which, his first wakening was in broad daylight, by King James standing over him. 'Malcolm,' he said, 'I have answered for you that you are discreet and trusty. A message of weight is to be placed in your hands. Come with me to the Duke of Bedford.'

Malcolm could only dress himself, and obediently follow to the chamber, where sat the Duke, his whole countenance looking as if the light of his life had gone out, but still steadfastly set to bear the heavy burden that had been placed on his shoulders.

He called Malcolm to him, and showed him a ring, asking

whether he knew it.

'The King's signet—King Harry's,' said Malcolm.

He was then reminded how, in the winter, Henry had lost
the ring, and after having caused another to be made at
Paris, had found it in the finger of his gauntlet. Very few
knew of the existence of this duplicate. Bedford himself
was not aware of it till it had been mentioned by James
and Lord Fitzhugh the chamberlain; and then search was
made for it, without effect, so that it evidently had been
left with the Queen. These private signets were of the
utmost importance, far more so than even the autograph;
for, though signatures were just acquiring individuality
enough to become the best authentication, yet up to this
very reign the seal was the only valid affirmation. Such
signets were always destroyed on a prince's death, and it
was of the utmost importance that the duplicate should
not be left in Queen Catherine's hands—above all, while
she was with her mother and her party, who were quite
capable of affixing it to forgeries.

Bedford, James, and Fitzhugh were all required at
Vincennes; the two latter at the lying-in-state in the
chapel. Most of the other trusty nobles had repaired to the
army; and, indeed, Bedford, aware of the terrible
jealousies that were sure to break out in the headless
realm, did not choose to place a charge that might here-
after prove invidious in the hands of any Englishman, or
to extend the secret any further than could be helped;
since who could tell what suspicion might not be thus cast
on any paper sealed by Henry?

In his perplexity, James had suggested young Malcolm,
who had assisted in the search for the lost ring, and been
witness to its discovery; and whom he could easily send
as bearer of his condolences to the widowed Queen; who

had indeed the *entree* of the palace, but had no political standing, was neither French nor English, and had shown himself discreet enough with other secrets to deserve confidence.

Bedford caught at the proposal. And Malcolm now received orders to take horse, with a sufficient escort, and hasten at once to Paris, where he should try if possible to obtain the ring from the Queen herself; but if he could not speak to her in private, he might apply to Sir Lewis Robsart. No other person was to be informed of the real object of the mission, and he was to get back to Vincennes as soon as possible.

Neither prince could understand the scared, distressed looks with which Malcolm listened to commands showing so much confidence in a youth of his years. They encouraged him by assurances that Sir Lewis Robsart, who had a curious kind of authority, half fatherly, half nurselike, over the Queen, would manage all for him. And King James, provoked by his reluctance, began, as they left Bedford's chamber, to chide him for ungraciousness in the time of distress, and insensibility to the honour conferred on him.

'Nay, nay,' disclaimed Malcolm, almost ready to weep, 'but I have a whole world of penance!'

'Penance! Plague on the boy's perverseness! What penance is so good as obedience?' said James, much displeased.

'Sir, Sir,' panted Malcolm, "tis not only that. Could any one but be sent in my stead? My returning alone is what Madame of Hainault bade—for—for some scheme on—'

His voice was choked, and his face was burning.

Charlotte M. Yonge

'Is the lad gone daft?' cried James, in great anger. 'If Madame of Hainault were so lost to decorum as to hatch such schemes at such a moment, I trow you are neither puppet nor fool in her hands for her to do what she will with. I'll have no more fooling!'

Malcolm could only obey.

In the brief space while the horses were preparing, and he had to equip and take food, he sped in search of Dr. Bennet, hoping, he knew not what, from his interference, or trusting, at any rate, to explain his own sudden absence.

But, looking into the chapel, he recognized the chaplain as one of the leading priests in one of the lengthiest of masses, which was just commencing. It was impossible to wait for the conclusion. He could but kneel down, find himself too much hurried and confused to recollect any prayer, then dash back again to don his riding-gear, before King James should miss him, and be angered again.

'Unabsolved—unvowed!' he thought. 'Sent off thither against my will. Whatever may fall out, it is no fault of mine!'

CHAPTER XIV

THE TROTH FLIGHT

Trembling and awed, the ladies waited at Paris. It was well known how the King's illness must end. No one, save the Queen, professed to entertain any hope of his amendment; but Catherine appeared to be too lethargic to allow herself to be roused to any understanding of his danger; and as to the personal womanly tendance of wife to suffering husband, she seemed to have no notion of it. Her mother had never been supposed to take the slightest care of King Charles; and Catherine, after her example, regarded the care either of husband or child as no more required of a royal lady than of a queen bee.

The little Lady Montagu, as Alice was now to be called, who had been scheming that her Richard should be wounded just enough to learn to call her his good little nurse-tender, was dreadfully scandalized, as indeed were wives of more experience, when they found all their endeavours to make their mistress understand how ill the King really was, and how much he wished for her, fall upon uncomprehending ears, and at last were desired by her mother Isabeau not to torment the poor Queen, or they would make her ill.

'Make her ill! I wish I could!' muttered Lady Warwick, as

Charlotte M. Yonge

she left the presence-chamber; 'but it is like my little Nan telling her apple-stock baby that all her kin were burnt alive in one castle. She heeds as much!'

But when at late evening Sir Lewis Robsart rode up to the hotel, and a hush went along with him, for all knew that he would never have left his King alive, Catherine's composure gave way. She had not imagination enough for apprehension of what was out of sight; but when she knew that she had lost her king, to whom she had owed the brief splendour of an otherwise dreary and neglected life, she fell into a passion of cries and tears, even at the mere sight of Sir Lewis, and continued to bewail her king, her lord, her husband, her light, her love, with the violence of an utterly unexpected bereavement.

But while her shrieks and sobs were rending the air, a hoarse voice gasped out, 'What say you? My son Henri dead!' and white and ghastly, the gray hair hanging wildly from the temples, the eyes roaming with the wistful gaze of the half insane, poor King Charles stood among them, demanding, 'Tell me I am sick again! Tell me it is but one of my delusions! So brave, so strong, so lively, so good to the poor old man! My son Henri cannot die! That is for the old, the sick!'

And when Sir Lewis with gentle words had made him understand the truth, he covered his face with his hands, and staggered away, led by his attendant knight, still murmuring in a dazed way, '*Mon fils Henri, mon bon fils Henri*—most loving of all my children!'

In truth, neither of his own sons had been thus mourned; nor had any person shown the poor crazed monarch the uniform deferential consideration he had received from Henry. He crept back to his own chamber, and for many days hardly spoke, save to moan for his *bon fils Henri*, scarcely tasting food, and pining away day by day. Those who had watched the likeness between the heroes of Monmouth and of Macedon, saw the resemblance carried out; for as the aged Persian queen perished away from grief for the courteous and gentle Alexander, so now the king of the conquered realm was actually wasting to death with mourning for his frank and kindly *bon fils Henri*.

As part of royal etiquette, Catherine betook herself to her bed, in a chamber hung with black, the light of day excluded, and ranks of wax tapers shedding a lugubrious light upon rows of gentlemen and ladies who had to stand there on duty, watching her as the mourners watched the King, though her lying-in-state was not always as silent; for though, there was much time spent in slumber, Catherine sometimes would indulge in a good deal of subdued prattle with her mother, or her more confidential attendants. But at other times, chiefly when first awaking, or else when anything had crossed her will, she would fall into agonies of passionate grief—weeping, shrieking, and rending her hair with almost a frenzy of misery, as she called herself utterly desolate, and screamed aloud for her king to return to her.

She was quite past the management of her English ladies on these occasions; and her mother, declaring that she was becoming crazed like her father, declined having anything to do with her. Even Sir Lewis Robsart she used to spurn aside; and nothing ever seemed effectual, but for the Demoiselle de Luxemburg, with her full sweet voice, and force of will in all the tenderness of strength, caressingly to hold her still, talk to her almost as to an infant, and sing away her violence with some long low ditty—sometimes a mere Flemish lullaby, sometimes a Church hymn. As Lady Warwick said, when the ladies were all wearied out with the endeavour to control their Queen's waywardness and violence, and it sighed away like a departing tempest

Charlotte M. Yonge

before Esclairmonde, 'It was as great a charity as ever ministering as a St. Katherine's bedeswoman could be.'

To the young Lady Montagu, the blow was astounding. It was the first realization that a great man could die, a great support be taken away; and, child-like, she moved about, bewildered and stunned, in the great household on which the dark cloud had descended—clinging to Esclairmonde as if to protect her from she knew not what; anything dreadful might happen, with the King dead, and her father and husband away.

Alas! poor Esclairmonde! She was in much more real danger herself, as came to the bride's mind presently, when, in the midst of her lamentations, she exclaimed, 'And, ah, Clairette! there ends his goodly promise about the sisterhood of good works at Paris.'

Esclairmonde responded with a gesture of sorrow, and the murmur of the '*In principibus non confide*' that is so often the echo of disappointment.

'And what will you do?' continued Alice, watching her anxiously, as her face, turning very pale, was nevertheless uplifted towards heaven.

'Strive to trust more in God, less in princes,' she breathed forth, clasping her hands, and compressing her lips.

'Nay, but does it grieve you so intensely?' asked Alice. 'Mayhap—'

'Alas! sweet one! I would that the fall of this device seemed like to be the worst effect to me of your good king's death. Pray for me, Alice, for now no earthly power stands between me and my kinsmen's will.'

Alice cried aloud, 'Nay, nay, lady, we are English still. There are my father; my lord, the Duke of Bedford; they will not suffer any wrong to be done.'

'Hush, Alice. None of them hath any power to aid me. Even good King Henry had no legal power to protect me; only he was so great, so strong in word or deed, that no man durst do before him what he declared a shame and a sin. Now it will be expedient more than ever that nothing be done by the English to risk offending the Duke of Burgundy. None will dare withhold me; none ought to dare, for they act not for themselves, but for their infant charge; and my countess is weary of me. There is nothing to prevent my uncles from taking me away with them; or—'

'Nothing!' cried Alice. 'It cannot be! Oh, that my father were here!'

'He could do nothing for me.'

'A convent!'

'No convent here could keep me against the Bishop of Therouenne.'

Alice wrung her hands. 'Oh, it cannot—shall not be!'

'No, Alice, I do not believe it will be. I have that confidence in Him to whom I have given myself, that I do not believe He will permit me to be snatched from Him, so long as my will does not consent.' Esclairmonde faltered a moment, as she remembered her wavering, crossed her hands on her breast, and ejaculated, 'May He deal mercifully with me! Yet it may be at an exceeding cost—at that of all my cherished schemes, of all that was pride and self-seeking. Alice, look not so terrified.

Nothing can be done immediately, or with violence, in this first mourning for the King; and I trust to make use of the time to disguise me, and escape to England, where I may keep my vow as anchoress, or as lay sister. Let me keep that, and my self-exalting schemes shall be all put by!'

The question whether this should be to England, or to the southern parts of France held by the Armagnacs, remained for decision, as opportunity should direct: Alice constantly urging her own scheme of carrying her friend with her as her tire-woman, if, as seemed likely, she were sent home; and Esclairmonde refusing to consent to anything that might bring the bride into troubles with her father and husband; and the debates being only interrupted when the Lady Montagu was required to take her turn among the weary ladies-in-waiting around Catherine's state bed.

Whenever she was not required to control, console, or persuade the Queen, Esclairmonde spent most of her time in a chamber apart from the chatter of Jaqueline's little court, where she was weaving, in the delicate point-lace work she had learnt in her Flemish convent, an exquisite robe, such as were worn by priests at Mass. She seldom worked, save for the poor; but she longed to do some honour to the one man who would have promoted her nearly vanished scheme, and this work she trusted to offer for a vestment to be used at his burial Mass. Many a cherished plan was resigned, many an act of self-negation uttered, as she bent over the dainty web; many an entreaty breathed, that her moment's wandering of fancy might not be reckoned against her, but that she might be aided to keep the promise of her infancy, and devote herself undivided to the direct service of God and of His poor, be it in ever so humble a station.

Here she sat alone, when steps approached, the door opened, and of all people he stood before her whom she least wished to see, the young Lord of Glenuskie.

Amazed as she was, she betrayed no confusion, and merely rose, saying quietly, 'This is an error. I will show you Madame's apartment.'

But Malcolm, who had begun by looking far more confused than she, cried earnestly, 'One moment, lady. I came not willingly; the Countess sent for me to her. But since I am here—listen while Heaven gives me strength to say it—I will trouble you never again. I am come to a better mind. Oh, forgive me!'

'What are you here then for, Sir?' said Esclairmonde, with the same defensive dignity.

'My king sent me, against my will, on a mission to the Queen,' panted Malcolm. 'I am forced to wait here; or, lady, I should have been this day doing penance for my pursuit of you. Verily I am a penitent. Mayhap Heaven will forgive me, if you will.'

'If I understand you aright, it is well,' said Esclairmonde, still gravely and doubtfully.

'It is so indeed,' protested Malcolm, with a terrible wrench to his heart, yet a sensation of freeing his conscience. 'Fear me no longer now. After that which I saw at Vincennes, I know what it is to be on the straight path, and—oh! what it is to have fallen from it. How could I dream of dragging you down to be with one so unworthy, becoming more worthless each day? Lady, if I never see you more, pardon me, pray for me, as a saint for a poor outcast on earth!'

Charlotte M. Yonge

'Hush,' said Esclairmonde; 'I am no saint—only a maiden pledged. But, Sir, I thank you fervently. You have lightened my heart of one of my fears.'

Malcolm could not but be cheered by being for once spoken to by her in so friendly a tone; and he added, gravely and resolutely: 'My suit, then, I yield up, lady— yield for ever. Am I permitted once to kiss that fair and holy hand, as I resign my presumptuous hopes thereof?'

'Mayhap it were wiser left undone,' said Esclairmonde. 'My mind misgives me that this meeting is planned to bring us into trouble. Farewell, my lord.'

As she had apprehended, the door was flung back, and Countess Jaqueline rushed in, clasping her hands in an affectation of merry surprise, as she cried, 'Here they are! See, Monseigneur! No keeping doves apart!'

'Madame,' said Esclairmonde, turning on her with cold dignity, 'I have been thanking Monsieur de Glenuskie for having resigned the suit that I always declared to be in vain.'

'You misunderstood, Clairette,' said Jaqueline. 'No gentleman ever so spoke! No, no; my young lord has kept his promise to me, and I will not fail him.'

'Madame,' faltered Malcolm, 'I came by command of the King of Scots.'

'So much the better,' cried Jaqueline. 'So he can play into our hands, for all his grandeur! It will lose him his wager, though! Here is bride—there is priest—nay, bishop!' pointing to him of Therouenne, who had accompanied her, but hitherto had stood silent.

'Madame,' said Malcolm, 'the time and state of the household forbid.'

'*Ma foi*! What is that to us? King Henry is neither our brother nor our father; and Catherine will soon laugh at it as a good joke.'

'Nay,' said the Bishop, with more propriety, 'it is the contract and troth-plight alone that could take place at present. That secure, the full solemnities will await a fitting time; but it is necessary that the troth be exchanged at once.'

'Monseigneur,' said Esclairmonde, 'mine is in other keeping.'

'And, Monseigneur,' added Malcolm, 'I have just told the lady that I repent of having fallen from my vocation, and persecuted her.'

'How, Sir!' said the Bishop, turning on him; 'do you thus lightly treat a lady of the house of Luxemburg? Beware! There are those who know how to visit an insult on a malapert lad, who meddles with the honour of the family.'

'Be not threatened, Lord Malcolm,' said Esclairmonde, with a gleam in her eye.

And Malcolm was Stewart enough to answer with spirit: 'My lord, I will meet them if needed. This lady is so affianced, that it is sacrilege to aspire to her.'

'Ah!' said the Bishop, in an audible aside to the giggling Countess: 'this comes of her having thrown herself at the youth's head. Now he will no more of her.'

Crimson with wrath, and also with a wild sense of hope

Charlotte M. Yonge

that the obligation had become absolute, Malcolm made a vehement incoherent exclamation; but Esclairmonde retained her composure.

'Monseigneur and Madame both know better,' she said. 'This is but another menace.'

'Peace, minion,' said the Bishop of Therouenne, 'and listen to me. If this young gentleman, after professing himself willing to wed you, now draws back, so much the worse for him. But if you terrify him out of it with your humours, then will my brother St. Pol and the Duke of Burgundy soon be here, with no King of England to meddle; and by St. Adrian, Sir Boemond will be daunted by no airs, like Monsieur there. A bride shall you be, Esclairmonde de Luxemburg, ere the week is out, if not to Monsieur de Glenuskie, to the Chevalier Boemond de Bourgogne.'

'Look not at me,' said Jaqueline. 'I am weary of your contumacy. All I shall do is to watch you well. I've suspected for some days that you were concocting mischief with the little Montagu; but you'll not escape again, as when I was fool enough to help you.'

The two stood a few paces apart, where they had been discovered; Esclairmonde's eyes were closed, her hands clasped, as if in silent prayer for aid.

'Girl—your choice!' said the Bishop, peremptorily. 'Wedlock on the spot to this gentleman, or to Sir Boemond a week hence.'

Esclairmonde was very white.

'My will shall not consent to a present breach of vow to save a future one,' she said, in a scarce audible voice.

A sudden thought darted into Malcolm's mind. With colour flooding his face to his very temples, he stepped nearer to her, and said, in a tremulous under-tone, 'Lady, trust me.'

The Bishop withheld Jaqueline almost by force, so soon as he saw that the pair were whispering together, and that there was something of relaxation in Esclairmonde's face as she looked up at him in silent interrogation.

He spoke low, but solemnly and imploringly. 'Trust me with your plight, lady, and I will restore it when you are free.'

Hardly able to speak, she however murmured, 'You will indeed do this?'

'So help me Heaven!' he said, and his eyes grew large and bright; he held his head with the majesty of his race.

'Heaven has sent you,' said Esclairmonde, with a long sigh, and holding out her hand to him, as though therewith she conferred a high-souled woman's full trust.

And Malcolm took it with a strange pang of pain and exultation at the heart. The trust was won, but the hope of earthly joy was gone for ever.

The Countess broke out with a shout of triumph: 'There, there! they have come to reason at last. There's an end of her folly.'

Malcolm felt himself a man, and Esclairmonde's protector, all at once, as he stood forth, still holding her hand.

'Monseigneur,' he said, 'this lady consents to intrust her

troth to me, and be affianced to me'—his chest heaved, but he still spoke firmly—'on condition that no word be spoken of the matter, nor any completion of the rite take place until the mourning for King Henry be at an end;' and, at a sort of shiver from Esclairmonde, he added: 'Not for a year, by which time I shall be of full age.'

'A strange bridegroom!' said Jaqueline; 'but maybe you do well to get her on what terms you can. Do you agree, Monseigneur?'

In truth, Monseigneur may have been relieved that the trial of strength between him and his ward had thus terminated. He was only anxious to have the matter concluded.

The agreement, binding Malcolm to accept a stated number of crowns in instalments, as the value of Esclairmonde's lands, under the guarantee of the Duke of Burgundy and King James of Scotland, had all been long ago signed, sealed, and secured; and there was nothing to prevent the *fiancailles*, or espousals, from taking place at once.

It was a much more real ceremony than a mere betrothal, being, in fact, in the eye of the civil law a marriage, though the full blessing and the sacramental words of union were deferred for the completion of the rite. It was the first part of the Marriage Service, binding the pair so indissolubly to one another, that neither could enter into wedlock with any one else as long as the other lived— except, of course, by Papal dispensation; and in cases of stolen weddings, it was all that was deemed needful.

All therefore that remained to be done was, that the Bishop summoned his chaplain to serve as a witness and as scribe; and then the two young people, in their deep mourning dresses, standing before the Bishop, vowed to belong to none other than to one another, and the betrothal rings being produced, were placed on their fingers, and their hands were clasped. Malcolm's was steady, as he felt Esclairmonde's rest in his untrembling, but with the quietness of one who trusted all in all where she trusted at all.

'Poor children! they have all to learn,' hilariously shouted the Countess. 'They have forgotten the kiss!'

'Will you suffer it, my sister?' said Malcolm, with burning cheeks.

'My brother and my guardian!' responded Esclairmonde, raising the white brow to his lips.

At that moment back went the door, and in flew Alice Montagu, crying aloud, 'Clairette! the Queen—oh, Madame, your pardon! but I am sent for Esclairmonde. The Queen is in worse fits than ever. Sir Lewis can't get the ring from her. They think she will rave like her father presently! Come!'

Esclairmonde could only hurry away at this; while Alice, grasping her hand, continued:

'Oh, have they been persecuting you? I dreaded it when I saw yon little wretch; but—oh, Esclairmonde, what is this?' in an utterly changed voice.

'He holds my faith in trust. He will restore it,' said Esclairmonde, hurriedly.

But Lady Montagu spoke not another word; and, indeed, they were hard upon the English queen's rooms, whence they already heard hysterical screams of passion.

Charlotte M. Yonge

Jaqueline had immediately set forth in the same direction out of curiosity; and Malcolm in much anxiety, since the mission that he had been cautioned to guard so jealously seemed in danger of being known everywhere. He had himself been allowed to stand by the Queen's bedside, and rehearse James's message; but when he had further hinted of his being sent by Bedford to bring the ring, the Queen, perhaps at the mention of the brother-in-law, pouted, knew nothing of any ring, and supposed M. le Duc meant to strip her, a poor desolate widow, of all her jewels.

Then Malcolm had spoken in private with Sir Lewis Robsart, who knew the ring was among her jewels, and promised to get it for him as soon as was possible; and it was while waiting for this that Malcolm had been summoned to the Countess of Hainault's apartments.

But ere Sir Lewis could get the ear of the Queen, as he now told Malcolm, her mother had been with her. Catherine was dull, jealous, unwilling to part with anything, but always easily coaxed over. Her mother Isabeau had, on the other hand, a good deal of low cunning and selfishness, and understood how valuable an instrument might be a duplicate seal of a deceased monarch. Therefore she instigated her daughter to deny that she possessed it, and worked her up into a state of impracticability, in which Sir Lewis Robsart was unable to deal with her, and only produced so wild a tempest of passion as perfectly to appal both him and her ladies.

That the Duke of Bedford had sent for a ring, which she would not give up, was known over the whole palace; the only matter still not perhaps known was, what was the value of that individual ring.

Robsart, however, promised to exonerate Malcolm from having shown any indiscretion; he charged it all on himself for having left his Queen for an instant to Isabeau.

Meanwhile, Malcolm and he, with other nobles and ladies, waited, waited in the outer chamber, listening to the fearful storm of shrieks and cries, till they began to spend themselves and die away; and then they heard Esclairmonde's low voice singing her lullaby, and every one breathed freer, as though relieved, and murmurs of conversation rose again. Malcolm moved across to greet the Lady Montagu; and though she looked at him with all the disdain her little gentle face could accomplish, he had somehow a spring and strength in him that could not now be brow-beaten.

He bent over her, and said, 'Lady, I see you know all. It is but a trust.'

'If you so treat it, Sir, you will do well,' responded the young matron, with as much stern gravity as she could assume; the fact being that she longed to break down and cry heartily, that Esclairmonde should so far have failed, and become like other people.

Long, long they waited—Malcolm with a strange dreamy feeling at his heart, neither triumph nor disappointment, but something between both, and peace above all. Dinner was served in the hall; the company returned to the outer apartment, yet still all was silent within; till at last, late in the afternoon, there came a black figure forth from under the black hangings, and Esclairmonde, turning to Lady Warwick, said, 'The Queen is awake, and desires her ladies' presence.' And then coming towards Malcolm, who was standing near Sir Lewis Robsart, she placed in his hand the signet-ring.

Both, while the attendants of the Queen filed back into her chamber, eagerly demanded how the ring had

Charlotte M. Yonge

been obtained.

'Poor lady!' said Esclairmonde, 'she was too much spent to withhold anything. She was weak and exhausted with cries and tears; and when she had slept, she was as meek as a lamb; and there was no more ado but to bid her remember that the blessed King her lord would have bidden her let the ring be broken up at once, lest it should be used so as to harm her son.'

That Esclairmonde had prevailed by that gentle force of character which no one could easily resist, could not, however, be doubted for a moment; and a fresh thrill of amazement, and almost of joy, came over Malcolm at the sense that he had become the protector of such a being, and that in a sort she belonged to him, and was in his power, having trusted herself to him.

Robsart advised, and Esclairmonde concurred in the counsel, that Lord Glenuskie should set forth for Vincennes immediately, before there should be time for any more cabals, or for Queen Isabeau to have made her daughter repent of having delivered up the signet-ring.

Malcolm therefore at once took leave of his affianced, venturing to kiss her hand as he looked wistfully in her face, and said, 'Dear lady, how shall I thank you for this trust?'

Esclairmonde gave her sweet grave smile, as she said, 'To God's keeping I commend you, Sir.' She would not even bid him be true to his trust; it would have seemed to her to insult him in whom her confidence was placed, and she only added: 'I shall ever bless you for having saved me. Farewell! Now am I bound for ever to pray for you and your sister.'

And it would be impossible to tell how the sense of Esclairmonde's trust, and of the resolute self-denial it would require of him, elevated Malcolm's whole tone, and braced his mind. The taking away of his original high purpose had rendered him as aimless and pleasure-loving as any ordinary lad; but the situation in which he now stood—guarding this saintly being for her chosen destiny, at the expense of all possible earthly projects for his own happiness or ambition—was such as to bring out that higher side of his nature that had well-nigh collapsed. As he stood alone in the ante-room, waiting until his horse and escort should be ready for his return, a flood of happiness seemed to gush over him. Esclairmonde was no more his own, indeed, than was King Henry's signet; but the trust was very precious, and gave him at least the power of thinking of her as joined by a closer link than even his sister Lilias. And towards her his conscience was again clear, for this very betrothal put marriage out of the question for him, and was a real seal of his dedication. He only felt as if his heart ought not to be so light and peaceful, while his penance was still unsaid, his absolution not yet pronounced.

Charlotte M. Yonge

CHAPTER XV

THE TRUST

James of Scotland and John of Bedford sat together in the twilight of a long and weary day, spent by the one in standing like a statue at the head of his deceased friend as a part of the pageant of the lying-in-state in the chapel, whither multitudes had crowded throughout the day to see the 'mighty victor, mighty lord, lie low on his funeral couch;' the nobles gazing with a certain silent and bitter satisfaction at him who had not only broken the pride of their country, but had with his iron hand repressed their own private exactions, while the poor and the peasants openly bewailed him as the father and the friend who had stood between them and their harsh feudal lords. By the other, the hours had passed in the press of toil and perplexity that had fallen on him as the yet unaccredited representative of English power in France, and in writing letters to those persons at home from whom he must derive his authority. The hour of rest and relaxation was welcome to both, though they chiefly spent it each leaning back in his chair in silence.

'Your messenger is not come back,' said Bedford, presently, rousing himself.

'It may have been no easy task,' replied James, not

however without uneasiness.

'I would,' said Bedford, presently, 'that I had writ the matter straight to Robsart. The lad is weak, and may be tampered with.'

'He knows that I have pledged my honour for him,' said James.

Bedford's thin lips moved at the corners.

'Nay,' said James, not angrily, 'the youth hath in some measure disappointed me. The evil in him shot forth faster than the good under this camp life; but methinks there is in him a certain rare quality of soul that I loved him for at the first, and though it hath lain asleep all this time, yet what he hath now seen seemed to me about to work the change in him.'

'It may be so,' said Bedford; 'and yet I would I had not consented to his going where that woman of Hainault might work on him to fret the Lady Esclairmonde.'

James started somewhat as he remembered overruling this objection of Malcolm's own making. 'She cannot have the insolence,' he said.

At that moment a hasty step approached; the door was opened with scant ceremony, and Ralf Percy, covered from head to foot with blood, hurried in breathless and panting.

'My lord Duke, your license! Here is Malcolm Stewart set upon in the forest by robbers and stabbed!'

'Slain? Dead?' cried both princes, springing up in horror.

Charlotte M. Yonge

'Alive still—in the chapel—asking for you, my lord,' said Percy. 'He bade us lay him there at the King's feet; and as it was the readiest way to a priest, we did his bidding.'

'My poor Malcolm!' sighed James; and he and Bedford hastened to obey the summons.

There was time on the way for Ralf Percy to give them the particulars. 'We had gone forth—Trenton, Kitson, altogether some half-dozen of us—for a mouthful of air in the forest after our guard all day in the chapel, when about a mile from the Castle we heard a scuffle, and clashing of arms. So breaking through the thicket, we saw a score of fellows on horseback fully armed, and in the midst poor Glenuskie dragged to the ground and struggling hard with two of them. We drew our swords, hallooed, and leapt out; and the knaves never stayed to see how many of us there were, but made off like the dastards they were, but not till one had dealt poor Stewart this parting stroke. He hath been bleeding like a sheep all the way home, and hath scarce spoken but a thanksgiving for our having come in time, as he called it, and to ask for Dr. Bennet and the Duke.'

The words brought them to the door of the chapel, where for a time the chants around King Henry had paused in the agitation of the new arrival. As the black and white crowd of priests and monks opened and made way for the King and Duke, they saw, in the full light of the wax tapers, laid on a pile of cushions not far from King Henry's feet, the figure of Malcolm, his riding-gown open at the breast, and kerchiefs dyed and soaked with blood upon it; the black of his garments and hair enhancing the ghastly whiteness of his face, and yet an air of peace and joy in the eyes and in the folded hands, as Dr. Bennet and another priest stood over him, administering those abbreviated rites of farewell blessing which the Church sanctioned in cases of sudden and violent death. The princes both stood aside, and presently Malcolm faintly said, 'Thank God! I trusted to His mercy to pardon! Now all would be well could I but see the Duke.'

'I am here, dear youth,' said Bedford, kneeling on one side of him; while James, coming to the other side, spoke to him affectionately; but to him Malcolm only replied by a fond clasp of the hand, giving his sole attention to Bedford, to whom he held the signet.

'It has cost too much,' said Bedford, sadly.

'Oh, Sir, this would be naught, save that I am all that lies between her—the Lady Esclairmonde—and Boemond of Burgundy;' and as at that moment Bedford saw the gold betrothal ring on the finger, his countenance lost something of the pitying concern it had worn. Malcolm detected the expression, and rallying his powers the more, continued: 'Sir, there was no help—they vowed that she must choose between Boemond and me. On the faith of a dying man, I hold her troth but in trust; I pledged myself to her to restore it when her way is clear to her purpose. She would never be mine but in name. And now who will save her? My life alone is between her and yonder wolf. Oh, Sir Duke, promise me to save her, and I die content.'

'This is mere waste of time!' broke in the Duke. 'Where are the knave chirurgeons?—See, James, if the lad dies, 'twill be from mere loss of blood; there is no inward bleeding; and if there be no more loitering, he will do well.'

And seeing the surgeons at hand, he would have risen to make way, but Malcolm held him fast, reiterating, 'Save her, Sir.'

Charlotte M. Yonge

'If your life guards her, throw it not away by thus dallying,' said Bedford, disengaging himself; while Malcolm groaned heavily, and turned his heavy eyes to his royal friend, who said kindly, 'Fear not, dear cousin; either thou wilt live, or he will be better than his word.'

'God will guard her, I know,' said Malcolm; 'and oh! my own dear lord, I need not ask you to be the brother to my poor sister you have been to me. At least all will be clear for her and Patie!'

'I trust not yet,' said James, smiling in encouragement. 'Thou wilt live, my faithful laddie.'

Malcolm was spent and nearly fainting by this time, and all his reply was a few gasps of 'Only say you pardon me all, my lord, and will speak for *her* to the Duke! ask *her* prayers for me!' and as James sealed his few words of reply with a kiss, he closed his eyes, and became unconscious; in which state he was conveyed to his bed.

'You might have set his mind at rest,' said James, somewhat hurt, to the Duke.

'Who? I!' said Bedford. 'I cannot stir a finger that could set us at enmity with Burgundy, for any lady in the land. Moreover, if she have found means to secure herself once, she can do so again.'

'I would you could have been more kind to my poor boy,' said James.

'Methought I was the most reasonably kind of you all! Had it not been mere murder to keep him there prating and bleeding, I had asked of him what indiscretion had blown the secret and perilled the signet. No robbers were those between Paris and Vincennes in our midst, but men who knew what he bore. I'll never—'

Bedford just restrained himself from saying, 'trust a Scot again;' but his manner had vexed and pained James, who returned to Malcolm, and left him no more till called by necessity to his post as King Henry's chief mourner, when the care of him was left to Patrick Drummond and old Bairdsbrae; and Malcolm was a very tranquil patient, who seemed to need nothing but the pleasure of looking at the ring on his finger. The weapon had evidently touched no vital part, and he was decidedly on the way to recovery, when on the second evening Bedford met James, saying: 'I have seen Robsart. It was no indiscretion of young Glenuskie's. It was only what comes of dealing with women. Can I see the boy without peril to him?'

Malcolm was so much better, that there was no reason against the Duke's admission, and soon Bedford's falcon-face looked down on him in all its melancholy.

'Thanks, my Lord Glenuskie,' he said; 'I thought not to be sending you on a service of such risk.'

'It was a welcome service,' said Malcolm.

Bedford's brows knitted themselves for a moment as he said, 'I came to ask whether you deem that this hurt was from a common robber or *routier*.'

'Assuredly not,' said Malcolm, but very low; and looking up into his face, as he added, 'This should be for your ear alone, Sir.'

They were left alone, and the Duke said: 'I have heard from Robsart how the ring was obtained. You may spare that part of the story.'

Charlotte M. Yonge

'Sir,' said Malcolm, 'when the Lady Esclairmonde' (for he was not to be balked of dwelling on that name with prolonged delight) 'had brought me the ring, Sir Lewis Robsart advised my setting forth without loss of time.'

'So he told me,' said the Duke; 'and likewise that you took his words so literally as to set out with only three followers.'

'Ay, Sir; but he knew not wherefore. My escort had gone forth into the city, and while they were being collected, a message bade me to the Lady Esclairmonde's presence. I went, suspecting naught, but I found myself in presence of Madame of Hainault, and of a veiled lady—who, my Lord—' He paused. 'She was broad in form, and had a trick of gasping as though over-fat.'

Bedford nodded. Every one knew Queen Isabeau by these tokens.

'She scarce spoke, my Lord; but the Countess Jaqueline pretended to be in one of her merry moods. She told me one good turn deserved another, and that, as in gratitude and courtesy bound, I must do her the favour of either lending her the signet, or, if I would not let it out of my hands, of setting it to a couple of parchments, which she declared King Henry had promised to grant.'

'The false woman!'

'Sir, words told not on her. She laughed and clapped her hands at whatever I said of honour, faith, or trust. She would have it that it was a jest—nay, romping fashion, she seized my hand, which I let her have, knowing it was only my own seal that was on it. Never was I so glad that the signet being too small for my fingers, it was in my bosom.'

'Knew you what the parchments bore?' asked, Bedford, anxiously.

'One—so far as I could see—was of the Duke of Orleans' liberty,' said Malcolm. 'The other—pardon me, Sir—it bore the names of Duke Humfrey and Countess Jaqueline.'

'The shameless wanton!' broke forth Bedford. 'How did you escape her at last, boy?'

'Sir,' said Malcolm, turning as red as loss of blood permitted, 'she had not kept her hands off me; therefore when she stood between me and the door, I told her that discourtesy was better than trust-breaking, and while she jeered at my talking out of a book of chivalry, I e'en took her by the hands, lifted her aside, opened the door, ran down-stairs, and so to the stables, where I mounted with the only three men I could get together.'

Bedford could not but laugh, as he added, 'Bravely done, Lord Malcolm; but, I fear me, she will never forgive you. What next?'

'I left word for the other fellows to join us at the hostel by the gate, and tarried for them till I feared being here after the gates were fast; then set out without them, and rode till, just within the forest, a band of men, how many I cannot tell, were on us, and before my sword was well drawn they had surrounded me, and seized my bridle. One of them bade me submit quietly, and they would not harm me, if I would yield up that which I wist of. I said I would sooner yield my life than my trust; whereupon they mastered me, and dragged me off my horse, and were rifling me, when I—knowing the Flemish accent of that drunken fellow of the Countess's—called out, "Shame on you, Ghisbert!" Then it was that he stabbed me, even at

Charlotte M. Yonge

the moment when the holy Saints sent brave Percy and the rest to rush in upon them.'

'You are sure it was Ghisbert?' repeated Bedford, anxiously.

'As certain as a man's voice can make me,' said Malcolm. 'Methinks, had I not named him, he would perhaps have bound me to a tree, and left it to be thought that they were but common thieves.'

'Belike,' said Bedford, thoughtfully. 'We are beholden to you, my Lord Glenuskie; the whole state of England is beholden to you for the saving of the confusion and evils the loss of that ring would have caused. You can keep counsel, I wot well. Then let all this matter of the Queen and Countess rest a secret.'

Malcolm looked amazed; and Bedford added: 'I cannot quarrel with the woman, nor banish her from Court. Did we accuse her, Holland would become Armagnac; nor is she subject of ours, to have justice done on her. It is for her interest to hush the matter up, and it must be ours too. If that knave Ghisbert ever gives me the chance, he shall hang like a dog; but for the rest—' he shrugged his shoulders.

'And,' said Malcolm, 'Ghisbert only meant to serve his lady. Any vassal of mine would do the like for me or my sister.'

Bedford half smiled; then sighed and said: 'Once we were like to get laws more obeyed than lords; but that is all over now! Yet you, young Sir, have seen a great pattern; you will have great powers!'

'Sir,' interrupted Malcolm, 'I pray you believe me, great

powers I shall not have. As I told you last night, I do but hold this precious troth in trust! It must be a secret, or it would not save her; but you—oh, Sir! you will believe that!'

'If it be so,' said Bedford, gravely, 'it is too sacred a trust to be spoken of. You will deserve greater honour if you keep your word, than ever you will receive from the world. Farewell—and recover fast.'

Malcolm did not meet with much encouragement from the few to whom he thought fit to confide the conditions of his espousal. The King allowed that he could not have acted otherwise, but was concerned at it, because of the hindrance that might for years be interposed in the way of his welfare; and secretly hoped that Malcolm, in his new capacity, would so gain on Esclairmonde's esteem and gratitude, as to win her affection, and that by mutual consent they would lay aside their loftier promises, and take up their espousal where they had left it.

And what James secretly desired, Sir Patrick Drummond openly recommended. In his eyes, Malcolm would be no better than a fool if he let his ladye-love, with all her lands, slip through his fingers, when she was lawfully his own. Patrick held that a monastery was a good place to be nursed in if wounded, and a convenience for disposing of dull or weakly younger sons; and he preferred that there should be some holy men to pray for those who did the hard and bloody work of the world; but he had no desire that any one belonging to himself should plunge into extra sanctity; and the more he saw Malcolm developing into a man among men, the more he opposed the notion of his dedicating himself.

A man! Yes; Malcolm was rising from his bed notably advanced in manliness. As the King's keen eye had seen from the first, and as Esclairmonde had felt, there was an elevation, tenderness, and refinement in his cast of character, which if left to his natural destiny would have either worn out his life early in the world, or carried him to the obscure shelter of a convent. In the novelty of the secular life, and temptations of all kinds, dread of ridicule, and the flood of excitements which came with reviving health, that very sensitiveness led him astray; and the elevated aims fell with a heavier fall when diverted from heavenly palaces to earthly ones. Self-reproach and dejection drove him further from the right course, and in proportion to the greater amount of conscience he had by nature, his character was the more deteriorating. His deeds were far less evil in themselves than those of many of his companions, but inasmuch as they were not thoughtless in him, they were injuring him more. But the sudden shock of Patrick's danger roused him to a new sense of shame. King Henry's death had lifted his mind out of the earthly atmosphere, and then the treasure of Esclairmonde's pure and perfect trust seemed to be the one thing to be guarded worthily and truly. It gave him weight, drew him out of himself, lifted him above the boyish atmosphere of random self-indulgence and amusement. To be the protector who should guard her vows for the heavenly Bridegroom to whom her soul was devoted, was indeed a championship that in his eyes could only have befitted Sir Galahad; and a Galahad would he strive to be, so long as that championship held him to the secular life. James and Bedford both told him he had won his spurs, and should have them on the next fit occasion; but he had ceased to care for knighthood, save in that half-consecrated aspect which he thought would render his guardianship less unmeet for Esclairmonde.

She had not shunned to send him a kind greeting on hearing of his wound, and by way of token a fresh leaf of vellum with a few more of those meditations from

Zwoll—meditations that he spelled over from Latin into English, and dwelt upon in great tranquillity and soothing of spirit during the days that he was confined to his bed.

These were not many. He was on his feet by the time the funeral cavalcade was in readiness to move from Vincennes to convey Henry of Monmouth to his last resting-place in Westminster Abbey. Bedford could not be spared to return to England, and was only to go as far as Calais; and James of Scotland was therefore to act as chief mourner, attended by his own small personal suite.

Sir Patrick Drummond—though, shrugging his shoulders, he muttered that he should as soon have thought of becoming mourner at the foul fiend's funeral as at the King of England's—could not object to swell the retinue of his sovereign by his knighthood; and though neither he nor Malcolm were in condition for a campaign, both could ride at the slow pace of the mournful procession.

The coffin was laid on a great car, drawn by four black horses, and surmounted by Henry's effigy, made in boiled leather and coloured to the life, robed in purple and ermine, crown on head, sceptre and orb in either hand. The great knights and nobles rode on each side, carrying the banners of the Saints; and close behind came James and Bedford, each with his immediate attendants; then the household officers of the King, Fitzhugh his chamberlain, Montagu his cup-bearer, Ralf Percy and his other squires, and all the rest. Four hundred men-at-arms in black armour, with lances pointed downwards, formed the guard behind; and the vanguard was of clergy, robed in white, bearing banners and wax lights, and chanting psalms. At the border of every parish, all the ecclesiastics thereto appertaining, parochial, chantry, and monastic, turned out to meet the procession with their tapers; escorted it to the principal church; performed Mass there,

　　　　Charlotte M. Yonge

if it were in the forenoon; and then accompanied the coffin to the other limit of their ground, and consigned it to the clerks of the next parish. At night, the royal remains always rested in a church, guarded by alternate watches of the English men-at-arms, and sung over by the local clergy, while the escort were quartered in the town, village, or abbey where the halt chanced to be made. Very slow was this progress; almost like a continual dream was that long column, moving, moving on—white in front, black behind—when seen winding over a hill, or, sometimes, the banners peering over the autumn foliage of some thicket, all composed to profound silence and tardy measured tread; while the chants rose and fell with the breeze, like unearthly music. Many moved on more than half asleep; and others of the younger men felt like Ralf Percy, who, for all his real sorrow for the King, declared that, were it not for rushing out, morning and evening, for a bathe and a gallop, to fly a hawk or chase a hare, he should some day run crazed, blow out all the wax lights, or play some mad prank to break the intolerable oppression. Malcolm smiled at this; but to him, still in the dreamy inertness of recovery, this tranquil onward movement in the still autumn weather had some thing in it of healing influence; and the sweet chants, the continual offices of devotion, were accordant with his present tone of mind, and deepened the purpose he had formed.

Queen Catherine and her ladies joined the funeral march at Rouen, or rather followed it at a mile's interval; but the two trains kept apart, and only occasional messages were sent from one to the other. Some of the gentlemen, who had a wife or sister in the Queen's suite, would ride at nightfall to pay her a hasty visit; but Malcolm—though he longed to be sent—durst not intrude upon Esclairmonde; and the Duke of Bedford was not only forced to spend all the evening and half the night in business, but was not loth to put off the day of the meeting with his dear sister

Catherine—to say nothing of the 'Woman of Hainault.'

Therefore it was not until all had arrived at Calais, where a fleet was waiting to meet them, that any visits were openly made by the one party to the other.

Bedford and James went together to the apartments of the Queen, and while they saw her in private, Malcolm came blushing towards Esclairmonde, and was welcomed by her with a frank smile, outstretched hand, and kind inquiry after his recovery.

She treated him indeed as a brother, as one on whom she depended, and had really wished to see and arrange with. She told him that Alice Montagu and her husband were returning to England, and that her little friend had so earnestly prayed her to abide with her at Middleham for the present, that she had consented—'until such time as the way be open,' said Esclairmonde, with her steady patient smile.

Malcolm bowed his head. 'I am glad you will not be forced to be with your Countess,' he said.

'My poor lady! Maybe I have spoken too plainly. But I owe her much. I must ever pray for her. And you, my lord?'

'I,' said Malcolm, 'shall go to study at Oxford. Dr. Bennet intends returning thither to continue his course of teaching, and my king has consented to my studying with him. It will not cut me off, lady, from that which you permit me to be. King Henry and his brothers have all been scholars there.'

'I understand,' said Esclairmonde, slightly colouring. 'It is well. And truly I trust that matters may be so guided, that

Charlotte M. Yonge

care for me may not long detain you from more lasting vows—be they of heaven or earth.'

'Lady,' said Malcolm, earnestly, 'none who had been plighted to you *could* pledge himself to aught else save One above!'

Then, feeling in himself, or seeing in Esclairmonde's face, that he was treading on dangerous ground, he asked leave to present to her his cousin, Patrick Drummond: and this was accordingly done; the lady comporting herself with so much sweet graciousness, that the good knight, as they left the hall, exclaimed: 'By St. Andrew, Malcolm, if you let that maiden escape you now she is more than half-wedded to you, you'll be the greatest fool in broad Scotland. Why, she is a very queen for beauty, and would rule Glenuskie like a princess—ay, and defend the Castle like Black Agnes of Dunbar herself! If you give her up, ye'll be no better than a clod.'

Malcolm and Patrick had been borne off by James's quitting the Castle; Bedford remained longer, having affairs to arrange with the Queen. As he left her, he too turned aside to the window where Esclairmonde sat as usual spinning, and Lady Montagu not far off, but at present absorbed by her father, who was to remain in France.

One moment's hesitation, and then Bedford stepped towards the Demoiselle de Luxemburg, and greeted her. She looked up in his face, and saw its settled look of sad patient energy, which made it full ten years older in appearance than when they had sat together at Pentecost, and she marked the badge that he had assumed, a torn-up root with the motto, 'The root is dead.'

'Ah! my lord, things are changed,' she could not help

saying, as she felt that he yearned for comfort.

'Changed indeed!' he said; 'God's will be done! Lady,' he added, 'you wot of that which once passed between us. I was grieved at first that you chose a different protector in your need.'

'You *could* not, my lord,' faltered Esclairmonde, crimson as she never had been when speaking to Malcolm.

'No, I *could* not,' said Bedford; 'and, lady, my purpose was to thank you for the generous soul that perceived that so it is. You spared me from a cruel case. I have no self any longer, Esclairmonde; all I am, all I have, all I can, must be spent in guarding Harry's work for his boy. To all else I am henceforth dead; and all I can do is to be thankful, lady, that you have spared me the sorest trial of all, both to heart and honour.'

Esclairmonde's eyes were downcast, as she said, 'Heaven is the protector of those of true and kind purpose;' and then gathering courage, as being perfectly aware to whom Bedford must give his hand if he would conciliate Burgundy, she added, 'And, verily, Sir, the way of policy is this time a happy one. Let me but tell you how I have known and loved gentle Lady Anne.'

Bedford shook his head with a half smile and a heavy sigh. 'Time fails me, dear lady,' he said; 'and I cannot brook any maiden's praise, even from you. I only wait to ask whether there be any way yet left wherein I can serve you. I will strive to deal with your kinsmen to restore your lands.'

'Hold!' said Esclairmonde. 'Never for lands of mine will I have your difficulties added to. No—let them go! It was a vain, proud dream when I thought myself most humble, to become a foundress; and if I know my kinsmen, they will be too much angered to bestow on me the dower required by a convent. No, Sir; all I would dare to inquire would be, whether you have any voice in choosing the bedeswomen of St. Katharine's Hospital?'

'The bedeswomen! They come chiefly from the citizens, not from princely houses like yours!' said John, in consternation.

'I have done with princely houses,' said Esclairmonde. 'A Flemish maiden would be of no small service among the many whom trade brings to your port from the Netherlands, and my longing has ever been to serve my Lord through His poor and afflicted.'

'It is my father's widow who holds the appointments,' said John. 'Between her and me there hath been little good-will, but my dear brother's last act towards her was of forgiveness. She may wish to keep well with us of the Regency—and more like still, she will be pleased that one of so great a house as yours should sue to her. I will give you a letter to her, praying her to remember you at the next vacancy; and mayhap, if the Lady Montagu could take you to visit her, you could prevail with her! But, surely, some nunnery more worthy of your rank—'

'There is none that I should love so well,' said Esclairmonde, smiling. 'Mayhap I have learnt to be a vagabond, but I cannot but desire to toil as well as pray.'

'And you are willing to wait for a vacancy?'

'When once safe from my kinsmen, in England, I will wait under my kind Alice's wing till—till it becomes expedient that yonder gentleman be set free.'

'You trust him?' said Bedford.

'Entirely,' responded Esclairmonde, heartily.

'Happy lad!' half sighed the Duke; but, even as he did so, he stood up to bid the lady adieu—lingering for a moment more, to gaze at the face he had longed for permission to love—and thus take leave of all his youth and joy, addressing himself again to that burthen of care which in thirteen years laid him in his grave at Rouen.

As he left the Castle and came out into the steep fortified street, Ralf Percy came up to him, laughing. 'Here, my lord, are those two honest Yorkshire knights running all over Calais to make a petition to you.'

'What—Trenton and Kitson! I thought their year of service was up, and they were going home!'

'Ay, my lord,' said Kitson, who with his comrade had followed close in Percy's wake, 'we were going home to bid Mistress Agnes take her choice of us; but this morn we've met a pursuivant that is come with Norroy King-at-arms, and what doth he but tell us that no sooner were our backs turned, than what doth Mistress Agnes but wed—ay, wed outright—one Tom of the Lee, a sneaking rogue that either of us would have beat black and blue, had we ever seen him utter a word to her? A knight's lady—not to say two—as she might have been! So, my lord, we not being willing to go home and be a laughing-stock, crave your license to be of your guard as we were of King Harry's, and show how far we can go among the French.'

'And welcome; no good swords can be other than welcome!' said Bedford, not diverted as his brother would have been, but with a heartiness that never failed to win respectful affection.

Charlotte M. Yonge

Long did James and Bedford walk up and down the Castle court together, while the embarkation was going on. The question weighed on them both whether they should ever meet more, after eighteen years of youth spent together.

'Youth is gone,' said Bedford. 'We have been under a mighty master, and now God help us to do his work.'

'You!' said James; 'but for me—it is like to be the library and the Round Tower again.'

'Scarcely,' said Bedford, 'the Beauforts will never rest till Joan is on a throne.'

James smiled.

'Ay,' said Bedford, 'the Bishop of Winchester will be no small power, you will find. Would that I could throw up this France and come home, for he and Humfrey will clash for ever. James, an you love me, see Humfrey alone, and remind him that all the welfare of Harry's child may hang on his forbearance—on union with the Bishop. Tell him, if he ever loved the noblest brother that ever lived, to rein himself in, and live only for the child's good, not his own. Tell him that Bedford and Gloucester must be nothing henceforth—only heads and hands doing Harry's will for his babe. Oh, James, what can you tell Humfrey that will make him put himself aside?'

'You have writ to him Harry's words as to Dame Jac?'

'The wanton! ay, I have; and if you can whisper in his ear that matter of Malcolm and the signet, it might lessen his inclination. But,' he sighed, 'I have little hope, James; I see nothing for Lancaster but that which the old man at York invoked upon us!'

'Yet, when I look at you and Humfrey, and think of the contrast with my own father's brethren, I see nothing but hope and promise for England,' said James.

'We must do our best, however heavy-hearted,' said John of Bedford, pausing in his walk, and standing steadfast. 'The rod becomes a palm to those who do not freshly bring it on themselves. May this poor child of Harry's be bred up so that he may be fit to meet evil or good!'

'Poor child,' repeated James. 'Were he not there, and you—'

'Peace, James,' said Bedford; 'it is well that such a weight is not added! While I act for my nephew, I know my duty; were it for myself, methinks I should be crazed with doubts and questions. Well,' as a messenger came up with tidings that all was ready, 'fare thee well, Jamie. In you I lose the only man with whom I can speak my mind, or take counsel. You'll not let me gain a foe, as well as lose a friend, when you get home?'

'Never, in heart, John!' said the King. 'As to hand— Scotland must be to England what she will have her. Would that I saw my way thither! Windsor will have lost all that made captivity well-nigh sweet. And so farewell, dear brother. I thank you for the granting to me of this sacred charge.'

And so, with hands clasped and wrung together, with tears raining from James's eyes, and a dry settled melancholy more sad than tears on John's countenance, the two friends parted, never again to meet; each to run a course true, brave, and short—extinguished the one in bitter grief, the other in blood.

On All Saints' Day, while James stood with Humfrey of

Charlotte M. Yonge

Gloucester at the head of the grave at Westminster, where Henry's earthly form was laid to rest amid the kings his fathers, amid the wail of a people as sorrowful as if they knew all the woes that were to ensue, Bedford was in like manner standing over a grave at the Royal Abbey of St. Denis. He, the victor's brother, represented all the princely kindred of Charles VI. of France, and, with his heart at Westminster, filled the chief mourner's place over the king who had pined to death for his conqueror.

The same infant was proclaimed king over each grave— heir to France and England, to Valois and Lancaster. Poor child, his real heirloom was the insanity of the one and the doom of the other! Well for him that there was within him that holy innocence that made his life a martyrdom!

CHAPTER XVI

THE CAGE OPEN

More than a year had passed, and it was March when Malcolm was descending the stone stair that leads so picturesquely beneath the archway of its tower up to the hall of the college of St. Mary Winton, then *really* New College. He had been residing there with Dr. Bennet, associating with the young members of the foundation educated at Winchester, and studying with all the freshness of a recent institution. It had been a very happy time for him, within the gray stone walls that pleasantly recalled Coldingham, though without Coldingham's defensive aspect, and with ample food for the mind, which had again returned to its natural state of inquiring reflection and ardour for knowledge.

Daily Malcolm woke early, attended Matins and Mass in the chapel, studied grammar and logic, mastered difficult passages in the Fathers, or copied out portions for himself in the chamber which he as a gentleman commoner, as we should call him, possessed, instead of living in a common dormitory with the other scholars. Or in the open cloister he listened and took notes of the lectures of the fellows and tutors of the college, and seated on a bench or walking up and down received special instructions. Then ensued the meal, spread in the hall; the period of

Charlotte M. Yonge

recreation, in the meadows, or in the licensed sports, or on the river; fresh studies, chapel, and a social but quiet evening over the supper in the hall. All this was varied by Latin sermons at St. Mary's, or disputations and lectures by notable doctors, and public arguments between scholars, by which they absolutely fought out their degrees. There were few colleges as yet, and those resident in them were the *elite*; beyond, there was a great mob of scholars living in rooms as they could, generally very poor, and often very disorderly; but they did not mar the quiet semi-monastic stillness within the foundations, and to Malcolm it seemed as if the truly congenial home was opened.

The curriculum of science began to reveal itself to him with all the stages so inviting to a mind conscious of power and longing for cultivation. The books, the learned atmosphere, the infinite possibilities, were delightful to him, and opened a more delightful future. His meta-physical Scottish mind delighted in the scholastic arguments that were now first set before him, and his readiness, appreciation, and eager power of acquiring surprised his teachers, and made him the pride of New College.

When he looked back at his year of court and camp, he could only marvel at having ever preferred them. In war his want of bodily strength would make real distinction impossible; here he felt himself excelling; here was absolute enjoyment, and of a kind without drawback. Scholarship must be his true element and study: the deep universal study of the sisterhood of science that the University offered was his veritable vocation. Surely it was not without significance that the ring that shone on his finger betrothed him to Esclairmonde, the Light of the World; for though in person the maiden was never to be his own, she was the emblem to him of the pure virgin light of truth and wisdom that he would be for ever wooing, and winning only to see further lights beyond. Human nature felt a pang at the knowledge that he was bound to deliver up the ring and resign his connection with that fair and stately maiden; but the pain that had been sore at first had diminished under the sense that he stood in a post of generous trust, and that his sacrifice was the passport to her grateful esteem. He knew her to be with Lady Montagu, awaiting a vacancy at St. Katharine's, and this would be the signal for dissolving the contract of marriage, after which his present vision was to bestow Lilias upon Patrick, make over his estates to them, take minor orders, and set forth for Italy, there to pursue those deeper studies in theology and language for which Padua and Bologna were famous. It was many months since he had heard of Lilias; but this did not give him any great uneasiness, for messengers were few, and letter-writing far from being a common practice. He had himself written at every turning-point of his life, and sent his letters when the King communicated with Scotland; but from his sister he had heard nothing.

He had lately won his first degree as Bachelor of Arts, and was descending the stair from the Hall after a Lenten meal on salt fish, when he saw below him the well-known figure of King James's English servant, who doffing his cap held out to him a small strip of folded paper, fastened by a piece of crimson silk and the royal seal. It only bore the words:—

'To our right trusty and well-beloved Cousin the Lord Malcolm Stewart of Glenuskie this letter be taken.

'DEAR COUSIN,

'We greet you well, and pray you to come to us without loss of time, having need of you, we being a free man

Charlotte M. Yonge

and no captive.

'Yours, 'JAMES R.

'Written at the Castle of Windsor this St. David's Day,
1424.'

'A free man:' the words kept ringing in Malcolm's ears
while he hastened to obtain license from Warden John
Bonke, and to take leave of Dr. Bennet. He had not left
Oxford since the beginning of his residence there.
Vacations were not general dispersions when ways and
means of transit were so scarce and tardy, and Malcolm
had been long without seeing his king. Joy on his
sovereign's account, and his country's, seemed to swallow
up all other thoughts; as to himself, when he bade his
friends and masters farewell, he declared it was merely
for a time, and when they shook their heads and augured
otherwise, he replied: 'Nay, think you I could live in the
Cimmerian darkness yonder, dear sirs? Our poor country
hath nothing better than mere monastery schools, and
light of science having once shone on me, I cannot but
dwell in her courts for ever! Soon shall I be altogether her
son and slave!'

Nevertheless, Malcolm was full of eagerness, and pressed
on rapidly through the lanes between Oxford and
Windsor, rejoicing to find himself amid the noble trees of
the forest, over which arose in all its grandeur the Castle
and Round Tower, as beautiful though less unique than
now, and bearing on it the royal standard, for the little
King was still nursed there.

Under the vaulted gateway James—with Patrick and
Bairdsbrae behind him—met Malcolm, and threw his
arms round him, crying: 'Ay, kiss me, boy; 'tis a king and
no caitiff you kiss now! Another six weeks, and then for

the mountain and the moor and the bonnie north countree.'

'And why not for a month?' was Malcolm's question, as hand and eye and face responded heartily.

'Why? Why, because moneys must be told down, and treaties signed; ay, and Lent is no time for weddings, nor March for southland roses to travel to our cold winds. Ay, Malcolm, you see a bridegroom that is to be! Did you think I was going home without her?'

'I did not think you would be in such glee even at being free, my lord, if you were.'

'And now, Malcolm, ken ye of ony fair Scottish lassie—a cousin of mine ain, who could be had to countenance my bride at our wedding, and ride with us thereafter to Scotland?'

'I know whom your Grace means,' said Malcolm, smiling.

'An if you do, maybe, Malcolm, sin she bides not far frae the border, ye'd do me the favour of riding with Sir Patrick here, and bringing her to the bridal,' said the King, making his accent more home-like and Scottish than Malcolm had ever heard it before.

The happiness of that spring afternoon was surpassing. The King linked his arm into Malcolm's, and walked up and down with him on the slopes, telling him all that had led to this consummation; how Walter Stewart and his brothers had become so insolent and violent as to pass the endurance of their father the Regent, as well as of all honest Scots; and how, after secret negotiations and vain endeavours to obtain from him a pledge of indemnity for all that had happened, the matter had been at length opened with Gloucester, Beaufort, and the Council. The

Scottish nation, with Albany at the head, was really recalling the King. This was the condition on which Henry V. had always declared that he should be liberated; these were the terms on which he had always hoped to return; and his patience was at last rewarded. Bedford had sent his joyful consent, and all was now concluded. James was really free, and waited only for his marriage.

'I would not tell you, Malcolm, while there might yet be a slip between cup and lip,' said the King; 'it might have hindered the humanities; and yet I needed you as much when I was glad as when all seemed like to fail!'

'You had Patrick,' said Malcolm.

'Patrick's a tall and trusty fellow,' said the King, 'with a shrewd wit, and like to be a right-hand man; but there's something in you, Malcolm, that makes a man turn to you for fellow-feeling, even as to a wife.'

Nevertheless, the King and Patrick had grown much attached to each other, though the latter, being no lover of books, had wearied sorely of the sojourn at Windsor, which the King himself only found endurable by much study and reflection. Their only variety had been keeping Christmas at Hertford with Queen Catherine; 'sorry pastime,' as Drummond reported it to him, though gladdened to the King by Joan Beaufort's presence, in all her charms.

'The Demoiselle of Luxemburg was there too, statelier than ever,' said James. 'She is now at Middleham Castle, with the Lady Montagu, and you might make it your way northward, and lodge a night there. If you can win her consent, it were well to be wedded when we are.'

'Never shall I, my lord. I should not dare even to speak

of it.'

'It is well; but, Malcolm, you merit something from the damsel. You are ten times the man you were when she flouted you. If women were not mostly witless, you would be much to be preferred to any mere Ajax or Fierabras; and if this damsel should have come to the wiser mind that it were pity to be buried to the world—'

'Sir, I pray you say no more. I were forsworn to ask such a thing.'

'I bid you not, only I would I were there to see that all be not lost for want of a word in season; and it is high time that something be done. Here be letters from my Lord of Therouenne, demanding the performance of the contract ere our return home.'

'He cannot reach her here,' said Malcolm.

'No; but his outcry can reach your honour; and it were ill to have such a house as that of Luxemburg crying out upon you for breach of faith to their daughter.'

Malcolm smiled. 'That I should heed little, Sir. I would fain bear something for her.'

'Why, this is mere sublimated devoir, too fine for our gross understandings,' said James, ironically. 'Mayhap the sight of the soft roseate cheek may bring it somewhat down to poor human flesh and blood once more.'

'Once I was tempted, Sir,' said Malcolm, blushing deeply; 'but did I not know that her holiness is the guardian of her earthly beauty, I would not see her again.'

'Nay, there I command you,' said the King; 'soon I shall

have subjects enough; but while I have but half a dozen, I cannot be disobeyed by them! I bid you go to Middleham, and there I leave all to the sight.'

The King spoke gaily, and with such kind good-humour that Malcolm, humiliated by the thought of the past, durst not make fresh asseverations. James, in the supreme moment of the pure and innocent romance of which he was the hero, looked on love like his own as the highest crown of human life, and distrusted the efforts after the superhuman which too often were mere simulation or imitation; but a certain recollection of Henry's warnings withheld him from pressing the matter, and he returned to his own joys and hopes, looking on the struggles he expected with a strong man's exulting joy, and not even counting the years of his captivity wasted, though they had taken away his first youth.

'What should I have been,' he said, 'bred up in the tumults at home? What could I have known better than Perth? Nay, had I been sent home when I came to age, as a raw lad, how would one or other by fraud or force have got the upper hand, so as I might never have won it back. No, I would not have foregone one year of study—far less that campaign in France, and the sight of Harry in war and in policy.'

James also took Malcolm to see the child king, his little master. This, the third king of James's captivity, was now a fair creature of two years old. He trotted to meet his visitor, calling him by a baby name for brother, and stretching out his arms to be lifted up and fondled; for, as Dame Alice Boteller, his *gouvernante*, muttered, he knew the King of Scots better than he did his own mother.

A retinue had been already collected, and equipments prepared, so that there was no delay in sending forth

Malcolm and Patrick upon their northward journey. At the nearest town they halted, sending forward a messenger to announce their neighbourhood to the old Countess of Salisbury and her grand-daughter Lady Montagu, and to request permission to halt for 'Mothering Sunday' at the Castle.

In return a whole band of squires and retainers came forth, headed by the knightly seneschal, to invite Lord Malcolm Stewart and his companion to the Castle; whereupon Sir Patrick proceeded to don his gayest gown and chaperon, and was greatly scandalized that Malcolm's preparation consisted in putting on his black serge bachelor's gown and hood of rabbit's fur such as he wore at Oxford, looking, as Patrick declared, no better than a begging scholar. But Malcolm had made up his mind that if he appeared before Esclairmonde at all it should be in no other guise; and thus it was that he rode like a black spot in the midst of the cavalcade, bright with the colours of Nevil and of Montagu, and was marshalled up the broad stairs by the silver wand of the seneschal.

Lord Montagu had gone back to the wars; so the family at home consisted of the grand, stately, and distant old Countess of Salisbury, and her young grand-daughter, the Lady Montagu, with her three months' old son. Each had an almost royal suite of well-born dames and damsels in attendance, among whom the Demoiselle de Luxemburg alone was on an equality with the mistresses of the house. Even Queen Catherine's presence-chamber had hardly equalled the grand baronial ceremony of the hall, where sat the three ladies in the midst of their circle of attendants, male and female ranged on opposite sides; and old Lady Salisbury knew the exact number of paces that it befitted her and Lady Montagu to advance to receive the royal infusion of blood that flowed in the veins of my Lord of Glenuskie. And yet it was the cheek, and not the hand, that were offered in salutation by both ladies, as well as by Esclairmonde. Malcolm, however, only durst kneel on one knee and salute her hand, and felt himself burning with crimson as the touch and voice brought back those longings that, as James had said, proved him human still. He was almost glad that etiquette required him to hand the aged Countess to her seat and to devote his chief attention to her.

Punctilio reigned supreme in such a house as this. Nowhere had Malcolm seen such observance of cere-mony, save in the court of the Duke of Burgundy, and there it was modified by the presence of rough and ready warriors; but an ancient dame like Lady Salisbury thought it both the due and the safeguard of her son's honour, and exacted it rigorously of all who approached her.

Alice of Montagu had the sweet fragile look of a young mother about her, but her frightened fawn air was gone; she was in her home, had found her place, and held it with a simple dignity of her own, quite ready to ripen into all the matronly authority, without the severe formality, of her grand-dame.

She treated Malcolm with a gentle smiling courtesy such as she had never vouchsafed to him before, and all the shyness that had once made her silent was gone, when at the supper-table, and afterwards seated around the fire, the tidings of the camp and court were talked over with all the zest of those to whom King Harry's last campaign was becoming 'old times'; and what with her husband's letters and opinions, little Alice was really the best-informed as to the present state of things. Esclairmonde took her part in the conversation, but there was no opportunity of exchanging a private or personal word between her and Malcolm in a party of five, where one was as vigilant and grave-eyed as my Lady Salisbury.

However, the next was a peculiar day, the Fourth Sunday in Lent, called 'Mothering Sunday' because on that day it was originally the custom for offerings to be carried from all the country round to the cathedral or mother church on that day. This custom had been modified, but it was still the rule that all the persons, who at other times worshipped at the nearest monastery chapel or at a private chapel in their own houses, should on that day repair to their parish church, and there make a special offering at the Mass—that offering which has since become the Easter dues. It was a festival Sunday too—'Refreshing Sunday'—then, as now, marked by the Gospel on the feeding of the multitude; and from this, as well as from the name, the pretty custom had begun of offering the mother of each house her rich simnal cake, with some other gift from each of her children.

Hearing a pattering of feet in the early morning, Malcolm looked out and beheld a whole troop of small children popping in and out of a low archway. If he could have peeped in, he would have known how many simnals Ladies Esclairmonde and Alice were sending down—with something more substantial—to be given to mothers by the children who as yet had nothing to bring of their own.

But when the household assembled in the castle hall, they did see fair young Lady Montagu kneel at the chair of the grave old Countess, and hold up a silver dish, wherein lay the simnal, mixed, kneaded, and moulded by her own hands, and bearing on it a rich ruby clasp, sent by her father, the Earl, as his special gift to his mother on this Sunday.

And then, when the old lady, with glistening eyes, had spoken her blessing on the fair young head bent down before her, and the grandchild rose up, there was the pretty surprise for her of her little swaddled son, lying in

Charlotte M. Yonge

Esclairmonde's arms, and between the small fingers, that as yet knew not how to grasp, the tiny simnal; and moreover a fair pearl devised in like manner by the absent Sir Richard as a gift for his wife's first 'Mothering Sunday.' There was no etiquette here to hinder sweet Alice from passionately clasping her child, and covering him with kisses, as many for his father as for himself, as she laughed at the baby smiles and helpless gestures of the future king-maker, whose ambition and turbulence were to be the ruin of that fair and prosperous household, and bring the gentle Alice to a widowed, bereaved, and attainted old age.

Well that none there present saw the future, as she proudly claimed the admiration of Malcolm for her babe!

She was equipped for the expedition to the parish church, as likewise were Esclairmonde and almost all the rest; but the aged Countess could not encounter the cold March winds, and had a dispensation; and thus Alice, being the lady of the procession, contrived at the same time to call Sir Patrick to her side, and bid Lord Malcolm lead the Lady Esclairmonde.

For as the weather was dry and cold, Lady Montagu had chosen to go on foot; and a grand procession it was that she led, of gentlemen and ladies, two and two, in their bright dresses and adornments that delighted the eyes of the homely yeomen and their wives, flocking in from their homesteads with baskets of offerings, often in kind.

Meantime, Malcolm, holding the tips of Esclairmonde's fingers, durst not speak till she began: 'This is a devout and pious household—full of peace and good government.'

'And your time goes happily here?' asked Malcolm.

'Yes, it has been a peaceful harbour wherein to wait,' said Esclairmonde. 'And even if Alice were called to her husband in France, my Lady Countess will keep me with her till there be a vacancy for me at St. Katharine's.'

'Have you the promise from Queen Joan?'

'Yes,' replied Esclairmonde. 'The Countess had been a lady of hers, and wrought with her, so that whenever the post of bedeswoman is in her gift I shall be preferred to it.'

'You, the heiress, accept the charity!' Malcolm could not help exclaiming.

'The better for all remnants of pride,' returned the lady. 'And you, my lord, has it fared well with you?'

Malcolm, happy in her interest, poured forth all that he had to tell, and she listened as Esclairmonde alone could listen. There was something in her very expression of attention that seemed to make the speaker take out the alloy and leave only his purest gold to meet her ears. Malcolm forgot those throbs of foolish wild hope that had shot across him like demon temptations to hermit saints, and only felt that the creature of his love and reverence was listening benignly as he told her of the exceeding delight that he was unravelling in learned lore; how each step showed him further heights, and how he had come to view the Light of the World as the light of wisdom, to the research of which he meant to devote his entire life, among universities and manuscripts.

'The Light of Wisdom,' repeated Esclairmonde—'so it may be, for Christ is Heavenly Wisdom; but I doubt me if the Light of the World lies solely in books and universities.'

Charlotte M. Yonge

'Nay,' said Malcolm. 'Once I was fool enough to fancy it was the light of glory, calling knights to deeds of fame and chivalry. I have seen mine error now, and—oh, lady, what mean you? where should that light be, save in the writings of wise and holy men?'

'Methinks,' said Esclairmonde, 'that the light is there, even as the light is also before the eyes of the true knight; but it is not only there.'

'Where is it then?' said Malcolm. 'In helmet or in cowl, I am the sworn champion of the Light of the World.'

'The Light,' said Esclairmonde, looking upwards, 'the true Light of the World is the Blessed Saviour, the Heavenly Wisdom of God; and His champions find Him and serve Him in camp, cloister, or school, or wherever He has marked their path, so as they seek not their own profit or glory, and lay not up their treasure for themselves on earth.'

'Then surely,' said Malcolm, 'the hoards of deep study within the mind are treasures beyond the earth.'

'Your schoolmen speak of spirit, mind, and body,' said Esclairmonde—'at least so I, an ignorant woman, have been told. Should not the true Light for eternity lighten the spirit rather than the mind?'

Malcolm pondered and said: 'I thought I had found the right path at last!'

'Nay—never, never did I say otherwise,' cried Esclairmonde. 'To seek God's Light in good men's words, and pursue it, must be a blessed task. Every task must be blessed to which He leads. And when you are enlightened with that light, you will hold it up to others. When you have found the treasure, you will scatter it here, and so lay it up above.'

Esclairmonde's words were almost a riddle to Malcolm, but his reverence for her made him lay them up deeply, as he watched her kneeling at the Mass, her upturned face beaming with an angelic expression.

His mind was much calmed by this meeting. It had had an absolutely contrary effect to what King James had expected, by spiritualizing his love, and increasing that reverence which cast out its earthliness. That first throb which had been so keen at meeting, and knowing her not for him, had passed away in the refining of that distant worship he had paid her in those days of innocence.

Lady Montagu was quite satisfied with him now. He was the Malcolm of her first acquaintance, only without his foolish diffidence, and with a weight and earnestness that made him a man and not a boy; and she cordially invited him to bring his sister with him, and rest, on the way southward. He agreed most thankfully, since this would be the only opportunity of showing Esclairmonde and Lilias one to the other, as well as one of his own few chances of seeing Esclairmonde.

Once they must meet, that their promises might be restored the one to the other; but as the betrothal remained the lady's security, this could not be done till she became pledged at St. Katharine's. When the opportunity came, she was to send Malcolm a messenger, and he would come to her at once. Until then he promised that he would not leave Great Britain.

On Monday the cousins proceeded, coming after a time to the route by which Malcolm had ridden three years before, and where he was now at home in comparison

Charlotte M. Yonge

with Patrick. How redolent it was with recollections of King Harry, in all his gaiety and grace, ere the shock of his brother's death had fallen on him! At Thirsk, Malcolm told of the prowess and the knighthood of honest Trenton and Kitson, to somewhat incredulous ears. The two squires had been held as clownish fellows, and the sentiment of the country was that Mistress Agnes was well quit of them, and the rough guardianship by which they had kept off all other suitors. As mine host concluded, "Tis a fine thing to go to the wars.'

Hearing that Kitson's mother lived not a mile out of his way, Malcolm rode to the fine old moated grange, where he found her sitting at her spinning, presiding over a great plentiful household, while her second son, a much shrewder-looking man than Sir Christopher, managed the farm.

The travellers were welcomed with eager hospitality so soon as it was understood that they brought tidings of 'our Kit'; and Malcolm's story was listened to with tears of joy by the old lady, while the brother could not get over his amazement at hearing that Trenton and Kitson had become a proverb in the camp for oneness in friendship.

'Made it up with Will Trenton! And never fought it out! I'd never know our Kit again after that!'

His steady bravery, his knighthood, and the King's praise, his having assisted in saving Lord Glenuskie's life against such odds, did not seem to strike Wilfred Kitson half as much as the friendship with Trenton, and Malcolm did not think the regret was very great at the two knights having given up their intention of returning. 'Our Kit's' place seemed to have closed up behind him; Wilfred seemed to be too much master to be ready to give up to the elder brother; and even the mother had learnt to do without him. 'I'll warrant,' quoth she, 'that now he is a knight and got used to fine French ways, he'll think nothing good enow for him. And if he brought Will Trenton with him, I'd not sit at the board with the fellow.—But ye'll ride over, Wilfred, and take care the minx Agnes knows what she's lost. Ay, and if you knew of a safe hand, Sir, when the shearing is over I'd send the lad a purse of nobles to keep up his knighthood in the camp, forsooth.'

'Certes,' said Malcolm, as after a salt-fish dinner he mounted again, 'if honest Kitson knew, he would scarce turn back from the camp, where he is somebody. Shall we find ourselves as little wanted when we get home, Patie?'

Patrick drew himself up with a happy face of secret assurance. Nothing could make Lilias forsake him, he well knew.

At Durham they found their good friend Father Akefield, erst Prior of Coldingham, but who had been violently dispossessed by the House of Albany in favour of their candidate, Drax, about a year before, and was thankful to have been allowed with a few English monks to retire across the Border to the mother Abbey at Durham.

The good father could hardly believe his eyes when he beheld Malcolm, now a comely and personable young gentleman, less handsome and graceful indeed than many, but with all his painful personal peculiarities gone, with none of the scared, imploring look, but with a grave thoughtful earnestness about his face, as though all that once was timid and wandering was now fixed and steadfast.

Father Akefield could tell nothing of Lilias since his own expulsion, but as the Prioress of St. Abbs was herself a Drummond, and no one durst interfere with her, he had no alarms for her safety. But he advised the two gentlemen to go straight to St. Abbs, without showing themselves at Coldingham, lest Prior Drax, being in the Albany interest, should make any demur at giving her up to the care of the brother, who still wanted some months of his twenty-first year.

Accordingly they pushed on, and in due time slept at Berwick, receiving civilities from the English governor that chafed Patrick's blood, which became inflammable as soon as he neared the Border; and rising early the next morning, they passed the gates, and were on Scottish ground once more, their hearts bounding at the sense that it was their own land, and would soon be no more a land of misrule. With their knowledge of King James and his intentions, well might they have unlimited hopes for the country over which he was about to reign.

They turned aside from Coldingham, and made for the sea, and at length the promontory of St. Abbs Head rose before them; they passed through the outer buildings intended as shelter for the attendants of ladies coming to the nunnery, and knocked at the gateway.

A wicket in the door was opened, and the portress looked out through a grating.

'*Benedicite*, good Sister,' said Malcolm. 'Prithee tell the Mother Abbess that Malcolm Stewart of Glenuskie is here from the King, and craves to speak with her and the Lady Lilias.'

'Lord Malcolm! Lady Lilias! St. Ebba's good mercy!' shrieked the affrighted portress. They heard her rushing headlong across the court, and looked on one another in consternation.

Patrick betook himself to knocking as if he would beat down the door, and Malcolm leant against it with a foreboding that took away his breath—dreading the moment when it should be opened.

The portress and her keys returned again, and parleyed a moment. 'You are the Lord Malcolm in very deed—in the flesh?'

'Wherefore not?' demanded Malcolm.

'Nay, but we heard ye were slain, my lord,' explained the portress—letting him in, however, and leading them across the court, to where the Mother Abbess, Annabel Drummond, awaited them in the parlour.

'Alas, Sirs, what grievous error has this been?' was her exclamation; while Malcolm, scarcely waiting for salutation, demanded, 'Where is my sister?'

'How? In St. Hilda's keeping at Whitby, whither the King sent for her,' said the Abbess.

'The King!' cried Malcolm, 'we come from the King! Oh, what treachery has been here?'

'And you, Lord Malcolm—and you, my kinsman, Sir Patrick of the Braes, how do I see you here? We had heard you both were dead.'

'You heard a lying tale then, good Mother,' said Patrick, gruffly, 'no doubt devised for the misery of the—of my—' He could not finish the sentence, and Malcolm entreated the Abbess to tell the whole.

It appeared that about a year previously the chaplain of the monastery had learnt at Coldingham that Sir John

Swinton of Swinton had sent home tidings that Patrick Drummond had been thrown from his horse and left behind in a village which the English had harried, and as he could not move, he was sure to have been either burnt or hung. This conclusion was natural, and argued no malice in the reporter; and while poor Lilias was still in her first agony of grief, Prior Drax sent over intelligence derived from the Duke of Albany himself that Malcolm Stewart of Glenuskie had been stabbed in the forest of Vincennes. This report Malcolm himself accounted for. He had heard a Scots tongue among his foes, though national feeling had made him utterly silent on that head to the Duke of Bedford, and he guessed it to belong to a certain M'Kay, whose clan regarded themselves as at feud with the Stewarts, and of whom he had heard as living a wild *routier* life. He had probably been hired by Ghisbert for the attack, and had returned home and spread the report of its success.

Some few weeks later, the Abbess Annabel continued, there had arrived two monks from Coldingham, with an escort, declaring themselves to have received orders from King James to transport the Lady Lilias to the nunnery at Whitby, where the Abbess had promised to receive her, till he could determine her fate.

The forlorn and desolate Lilias, believing herself to stand alone in the world, was very loth to quit her shelter and her friends at St. Abbs; but the Abbess, doubting her own ability to protect her from the rapacious grasp of Walter Stewart, now that she had, as she believed, become an heiress, and glad to avert from her house the persecution that such protection would bring upon it, had gratefully heard of this act of consideration on the King's part, and expedited her departure. The two monks, Simon Bell and Ringan Johnstone, had not returned to the monastery, but had been thought to be in the parent house at Durham; but

Malcolm, who knew Brother Simon by sight, was clear that he had not seen him there.

All this had taken place a year ago, and there could be no doubt that some treachery had been exercised. Nothing had since been heard of Lilias; none of Malcolm's letters had reached St. Abbs, having doubtless been suppressed by the Prior of Coldingham; and all that was certain was that Walter Stewart, to whom their first suspicions directed themselves, had not publicly avouched any marriage with Lilias or claimed the Glenuskie estates, or the King, who had of late been in close correspondence with Scotland, must have heard of it. And it was also hardly possible that the Regent Murdoch and his sons, though they might for a few weeks have been misled by M'Kay's report, should not have soon become aware of Malcolm's existence.

Unless, then, Walter had married her 'on the first brash,' as Patrick called it, he might not have thought her a prize worth the winning; but the whole aspect of affairs had become most alarming, and Malcolm turned pale as death at the thought that his sister might be suffering retribution for the sin he had contemplated.

The danger was terrible! He could not imagine Lilias to have the moral grandeur and force of Esclairmonde. Moreover, she supposed her lover dead, and had not the same motive for guarding her troth. Forlorn and despairing, she might have yielded, and Walter Stewart was, Malcolm verily believed, worse to deal with than even Boemond. As the whole danger and uncertainty came over him, his senses seemed to reel; he leant back in his seat, and heard as in the midst of a dream his sister's sobs and groans, Patrick's fierce and furious exclamations, and the Abbess's attempts at consoling him. Dizzy with horror at the scene he realized, Lilias's cries and shrieks of

Charlotte M. Yonge

entreaty were ringing in his ear, when suddenly a sweet full low voice seemed to come through them, 'I am bound ever to pray for you and your sister.' Mingled with the cry came ever the sweet soft Litany cadences—'For all that are desolate and oppressed: we beseech Thee to hear us, good Lord.' Gradually the cries seemed to be swallowed up, both voices blended in *Kyrie eleison* and then in the *Gloria*, and at that moment he became aware of Patrick crying, 'I will seek her in every castle in Scotland.'

'Stay, Patrick,' he said, rising, though forced to hold by his chair; 'that must be my part.'

'You—why, the laddie is white as a sheet! He well-nigh swooned at the tidings. You seek her, forsooth!' and Patrick laughed bitterly.

'Yes, Patie,' said Malcolm, 'for this I am strong. It is my duty and not yours, and God will strengthen me for it.'

Patrick burst out at this: 'Neither man nor devil shall tell me it is not mine!'

'You are the King's prisoner still,' said Malcolm, rising to energy; 'you are bound to return to him. The tidings must be taken to him at once.'

'A groom could do that.'

'Neither so swiftly nor surely as you. Moreover, your word of honour binds you not to wander at your own pleasure.'

'My honour binds me not to trust you—wee Malcolm—to wander into the wolf's cage alone.'

'I am not the silly feckless callant I once was, Patie,'

answered Malcolm. 'There are many places where my student's serge gown will take me safely, where your corslet and lance would never find entrance. No one will know me again as I am now: will they, holy Mother?'

'Assuredly not,' said the Abbess.

'A student is too mean a prey to be meddled with,' proceeded Malcolm, 'and is sure of hospitality in castle or convent. I can try at Coldingham to find out whither the two monks are gone, and then follow up the track.'

Patrick stormed at the plan, and was most unwilling it should be adopted. He at least must follow, and keep watch over his young cousin, or it would be a mere throwing the helve after the hatchet—a betrayal of his trust.

But a little reflection convinced him that thus to follow would only bring suspicion on Malcolm and defeat his plans; and that it were better to obtain some certain information ere the King should come home, and have to interfere with a high hand; and Malcolm's arguments about his obligations as a captive, too, had their effect. He perceived his own incapacity to act; and in his despair at nothing being done consented to risk Malcolm in the search, while he himself should proceed to the King, only ascertaining on the way that Lilias was not at Whitby. And so, in grief and anxiety, the cousins parted, and Malcolm alone durst speak a word of hope.

Charlotte M. Yonge

CHAPTER XVII

THE BEGGING SCHOLAR

'The poor scholar,' now only existing in Ireland and Brittany—nay, we believe extinct there since the schoolmaster has become not abroad, but at home, in Government colleges—was to be found throughout the commonwealth of Europe in the Middle Ages. Young lads, in whom convent schools had developed a thirst for learning, could only gratify it by making their way to some university, where between begging, singing, teaching, receiving doles, earning rewards in encounters of wit and learning, doing menial services and using all manner of shifts, they contrived to live a hard life, half savage on the one side, highly intellectual upon the other. They would suck the marrow of one university, and then migrate to another; and the rank they had gained in the first was available in the second, so that it was no means uncommon for them to bring away degrees from half the universities in Europe, all of which formed one general system—all were like islands of one country, whose common language was queer Latin, and whose terms, manners, and customs were alike in all main points.

Scotland contributed many of her sons to this curious race of vagabond students, when she herself was without any university to satisfy the cravings of her thoughtful and intellectual people. 'No country without a Scot or a flea' was an uncomplimentary proverb due to the numerous young clerks, equally fierce for frays and for lectures, who flocked to the seats of learning on the Continent, and sometimes became naturalized there, sometimes came home again, to fight their way to the higher benefices of the Church, or to become councillors of state.

It was true that Malcolm was an Oxford scholar, or rather bachelor, and that Oxford and Cambridge were almost the only universities where Scots were not—their place being taken by multitudinous Irish; yet not only were all universities alike in essentials, but he had seen and heard enough of that at Paris to be able to personate a clerk from thence.

It was no small plunge for one hitherto watched, tended, and guarded as Malcolm had been, to set forth entirely alone; but as he had approached manhood, and strengthened in body, his spirit had gained much in courage, and the anxiety about his sister swallowed up all other considerations. Even while he entreated the prayers of the Abbess, he felt quite sure that he had those of Esclairmonde; and when he had hunted out of his mails the plain bachelor's rabbit-skin hood and black gown—which, perhaps, was a little too fine in texture for the poor wanderer—and fastened on his back, with a leathern thong, a package containing a few books and a change of linen, his pale and intellectual face made him look so entirely the young clerk, that Patrick hardly believed it was Malcolm.

And when the roads parted, and Drummond and his escort had to turn towards Berwick, while Malcolm took the path to the monastery, it was the younger who was the stronger and more resolute of the two; for Patrick could neither reconcile himself to peril the boy, who had always been his anxious trust, nor to return to the King without him; and yet no one who loved Lilias could withhold him from his quest.

Malcolm did not immediately speed to the monastery on taking leave of Patrick. He stood first to watch the armour flashes gradually die away, and the little troop grow smaller to his eye, across the brown moor, till they were entirely out of sight, and he himself left alone. Then he knelt by a bush of gorse, told his beads, and earnestly entreated direction and aid for himself, and protection for his sister; and when the sun grew so low as to make it time for a wanderer to seek harbour, he stained and daggled his gown in the mire and water of a peat-moss, so as to destroy its Oxford gloss, took a book in his hand, and walked towards the monastery, reciting Latin verses in the sing-song tone then universally followed.

As he came among the fields, he saw that the peasants, and lay brethren who had been working among them, were returning, some from sowing, others from herding the cattle, which they drove before them to the byre within the protecting wall of the monastery.

A monk—with a weather-beaten face and athletic figure, much like a farmer's of the present day—overtook him, and hailed him with 'Benedicite, you there and welcome to your clerkship! Are you coming for supper and bed in the convent?'

Malcolm knew good-natured Brother Nicolas, and kept his hood well over his face after the first salutation; though he felt confident that Lord Malcolm could hardly be recognized in the begging scholar, as he made reply, 'Salve, reverende frater. Venio de Lutetia Parisiorum.' {1}

'Whisht with your Latin, laddie,' said the brother. 'Speak out, if you've a Scots tongue in your head, and have not left it in foreign parts.'

'For bed and board, holy father, I shall be most thankful,' replied Malcolm.

'That's more like it,' said the brother, who acted as a kind of farming steward, and was a hearty, good-natured gossip. 'An' what's the name of ye?'

He gave his real Christian name; and added that he came from Glenuskie, where the good Tutor of Glenuskie had been kind enough to notice him.

'Ay,' said Brother Nicolas, 'he was a guid man to all towardly youths. He died in this house, more's the pity.'

'Yea, Sir—so I heard say,' returned Malcolm. 'He was a good friend to me!' he added, to cover his heavy sigh. 'And, Sir, how went it with the young laird and leddy?'

'For the young laird—a feckless, ugsome, sickly wean he was, puir laddie—a knight cam by, an' behoved to take him to the King. Nay, but if you've been at Parish—if that's what ye mean with your Lutetia—ye'll have seen him an' the King.'

'I saw the King,' answered Malcolm; 'but among the Englishry.'

'A sorry sight enow!' said the monk; 'but he'll soon find his Scots heart again; and here we've got rid of the English leaven from the house, and be all sound and leal Scots here.'

'And the lady?' Malcolm ventured to ask. 'She had a

Charlotte M. Yonge

winsome face.'

'Ho! ho! what have young clerks to do wi' winsome faces?' laughed the Benedictine.

'She was good to me,' Malcolm could truly say.

'They had her in St. Abbs yonder,' said the monk.

'Is she there?' asked Malcolm. 'I would pay my duty and thanks to her.'

'Now—there I cannot say,' replied Brother Nicolas. 'My good Mother Abbess and our Prior are not the friends they were in Prior Akefield's time; and there's less coming and going between the houses. There was a noise that Lord Malcolm had been slain, and I did hear that, thereupon, she had been claimed as a ward of the Crown. But I cannot say. If ye gang to St. Abbs the morn, ye may hear if she be there—and at any rate get the dole.'

It was clear that the good brother knew no more, and Malcolm could only thank him for his condescension, and follow among the herdsmen into the well-known monastery court.

Here he availed himself of his avowed connection with Glenuskie, to beg to be shown good old Sir David Drummond's grave. A flat gray stone in the porch was pointed out to him; and beside this he knelt, until the monks flocked in for prayers—which were but carelessly and hurriedly sung; and then followed supper. It was all so natural to him, that it was with an effort that he recalled that his place was not at the high table, as Lord Malcolm Stewart, but that Malcolm, the nameless begging scholar, must be trencher-fellow with the servants and lay brethren. He was the less concerned, that here there was less danger of recognition, and more freedom of conversation.

Things were evidently much altered. A novice was indeed, as usual, placed aloft in the refectory pulpit, to read aloud to the brethren during their repast, but no one seemed to think it needful to preserve the decorous silence that had been rigidly exacted during Prior Akefield's time, and there was a continual buzz of conversation. Lent though it was, the fish was of the most esteemed kinds, and it was evident that, like the monks of Melrose, they 'made gude kale.' Few of the kindly old faces that Malcolm remembered were to be seen under their cowls. Prior Drax himself had much more the countenance of a moss-trooper than of a monk—mayhap he was then meditating that which he afterwards carried out successfully, *i.e.* the capture and appropriation of a whole instalment of King James's ransom, on its way across the Border; and there was a rude recklessness and self-indulgence about the looks, voices, and manners of the brethren he had brought with him, such as made Malcolm feel that if he had had his wish, and remained at Coldingham, he should soon have found it no haven of peace.

The lay-brothers and old servants were fixtures, but the old faithful and devout ones looked forlorn and unhappy and there had been a great importation of the ruffianly men-at-arms, whom the more pugnacious ecclesiastics, as well as nobles, of Scotland, were apt to maintain. Guards there had been in old times, but kept under strict discipline; whereas, in the rude conduct of these men, there was no sign that they knew themselves to be in a religious house. Malcolm, keeping aloof from these as much as might be, gave such an account of himself as was most consistent with truth, since it was necessary to account for his returning so young from his studies. He

Charlotte M. Yonge

had, he said, been told that there was an inheritance fallen due to him, and that the kinsman, in whose charge his sister had been left, was dead; and he had come home to seek her out, and inquire into the matter of his heirship.

Rude jokes, from some of the new denizens of the monastery, were spent on the improbability of his finding sister or lands; if it were in the Barony of Glenuskie, the House of Albany had taken the administration of that into their own hands.

'Nay—but,' said Malcolm, 'could I but see my young Lady Lilias, she might make suit for me.'

The gray-headed lay-brother, to whom he addressed himself, replied that it was little the Lady Lilias could do, but directed him to St. Abbs to find her; whereat one of the men-at-arms burst out laughing, and crying, 'That's a' that ye ken, auld Davie! As though the Master of Albany would let a bonnie lassie ware hersel' and her tocher on stone walls and dour old nuns.'

'Has she wedded the Master of Albany, then?' asked Malcolm, concealing his anxiety as best he might.

'That's as he pleases; and by my troth he took pains enow to get her!'

'What pains?'

'Why, once she slipped out of his very fingers; that time that he had laid hands on her, and the hirpling doited brother of hers cam down with a strange knight, put her into St. Abbs, and made off for England—so they said. Some of the rogues would have it 'twas St. Andrew in bodily shape, and that he tirled the young laird, as was only fit for a saint, aff to heaven wi' him; for he was no more seen in these parts.'

'Nay, that couldna be,' put in another soldier. 'Sandy M'Kay took his aith that he was in the English camp—more shame till him—an' was stickit dead for meddling between King Harry's brother and his luve. It sorted him weel, I say.'

'Aweel!' continued the first; 'gane is he, and sma' loss wi' him! An' yon old beldame over at St. Abbs, she kens weel how to keep a lass wi' a tocher—so what does the Master but sends a letter ower to our Prior, bidding him send two trusty brethren, as though from the King, to conduct her to Whitby?'

'Ha!' said Malcolm; 'but that's ower the Border.'

'Even so; but the Glenuskies are all English at heart, and it sicker trained away the silly lassie.'

'And then?'—the other man-at-arms laughed.

'Why, at the first hostelry, ye can guess what sort of nuns were ready to meet her! I promise ye she skirled, and ca'ed Heaven and earth to help; but Brother Simon and Brother Ringan gave their word they'd see nae ill dune to her, and she rade with them on each side of her, and us tall fellows behind and before, till we cam to Doune.'

'And what became of her, the poor lassie, then?' inquired Malcolm, steadying his voice with much effort.

'Ye maun ask the Master that,' said the soldier. 'I ken nae mair; I was sent on anither little errand of the Earl of Fife into the Highlands, and only cam back hither a week syne, to watch the Border.'

Charlotte M. Yonge

'Had it been St. Andrew that saved her before, he wad hae come again,' pondered the lay-brother. 'He'd hardly hae given her up.'

'Weel, I heard the lassie cry on the Master to mind the aith he had made the former time; an' though he tried to laugh her to scorn, his eyes grew wild, and there were some that tell'd me they lookit to see that glittering awsome knight among them again! My certie, they maun hae been feared enow the time he did come.'

Malcolm had now had his fears and suspicions so far confirmed, that he perceived what his course should next be. Strange to say, in spite of the horror of knowing his sister to have been a whole year in Walter Stewart's power, he was neither hopeless nor disheartened. Lilias seemed to have kept her persecutor at bay once, and she might have done so again—if only by the appeal to the mysterious relic, on which his oath to abstain from violence had been sworn. And confidence in Esclairmonde's prayers continued to buoy him up, as he recited his own, and formed his designs for ascertaining whether she were to be found at Doune—either as wife, or as captive, to Walter, Earl of Fife and heir of Albany.

So soon as the doors of Coldingham Priory were opened, he was on his way northward. It was a sore and trying journey, in the bitter March weather, for one so little used to hardship. He did not fail in obtaining shelter or food; his garb was everywhere a passport; but he grew weary and footsore, and his anxiety greatly increased when he found that fatigue was bringing back the lameness, which greatly enhanced the likelihood of his being recognized. Kind monks, and friendly gude-wives, hospitably persuaded the worn student to remain and rest, till his blistered feet were whole; but he pressed on whenever he found it possible to travel, and after the first week found his progress less tardy and painful.

Resting at Edinburgh for Passion-tide and Easter Day, he found that the Regent Albany himself, with all his family, were at Doune, and he accordingly made his way thither; rejoicing that he had had some little time to perfect himself in his part, before rehearsing it to the persons most likely to detect his disguise.

Along the banks and braes of bonny Doune he slowly moved, with weary limbs; looking up to the huge pile of the majestic castle in sickening of heart at the doubt that was about to become a certainty, and that involved the happiness or the absolute misery of his sister's life. Nay, he would almost have preferred to find that she had perished in her resistance, rather than have become wife to such a man as Walter Stewart.

The Duke of Albany, as representing majesty, kept up all the state that Scottish majesty was capable of, in its impoverished irregular state. Hosts of rough lawless warriors, men-at-arms, squires and knights, lived at free quarters, in a sort of rude plenty, in and about the Castle; eating and drinking at the Regent's expense, sleeping where they could, in hall or stable, and for clothing and armour trusting to 'spulzie'; always ready for violence, without much caring on whom exercised—otherwise hunting, or lounging, or swelling their master's disorderly train.

This retinue was almost at its largest at this time, being swelled by the following of the two younger sons of Murdoch, Robert and Alexander; and the courts of the Castle were filled with rude, savage-looking men, some few grooming horses, others with nothing to do but to shout forth their jeers at the pale, black-gowned student, who timidly limped into their lair.

Timidly—yes; for the awful chances heavily oppressed him; and the horrible scurrility and savagery that greeted him on all sides made his heart faint at the thought of his Lily in this cage of foul animals. He did not fear for himself, and never paused until a shouting circle of idle ruffians set themselves full in his way, to badger and bait the poor scholar with taunts and insults—hemming him in, bawling out ribald mirth, as a pack of hounds fall on some stray dog, or, as Malcolm thought, in a moment half of sick horror, half of resolute resignation, like wild cattle—fat bulls of Bashan closing in on every side. So horrible a moment of distress he had never known; but suddenly, as he stood summoning all his strength, panting with dismay, inwardly praying, and trying to close his ears and commend himself to One who knew what mockery is, there was an opening of the crowd, a youth darted down among them, with a loud cry of 'Shame! Out on you! A poor scholar!' and taking Malcolm's hand, led him forward; while a laugh of mockery rose in the distance—'Like to like.'

'Ay, my friend and brother, I am Baccalaureus, even as you are,' eagerly said the young gentleman, in whom Malcolm, somewhat to his alarm, recognized his cousin, James Kennedy, the King's nephew, a real Parisian '*bejanus*,' or *bec jaune*, {2} when they last had met in the Hotel de St. Pol; and thus not only qualified to confute and expose him, should he show any ignorance of details, but also much more likely to know him than those who had not seen him for many months before he had left Scotland.

But James Kennedy asked no questions, only said kindly, in the Latin that was always spoken in the University, 'Pray pardon us! *Mores Hyperboreis desunt.* {3} The Regent would be grieved, if he knew how these *scelerati* {4} have sorted you. Come, rest and wash—it will soon be supper-time.'

He took Malcolm to an inner court, filled for him a cup of ale, for his immediate refreshment, and led him to a spout of clear water, in the side of the rock on which the Castle stood; where a stone basin afforded the only facilities for washing that the greater part of the inhabitants of the Castle expected, and, in effect, more than they commonly used. Malcolm, however, was heartily glad of the refreshment of removing the dust from his weary face and feet—and heartily thanked his protector, in the same dog-Latin. Kennedy waited for him, and as a great bell began to ring, said 'Pro caena,' {5} and conducted him towards the great hall while Malcolm felt much impelled to make himself known, but was conscious that he had not so comported himself towards his cousin at Paris as to deserve much favour from him.

A high table was spread in the hall, with the usual appliances befitting princes and nobles. The other tables, below the dais, were of the rudest description, and stained with accumulations of grease and ale; and no wonder, since trenchers were not, and each man hacked a gobbet for himself from the huge pieces of beef carried round on spits—nor would the guests have had any objection, during a campaign, to cook the meat in the fashion described by Froissart, between themselves and the saddle. These were the squirearchy; Malcolm's late perse-cutors did not aspire to the benches around these boards, or only at second hand, and for the most part had no seat but the unclean straw and rushes that strewed the floor.

As James Kennedy entered the hall with Malcolm, there came from another door, marshalled by the seneschal in full feudal state, the Regent Duke of Albany himself, his wife, a daughter or two, two sons—and Malcolm saw, with beating heart, Lilias herself, pale worn, sorrowful-looking, grievously altered, but still his own Lily. Others followed, chiefly knights and attendants, but Malcolm saw no one but Lily. She took her place dejectedly, and never raised her eyes towards him, even when, on the Regent's question, 'What have ye there, Jamie?' Kennedy stood forth and answered that it was a scholar, a student, for whom he asked the hospitality of his kinsman.

'He is welcome,' said the Regent, a man of easy good-nature, whose chief misfortune was, that being of weak nature, he came between a wicked father and wickeder sons. He was a handsome man, with much of the stately appearance of King James himself, and the same complexion; but it was that sort of likeness which was almost provoking, by seeming to detract from the majesty of the lineaments themselves, as seen in him who alone knew how to make them a mask for a great soul. His two sons, Robert and Alexander, laughed as they saw Kennedy's companion, and called out, 'So that's the brotherhood of learning, is it, Jamie?—forgathering with any beggar in the street!'

'Yea,' said Kennedy, nothing daunted, 'and finding him much better mannered than you!'

'Ay!' sighed Murdoch, feebly; 'when I grew up, it was at the Castles of Perth and Doune that we looked for the best manners. Now—'

'We leave them to the lick-platters that have to live by them,' said Alexander, rudely.

Kennedy, meanwhile, gave the young scholar in charge to a gray-headed retainer, who seemed one of the few who had any remains of good-breeding; and then offered to say Grace—he being the nearest approach to an ecclesiastic present—as the chaplain was gone to an Easter festivity at his Abbey. Malcolm thus obtained a seat at the second table, and a tolerable share of supper; but he could hardly eat, from intense anxiety, and scarcely knew whether to be glad or sorry that he was out of sight of Lily.

By and by, a moment's lull of the universal din enabled Malcolm to hear the Regent saying, 'Verily, there is a look of gentle nurture about the lad. Look you, James, when the tables are drawn, you shall hold a disputation with him. It will be sport to hear how you chop logic at your Universities yonder.'

Malcolm's spirit sank. Such disputations were perfectly ordinary work at both Oxford and Paris, and, usually, he was quite capable of sustaining his part in them; but his heart was so full, his mind so anxious, his condition so dangerous, that he felt as if he could by no means rally that alertness of argument, and readiness of quotation, that were requisite even in the merest tyro. However, he made a great effort. He secretly invoked the Light of Wisdom; tried to think himself back into the aisles of St. Mary's Church, and to call up the key-notes of some of the stock arguments; hoping that, if the selection of the subject were left to Kennedy, he would hit on one of those most familiar at Oxford.

The supper was ended, the tables were removed, and the challenge took place. Duke Murdoch, leaning back in his high chair by the peat-fire, while the ladies sat round at their spinning, called for the two young clerks to begin their tourney of words. They stood opposite one another, on the step of the dais; and Kennedy, as host and challenger, assigned to his opponent the choice of a subject, when Malcolm, brightening, proposed one that he had so often heard and practised on, as to have the arguments at his fingers' ends; namely, that the real

Charlotte M. Yonge

consists only in that which is substantial to the senses, and which we see, hear, taste, smell, or touch.

Kennedy's shrewd gray eye glanced at him in a manner that startled him, as he made reply, 'Fellow-*alumnus*, you speak as Oxford scholars speak; but I rede ye well that the real is not that which is grossly tangible to the corporeal sense, but the idea that is conceived within the immortal intelligence.'

The argument was carried on in the vernacular, but there was an unlimited license of quotation from authors of all kinds, classics, Fathers, and schoolmen. It was like a game at chess, in which the first moves were always so much alike, that they might have been made by automatons; and Malcolm was repeating reply and counter-reply, almost by rote, when a citation brought in by Kennedy again startled him.

'Outward things,' said James, 'are the mere mark; for have we not heard how

> "Telephus et Peleus, quum pauper et exsul uterque,
> Projicit ampullas et sesquipedalia verba"?' {6}

Was this to prove that he recognized a wandering prince in his opponent? thought Malcolm; but, much on his guard, he made answer, as usual, in his native tongue. 'That which is not touched and held is but a vain and fleeting shadow—"*solvitur in nube.*" {7}

'*Negatur*, it is denied!' said Kennedy, fixing his eyes full upon him. 'The Speculum of the Soul, which is immortal, retains the image even while the bodily presence is far away. Wherefore else was it that Ulysses sat as a beggar by his paternal hearth, or that Cadmus wandered to seek his sister?'

This was anything but the regular illustration—the argument was far too directly *ad hominem*—and Malcolm hesitated for a moment, ere framing his reply. 'If the image had satisfied the craving of their hearts, they had never wandered, nor endangered themselves.'

'Nor,' said Kennedy, 'endeared themselves to all who love the leal and the brave, and count these indeed as verities for which to live.'

From the manner in which these words were spoken, Malcolm had no further doubt either that Kennedy knew him, or that he meant to assist him; and the discussion thenceforth proceeded without further departures from the regular style, and was sustained with considerable spirit, till the Regent grew weary of it, and bed-time approached, when Kennedy announced his intention of taking his fellow-student to share his chamber; and, as this did not appear at all an unnatural proposal, in the crowded Castle, Malcolm followed him up various winding stairs into a small circular chamber, with a loop-hole window, within one of the flanking towers.

Carefully closing the heavy door, Kennedy held out his hands. 'Fair cousin,' he said, 'this is bravely done of you.'

'Will it save my sister?' asked Malcolm, anxiously.

'It should,' said his kinsman; 'but how can it be? Whatever is done, must be ere Walter Stewart returns.'

'Tell me all! I know nothing—save that she was cruelly lured from St. Abbs.'

'I know little more,' said Kennedy. 'It was on a false report of your death, and Walter had well-nigh obtained a forcible marriage; when her resistance and cries to

Charlotte M. Yonge

Heaven daunted the monk who was to have performed the rite, so that he, in a sort, became her protector. When she was brought here, Walter swore he would bend her to his will; shut her up in the old keep, and kept her there, scantily fed, and a close prisoner, while he went forth on one of his forays. The Regent coming here meantime, found the poor maiden in her captivity, and freed her so far that she lives, to all appearance, as becomes his kinswoman; but the Duchess is cruelly strict with her, being resolved, as she says, to take down her pride.'

'They must know that I live,' said Malcolm.

'They do; but Walter is none the less resolved not to be balked. Things came to a wild pass a few weeks syne. The Regent had never dared tell him how far matters had gone for bringing back the King, when one day Walter came in, clad for hawking; and, in his rudest manner, demanded the falcon that was wont to sit on his father's wrist, and that had never been taken out by any other. The Regent refused to part with the bird, as he had oft done before; whereupon his son, in his fury, snatched her from his wrist, and wrung her head off before all our eyes; then turning fiercely on your poor sister, told her that "yon gled should be a token to her, of how they fared who withheld themselves from him." Then rose the Duke, trembling within rage; "Ay, Wat," said he, "ye hae been owermuch for me. We will soon have ane at home that will ken how to guide ye." Walter looked at him insolently, and muttered, "I've heard of this before! They that wad have a master, may live under a master—but I'm not ane of them;" and then, turning upon Lady Lilias, he pointed to the dead hawk, and told her that, unless she yielded to him with a good grace, that bird showed her what she might expect, long ere the King or her brother were across the border.'

'And where is he now?'

'In Fife, striving to get a force together to hinder the King's return. He'll not do that; men are too weary of misrule to join him against King James; but he is like, any day, to come back with reivers enough to terrify his father, and get your sister into his hands—indeed, his mother is ready to give her up to him whenever he asks. He has sworn to have her now, were it merely to vex the King and you, and show that he is to be daunted neither by man, heaven, nor hell.'

'And he may come?'

'Any day or any night,' said James. 'Since he went I have striven, in vain, to devise some escape for your sister; but Heaven has surely sent you to hinder so foul a wrong! Yet, if you went to Glenuskie and raised your vassals—'

'It would be loss of time,' said Malcolm; 'and this matter may not be put to the doubtful issue of a fray between my men and his villains. Out of this place must she go at once. But, alas! how win to the speech of her?'

'That can I do,' said Kennedy. 'For a few brief moments, each day, have I spoken to her in the chapel. Nay, I had left this place before now, had she not prayed me to remain as her only friend.'

'Heaven must requite you, Cousin James,' said Malcolm, warmly. 'I deserved not this of you.'

'All that I desire,' said Kennedy, 'is to see this land of ours cease to be full of darkness and cruel habitations. Malcolm, you know the King better than I; may we not trust that he will come as a redresser of wrongs?'

'Know you not his pledge to himself?—"I will make the key keep the castle, and the bracken bush keep the cow, though I live the life of a dog to bring it about!"'

'God strengthen his hand,' said Kennedy, with tears in his eyes; 'and bring better days to our poor land. Cousin, has not your heart burnt within you, to be doing somewhat to bring these countrymen of ours to better mind?'

'I have grieved,' said Malcolm. 'The sight has been the woe and horror of my whole life; and either it is worse now than when I went away, or I see it clearer.'

'It is both,' said Kennedy; 'and, Malcolm, it is borne in on me that we, who have seen better things, have a heavy charge! The King may punish marauders, and enforce peace; but it will be but the rule of the strong hand, unless men's hearts be moved! Our clergy—they bear the office of priests—but their fierceness and their ignorance would scarce be believed in France or England; and how should it be otherwise, with no schools at home save the abbeys—and the abbeys almost all fortresses held by fierce noblemen's sons?'

Malcolm would much rather have discussed the means of rescuing his sister, but James Kennedy's heart was full of a youth's ardent plans for the re-awakening of religion in his country, chiefly through the improved education of the clergy, and it was not easy to bring his discourse to a close.

'You—you were to wed a great Flemish heiress?' he said. 'You will do your part, Cousin, in the founding of a University—such as has changed ourselves so greatly.'

Malcolm smiled. 'My only bride is learning,' he said; 'my other betrothal is but in name, for the safety of the lady.'

'Then,' cried Kennedy joyfully, 'you will give yourself. Learning and culture turned to God's service, for this poor country's sake, in one of birth like you, may change her indeed.'

Was this the reading of Esclairmonde's riddle? suddenly thought Malcolm. Was the true search for heavenly Light, then, to consist in holding up to his countrymen the lamp he was kindling for himself? Must true wisdom consist in treasuring knowledge, not for his own honour among learned men, or the delectation of his own mind, but to scatter it among these rude northern souls? Must the vision of learned research and scholarly calm vanish, as cloistral peace, and chivalrous love and glory, had vanished before? and was the lot of a hard-working secular priest that which called him?

CHAPTER XVIII

CLERK DAVIE

For Malcolm to speak with his sister was well-nigh an impossibility. Had he been detected, he would have been immediately treated as a spy, and the suspicion thus excited would have been a dangerous preparation for the King as well as for himself; nor was there any pretext for giving the wandering scholar an interview with her.

But harsh and strict as was the Duchess of Albany—a tall, raw-boned, red-haired woman, daughter of the fierce old Earl of Lennox—and resolved as she was to bend Lilias by persecution to accept her son, she could not debar a young gentleman of the royal kindred, like James Kennedy, from entering the apartment where the ladies of the family sat with their needles; and the Regent, half from pity, half from shame, had refused to permit Lilias Stewart's being treated as a mere captive.

Thus Malcolm remained in Kennedy's room in much anxiety, while his cousin went forth to do his best in his cause, and after some hours returned to him with the tidings that he had succeeded in letting Lily know that he was in the Castle. Standing over her while she bent over her embroidery, and thus concealing her trembling agitation, he had found it possible to whisper in her ears the tidings of her brother having come to save her, and of hearing her insist that Malcolm, 'wee Malcolm, must run no peril, but that she would do and dare everything—nay, would prefer death itself to Walter Stewart.'

'Have you any device in this matter?' demanded James Kennedy, when he had thus spoken.

'Have you your college gown here?' inquired Malcolm.

'I have, in yon kist,' said Kennedy. 'Would you disguise her therein? You and she are nearly of a height.'

'Ay,' said Malcolm. 'The plot I thought on is this—the worst is that the risk rests with you.'

'That is naught, less than naught,' said Kennedy. 'I had risked myself ten times over had I seen any hope for her in so doing.'

Malcolm then explained his plan, namely, that if Lilias could have Kennedy's gown conveyed to her, she should array herself therein, and be conducted out of the castle by her cousin by one gate, he himself in secular garb going by another, and joining at some place of meeting, whence, as a pair of brothers, Malcolm and she might gain the English border.

James Kennedy considered, and then added that he could improve on the plan. He had long intended leaving Doune for his brother's castle, but only tarried in case he could do anything for Lilias. He would at supper publicly announce to the Regent his departure for the next day, and also say that he had detained his fellow-scholar to go within him. Then arranging for Malcolm's exit in a secular dress among his escort, as one of the many unobserved loungers, Lilias should go with him in very early morning

Charlotte M. Yonge

in the bachelor's gown, which he would place in a corner of a dark passage, where she could find it. Then if Malcolm and she turned aside from his escort, as the pursuit as soon as her evasion was discovered would be immediately directed on himself, they would have the more time for escape.

It was a complicated plan, but there was this recommendation, that Malcolm need not lose sight of his sister. Clerk as he was, young Kennedy could not ride without an escort, and among his followers he could place Malcolm. Accordingly at supper he announced his desire to leave Doune at dawn next morning, and was, as a matter of course, courteously pressed to remain. Malcolm in the meantime eluded observation as much as possible while watching his sister, who, in spite of all her efforts, was pale and red by turns, never durst glance towards him, and trembled whenever any one went near him.

The ladies at length swept out of the hall, and Robert and Alexander called for more wine for a rere-supper to drink to James's good journey; but Kennedy tore himself from their hospitable violence, and again he and Malcolm were alone, spending a night of anxiety and consultation.

Morning came; Malcolm arrayed himself in a somewhat worn dress of Kennedy's, with the belt and dirk he had carried under his scholar's garb now without, and a steel cap that his cousin had procured for him on his head. With a parcel in his arms of Kennedy's gear, he might pass for a servant sent from home to meet him; and so soon as this disguise was complete, Kennedy opened the door. On the turret stair stood a hooded black figure, that started as the door opened.

Malcolm's heart might well seem to leap to his lips, but both brother and sister felt the tension of nerve that caution required too much to give way for a moment.

Kennedy whispered, 'Your license, fair Cousin,' and passed on with the free step of lordly birth, while a few paces behind the seeming scholar humbly followed, and Malcolm, putting on his soldier's tread and the careless free-and-easy bearing he had affected before Meaux, brought up the rear with Master Kennedy's mails.

As they anticipated, the household was not troubling itself to rise to see the priest off. Not that this made the coast clear, for the floor of the hall was cumbered with snoring sleepers in all sorts of attitudes—nay, at the upper table, the flushed, debauched, though young and handsome, faces of Robert and Alexander Stewart might have been detected among those who lay snoring among the relics of their last night's revel.

The old steward was, however, up and alert, ready to offer the stirrup-cup, and the horses were waiting in the court; but what they had by no means expected or desired was that Duke Murdoch himself, in his long furred gown, came slowly across the hall to bid his young kinsman Kennedy farewell.

'Speed you well, my lad,' he said kindly. 'I ask ye not to tarry in what ye must deem a graceless household;' and he looked sadly across at his two sons, boys in age, but seniors in excess. 'I would we had mair lads like you. I fear me a heavy reckoning is coming.'

'You have ever been good lord to all, Sir,' said Kennedy, affectionately, for he really loved and pitied the soft-hearted Duke.

'Too good, maybe,' said Murdoch. 'What! the scholar goes with you?' and he fixed a look on Lily's face that brought the colour deep into it under her hood.

'Yes, Sir,' answered Kennedy, respectfully. 'Here, you Tam,' indicating Malcolm, 'take him behind you on the sumpter-horse.'

'Fare ye weel, gentle scholar,' said Murdoch, taking the hand that Lily was far from offering. 'May ye win to your journey's end safe and sound; and remember,' he added, holding the fingers tight, and speaking under the hood, 'if ye have been hardly served, 'twas to make ye the second lady in Scotland. Take care of her—him, young laddie,' he added, turning on Malcolm: "tis best so; and mind' (he spoke in the same wheedling tone of self-excuse), 'if ye tell the tale down south, nae ill hath been dune till her, and where could she have been mair fitly than beneath her kinsman's roof? I'd not let her go, but that young blude is hot and ill to guide.'

An answer would have been hard to find; and it was well that he did not look for any. Indeed, Malcolm could not have spoken without being heard by the seneschal, and therefore could only bow, take his seat on the baggage-horse, and then feel his sister mounting behind him in an attitude less unfamiliar on occasion even to the high-born ladies of the fifteenth century than to those of our day. Four years it was since he had felt her touch, four years since she had sat behind him as they followed the King to Coldingham! His heart swelled with thankfulness as he passed under the gateway, and the arms that clung round his waist clasped him fervently; but neither ventured on a word, amid Kennedy's escort, and they rode on a couple of miles in the same silence. Then Kennedy, pausing, said, 'There lies your way, Brother. Tam, you may show the scholar the way to the Gray Friars' Grange, bear them greetings frae me, and halt till ye hear from me. Fare ye well.'

Lilias trusted her voice to say, 'Blessings on ye, Sir, for all ye have done for me,' but Malcolm thought it wiser in his character of retainer to respond only by a bow.

Of course they understood that the direction Kennedy gave was the very one they were not to take, but they followed it till a tall bush of gorse hid them from the escort; and then Malcolm, grasping his sister's hand, plunged down among the rowans, ferns, and hazels, that covered the steep bank of the river, and so soon as a footing was gained under shelter of a tall rock, threw his arms round her, almost sobbing in an under-tone, 'My Lily, my tittie!—safe at last! Oh, God be thanked! I knew her prayers would be heard! Oh, would that Patrick were here!' Then, as her face changed and quivered ready to weep, he cried, 'Eh, what! art still deeming him dead?'

'How!' she cried wildly. 'He fell into the hands of your English, and—'

'He fell into the hands of your King and mine,' said Malcolm. 'Yes, King James dragged him out of the burning house, and wrung his pardon out of King Harry. He came with me to St. Abbs to fetch you, Lily, and only went back because his knighthood would not serve in this quest like my clerkship.'

'Patrick living, Patrick safe! Oh!' she fell on her knees among the ferns, hid her face in her hands, and drew a long breath. 'Malcolm, this is joy overmuch. The desolation of yesterday, the joy to-day!'

Malcolm, seeing her like one stifled by emotion, fell on his knees beside her, and whispered forth a thanksgiving. She rested with her head on his shoulder in content till he started up, saying in a lively manner, 'Come, Lily, we must be on our way. A very bonnie young clerk you are,

Charlotte M. Yonge

with your berry-brown locks cut so short round your face.'

Lilias blushed up to the short dark curls she had left herself. 'Had I thought he lived, I could scarce have done it.'

'What, not to get to him, silly maid? Here,' as he shook out and donned the gown he had brought rolled up, 'now am I a scholar too. Stay, you must take off this badge of the bachelor; you have only been in a monastery school, you know; you are my young brother—what shall we call you?'

'Davie,' softly suggested Lilias.

'Ay, Davie then, that I've come home to fetch to share my Paris lear. You can be very shy and bashful, you know, and leave all the knapping of Latin and logic to me.'

'If it is such as you did with Jamie Kennedy,' said Lilias, 'it will indeed be well. Oh, Malcolm, I sat and marvelled at ye—so gleg ye took him up. How could ye learn it? And ye are a brave warrior too in battles,' she added, looking him over with a sister's fond pride.

'We have had no battle, no pitched field,' said Malcolm 'but I have seen war.'

'So that ugly words can never be flung in your face again!' cried Lilias. 'Are you knighted, brother?'

'No, but they say I have won my spurs. I'll tell you all, Lily, as we walk. Only let me bestow this iron cap where some mavis may nestle in it. Ay, and the boots too, which scarce befit a clerk. There, your hand, Clerk Davie; we must make westward to-day, lest poor Duke Murdoch be forced to send to chase us. After that, for the Border and Patie.'

So brother and sister set forth on their wandering—and truly it was a happy journey. The weather favoured them, and their hearts were light. Lilias, delivered from terrible, hopeless captivity, her brother beside her, and now not a brother to be pitied and protected, but to protect her and be exulted in, trod the heather with an exquisite sense of joy and freedom that buoyed her up against all hardships; and Malcolm was at peace, as he had seldom been. His happiness was not exactly like his sister's in her renewed liberty and restoration to love and joy, for he had known a wider range of life, and though really younger than Lily, his more complicated history could not but make him older in thought and mind. Another self-abnegation was beginning to rise upon him, as he travelled slowly southwards by stages suited to his sister's powers, and by another track than that by which he had gone. On the moor, or by the burn side, there was peace and brightness; but wherever he met with man he found something to sadden him. Did they rest in a monastery, there was often irregularity, seldom devotion, always crass ignorance. The manse was often a scene of such dissolute life that Malcolm shunned to bring his sister into the sight of it; the peel tower was the dwelling of savagery; the farm homestead either rude and lawless or in constant terror; the black spaces on many a brae side showed where dwellings had been burned; more than once they passed skeletons depending from the trees or lying rotting by the way-side. And it was frightful to Malcolm, after his four years' absence, to find how little Lilias shared his horror, taking quite naturally what to Alice Montagu would have seemed beyond the bounds of possibility, and would have set Esclairmonde's soul on fire, while Lilias seemed to think it her brother's amiable peculiarity to be shocked, or to long to set such things straight.

Charlotte M. Yonge

He felt the truth of James Kennedy's words—that reformation could not be the sole work of the King, but that his hands must be strengthened by all the few who knew that a different state of things was possible, and that, above all, the clergy needed to be awakened into vigour and intelligence. Formerly, the miserable aspect of the country had merely terrified him, and driven him to strive to hide his head in a convent; but the strength and the sense of duty he had acquired had brought his heart to respond to Kennedy's call to work.

Esclairmonde's words wrought within him beyond her own ken or purpose in speaking them. He began to understand that to bury himself in an Italian university and dive into Aristotle's sayings, to heap up his own memory with the stores of thought he loved, or to plunge into the mazes of mathematics, philosophy, and music, while his brethren in his own country were tearing one another to pieces for lack of any good influence to teach or show them better things, would be a storing of treasure for himself on earth, a pursuit of the light of knowledge indeed, but not a wooing of the light of Wisdom, the true Light of the World, as seen in Him who went about doing good. To complete his present course was, he knew, necessary. He had seen enough of really learned scholars to know the depths of his own ignorance, and to be aware that certain books must be read under guidance, and certain studies gone through, before his cultivation would be on a level with the standard of the best working clergy of the English Church—such as Chicheley, Waynflete, or the like. He would therefore remain at Oxford, he thought, long enough to take his Master of Arts degree, and then, though to his own perceptions only the one-eyed among the blind, he would make the real sacrifice of himself in the rude and cruel world of Scotland.

He knew that his king was well satisfied with Patrick, and

also that a man of sound heart and prompt, hard hand was far fitter to rule as a secular lord than his own more fine-drawn mature could ever be; but as a priest, with the influence that his birth and the King's friendship would give him, he already saw chances of raising the tone of the clergy, and thus improving the wild and lawless people.

A deep purpose of self-devotion was growing up in his soul, but without saddening him, only rendering him more energetic and cheerful than his sister had ever known him.

As they walked together over the long stretches of moor, many were Lily's questions; and Malcolm beguiled the way with many a story of camp and court, told both for his own satisfaction in her sympathy, and with the desire to make the Scottish lassie see what was the life and what the thoughts of ladies of her own degree in other lands, so that the Lady of Glenuskie might be awake to somewhat of the high purpose of virtuous home government to which Alice of Salisbury had been trained.

As to the Flemish heiress, no representation would induce Lilias to love her. Reject Malcolm for a convent's sake! It was unpardonable; and as to a bedeswoman, working uncloistered in the streets, Lily viewed that as neither the one thing nor the other, neither religious nor secular; and she was persuaded that a little exertion on the part of the brother, whom she viewed as a paladin, would overcome all coyness on the lady's part.

Malcolm found it vain to try to show his sister his sense of his own deserts, and equally so to declare that if the maiden should so yield, she would indeed be the Demoiselle de Luxemburg to whom he was pledged, but not the Esclairmonde whom his better part adored. So he let the matter pass by, and both enjoyed their masquing in one another's company as a holiday such as they could never have again.

They had no serious alarms; the pursuit must have been disconcerted, and the two young scholars were not worth the attention of freebooters. Their winsomeness of manner won them kindness wherever they harboured; and thus, after many days, without molestation they came to the walls of Berwick. And now, while Malcolm thought his difficulties at an end, a horror of bashfulness fell upon Lilias. She had been Clerk Davie merrily enough while there was no one to suspect her, but the transmutation into her proper self filled her with shame.

She hung back, and could be hardly dragged forward to the embattled gateway of the bridge by her brother—who, as the guards, jealously cautious even in this time of peace, called out to him to stand, showed his ring bearing the royal arms, and desired to speak within the captain of the garrison, who was commanding in the name of the Earl of Northumberland, Governor of Berwick and Warden of the Marches, and who had entertained him on his way north, and would have been warned by Patrick of his probable return in this guise.

Instead of the stalwart form of the veteran sub-governor, however, a quick step came hurrying to the gateway, and the light figure of a young knight stood before him, with outstretched hands, crying: 'Welcome to the good town of Berwick-upon-Tweed, dear comrade!' And he added in a lower tone: 'So you have succeeded in your quest—if, as I trow, this fairest of clerks be your lady sister. May I—'

'Hold!' softly said Malcolm. 'She is so shamefast that she cannot brook a word;' and in fact Lilias had pulled her hood over her face, and shrunk behind him, at the first approach of the young gentleman.

'We will to my mother,' said Ralf, aloud. 'She has always a soft corner in her heart for a young clerk or a wanderer.'

And so saying, without even looking at the disguised figure, he gave the pass-word, and holding Malcolm by the arm, led him, followed by Lilias, through the defences and into the court of the castle, then to a side-door, where, bounding up several steps at once of a stone stair, he opened a sort of anteroom door, and bade the two strangers wait there while he fetched his mother.

'That is well! Who would have looked to see him here!' cried Malcolm, joyously. 'What, you knew him not? It was Ralf Percy, my dear old companion!'

'Ralf Percy! he that was so bold and daring?' cried Lilias. 'Nay, but how can it be, he was as meek and shamefast—'

'As yourself,' smiled Malcolm. 'Ah, sister, you have much to learn of the ways of an English gentleman among ladies.'

Before many further words could be exchanged, there entered a fair and matronly dame in the widow's veil she had worn ever since the fatal day of Shrewsbury—that eager, loving, yet almost childish woman whom we know so well as Hotspur's gentle Kate (only that unfortunately her name was Elizabeth); fondling, teasing, being fondled and teased in return, and then with all her pretty puerilities scorched away when she upbraids Northumberland with his fatal delay. Could Malcolm and Lilias have known her as we do in Shakespeare, they would have been the more gratified by her welcome, whereas they only saw her kind face and the courtly sweep of her curtsey, as, going straight up to the disguised girl, blushing and trembling now more than ever, she said: 'Poor child, come with me, and we will soon have you yourself again, ere any other eye see you;' and then moved away again, holding Lily by the hand, while Ralf, who had followed close behind her, again grasped Malcolm's hand.

'Well done, Glenuskie; you have all the adventures! They seek you, I believe! So you have borne off your damosel errant, and are just in time to receive your king.'

'Is he wedded then?'

'Ay, and you find us all here in full state, prepared to banquet him and lodge him and his bride for a night, and then I fancy my brother is to go through some ceremony, ere giving him up to his own subjects. We are watching for him every day. Come to my chamber, and I'll apparel you.'

'Nay, but what brings you here, Ralf?—you, whom I thought in France.'

"Twas a Scottish bill that brought me,' answered Ralf. 'What, are you too lost in parchment at Oxford to hear of us poor soldiers, or knew you not how we fought at Crevant?'

'I heard of the battle, and that you were hurt, but that was months ago, and I deemed you long since in the field again. Was it so sore a matter?'

'Chiefly sore for that it hindered me from taking the old rogue Douglas, and meriting my spurs as befitted a Percy. I was knighted while the trumpet was sounding, and I did think that I was on the way to prowess, for fully in the *melee* I saw a fellow with the Douglas banner. I made at it, thinking of my father's and of Otterburn; and, Malcolm, this very hand was on the staff, when what must a big

Scot do but chop at me with his bill like a butcher's axe. Had it fallen on mine arm it would have been lopped off like a bough of a tree, but, by St. George's grace, it lit here, between my neck and shoulder, and stuck fast as I went down, and the fellow was swept away from me. 'Twas so fixed in the very bone, that they had much ado to wrench it out, when there was time after the fight to look after us who had come by the worse. And what d'ye think they found, Malcolm? Why, those honest Yorkshiremen, Trenton and Kitson, stark dead, both of them. Trenton must have gone down first, with a lance-thrust in the throat; and there was Kitson over him, his shield over his head, and his own cleft open with an axe! They laid them side by side—so I was told—in their grave; and sure 'twas as strange and as true a brotherhood as ever was between two brave men.'

'The good fellows!' cried Malcolm. 'Nay, after what I saw I can hardly grieve. I went to Kitson's home, where they knew as little as I did of his death, and verily his place had closed up behind him, so that I scarce think his mother even cared to see him more, and the whole of them seemed more concerned at his amity with Trenton than proud of his feats of arms. I was marvelling if their friendship would be allowed to subsist at home, even when they, poor fellows, were lying side by side in their French grave.'

'We warriors should never come home,' said Percy; 'we are spoilt for aught but our French camp. I am wearying to get back once more, but so long as I cannot swing my sword-arm I must play the idler here.'

'It must have been a fearsome wound,' said Malcolm. 'The marvel is your overgetting it.'

'So say they all; and truly it has lasted no small time. They shipped me off home so soon as I could leave my bed, and bade me rest. Nay, and my mother herself came even to London, when my brother was summoned to Parliament,—she who had never been there since the first year after she was wedded!'

'You can scarce complain of such kin as that,' said Malcolm.

"Tis not the kin, but this petty Border life, that frets me. Here we move from castle to castle, and now and then come tidings of a cattle lifting, and Harry dons his helm and rides forth, but nine times out of ten 'tis a false alarm, or if it be true, the thieves have made off, and being time of peace, he, as Warden, cannot make a raid in return. I'm sick of the life, after the only warfare fit for a knight, with French nobles instead of Border thieves; and back I will. If my right arm will not serve me, the left shall. I can use a lance indifferent well already.'

As Sir Ralf Percy spoke, a bugle-call rang through the castle. He started. 'Hark! that's the warder's horn,' and flying to the door, he soon returned crying—'Your king is in sight, Malcolm!'

'How soon will he be here?'

'In less than half an hour. There's time to array yourself. I'll take you to my chamber.'

'Thanks,' said Malcolm; 'but this gown is no disguise to me. I had rather meet the King thus, for it is my fitting garb. Only I would remove the soil of the journey, and then take my sister by the hand.'

For this there was ample time, and Malcolm had arranged his hair, and brushed away the dust from his gown, washed his face and hands, and made himself look more like an Oxford bachelor, and less like a begging clerk, than he had of late judged it prudent to appear, ere Ralf took him to the great hall, where he found Lord Northumberland and the chief gentlemen of his household, with his mother, Lady Percy, and his young wife, together with their ladies, assembling for the reception of their royal guests.

Malcolm was presented to, and kindly greeted by, each of the principal personages, and then the Earl, Sir Ralf, and their officers went forth to meet the King at the gateway. Malcolm, however, at his sister's entreaty, remained with her, for in the doubt whether Patrick were really at hand, and a fond unreasonable vexation that he had had no part in her liberation, her colour was coming and going, and she looked as if she might almost faint in her intense excitement.

But when, marshalled by the two Percies, King James and Queen Joan had entered the hall, and the blare of trumpets without and rejoicings within, and had been welcomed with deep reverences by the two ladies, Ralf said: 'Sir, methinks you have here what you may be glad to see.'

And standing aside, he made way for the two figures to stand forth, one in the plain black gown and hood, the other in the rich robes of a high-born maiden, her dark eyes on the ground, her fair face quivering within emotion, as both she and her brother bent the knee before their royal master.

'Ha!' cried James, 'this is well indeed. Thou hast her, then, lad? See, Patrick! Where is he? Nay, but, fair wife, I must present thee the first kinswoman of mine thou hast seen. How didst bring her off, Malcolm?' And he embraced Malcolm with the ardour of a happy man, as he added,

'This is all that was wanting.'

Truly James looked as if nothing were wanting to his joy, as there he stood after his years of waiting, a bridegroom, free, and on the borders of his native land. His eyes shone with joy, and there was a bright energy and alacrity in his bearing that, when Malcolm bethought him of those former grave movements, and the quiet demeanour as though only interested by an effort, marked the change from the captive to the free man. And beautiful Joan, lovelier than ever, took on her her queenly dignity with all her wonted grace and graciousness.

She warmly embraced Lilias, hailing her as cousin, and auguring joyously of the future from the sight of this first Stewart maiden whom she had seen; and the next moment Patrick Drummond, hurrying forward, fell on his knee before his lady, grasped, kissed, fondled her hand, and struggled and stammered between his rejoicing over her liberation and despair that he had no part in it.

'Yea,' said the King 'it was well-nigh a madman whom you sent home to me, Malcolm. He was neither to have nor to hold; and what he would have had me do, or have let him do, I'll not say, nor doth he know either. I must hear your story ere I sleep, Malcolm.'

The King did not ask for it then: he would not brook the exposure of the disunion and violence of Scotland to the English, especially the Percies; and it was not till he could see Malcolm alone that he listened to his history.

'Cousin,' he said, 'you have done both bravely and discreetly. Methinks you have redeemed my pledge to your good guardian that in the south you should be trained to true manhood; though I am free to own that 'twas not under my charge that you had the best training. How is it to be, Malcolm? Patrick tells me you saw the Lady of Light.'

'Ay, Sir, but neither her purpose nor mine is shaken. My lord, I believe I see how best to serve God and yourself. If you will consent, I will finish my first course at Oxford, and then offer myself for the priesthood.'

'Not hide thyself in cloister or school—that is well!' exclaimed the King.

'No, Sir. Methinks I could serve yonder rude people best if I were among them as a priest.'

James considered, then said: 'I pledged myself not to withstand your conscience, Malcolm; and though I grieve that the lady should be lost, she has never wavered, and cannot be balked of her will. Godly and learned priests will indeed be needed; and between you and James Kennedy, when both are come to elder years, we may perchance lift our poor Scottish Church to some clearer sense of what a church should be. Meanwhile—' The King stopped and considered. 'Study in England! Ay! You see, Malcolm, I must take my seat, and have the reins of my unruly steed firm in my hand, ere I take cognizance of these offences. The caitiff Walter—mansworn that he is— he shall abye it; but that can scarce be as yet, and methinks it were not well that I entered Scotland with you and your sister at my side, for then must I seem to have overlooked an offence that, by this holy relic, I will never pardon. So, Malcolm, instead of entering Scotland with me—bonnie land, how sweet its air blows from the north!—ye must e'en turn south! But how to dispose of your sister? Some nunnery—'

'Poor Lily, she is weary of convents,' said Malcolm 'but if Lady Montagu would let her be with her and the Lady

Esclairmonde, then would she learn somewhat of the ways of a well-ordered English noble house. And I could well provide for her being there as befits her station.'

'Well thought of! The gentle Lady Alice will no doubt welcome her,' said the King; 'and Patrick must endure.'

Thus then was it fixed. The King and Queen, stately and beautiful, royally robed, and mounted on splendid steeds, were escorted the next morning to the Scottish gate of Berwick by Lord Northumberland and his retinue, and they were met by an imposing band of Scottish nobles, with the white-haired Earl of Lennox at their head. To these the captive was formally surrendered by Northumberland; and James, flinging himself from his horse, kissed his native soil, and gave thanks aloud to God, ere he stood up and received the homage of his subjects, to most of whom he was a total stranger.

Malcolm and Lilias on the walls could see all, but could not hear, and finally beheld the glittering troop wind their way over the hills to make ready for the coronation of James and Joan as king and queen of Scotland.

CHAPTER XIX

THE LION'S WRATH

It was the 24th of May, 1425, when in the vaulted hall of the Castle of Stirling the nobles of Scotland were convened to try, as the peers of the realm, men of rank— no less than Murdoch, Duke of Albany, his sons Walter and Alexander, the Earl of Lennox, and twenty-two other nobles, most of whom had been arraigned in the Parliament of Perth two months previously, and had been shut up in different castles. Robert Stewart had escaped to the Highlands; and Walter—who had neither been at the Coronation of Scone, nor at the Parliament of Perth, nor indeed had ever bowed his pride so as to present himself to the King at all—had been separately arrested, and shut up for two months in the strong castle on the Bass Rock.

The charge was termed treason and violence; and assuredly there had been perpetual acts of spoil and barbarous infractions of the law by men who deemed themselves above all law. The only curiosity was, for which of these acts they were to be tried, and this affected many of their judges likewise; for there was hardly a man in that court who was not conscious of some deed that would not exactly bear to be set beside the code of Scotland, and who had not been in the habit of regarding those laws as all very well for burghers, but not meant

Charlotte M. Yonge

for gentlemen.

There, on seats behind the throne, sat the twenty-one jurors, Earl Douglas among them—a new earl, for the grim old Archibald had died in the battle of Verneuil some months before. Angus, March, and Mar, and all the most powerful names in Scotland, were there; and upon his throne, in regal robes of crimson and ermine, the crown upon his brow, the sceptre in his hand, the sword of state held before him, sat King James, the most magnificent-looking king then reigning in Europe, but with the sternest, saddest, most resolute of countenances, as one unalterably fixed upon the terrible duty of not bearing the sword in vain. Something of Henry's avenging-angel look seemed to have passed into his face, but with far more of melancholy weight.

Walter Stewart was led into the court. He too was a man of lofty stature and princely bearing, and his grand Stewart features were set in an expression of easy nonchalance and scorn; aware as he was that of whatever he might be accused, there were few of his judges that did not share the guilt, and moreover persuaded that this was a mere ceremony, and that the King would never dare to go beyond this futile attempt to overawe him. He stood alone—his father and the others were reserved for another trial; and as, richly arrayed, he stood opposite to the jury, gazing fixedly first at one, then at the other, as though challenging their right to sit in judgment on him, one eye after another fell beneath his gaze.

'Walter Stewart of Albany, Earl of Fife,' proclaimed the crier's voice. 'You stand here arraigned of murder and of robbery.'

'At whose suit?' demanded Walter, undaunted.

'At the suit of Malcolm and Lilias Stewart of Glenuskie; and of Patrick Drummond of the Braes,' returned the crier, an ecclesiastic, as were all lawyers; and at the same moment three figures came forward, namely, a tall knightly gentleman with gold chain and spurs, a lady whose veil disclosed a blushing dark-eyed face, and a slender youth of deep and earnest countenance. 'At the suit of these here present you stand arraigned, Sir Walter Stewart of Albany, for having feloniously, and of malice aforethought, on the Eve of the Annunciation of our Lady, of the year of grace 1421, set upon the said Malcolm and Lilias Stewart, Sir David Drummond of the Braes, Tutor of Glenuskie, and divers other persons, on the muir of Hetherfield; and having there cruelly and maliciously wounded the said David of the Braes to the death; and of having forcibly stolen and abducted the person of the said Lilias Stewart—'

The crier was not permitted to proceed, for Walter Stewart broke forth, passionately addressing the jurors. 'So this is all that can be found to be laid against me. This is the way that matters of five years back are raked up to vex the princes and nobles of Scotland. I am sorry for you, lords and gentlemen, if this is the way that vexatious are to be stirred up against those who have defended their country so long.'

'This is no answer to the accusation, Sir Walter,' said the Earl of Mar.

'Accusation, forsooth!' said Walter Stewart scornfully. 'Who dares to bear witness, if I *did* maintain my father's lawful authority over peevish runaway wards of the Crown?'

'Sir Walter,' said the King, 'you would have done better to have waited and heard the whole indictment ere

Charlotte M. Yonge

answering one charge. But since you demand who will dare to bear witness in this matter of the murder of Sir David Drummond of the Braes, and of the seizure of the Lady Lilias, here is one.'

So saying, and rising as he spoke, he held forth the reliquary that hung from a chain round his neck, keeping his gleaming tawny eyes fixed steadily straight upon Walter Stewart's face.

That face, as he first had stood up, expressed the utmost amazement, and this gradually, under the lion glance, became more and more of dismay, quailing, collapsing visibly under the passionless gravity of that look. Even the tall form seemed to shrink, the eyes dilated, the brows drew closer together, and the chest seemed to pant, as the relic was held forth. There was a dead silence throughout the court as the King ceased to speak; only he continued to bend that searching gaze upon his prisoner.

'Was it you?—was it your own self, my lord?' he stammered forth at last, in the tone of one stricken.

'Yea, Walter Stewart. To me it was, and on this holy relic, that you made oath to abstain from all further spoil and violence until the King should come again in peace. How that oath has been kept the further indictments will show.'

'I deemed it was St. Andrew,' faltered the prisoner.

'And therefore that the oath to a heavenly saint would better bear breaking than one to an earthly sinner,' replied James gravely. 'Read on, Clerk of the Court.'

The roll continued—a long and terrible record of violence and cruelty; the private warfare of the lawless young prince, the crimes of reckless barbarity and of savage passion—a deadly roll, in which indeed even the second abduction of Lilias was one of the least acts laid to his charge.

No lack of witnesses were there to prove deeds that had been done in the open face of day, in utter fearlessness of earthly justice, and defiance of Heaven. The defence that the prisoner seemed to have been prepared to us?—that those who sat to judge him had shared in his offences, and his daring power of brow-beating them, as he had so often done before, as son of the man who sat in the King's seat—had utterly failed him now. He was mute; and the forms of the trial were gone through as of one whose doom was already sealed, but who must receive his sentence according to the strictest form of law, lest the just reward of his deeds should partake of their own violence. By the end of the day the jurors had found Walter Stewart guilty; and the doomster, a black-robed clerk, rising up, pronounced the sentence that condemned Walter Stewart of Albany to suffer death by beheading.

Even then no one believed that the doom would be inflicted. Royal blood had never flowed beneath the headsman's axe; and it would have been infinitely more congenial to Scottish feelings if the King had sent a party of men-at-arms to fall on the Master in the high road, and cut him off, or had burnt him alive in his castle. The verdict 'served him right' would have been universally returned, and rejoiced in; but a regular trial of a man of such birth was unheard of, and shocking to the feelings even of those whom that irresistible force of the King's had compelled to sit in judgment upon him. No one could avow it face to face with the King; but every one felt it an outrage to find that no rank was exempt from law.

Duke Murdoch, his son Alexander, and his father-in-law Lennox, were tried the next day, and many a deed of dark

Charlotte M. Yonge

treason was laid to their charge. The Earl of Lennox had been the scourge of Scotland for more than half the eighty years of his life, but his extreme age might have excited some pity; Murdoch had erred rather negatively than positively; and Alexander, ruffian as he was, had been bred to nothing better. Each had deserved the utmost penalty of the law again and again, and yet there did seem more scope for mercy in their case than in that of Walter.

But the King was inexorable. He set Malcolm aside as he had set others.

'I know what you would say, lad. Lennox is old, and Alexander is young, and Albany is a fool; and Walter has injured you, so you are bound to speak for him. Take it all as said. But these are the men who have been foremost in making our country a desert! Did I pardon them, with what face could I ever make any man suffer for crime? And, in the state of this land, ruth to the guilty high would be treason to the sackless low.'

So Stirling saw the unprecedented sight of three gene-rations suffering for their crimes upon the same scaffold—the white-haired Lennox, the Duke of Albany in the prime of life, Walter in the flush and strength of early manhood, Alexander in the bloom of youth. They all met their fate undauntedly; for if Murdoch's heart in any measure failed him, he was afraid to give way in presence of the proud bold Walter, who maintained an iron rigidity of demeanour with the wild fortitude of a Red Indian at the stake, and in like manner could by no means comprehend that King James acted from any motive save malice, for having been so long kept out of his kingdom. 'It was his turn now,' said poor Murdoch, even when most desirous of bringing himself to die in a state of Christian forgiveness; nor could any power on earth show any of the criminals that the King acted in the eternal interests of right and justice.

Thus it was with the whole country; and when the four majestic-looking men stood bare-headed on the scaffold, in view even of their own fair towers of Doune, and one by one bowed their heads on the block, perverse Scottish nature broke out into pity for their fate, and wrath against the King, who could thus turn against his own blood, and disgrace the royal lineage.

On that same day Malcolm received Esclairmonde's token, there being at present full peace with England, and set forth on her summons. He met her at Pontefract, where she was residing with the Dowager Queen Joan of Navarre, Alice of Salisbury having been summoned to return to her husband in France.

There then it was that Malcolm and Esclairmonde, in presence of the chaplain, gave each other back the rings, and therewith their troth to wed none other, and were once more declared free.

Esclairmonde held out her hand to Malcolm, saying, 'The thanks I owe you, Sir, are beyond what tongue can tell. May He to Whom my first vows were due requite it to you.'

And Malcolm, with his knee to the ground, pressing for the last time that fair hand, said, 'The thanks, lady, are mine. Had you been one whit lower in aims or in constancy, what had I been? You were my light of the world, but to light me to seek that higher Light that shone forth in you, and which may I show truly to the darkened spirits of my countrymen! Lady, you will permit me to take to myself the ring you have worn so long. It will be my token of my betrothal to that true Light.'

Charlotte M. Yonge

Such was their parting, when the one went forth to her tasks of charity among the poor in London, the other to divest himself of land and lordship on behalf of his sister and her husband, and then to begin his task in the priesthood, of trying to hold up the true Light to hearts darkened by many an age of crime and ignorance.

Lived very happy ever after! Yes, we would fain always leave the creatures with whom our thoughts have been busy in such felicity; but when we have linked them with real events, the sense of the veritable course of history reminds us that we cannot even suppose beings possible in real life without endowing them with the common lot of humanity; and the personages of our tale lived in a time of more than ordinary reverse and trouble.

Yet Sir Patrick Drummond and Lilias his wife, the Lord and Lady of Glenuskie, nearly did fulfil these conditions. They had not feelings beyond their age, but they were good specimens of that age, and they did their duty in it; he as a trustworthy noble, ready to aid in council or war, and she as the beneficent dame, bringing piety and charity to heal the sufferings of her vassals and serfs. His hand was strong enough to repel the attacks of his foes; her intelligence, backed by Malcolm's counsel, introduced improvements; and the little ravine of Glenuskie was a happy valley of peace and prosperity for many years among the convulsions of Scotland.

Nor was Esclairmonde de Luxemburg's life in the Hospital of St. Katharine otherwise than the holy and beneficent career that she had always longed for— worshipping in the fair church, and going forth from thence 'into the streets and lanes of the city,' to fulfil Queen Philippa's pious behest, to seek out the suffering and the ignorant, and to tend and instruct them. The tall form and beautiful countenance of Sister Clare were loved and reverenced as those of an angel messenger among the high houses and courts that closed in on the banks of the Thames; and while Luxemburgs in France and Flanders intrigued and fought, plotted and fell, their kinswoman's days passed by in busy alms-deeds and ever loftier devotion, till those who watched her steps felt that she was verily a light of the world, manifesting forth the true Light in many a dark place.

And her light of sympathy shone upon many an old friend both in joy and in grief. When the dissensions of Gloucester and Beaufort had summoned Bedford to England to endeavour to appease their strife, his Burgundian Duchess sought out her early friend, and Esclairmonde saw her gentle companion, the Lady Anne, fulfilling her daily task of mediation, and living a life, not indeed very sunshiny, but full of all that esteem and respect could give her, and of calm gratitude and affection, although Anne, like all others, believed that John of Bedford's heart had been buried in his brother's grave, and that of youthful love he had none to give. His whole soul was absorbed in his care for the welfare of the pale, gentle, dreamy, inanimate boy, who, from his very meekness and docility, gave so little promise of representing the father whose name he bore.

The loving Alice of Montagu, though the mother of many a bold boy and girl, and busy with all the cares of the great Nevil household, regarded as the chief delight in a journey to court the sight of her dear Sister Clare. It was to Sister Clare that Alice turned for comfort when her brave old father died at the siege of Orleans; and it was while daily soothing and ministering to her sorrow that Esclairmonde heard the strange wild tales of the terrible witch maiden who had appeared on behalf of the French, and turned whole English armies to flight, by power that the French declared to come from the saints, but which the English never doubted to be infernal. Maimed and wounded soldiers, whom Esclairmonde relieved and tended as they returned from lost battles, gave her fearful accounts of the panic that La Pucelle inspired. Even the hardy veteran, Sir John Fastolfe, had not been able to withstand her spells, but had fled from the field of Jergeau, where gallant Sir Ralf Percy had died, in a vain attempt to gather the men to resist the irresistible maiden. His groom, who had succumbed for a time to wounds and weakness on his way home to Alnwick, was touched by the warmth and emotion with which the kind bedes-woman listened to his lamentation over the good and loyal knight, whom she pictured to herself resisting the enchantress's dread power as dauntlessly as he had defied the phantoms of the Dance of Death.

No whisper ever reached Esclairmonde that the terrible Pucelle was a maiden as pure and high-souled as herself. All that she heard more was that this terror of the English and Burgundians was taken, imprisoned for a time by her own Luxemburg kindred, and then carried to Rouen, where the kind Duchess Anne of Bedford did her best to persuade her to overcome the superstition that kept her in male garments, thus greatly tending to increase the belief in her connection with the powers of evil. French and Burgundian bishops, and even the University of Paris, were the judges of the maiden; and the dastard prince she had crowned never stirred a finger nor uttered a protest in her behalf. Bedford, always disposed to belief in witchcraft, acquiesced in the decision of Churchmen, which was therefore called the judgment of the Church; but when he removed himself and his duchess from Rouen, and left the conduct of the matter to the sterner and harder Beauchamp, Earl of Warwick, it was with little thought that after-generations would load his memory with the fate of Jeanne d'Arc, as though her sufferings had proceeded from his individual malice.

Esclairmonde never saw Bedford again, and only heard through Alice, now Countess of Salisbury, how when good Duchess Anne was dead, and her gentle influence removed, Burgundy's disinclination to the English cause was no longer balanced; and how Bedford, perplexed, disheartened, broken in health, but still earnest to propitiate friends for his helpless nephew, had listened to the wily whisper of the Bishop of Therouenne, that his niece, Jaquette, would secure the devotion of the Count de St. Pol, and that she was moreover like unto another Demoiselle de Luxemburg.

How like, Esclairmonde could judge, when her kins-woman, widowed in her eighteenth year, at six months' end, came to London to claim her dower. Never, since her days of wandering and anxiety, had Esclairmonde felt such pain as when she perceived how little store the thoughtless girl had set by the great and noble spirit that had been quenched under the load of toil and care with which it had battled for thirteen long years. Faithful, great-hearted Bedford, striving to uphold a losing cause, to reconcile selfish contentions, to retain conquests that, though unjustly made, he had no power to relinquish; and all without one trustworthy relation, with friends and fellow-warriors dying, disputing, betraying, or deserting, his was as self-devoted and as mournful a career as ever was run by any prince at any age of the world; and while he slept in his grave at Rouen, that grave which even Louis XI. respected, Esclairmonde, as, like a true bedeswoman of St. Katharine, she joined in the orisons for the repose of the souls of the royal kindred, never heard the name of the Lord John without a throb of prayer, and a throb too that warmed her heart with tenderness.

It was some four years later, and the even tenor of Sister Clare's course had only been interrupted by her kinswoman, Jaquette, making her way to her to confess her marriage with Richard Wydville, and to entreat her intercession with the Luxemburg family; when one summer night she was called on to attend a pilgrim priest from the Holy Land, who had been landed from a Flemish vessel, and lay dangerously sick at the 'God's house,' or hospital, by the river side. He was thought by his accent to be foreign, and Sister Clare was always called on to wait upon the stranger.

As she stood by his bedside, she beheld a man of middle age, but wasted with sickness, and with a certain strange look of horror so imprinted on his brow, that even as he lay asleep, though his mouth was grave and peaceful, the lines were still there, and the locks that hung from around his tonsure were of a whiteness that scarce accorded with the features. It was a face that Esclairmonde could not look at without waking strange memories; but it was not till the sleeper awakened, opened two dark eyes, gazed on her with dreamy doubtful wonder, and then clasped his hands with the murmured thanksgiving, 'My God, hast Thou granted me this? Light of my life!' that she was assured to whom she was speaking.

Malcolm Stewart it verily was. Canon Malcolm Stewart of Dunkeld was his proper title, for he had, as she knew, long ceased to be Lord of Glenuskie. It was not at first that she knew how he had been brought where she now saw him; but after some few days of her tender care and skilful leechcraft, he somewhat rallied, and she gathered his history from his conversation when he was able to speak.

He had had a time of happy labour in Scotland, fully carrying out the designs with which he and his cousin James Kennedy had taken upon them the ministry. Their own birth, and the appointments their King gave them, so soon as their age permitted, made them able to exert an influence that told upon the rude and unenlightened clergy around. It had been almost a mission of conversion, to awaken a spirit of Christianity in the country, that had so long been a prey to anarchy. The King's declaration, 'I will make the key keep the castle, and the bracken-bush keep the cow, though I live the life of a dog to bring it about,' had been the moving spring of their lives. James had fought hour by hour with the foul habits of lawlessness, savagery, and violence, that had hitherto been absolutely unchecked; and while he strove with the sword of justice, the two young priests worked within the Word of truth, to implant some sense of conscience in the neglected people.

It had been a life of constant exertion, but full of hope and cheerfulness. Amid that rude country, James's own home was always a bright spot of peace, sunshine, and refinement. With his beloved queen, and their fair little brood of children, the King cast aside his cares, and was all, and more than all, he had been as the ornament of Henry's Court. There all that was sweet, innocent, and beautiful was to be found; and there Malcolm, his royal kinsman's confidant, counsellor, and chaplain, was always welcome as one of the home circle and family, till he broke away from such delights to labour in his task of reviving religion in the land. A little band of men were gathering round, clergy awakening from their sloth or worldliness, young nobles who began to see what chivalry meant, burghers who rejoiced in order; and hope and encouragement strengthened the hands of the three kinsmen.

But, alas! there were those who deemed James's justice on the savage prince and noble mere sacrilege on high blood, and who absolutely hated and loathed peace and order. Those thirteen years of cheerful progress ended in that murder so unspeakably horrible in all its circumstances,

Charlotte M. Yonge

which almost merits the name of a martyrdom to right and justice. Malcolm so shuddered when he did but touch on it, and was so rent with agitation, that Esclairmonde perceived that when his beloved King had perished, he had indeed received the death-wound to his own fragile nature.

He had been actually in the Abbey of Perth; and had been one of those who lifted the mangled corpse from the vault, and sought in vain for a remnant of life, if but to grant the absolution, for which the victim had so piteously besought his murderers. No wonder that Fastern's E'en had whitened Malcolm's hair!

But when the assassins were captured, and Joan of Beaufort was resolved that their death should be as atrocious as their crime, it was Malcolm who strove to bend her to forgiveness. He bade her recollect King Henry, and how, when dealing with that cruel monster, the Castellane of Meaux, he had merely required death, without enhancing the agony; but Joan, in her rage and misery, had left the Englishwoman behind her, and was implacable. All that human cruelty could invent was to be the lot of Robert Graham and his associates; and whereas they had granted no priest to their victim, none should be granted to them.

And then it was that all Malcolm had learnt of the true spirit of the Christian triumphed—not only over the dark Keltic spirit of revenge, but over the shuddering of a tender and pitiful nature. Where no other priest durst venture, he went. Through all the frightful and protracted sufferings of Athol, Graham, Hall, and the rest, it was Malcolm Stewart who, never flinching, prayed with and for them; gathered their agonized sobs of confession, or strove to soften their hardness; spoke the words of absolution, and commended their departing souls.

When he awoke from the long unconsciousness and delirium that ensued upon the force he had put on himself, he found himself tended by his sister at Glenuskie. Patrick Drummond had transported him thither; finding that the angry Queen, in the madness of her vindictiveness, was well-nigh disposed to connect him with the treasonable designs of Athol and Graham. He slowly and partially recovered, but his influence was gone; the Queen would not brook the sound of his name, the little king was beyond his reach, James Kennedy was biding his time, and the country was returned to its state of misrule and violence, wherein an individual priest could do little: yet Malcolm would have held by his post, had not his health been so utterly shattered that he was incapable of the work he had hitherto done, as a confessor and a preacher. And therefore, as the state of his beloved King, 'sent to his account unhouselled, disappointed, unannealed,' hung heavy on his mind, he determined, so soon as he was in any degree convalescent, to set forth on pilgrimage to Jerusalem, the object of so many dreams of King Henry; there to offer masses and prayers for the welfare of his departed prince, as well as of the unhappy murderers, and for the country in its distracted condition.

And there, at the Holy Sepulchre, had Malcolm, in the fervour of his heart, offered the greatest treasure he possessed—nay, the only one that he still really cared for—namely his betrothal ring, which Esclairmonde had worn for so long and had returned to him. As a priest, he had deemed that it was not unlawful for him to retain the memorial of the link that had bound him to her who had been the light that led him to the true Light beyond; but as youth passed away, as devotion burned brighter, as the experiences of those years became more dream-like, and the horror, grief, and misery of his King's death had been assuaged only by the steadier contemplation of the Light of Eternity, he had felt that this last pledge of his once

Charlotte M. Yonge

lower aims and hopes ought to be resigned; and that if it cost him a pang, it was well that it should be so, to render the offering a sacrifice. So the ring that had once been Esclairmonde's protection was laid on the altar of the Holy Tomb.

There Malcolm had well-nigh died, under the influences of agitation, fatigue, and climate; but he had revived enough to set out on his return from his pilgrimage, and had made his way tardily and wearily, losing his attendants through death and desertion on the road; and passing from one religious house to another, as his strength and nearly exhausted means served him. Unable to find any vessel bound for Leith, he had taken ship for London; concealing his quality, lest, in the always probable contingency of a war, it might lead to his being made prisoner; and thus he had arrived, sick indeed unto death, but peaceful, rejoicing, and hopeful.

'Sister,' he said, 'the morn that I had offered my ring, I was feeble and faint; and when I knelt on before the altar in continued prayer—I know not whether I slept or whether it were a vision, but it was to me as though I were again on the river, and again the hymn of Bernard of Morlaix was sung around and above me, by the voice I never thought to hear again. I looked up, and behold it was I that was in the boat—my King was there no more. Nay, he stood on the shore, and his eyes beamed on me; while the ghastly wounds that I once strove in anguish to staunch shone out like a ruby cross on his breast—the hands, that were so sorely gashed, were to me as though marked by the impress of the Sacred Wounds. He spake not; but by his side stood King Henry, beautiful and spirit-like, and smiled on me, and seemed as though he pointed to the wounds, as he said, "Blessed is the king who died by his people's hand, for withstanding his people's sin! Blessed is every faint image of the true King!"

'Then methought they held out their arms to me; and I would have come to them on their shore of rest, but the river bore me away—and I looked up, to find I was as yet only in the earthly Jerusalem; but I watch for them every hour, to call me once and for ever.'

Charlotte M. Yonge

FOOTNOTES

{1} 'Hail, reverend brother. I come from Paris.'

{2} Student of the first year.

{3} Manners are lacking to the Northerners.

{4} Wretches.

{5} For supper.

{6} Telephus and Peleus, when both are poor and exiled, dismiss boasting and six-foot words.

{7} It is dispersed in a cloud.

Choose from Thousands of 1stWorldLibrary Classics By

A. M. Barnard
Ada Leverson
Adolphus William Ward
Aesop
Agatha Christie
Alexander Aaronsohn
Alexander Kielland
Alexandre Dumas
Alfred Gatty
Alfred Ollivant
Alice Duer Miller
Alice Turner Curtis
Alice Dunbar
Allen Chapman
Alleyne Ireland
Ambrose Bierce
Amelia E. Barr
Amory H. Bradford
Andrew Lang
Andrew McFarland Davis
Andy Adams
Angela Brazil
Anna Alice Chapin
Anna Sewell
Annie Besant
Annie Hamilton Donnell
Annie Payson Call
Annie Roe Carr
Annonaymous
Anton Chekhov
Archibald Lee Fletcher
Arnold Bennett
Arthur C. Benson
Arthur Conan Doyle
Arthur M. Winfield
Arthur Ransome
Arthur Schnitzler
Arthur Train
Atticus
B.H. Baden-Powell
B. M. Bower
B. C. Chatterjee
Baroness Emmuska Orczy
Baroness Orczy
Basil King
Bayard Taylor
Ben Macomber
Bertha Muzzy Bower
Bjornstjerne Bjornson

Booth Tarkington
Boyd Cable
Bram Stoker
C. Collodi
C. E. Orr
C. M. Ingleby
Carolyn Wells
Catherine Parr Traill
Charles A. Eastman
Charles Amory Beach
Charles Dickens
Charles Dudley Warner
Charles Farrar Browne
Charles Ives
Charles Kingsley
Charles Klein
Charles Hanson Towne
Charles Lathrop Pack
Charles Romyn Dake
Charles Whibley
Charles Willing Beale
Charlotte M. Braeme
Charlotte M. Yonge
Charlotte Perkins Stetson
Clair W. Hayes
Clarence Day Jr.
Clarence E. Mulford
Clemence Housman
Confucius
Coningsby Dawson
Cornelis DeWitt Wilcox
Cyril Burleigh
D. H. Lawrence
Daniel Defoe
David Garnett
Dinah Craik
Don Carlos Janes
Donald Keyhoe
Dorothy Kilner
Dougan Clark
Douglas Fairbanks
E. Nesbit
E. P. Roe
E. Phillips Oppenheim
E. S. Brooks
Earl Barnes
Edgar Rice Burroughs
Edith Van Dyne
Edith Wharton

Edward Everett Hale
Edward J. O'Biren
Edward S. Ellis
Edwin L. Arnold
Eleanor Atkins
Eleanor Hallowell Abbott
Eliot Gregory
Elizabeth Gaskell
Elizabeth McCracken
Elizabeth Von Arnim
Ellem Key
Emerson Hough
Emilie F. Carlen
Emily Bronte
Emily Dickinson
Enid Bagnold
Enilor Macartney Lane
Erasmus W. Jones
Ernie Howard Pie
Ethel May Dell
Ethel Turner
Ethel Watts Mumford
Eugene Sue
Eugenie Foa
Eugene Wood
Eustace Hale Ball
Evelyn Everett-green
Everard Cotes
F. H. Cheley
F. J. Cross
F. Marion Crawford
Fannie E. Newberry
Federick Austin Ogg
Ferdinand Ossendowski
Fergus Hume
Florence A. Kilpatrick
Fremont B. Deering
Francis Bacon
Francis Darwin
Frances Hodgson Burnett
Frances Parkinson Keyes
Frank Gee Patchin
Frank Harris
Frank Jewett Mather
Frank L. Packard
Frank V. Webster
Frederic Stewart Isham
Frederick Trevor Hill
Frederick Winslow Taylor

Friedrich Kerst
Friedrich Nietzsche
Fyodor Dostoyevsky
G.A. Henty
G.K. Chesterton
Gabrielle E. Jackson
Garrett P. Serviss
Gaston Leroux
George A. Warren
George Ade
Geroge Bernard Shaw
George Cary Eggleston
George Durston
George Ebers
George Eliot
George Gissing
George MacDonald
George Meredith
George Orwell
George Sylvester Viereck
George Tucker
George W. Cable
George Wharton James
Gertrude Atherton
Gordon Casserly
Grace E. King
Grace Gallatin
Grace Greenwood
Grant Allen
Guillermo A. Sherwell
Gulielma Zollinger
Gustav Flaubert
H. A. Cody
H. B. Irving
H.C. Bailey
H. G. Wells
H. H. Munro
H. Irving Hancock
H. R. Naylor
H. Rider Haggard
H. W. C. Davis
Haldeman Julius
Hall Caine
Hamilton Wright Mabie
Hans Christian Andersen
Harold Avery
Harold McGrath
Harriet Beecher Stowe
Harry Castlemon
Harry Coghill
Harry Houidini

Hayden Carruth
Helent Hunt Jackson
Helen Nicolay
Hendrik Conscience
Hendy David Thoreau
Henri Barbusse
Henrik Ibsen
Henry Adams
Henry Ford
Henry Frost
Henry James
Henry Jones Ford
Henry Seton Merriman
Henry W Longfellow
Herbert A. Giles
Herbert Carter
Herbert N. Casson
Herman Hesse
Hildegard G. Frey
Homer
Honore De Balzac
Horace B. Day
Horace Walpole
Horatio Alger Jr.
Howard Pyle
Howard R. Garis
Hugh Lofting
Hugh Walpole
Humphry Ward
Ian Maclaren
Inez Haynes Gillmore
Irving Bacheller
Isabel Cecilia Williams
Isabel Hornibrook
Israel Abrahams
Ivan Turgenev
J.G.Austin
J. Henri Fabre
J. M. Barrie
J. M. Walsh
J. Macdonald Oxley
J. R. Miller
J. S. Fletcher
J. S. Knowles
J. Storer Clouston
J. W. Duffield
Jack London
Jacob Abbott
James Allen
James Andrews
James Baldwin

James Branch Cabell
James DeMille
James Joyce
James Lane Allen
James Lane Allen
James Oliver Curwood
James Oppenheim
James Otis
James R. Driscoll
Jane Abbott
Jane Austen
Jane L. Stewart
Janet Aldridge
Jens Peter Jacobsen
Jerome K. Jerome
Jessie Graham Flower
John Buchan
John Burroughs
John Cournos
John F. Kennedy
John Gay
John Glasworthy
John Habberton
John Joy Bell
John Kendrick Bangs
John Milton
John Philip Sousa
John Taintor Foote
Jonas Lauritz Idemil Lie
Jonathan Swift
Joseph A. Altsheler
Joseph Carey
Joseph Conrad
Joseph E. Badger Jr
Joseph Hergesheimer
Joseph Jacobs
Jules Vernes
Julian Hawthrone
Julie A Lippmann
Justin Huntly McCarthy
Kakuzo Okakura
Karle Wilson Baker
Kate Chopin
Kenneth Grahame
Kenneth McGaffey
Kate Langley Bosher
Kate Langley Bosher
Katherine Cecil Thurston
Katherine Stokes
L. A. Abbot
L. T. Meade

L. Frank Baum
Latta Griswold
Laura Dent Crane
Laura Lee Hope
Laurence Housman
Lawrence Beasley
Leo Tolstoy
Leonid Andreyev
Lewis Carroll
Lewis Sperry Chafer
Lilian Bell
Lloyd Osbourne
Louis Hughes
Louis Joseph Vance
Louis Tracy
Louisa May Alcott
Lucy Fitch Perkins
Lucy Maud Montgomery
Luther Benson
Lydia Miller Middleton
Lyndon Orr
M. Corvus
M. H. Adams
Margaret E. Sangster
Margret Howth
Margaret Vandercook
Margaret W. Hungerford
Margret Penrose
Maria Edgeworth
Maria Thompson Daviess
Mariano Azuela
Marion Polk Angellotti
Mark Overton
Mark Twain
Mary Austin
Mary Catherine Crowley
Mary Cole
Mary Hastings Bradley
Mary Roberts Rinehart
Mary Rowlandson
M. Wollstonecraft Shelley
Maud Lindsay
Max Beerbohm
Myra Kelly
Nathaniel Hawthrone
Nicolo Machiavelli
O. F. Walton
Oscar Wilde

Owen Johnson
P.G. Wodehouse
Paul and Mabel Thorne
Paul G. Tomlinson
Paul Severing
Percy Brebner
Percy Keese Fitzhugh
Peter B. Kyne
Plato
Quincy Allen
R. Derby Holmes
R. L. Stevenson
R. S. Ball
Rabindranath Tagore
Rahul Alvares
Ralph Bonehill
Ralph Henry Barbour
Ralph Victor
Ralph Waldo Emmerson
Rene Descartes
Ray Cummings
Rex Beach
Rex E. Beach
Richard Harding Davis
Richard Jefferies
Richard Le Gallienne
Robert Barr
Robert Frost
Robert Gordon Anderson
Robert L. Drake
Robert Lansing
Robert Lynd
Robert Michael Ballantyne
Robert W. Chambers
Rosa Nouchette Carey
Rudyard Kipling
Saint Augustine
Samuel B. Allison
Samuel Hopkins Adams
Sarah Bernhardt
Sarah C. Hallowell
Selma Lagerlof
Sherwood Anderson
Sigmund Freud
Standish O'Grady
Stanley Weyman
Stella Benson
Stella M. Francis

Stephen Crane
Stewart Edward White
Stijn Streuvels
Swami Abhedananda
Swami Parmananda
T. S. Ackland
T. S. Arthur
The Princess Der Ling
Thomas A. Janvier
Thomas A Kempis
Thomas Anderton
Thomas Bailey Aldrich
Thomas Bulfinch
Thomas De Quincey
Thomas Dixon
Thomas H. Huxley
Thomas Hardy
Thomas More
Thornton W. Burgess
U. S. Grant
Upton Sinclair
Valentine Williams
Various Authors
Vaughan Kester
Victor Appleton
Victor G. Durham
Victoria Cross
Virginia Woolf
Wadsworth Camp
Walter Camp
Walter Scott
Washington Irving
Wilbur Lawton
Wilkie Collins
Willa Cather
Willard F. Baker
William Dean Howells
William le Queux
W. Makepeace Thackeray
William W. Walter
William Shakespeare
Winston Churchill
Yei Theodora Ozaki
Yogi Ramacharaka
Young E. Allison
Zane Grey